SUMMIT

WALTER ERHARDT: Professional, disciplined, and brilliant, he is a German submarine commander of unmatched skill, dedicated to avenging his lost love. He's honing his rogue crew and lethal submarine to a fine, killing edge—to turn them into instruments of world-shaking terror. . . .

LT. COMMANDER JAKE STEELE: The senior SEAL officer aboard the helicopter carrier *Wasp,* he's the key player of the first U.S. response team in the Mediterranean. He lives for action—and now he is going to get it. . . .

PRAISE FOR CHARLES D. TAYLOR'S *BOOMER*

"Tom Clancy, move over. . . . One of the best naval thrillers since *Red October*. . . . Gripping reading from the first intriguing page to the edge-of-your-chair finale."

—Nelson DeMille

"Taylor ratchets the suspense well past the breaking point. . . . *Boomer* is a hell of a fine sea story!"

—Stephen Coonts

WILL RILEY: He came out of the FBI and survived the drug wars of Latin America. The former right-hand man to the Secretary of State—who was murdered at the hands of terrorists—Riley knows how to play hardball to make the President's peace plan come true. . . .

SORAYA: She believes she is more powerful than any man. A dedicated terrorist and a passionate lover, she adores violence—killing is her only real pleasure. . . .

PRAISE FOR CHARLES D. TAYLOR'S

SHADOW WARS

"A page-turner. . . . The pacing is fast and the action furious and detailed."

—*Publishers Weekly*

SIGHTINGS

"Meticulous crafting, furious pacing, and strong characters, both male and female, distinguish Taylor's military thriller."

—*Publishers Weekly*

LT. HUGO SCHROEDER: He was the finest weapons officer in the German Navy, and Erhardt needed him. Trapped aboard a submarine controlled by terrorists, he must stay alive long enough to alert the outside world. . . .

PHILIP SALKIN: The U.S. President has lost his best friend and Secretary of State to a bomb blast, and now he's determined to make peace in the Middle East. He's kept his presence in the Mediterranean a secret, but someone knows where he is. . . .

PRAISE FOR CHARLES D. TAYLOR'S *DEEP STING*

"Taylor hurtles international intrigue and underwater adventure to America's shore. *Deep Sting* explodes with suspense."

—Clive Cussler

"Spellbinding, superbly written. . . . An original, hard-to-put-down saga of today's and tomorrow's navy."

—Nelson DeMille

Books by Charles D. Taylor

Show of Force
The Sunset Patriots
First Salvo
Choke Point
Silent Hunter
Shadow of Vengeance
(pen name: David Charles)
Counterstrike
Warship
Boomer*
Deep Sting*
Shadow Wars*
Sightings*

*Published by POCKET BOOKS

For orders other than by individual consumers, Pocket Books grants a discount on the purchase of **10 or more** copies of single titles for special markets or premium use. For further details, please write to the Vice-President of Special Markets, Pocket Books, 1633 Broadway, New York, NY 10019-6785, 8th Floor.

For information on how individual consumers can place orders, please write to Mail Order Department, Simon & Schuster Inc., 200 Old Tappan Road, Old Tappan, NJ 07675.

SUMMIT

CHARLES D. TAYLOR

POCKET **STAR** BOOKS
New York London Toronto Sydney Tokyo Singapore

This book is a work of fiction. Names, characters, places and incidents are products of the author's imagination or are used fictitiously. Any resemblance to actual events or locales or persons, living or dead, is entirely coincidental.

An *Original* Publication of POCKET BOOKS

A Pocket Star Book published by
POCKET BOOKS, a division of Simon & Schuster Inc.
1230 Avenue of the Americas, New York, NY 10020

ISBN: 0-671-87579-5

First Pocket Books printing August 1996

10 9 8 7 6 5 4 3 2 1

Cover art by John Stephens

Printed in the U.S.A.

This book is for
Captain Lee M. Laitala (USNR), ret.,
who served his country
through four decades

ACKNOWLEDGMENTS

If an author hasn't "done" his subject, he has to learn by reading and consulting with the experts. Lieutenant Commander Greg (Jake) Jaquith, USN, was my guide through his world of SEALs and special boat sailors and "gators." He then read and reread the manuscript, not to mention providing a roof and sustenance during research; there wouldn't be a book without him. Having said that, creating a story sometimes overrides technical accuracy: the Type-212 submarine functions as Captain Erhardt demands; the German Navy's message format I have employed is for easy reading; *Calm Seas* modernization appears simpler than it really would be; Admiral Turner's task force does not necessarily maneuver according to current tactical doctrine; and neither I nor Jake Steele care to detail his SEALs' exact tactics. However, the time has come for our experts to appreciate the abilities of diesel submarines like *Heinz Waller,* for they are going to have a tremendous impact on sea power as we understand it.

Let me apologize first to anyone I have forgotten and then mention those who gave freely of their time. Thanks to Lieutenant Commander Ted Dill, Lieutenant Scott Templeton, "Gunner" Robert Adams, and the men of Special Boat Squadron Two who gave me the ride of my life; to Lieutenant Todd Senniff and Chief Pianna of SEAL Team Two; to Lieutenant Commander Rich Arnold, USCG, who discussed boarding and rescue methods, which I adapted to my own needs; to the officers and men of U.S.S. *Ashland* (LSD-48) and their great ship; to Bob Cutting, USNI Military Database; to Bill McDonald, who remains my guide through the intricacies of the military/political world; to Dan Mundy and Phil Craig for their comments; and to the administrative efforts of Dominick Abel, Paul McCarthy, Doug Grad, and Tris Coburn.

And to the denizens of The Reef and dear old friends who travel through these pages with me, I hope you enjoy the trip! As always, wife and best friend, Georgie, stood by when standing by was needed.

A terrific force lifted the commanding officer's Aegis warship out of the water, broke her back, and unceremoniously dumped her back into the unforgiving ocean. . . .

. . . the captain's mind raced to explain his fate.

He vowed to share his revelations with those who could promote change—if he survived. . . .

Elevate diesel submarine proliferation to its deserved level of concern.

—excerpted from *Contingency Blues*
by Commander Eric Rosenlof, USN
U.S. Naval Institute Proceedings
January 1995

PROLOGUE

If ever credit was given to those who fought for justice in the world, Rupert Daniels's name should be at the top of the list.

But Rupert Daniels was dead.

Minute shreds of flesh and blood and bone that once distinguished the gentleman had been blasted through the immense cavity in the Key Bridge to float down the Potomac toward the sea.

Those bizarre, repetitive thoughts ran through the saddened, troubled mind of Philip Salkin, the President of the United States. Rupert Daniels had been his best friend. If, Salkin pondered, he hadn't made the decision to run for the office—and then won—Rupert Daniels, as much of a brother as a brother could be, wouldn't be dead now. Salkin considered the immense burdens of the presidency, and for the moment, the death of his friend-since-childhood seemed much the greater burden.

Rupert Daniels had died for Phil Salkin.

Salkin wearily removed his glasses and lay them on top of the memo placed precisely in the middle of his desk blotter. He leaned forward, elbows on the desk, and massaged tired eyes with the heels of his hands. Then those once-callused hands slid down his cheeks until his chin balanced in his palms. He was a tired man, exhausted—not physically, mentally.

This was the third year of Phil Salkin's first term, and there was as yet no major international event that he could claim personal responsibility for as a turning point in world history. He was a decent, peaceful man who desperately visualized "good will toward men" as his singular contribution to world peace. And that was the mission with which he had charged his Secretary of State, Rupert Daniels, just months ago—"I will go anywhere, meet with any leader, anytime, in an effort to bring a final, peaceful solution to the Middle East. You know me well enough, Rupert, to speak for me if promises must be exacted from the United States to accomplish this." In retrospect, that sounded so pompous that he recalled Daniels to his office that afternoon. "Rupert, forget that bullshit! Here's a letter stating that your words are my words, your promises my promises. If you can bring them together, I, the United States, however you see fit to verbalize it, will go to whatever lengths possible to mediate a solution." At the time, it had seemed so simplistic . . . so logical . . . soooo . . .

It was winter now and "good will toward men" would be Rupert Daniels's epitaph, not Philip Salkin's. Phil Salkin would have to find another personal maxim.

The President smoothed the single sheet of paper on his blotter and reread that terse, yet historic, memo from Rupert Daniels:

TOP SECRET—HAND DELIVER

To: The President of the United States
Fm: Secretary of State
Re: Your Middle East Initiative

As of the writing of this memo, my Assistant Secretary for Mideast Affairs, Will Riley, is returning from the final stop on his leg of our mutual journey. I have just finished conversing with him on the scrambler. He has spent the past two weeks in the capitals of Turkey, Lebanon, Egypt, Tunisia, Algeria, and Morocco. During that period, I visited Amman, Jerusalem, Damascus, Baghdad, Tehran, Kuwait City, and Riyadh. Although we were not allowed to visit Tripoli, the Iraqis assure us the Libyans will send a delegation.

I am pleased to report that our mission was successful beyond imagination. The example set by the PLO and the Israelis convinced the other nations that peace throughout the region can become a reality before the turn of the century. Every leader has agreed to a summit conference to convene next April, dates to be confirmed, somewhere afloat in the Mediterranean. Each individual concurred that international waters would be the most logical site. Your short, simple letter bore the fruit of peace. It was a masterpiece of good will that appears to have isolated the source of humanity in each individual we met. They will come—I hope with open minds and clear hearts.

If you remember how long the preparatory stages for the Israeli/PLO accord took, I believe it is necessary to commence preparations at once for this historic summit. Because there are so many enemies, so many cross purposes extant in the cabinets and ministries of these Arab nations, absolute secrecy is vital if we are to have a chance of success. Some of these leaders would not survive until next April if it was known that they were willing to attend such a conference.

Once Will Riley has had a chance to wind down with his family, he will undertake the selection of a suitable ship. Both Will and I agree a navy ship would attract too much attention. You and I must discuss all of this as soon as possible, tomorrow A.M. if you concur.

One final word. I want you to know from the bottom of my heart that your magnanimous offer was accepted with a sense of relief by every individual Will and I encountered. An honest mediator—honest mediation—is what each one of these leaders has been hoping for.

Sincerely,
(ss) Rupert

But before that meeting with his dearest friend could ever take place, Rupert Daniels had literally been atomized as his limo crossed the Key Bridge.

Security? Peace dividend? Mutual pacts? *Garbage . . . foolishness . . . none of it exists in today's world!*

Phil Salkin's lips barely moved as he murmured a silent prayer for Rupert. At the end, rather than "amen," he mouthed the words "good will toward men."

Unashamed tears ran down his cheeks.

PART ONE

FEBRUARY

The Following Year

CHAPTER ONE

The two men, voyeurs so taken with the scene before them that they were afraid to even blink their eyes, stared breathlessly at the couple performing on the bed. The woman, long, silky, black hair rippling across damp shoulders, was astride the man.

She knew they were there, Hussein's people, knew they were studying her every move salaciously from behind the one-way mirror. Yet she was totally involved in the act. She would arch her back, eyes closed, balanced backward on her hands, palms flat on the mattress—enticing the man, forcing him to savor her magnificent body and actually watch himself disappear inside her. Then she would fall forward, her mane of thick, ebony hair enveloping his head, and rub her breasts across his chest until his frantic hands came up to massage them.

The man, young, blond, his pink skin aglow with sweat, was fascinated by the mirror, reveling in the sight of this gorgeous creature, black hair and dusky skin contrasting so captivatingly, totally involved in bringing him to the point of ecstasy. It was a sight he knew he would never experience in his own home. He would treasure this memory forever, and he told her so again and again.

She smiled back wordlessly. *If only you knew, Hans.* Even if she'd asked him if he minded people observing, he would never have believed there were actually two fully dressed men—her bodyguards—brazenly watching her every move.

She raised herself slightly above his belly so he might look between their bodies at the mirror, but he heaved upward.

"No, Hans. Remember, no motion. Tonight I am the aggressor. Tonight I am your sex slave," she purred. "You promised to let me do it all." She fell forward again and pressed her right breast into his face. "That's it, Hans. Don't move your hips. But use your tongue if you want. I'd like that. Yes, oh, yes, that's wonderful, Hans. You're wonderful. You are a perfect lover." Her voice was deep and soothing, and she could feel the man beneath her tensing as she lifted herself up and down on him. "But I want you to feel pleasure like you've never experienced in your life," she whispered. She lifted slowly, paused for an instant, then intensified her rhythm as he trembled in anticipation. She dug her fingernails into his shoulders to maximize the sensation.

One of the men studying the scene from behind the mirror licked his bushy mustache and moaned in concert with the German officer on the bed. His own hands clenched into fists as the man beneath the woman bared his teeth and shouted out something in German. The reason he was there was a memory for the moment.

"Soraya . . . she knows how to . . ." the other man murmured in admiration as the final words escaped him. "She's absolutely in control," he finished.

The German's body was still convulsing in pleasure as the woman leaned over to one side and pulled open her bedside drawer. He was so occupied in shaking his face back and forth between her breasts that he never saw the small Glock handgun she extracted. By the time awareness began to dawn, she was upright again, the cool barrel of the gun nestled beneath his chin.

"Soraya!" The German officer gurgled. His shock, as he recognized the intense look of hatred in the woman's eyes, was coupled with the sensation of the gun barrel jammed tightly against his windpipe and the explosion as she pulled the trigger. That was her climax—the moment of death!

Both of the men behind the mirror, even though they anticipated the event, exclaimed at the same time as the top of the blond head exploded into the pillow.

The woman sat upright, her right arm crooked, the gun now pointed at the ceiling, and snapped her head back, shaking her hair until it flowed down her back in a shiny, raven cascade. She turned her head slowly until she was staring directly into the mirror, then pursed her lips into a kiss for the observers she knew were still watching with rapt attention.

Her gaze returned briefly to the limp body beneath her before she lifted herself up and climbed off the bed. She pirouetted, facing the mirror, and threw her shoulders back like a soldier. Then she raised the gun, her index finger still on the trigger, and aimed it at the center of the mirror. She walked slowly forward until the barrel touched the glass. "Bang . . . bang . . ." she murmured. "You're dead . . . too." Her tongue flicked enticingly toward the invisible figures behind the mirror. What a pity that they found no pleasure in death—Soraya had built her reputation around it.

Both men had ducked instinctively. One reached forward and pressed a button down. "Soraya! In the name of Allah, put that thing down."

She gazed back provocatively at her own reflection. Slowly, her arm dropped down until the gun rested on the bureau beneath the mirror. "Well, are you satisfied?" She tilted her head to one side, flicking her tongue again, knowing they would be unable to take their eyes off her naked body.

"No . . . no, everything was perfect . . . no doubt . . ." He searched for words, found himself speechless. What . . . what could you say after something like that? Yet she'd insisted, and leadership had concurred, that this method was the only perfect way to accomplish Preminger's disappearance. *The woman was absolutely without conscience. She was like a . . . a jungle cat.* He never wanted to see anything like that again. Never!

"So, now Walter has a new job," she commented matter-of-factly.

"Yes . . . yes, he does," the invisible voice murmured. He had never met Walter Erhardt and was sure he never would. All he knew was that Erhardt, the darling of the new German submarine force, had been assured six months before of the next available command. There was now a command available—that of the man who now stared lifelessly at the ceiling.

Neither of the two men behind that mirror would ever know how Walter Erhardt had become associated with their group. Nor would they know what the purpose was for this strange liaison between a German submariner and an obscure organization of fundamentalist Muslims. There were so few Muslims who knew of Hussein's league that it seemed incomprehensible that a man like Walter Erhardt should be aware of them. It was not their place to question why unbelievers were involved, and the leadership wasn't about to make them aware. The less each member knew, the less chance that the names of other members or their targets would be known—and the better chance that member had of staying alive. They hadn't the slightest access to information that Soraya was already privy to—that they would soon be sacrificed, taking their knowledge of Hans Preminger's murder to the grave with them. They'd served the league's purpose. If, for some reason, Soraya hadn't successfully completed her mission, or if Preminger suddenly became aware of the trap, they were to act. They would have killed Preminger. From one source or the other, the leader would have proof that this step in his incredible scheme had been successful. Now, they were no longer needed.

"Are you finished staring at me then?" There was only one Soraya, only one woman in the organization with her ruthless talents.

"Get a shower and get dressed, Soraya," one of them said bravely yet tentatively. How could they know that they were just soldiers, placed there to protect her if something had gone awry, and now better dead with their frightful knowledge?

Soraya appreciated the tremor in the man's voice. She was in full control. There had been moments with the German—it would have been so easy to let herself go—*but to have such control of a man!* That was close to ecstasy. And it would have been nearly impossible to exterminate a man as critical as Preminger in any other manner. It was the only means of forcing him to elude the system that had been devised to protect him.

No, it wasn't quite ecstasy, but so close. She would save that moment of ecstasy for Michael. It might happen the following day. It might be a week. A month. She and Michael never knew. It just happened. But when it came, she would take that moment from him.

She went into the bathroom and twirled the hot water faucet on full. When the room was thick with steam, she reached in and turned the cold just enough to avoid scalding herself. Then she stood under the searing stream until her dusky skin achieved a pinkish luster.

Soraya did not know who the leaders of the organization were either, nor did she want to. She also wasn't aware of the location of their headquarters. If there was something she should know, then they would tell her. This willingness to adjust to the directives of the leadership, plus her incredible talents, were the major reasons she had survived and was considered indispensable. So many ideas had been conceived over the years, yet so few had been seen through to the end. Michael had explained that contacts like Walter Erhardt were nurtured years in advance with the hope that someday they might be used. She had no idea what the leaders had in mind this time, only that Erhardt's talents as a submariner could finally be employed on a specific mission.

Now, as the steaming water pulsated against her skin, Soraya erased Hans Preminger from her mind. When she reported to Michael, she would be ready for whatever assignment they had for her.

INITIAL REPORT TO DIRECTOR, HOMICIDE, KIEL

HEADQUARTERS RECEIVED A TELEPHONE CALL AT 0027 THIS MORNING FROM THE NIGHT MANAGER OF THE BODO CABARET REPORTING A SUSPICIOUS INCIDENT IN THE ALLEY DIRECTLY BEHIND HIS PLACE OF BUSINESS. CALLER REPORTED THAT AS HE ENTERED THE ALLEYWAY TO DEPOSIT THE LAST OF THE

EVENING TRASH HE WITNESSED TWO MEN CARRYING A LONG AWKWARD OBJECT WRAPPED IN A BLANKET DOWN THE FIRE ESCAPE OF THE BUILDING ACROSS FROM HIS REAR DOOR. WITNESS REMAINED IN THE SHADOWS AND IS CERTAIN HE WAS NOT OBSERVED. WITNESS REPORTED THAT HE CLEARLY IDENTIFIED A HUMAN FOOT HANGING FROM ONE END OF THE BLANKET. HE ALSO MAINTAINS THAT HE COULD SEE DARK STAINS ON THE OPPOSITE END OF THE BLANKET. SINCE HE WAS FRIGHTENED HE REMAINED IN PLACE UNTIL THE OBJECT IN THE BLANKET WAS PLACED IN THE BACK END OF AN UNIDENTIFIED AUTOMOBILE—NO LICENSE NUMBER AVAILABLE.

A CHECK OF THE ADDRESS IN QUESTION INDICATES THAT THE BUILDING HAS COMMERCIAL BUSINESSES ON THE STREET LEVEL AND SMALL APARTMENTS ON THE THREE FLOORS ABOVE. RESIDENTS ARE APPARENTLY TRANSIENT. INTERVIEWS TO BE CONDUCTED TODAY BY THIS DEPARTMENT.

CONCLUSION: SINCE WITNESS IS A RECOVERING ALCOHOLIC AND INTERVIEWING OFFICER MAINTAINS WITNESS WAS SOBER WE ARE CONTINUING AN UNOFFICIAL INVESTIGATION. HOWEVER THERE IS NO EVIDENCE TO SUBSTANTIATE THAT A CRIME HAS BEEN COMMITTED NOR IS THERE A CORPSE. A CODE THREE REPORT WILL BE DIRECTED TO YOUR OFFICE WITHIN TWENTY-FOUR HOURS.

FEDERAL REPUBLIC OF GERMANY

CLASSIFICATION: SECRET

TO: COMMANDING OFFICER, SUBMARINE FLOTILLA
FM: COMMANDING OFFICER, SUBMARINE SQUADRON FOUR

INFO: INSPECTOR OF THE NAVY/COMMANDING OFFICER, NORTHERN NAVAL DISTRICT/ DIRECTOR, ADMIN/LEGAL AFFAIRS

1) COMMANDING OFFICER S-252, COMMANDER HANS PREMINGER, DEPARTED SHIP LAST EVENING AT 1752 LOCAL TIME AFTER INFORMING EXECUTIVE OFFICER THAT HE COULD BE CONTACTED AT HIS HOME AT ANY TIME.

2) CAPTAIN PREMINGER'S WIFE CALLED SHIP'S QUARTERDECK AT APPROXIMATELY 2000 TO SPEAK TO HER HUSBAND. WHEN DUTY OFFICER TOOK HER CALL SHE INQUIRED AS TO WHEN THE CAPTAIN WOULD BE RETURNING HOME THAT EVENING. SHE WAS TOLD CAPTAIN PREMINGER HAD BEEN LOGGED OFF THE SHIP AT 1752 AND DUTY OFFICER INDICATED HE WOULD CONTACT THE EXECUTIVE OFFICER AND WOULD ALSO CALL MRS. PREMINGER WITH ANY FURTHER INFORMATION IF THE CAPTAIN HAD BEEN DETAINED. HE ALSO REQUESTED THAT CAPTAIN PREMINGER CALL THE QUARTERDECK WHEN HE RETURNED HOME.

3) CAPTAIN PREMINGER'S WIFE CALLED THE EXECUTIVE OFFICER AT HOME JUST BEFORE MIDNIGHT TO REPORT THAT HER HUSBAND STILL HADN'T RETURNED HOME. SHE WAS TOLD BY EXECUTIVE OFFICER THAT HE WOULD INSTIGATE A SEARCH IMMEDIATELY AND WOULD REPORT ANY INFORMATION DIRECTLY TO HER. HE THEN INFORMED SQUADRON DUTY OFFICER OF THE SITUATION AND RETURNED TO S-252 SHORTLY BEFORE 0030.

4) CAPTAIN PREMINGER FAILED TO REPORT TO ALL-CAPTAIN MEETING AT SQUADRON HEADQUARTERS SCHEDULED FOR 0830 THIS DATE. EXECUTIVE OFFICER HAS ASSUMED DUTIES AS ACTING COMMANDING OFFICER.

5) FOLLOW-UP REPORT NO LATER THAN

TWENTY-FOUR HOURS. INTERIM REPORTS UPON RECEIPT OF FURTHER VALID INFORMATION.

A stiff northeast breeze churned the harbor's gray surface into foamy whitecaps, then spun the froth skyward into raw, increasingly damp air that settled mercilessly over the city. Eckernforde, home port of the Bundesmarine's (German navy) Submarine Flotilla, lay under this colorless chill with a new coat of snow not yet darkened by the factory smoke that would blend with the heavy air. Her citizens slogged through the streets of the city with heads down against the wind and chill that penetrated so quickly into the bones.

S-252, the *Heinz Waller,* bumped gently against the woven bumpers alongside her pier. The rounded black hull of the submarine appeared motionless, and only the soft grinding sound of metal against hemp indicated that she was a separate and distinct entity in the dark oily water. There was a gangway secured to quarterdeck stanchions. Its pierside wheels turned slowly, squeaking for oil as S-252—her name in large white numerals on the conning tower rising from her rounded hull—heaved on the indistinct swell. An officer, a scarf pulled over his chin and the collar of his bridge coat up against his ears, huddled against the ship's high tower to ward off the wind.

A sailor in foul-weather gear appeared from a hatch just to one side of the officer. He carried two mugs of steaming coffee. "There you go, sir. That'll take the nip out of the air."

"Thanks, Neuner." He held the mug in both hands and inhaled the rising steam before sipping cautiously. "Doesn't change the weather, but it makes the gut feel better."

The two men returned to silence, each coping with the winter chill in his own way. They watched the pierside activity without interest—messengers on bicycles peddling through steam clouds generated by shoreside power units, trucks hauling supplies to various ships, work parties hustling goods from truck to pierside to the human chains that passed each item below. It was a typical day for any naval base anywhere in the world, the same work, the same grumbling, the same sights. The only difference was that it was February in Eckernforde and it was cold and raw and miserable.

The sailor moved over in the lee of the sail by the officer of the watch. "Hear anything more about the captain, sir?" he asked, even though he knew before he spoke that there'd been nothing more since they assumed the quarterdeck watch that morning.

The officer knew that the sailor was aware there had been no further word concerning the whereabouts of S-252's commanding officer, but he also shared the concern for the popular Captain Preminger. "Nothing yet, Neuner, but you can be sure the executive officer will pass the word the moment he hears something."

Every man aboard *Heinz Waller* knew that Captain Preminger's wife had called the submarine's duty officer around 2000 last night to inquire if her husband was coming home for dinner, and had been informed that the captain was logged off *Waller*'s quarterdeck before 1800 that evening. They also knew she called the executive officer at his apartment in town just before midnight and learned only that her husband had voiced no plans to him other than to return directly home that night. The crew was aware, too, that at 0830 on this chill morning, the squadron commander had called *Waller*'s quarterdeck to ask if Captain Preminger planned to join the others at the commanding officers' conference about to begin. The executive officer had departed instantly to attend in the captain's place while the weapons officer, the next senior, contacted the captain's now-hysterical wife to assure her that the navy had already initiated an investigation. There was nothing critical to S-252 that her crew wouldn't be aware of almost instantly. Every individual, from captain to the newest seaman, was equally important on a submarine.

"Strange isn't it, sir? So unlike Captain Preminger." The sailor hugged himself for warmth. "He's always so predictable. When I was below for the coffee, I heard someone say you could always set your watch to the captain and you couldn't go wrong."

It was true. The captain was almost machinelike in his actions. It seemed there was nothing that could deviate him from the schedule he set for himself and for S-252. *Waller* was by far the most efficient submarine in the squadron, probably the finest in the German navy as far as her captain and crew were concerned. It was really so unlike the man. The duty officer glanced unconsciously at his watch. "That's right. You really can set your watch by him. I'm sure he'll be back aboard during our watch, certainly no later than the next one. And with a perfectly sound reason for whatever detained him, too," he added reassuringly, for he knew whatever he said would be repeated below decks.

A light snow began to fall again, the icy northeast wind blowing little rivulets of it across the rounded hull and into the harbor. The naval base went on about its routine—the trucks, the messengers on bicycles, the working parties, the squadron captain's meeting—all without Captain Hans Preminger.

In the chill mountains of Lebanon, east of Beirut near the town of Biskinta, six men squatted for warmth around a campfire and talked among themselves. They would have been warmer in the peasant hut nearby, but their leader decreed that was to be reserved for eating and sleeping. Besides, they intuitively preferred the companionship and security of the fire just as their ancestors had before them. Many generations earlier, men like themselves had stared into the flames and planned the acts that would bring justice for their people according to the ancient Shari'ah, and this evening would be no different. Planning would be done just as their forebears had done it. Victory would be accomplished by the most modern of means.

"Michael and Soraya have both been in contact with Erhardt now. His attitude is unchanged. Revenge is foremost in his mind. He remains a driven man." The speaker was dressed, as were the others, in the robes any Arab would wear that time of year in the mountains. He was their leader and was known only by a single title, Hussein, a common name in the Arabic world, and he limited it to that to preserve his anonymity.

"When will he learn of his mission?" asked the one who had arrived just hours before. He was constantly late, always impatient.

"Not until they are actually close to their target," Hussein cautioned. "Erhardt, himself, asked that we not tell him. He is very strange, very different from us. There is an extremely fine line there that we must understand. He is a German naval officer first. This submarine is his first command and it is an objective he has cherished all his life." He fed another stick into the flames. "He made it quite clear that he must work with the men on his ship and learn everything he can about them—there are some, technicians, who know that type of submarine better than the others, whom he may have to keep. He understands that we have recruited the majority of the final crew." Hussein looked over to the impatient one. "His methods are no different than ours. Our own men have no idea of what we will require from them while they train. If no one knows," he added, "security is absolute."

"Fortune has indeed smiled upon us," commented the eldest, who sincerely believed there was a theological explanation for everything. He cared nothing for modern technology. He was the savant of the group, the mullah, their religious leader.

"Fortune and superb planning," Hussein remarked. "Erhardt's no quirk of fate. I discovered him and nurtured him for years. He is superb in his profession."

"And still dedicated to us?" It was a legacy of their culture not to trust an outsider.

"He has never been dedicated to us. He is dedicated to his own revenge."

Walter Erhardt possessed one of the finest young minds in the German submarine force. And, as austere as he was, he was also an extremely popular officer. While he adhered to a rigid military decorum that, coupled with his brilliance, gratified his seniors, he retained the respect of his fellow officers. His professionalism and devotion to duty was unquestioned. There was absolutely nothing in his background that would lead any of his seniors to doubt that he should have the next available submarine command. It had been general knowledge that Walter Erhardt would receive that opportunity. Although it was assumed that would be

S-259, since her captain was scheduled to rotate ashore the following summer, fate had brought him to S-252, the *Heinz Waller.*

Erhardt was the perfect man for a difficult situation.

But every man has a skeleton in his closet. What no one in the German navy was aware of, not even the intelligence experts who conducted background investigations of all officers destined for submarine duty, was that Erhardt had once been deeply in love with a girl of the Islamic faith. It had been his first and only love and one that he would never recover from. Her memory was the spirit that drove Walter Erhardt, the spirit that allowed him to maintain the appearance of total devotion to the German navy. His entire life appeared to revolve around the submarine service.

Darra Paddha was an Iranian—born and raised in Rey, a suburb of Tehran—and so light-skinned that she might have lived unquestioned in Germany as a native. Her hair was long and dark, her eyes a liquid brown, her nose short and rounded, her cheekbones pronounced, and her complexion olive yet pale enough for occasional freckles on her nose and cheeks. She was beautiful by any standard and she enchanted Walter Erhardt the summer they met in Malta, when he was a new junior officer on leave.

The Maltese possess a diverse cultural background—northern Africa, southern Europe, the Middle East's Levant. They take pride in their Arabic heritage, which influences their language, customs, and religious background, and as a result, they maintain close ties with Arab nations. It was therefore a combination of trust and heritage that convinced Darra's family to allow her to travel to Malta. It was a safe haven for a modern Iranian girl who had completed her education and whose family did not practice strict Islamic conformity to the ancient laws. It was also equally natural for Erhardt to be there because the island was a destination for vacationing Germans. That they met and fell in love was seen by both of the young people as their good fortune, since neither possessed the religious intensity that should have kept them apart.

If two young people could be naive about love and sex, it was Walter and Darra. They were a couple destined for each other, a couple who laughed at the joys of learning about the mysteries of love through their own fumbling and experimentation. Their meeting on a Mediterranean island was like a summer romance except they both knew this one would have no end when they parted. They believed they were destiny's children and they sensed it even before they were able to express it to each other. The concept of *eternal love* quite suddenly provided meaning for their young lives.

Their two weeks of bliss ended when Erhardt's leave was up and he returned to duty at the submarine base thirty kilometers north of Kiel in Eckernforde, and it was shattered forever when Darra was killed on her flight back home. The first leg of her trip was on a Syrian airliner destined for Damascus where she would change planes for the final leg to Tehran. But it occurred on a day when the Israelis and the Syrians were involved in another of their perpetual misunderstandings. Initially, it began as a border incident that should have been solved by the negotiations of older men. But it was the impetuosity of youth that caused the destruction of an Israeli helicopter by a missile prematurely launched from Syrian territory. While the politicians postured, the Israeli military seethed, and that was how the Syrian A-300 Darra was aboard was blown out of the Mediterranean sky by an Israeli missile boat positive that their airspace was about to be penetrated by a Syrian military plane.

The shock of her loss overwhelmed Walter Erhardt. From the second he learned of Darra's death, he made a covenant with his own personal devil that her loss—*his loss*—would be avenged and someday there would be a greater price paid than any man might comprehend. His goal was as pure and simple as their love had been, and the objective was a vengeance beyond even his own comprehension. Israeli or Arab—it didn't matter. Through their mutual hatred of each other, they'd destroyed the one love of his life.

Erhardt briefly toyed with the Muslim faith because it had meant enough to Darra that he had agreed to study it. It hadn't been a promise to convert, simply an understanding between two lovers to fully comprehend the background of the other. But all he could gain from Islam's pronouncements after her tragic death, perhaps all he cared to understand, was *an eye for an eye.* He would honor her memory by never loving another. His singular goal became an uncontrollable and uncompromising vengeance.

Eventually, he saw that his mission could be twofold and that the first part might just balance the other. *By becoming the best submariner in the German navy, would he position himself to avenge his lost love?*

FEDERAL REPUBLIC OF GERMANY

CLASSIFICATION: SECRET

TO: COMMANDING OFFICER, NORTHERN NAVAL DISTRICT/COMMANDING OFFICER, SUBMARINE FLOTILLA/COMMANDING OFFICER, SUBMARINE SQUADRON FOUR
FM: DIRECTOR, ADMIN/LEGAL AFFAIRS
INFO: FEDERAL MINISTER OF DEFENSE/ INSPECTOR OF THE NAVY

REF: A) DISAPPEARANCE OF COMMANDING OFFICER S-252
B) TWENTY-FOUR-HOUR FOLLOW-UP REPORT

1) THIS COMMAND INITIATED CONTACT WITH KIEL LAW ENFORCEMENT AGENCIES ON THE SAME DATE AS THE DISAPPEARANCE OF COMMANDER HANS PREMINGER ON THE ASSUMPTION THAT FOUL PLAY MAY HAVE BEEN INVOLVED.

2) NO TRACE OF CAPTAIN PREMINGER HAS BEEN FOUND.

3) KIEL AUTHORITIES REPORT ONE POSSIBLE CASE THAT MAY BE RELATED. WITNESS REPORTED WHAT MAY HAVE BEEN A CORPSE LOADED INTO AUTOMOBILE TRUNK ON THE EVENING OF PREMINGER'S DISAPPEARANCE. THERE REMAINS NO SUBSTANTIATION THAT A CRIME ACTUALLY OCCURRED. THERE IS NO INDICATION THAT PREMINGER MAY NECESSARILY HAVE BEEN INVOLVED. MOST RECENT POLICE REPORT BEING SENT UNDER SEPARATE COVER FOR YOUR INFORMATION.

4) RECOMMENDATIONS: A) CONTINUE INVESTIGATION IN CONJUNCTION WITH LOCAL AUTHORITIES; B) APPOINT NEW S-252 COMMANDING OFFICER ON EITHER AN INTERIM OR PERMANENT BASIS DEPENDING ON NEEDS OF SUBMARINE FORCE; C) ASSIGN QUALIFIED SUBMARINER TO S-252 AS INVESTIGATING OFFICER TO DETERMINE IF ANY MEMBER OF THE CREW MAY BE INVOLVED IN DISAPPEARANCE.

5) INTERIM REPORTS FOLLOW UPON RECEIPT OF FURTHER VALID INFORMATION.

Walter Erhardt watched the evening news in his tiny bachelor apartment in Kiel without really seeing it. Whenever thoughts of Darra gained control of his mind, something seemed to snap—something deep within his soul that he had never quite been able to comprehend—and when this happened, he understood that his most important reason for living was to exact vengeance for her death. Although he was certain command of the S-252 would be his, something else occupied his mind.

His thoughts drifted back to those horrible, confusing days after Darra's plane had been shot down. When traditional religious services were held in Rey for Darra Paddha, Erhardt was the sole Christian present. He was there because Darra had taken her only sister into her confidence during an excited phone conversation between Malta and Tehran. Somehow that sister had understood the depths of their love affair and had been able to contact Walter. There were two sleepless days filled with anguish and confusion as he traveled back and forth to Tehran without anyone being aware of his whereabouts.

He was allowed into Iran because of her family's influence, but he had remained unobtrusive at the sister's suggestion, appearing at the Islamic services only after they had begun. He would never have been noticed if a Palestinian named Hussein hadn't been informed of a German's arrival in Tehran. Hussein got close enough to Erhardt to recognize the unfathomable hatred radiating from his eyes.

The young German had a square chin that thrust out slightly, expressive lips around a small mouth, cheekbones that emphasized his thin angular face, and deep-set, blue eyes that were soft and almost sad, except for those moments he thought of his lovely Darra. Erhardt had thin dark hair, short and efficiently parted, and his pale complexion caused his dark beard to stand out no matter how closely he shaved.

Hussein was the one who six months later made the initial contact with Erhardt and began the process of nourishing that hatred. How could Hussein have possibly known that S-252 would become available, unless . . .

FEDERAL REPUBLIC OF GERMANY

CLASSIFICATION: UNCLASS

TO: COMMANDER WALTER ERHARDT, FRGN
FM: DIRECTOR, ADMIN/LEGAL AFFAIRS
INFO: FEDERAL MINISTER OF DEFENSE/INSPECTOR OF THE NAVY/COMMANDING OFFICER, NORTHERN NAVAL DISTRICT/COMMANDING OFFICER, SUBMARINE FLOTILLA/COMMANDING OFFICER, SUBMARINE SQUADRON FOUR

1) YOU ARE HEREBY ORDERED TO ASSUME COMMAND OF FRG(SS) HEINZ WALLER (S-252) EARLIEST POSSIBLE.

2) UPON REPORTING YOU WILL IMMEDIATELY RELIEVE INTERIM COMMANDING OFFICER.

3) INTERIM COMMANDING OFFICER WILL RESUME DUTIES AS EXECUTIVE OFFICER.

4) UPON ASSUMPTION OF COMMAND S-252 REPORT TO COMMANDING OFFICER, SUBMARINE SQUADRON FOUR FOR ORDERS.

CHAPTER TWO

The watch officer on the bridge of MV *Calm Seas* awoke Captain Waters in his cabin at five forty-eight on a pleasant spring morning to report visual landfall. Bridge personnel had actually acquired the coastline of Israel on radar an hour and a half before and had reported into the Israeli Sea Defense Network shortly afterward. But there'd been no reason to interrupt the captain until the first rays of early morning sun reflected off the distant skyline of Haifa.

Calm Seas was a magnificent private yacht, brilliant white from keel to mast head, her dolphin-nosed bow balanced by dramatically sweeping lines. Christened in 1992, she was designed to provide the ultimate in creature comforts to the wealthiest people in the world, who willingly paid a great deal of money to savor her luxury. She was over two hundred feet in length and thirty feet wide. *Calm Seas* was heavy, almost a thousand tons fully loaded, and she cruised with all four diesel engines at eighteen knots, although a friendly current could make her a knot or two faster during ocean crossings. Computer-controlled stabilizers on either side of her hull insured smooth passage in all but the foulest weather. A crew of twenty pampered her fortunate passengers. In an article about the most exotic vacations available to the rich, *Fortune* quoted *Yachting Magazine: "Calm Seas* surpasses every private vessel at sea in true elegance. Nothing afloat or ashore can match the unusual amenities that her staff believes each passenger deserves during their stay aboard."

Early morning breezes floated the aroma of orange blossoms across the Mediterranean to presage a perfect spring day so early in February. The watch officer studied the changing colors of the sunrise in a cloudless sky. Spring seemed to be coming early to the Mediterranean after a mild winter. That was why *Calm Seas'* owners had agreed to allow their current charter to debark in Haifa. Normally, she remained in warm waters until April, but the six wealthy couples who'd chartered her wanted to finish their Caribbean vacation with an ocean crossing and a visit to Israel. There was no reason, the owners agreed, to deny those who were paying the bill if the weather was within reason.

And then there were the next few months to consider. The night before, the captain had shared a message from the owners with his senior crew. The majority partner was to meet the ship at the dock in Haifa with an individual who might be willing to charter *Calm Seas* for the next six months; there was also the distinct possibility of a dry-dock period for structural alterations during that time. Since there were two other charters and a wedding scheduled before they were to enter dry dock in Naples for overhaul, that meant this individual had offered so much money that the owners didn't mind canceling out on someone who had already made an extensive down payment.

The idea was exciting. Some of the people who spent a week or two aboard could be stimulating. Sometimes, the younger women grew tired of their wealthy companions, who were generally old enough to be their fathers, and found members of the crew most accommodating.

Who was this individual who found no problem in parting with millions of dollars for a few weeks at sea?

Haffar Qusuriyah Almamoudi had been bigger than most children his age and obtained immediate respect because of his size. As an adolescent, he was not only bigger and better looking than the other boys his age but he also possessed an inherent maturity that was instinctively recognized by the teenage girls who noted such traits. When he attained manhood, he still was taller than many men and he had filled out physically into a powerful individual handsome enough to become a movie star, if he cared. His black hair, at one time thick and curly, had been trained since he was sixteen to look more Western. He became an Omar Sharif–type Arab. His nose was broad and straight, his dark eyes set wide under heavy eyebrows, and his jaw strong and square. He had always taken care of his teeth and his complexion so that now even men marveled at his dark appealing looks.

When necessary, Almamoudi could be only as Arab as a Westerner would hope a friendly Arab would appear. Yet he was anything but friendly toward Westerners, even though he had assumed a Western name—Michael. That was a convenience chosen by the leader of the Palestinian organization that recruited him. That leader, known only as Hussein, believed that youth was more important than maturity in a violent world. The old men could think and they could plan, but it was the young people, men and women alike, who could act.

Michael's original beliefs had been naive and his goals ingenuous. A year in an Italian jail after his twentieth birthday altered his objectives considerably. He now believed, thanks to Hussein and his invisible organization, that the respect Arabs deserved in the modern world was impossible as long as Israel maintained her borders and established the rules in the Middle East, and moderate Arabs allowed that. Hussein taught that the latter were no better than the Jews. Michael never expected to change the world during however many years he survived, but he did plan to make things easier for those Arabs who would be in a position to change it in the future. That unselfish attitude had brought him to Hussein's attention.

Michael looked up from his notepad, aware that Soraya had been speaking to him, yet totally unaware of what she'd said. ". . . that Walter . . . he will lose interest in us. His whole world is that submarine. It is all he ever aspired to," Soraya insisted vehemently, her voice rising when she noticed he hadn't been paying attention. She hated to be ignored.

Michael didn't care to argue with her. "Was, Soraya," he said patiently. "Until his Darra died, a submarine was all he cared about. Now there are two things in his world and they are inextricably bound to each other. His beloved submarine is, of course, one, and somehow he believes that through it he will gain the second, the vengeance he must seek for his beloved Darra. Hussein says it's a crusade of some kind. He calls Walter the lone crusader. Who knows why he's so possessed? I imagine that's also why he's incapable of making love to any woman."

"How do *you* know he can't?" Soraya retorted.

Michael couldn't resist twisting the knife just a little bit. "Maybe after he's gotten that out of his system he'll screw you until it hurts to get up off your back." He smiled widely at the anger that flashed momentarily in Soraya's eyes. He relished the fact that Walter Erhardt found it so easy to resist her. It was even more amusing as he watched her temper flare because she knew exactly why he was smiling. Erhardt's refusal of her was that much more infuriating because she believed she was more powerful than any man.

"It's not funny, Michael," she snapped. Even Almamoudi's own people were accustomed to referring to him by his Western name. "You have a sick sense of humor."

"What's not funny?" he teased.

"I don't know how you can see humor in what I'm saying. Sometimes I agree with the others. You're almost too Westernized." She glared at him, then turned away, more angry at herself than Michael because she'd allowed him to succeed with his male humor.

She craved a respect from Michael that would make them equals. While she believed that as a Muslim warrior she would go to heaven as a martyr, she also believed in setting her own standards. The Islamic code for women covered those who were controlled by men. No man controlled Soraya. With the exception of Michael, she used sex as a weapon, actually coming in intimate physical contact with her victims before killing them. He'd never dared comment on that, but she intuitively knew, from his facial expression if nothing else, that her actions mystified him. And that was the way it should be.

The relationship she and Michael maintained was a

strange blend of common sense and carnal behavior. Initially they had been drawn to each other by one thing, animal magnetism. Both were dedicated terrorists, neither believed they would survive to even middle age, and their sporadic lovemaking was almost feral in nature from the moment of their first embrace. Each intended to possess the other, yet they both failed in that regard. They couldn't live together as lovers, but they proved to be a superb team within Michael's part of the organization. How could such a relationship work when there were still times that basic human needs overwhelmed them? There appeared to be no answer and both Michael and Soraya determined to allow those moments. When this happened, Michael compared it to two lions fighting over fresh kill.

"Are you sorry for what you said . . . for what you were thinking a moment ago?" she asked.

"Why does it matter?"

"I have a deep respect for you, Michael," she responded, rising from her chair. "I would hope you have the same regard for me." For some reason she didn't immediately perceive, her voice had mellowed. Husky. "We have to understand each other." There it was again, husky, not guttural . . . but so deep. She was sure it was unintentional.

"We do." Michael, noting the change in her voice, was surprised that it affected him also. He rose to his feet and extended his hand to her as he came from behind the desk. "I guess if you feel that whatever I said lowered you in my eyes, then I am indeed sorry," he said apologetically. "Nothing will work in this organization without the two of us . . . on an equal basis." This was unnerving. What was there about her that could so quickly gain control of him?

Soraya reached for his hand, the same fervor creating a knot in her chest. They turned into each other at the same moment, their bodies coming into contact even before their arms reached out. Neither would be able to say afterward which of them initiated it. They were suddenly one person, tongues probing deeply into each other's mouth. Then they were moving, still as one, to the old sofa that often had served them as a bed.

Clothes fell to the floor. They were both naked below the waist, grinding rhythmically against each other. Michael's hands reached under her blouse and pushed her bra up, roughly kneading her breasts. Then they were down on the cushions, Soraya on top, fingernails digging through his shirt as she rode him with her head back, eyes closed, purring deeply like a cat.

Michael felt himself peaking too quickly, and with a surge of strength, he forced her upward and back. Now he was on top of her. He bit her lip. He bit her nipples. Her fingernails dug deeply into his shoulders, raking away strips of skin. As suddenly as it had started, it was over with an animal howl of gratification escaping Soraya's lips. Michael's full weight enveloped her as he relaxed and sucked in deep, almost painful breaths. Drops of blood from his shoulders fell across her breasts.

It had indeed been much like two lions fighting over fresh kill.

Otto Rather had been executive officer of S-252, a modern Type-212 diesel submarine, six months before Hans Preminger reported aboard as commanding officer. Preminger had been as different from the previous captain as night and day, yet Rather managed to adapt to him quickly, as a good executive officer was expected to do. It was no more than Rather would have expected of his number two when he one day commanded his own submarine. All captains were unique and he'd expected the new one would be no different.

Walter Erhardt's reputation had proceeded him. He was brilliant, tough, and demanding, yet he also made clear from his first day on board that he would expect no more of any man than he would of himself. It was said that Erhardt was so good that he would be selected early as an admiral, that he would return the German submarine force to the glory it had once known, and even that the FRG Navy might again be the dominant seagoing force. It would be difficult to serve under him. It also seemed that it would be rewarding for each crewman of S-252.

But Rather would never forget their first few days at sea with Erhardt commanding. The new captain had requested a training cruise his first week on board.

"Ninety meters," the new captain ordered as they slipped

beneath the surface of the shallow North Sea on the first dive.

There was a momentary and absolute silence in S-252's control room as Captain Erhardt's order rang out. Erhardt's eyebrows knit quizzically and he glanced at his executive officer. Then the diving officer echoed the command. "Ninety meters, aye. Make your angle fifteen degrees," he ordered the man on the bow planes as he adjusted the valves to flood the ballast tanks.

"Otto, I think maybe Preminger never took this boat to sea." Walter Erhardt effected a mirthless smile. "Did you spend most of your time alongside the pier?" It was difficult to tell if he was joking. His face reflected neither anger nor humor.

"Certainly not, Captain." *Heinz Waller*'s executive officer answered vigorously. "We have been the finest submarine in the squadron. Our efficiency ratings are some of the highest ever accumulated in the fleet." Otto Rather appeared anything but the spit-and-polish officer Erhardt had hoped for as his number two. He was a short man, solidly built like a wrestler. His unruly thatch of brown hair seemed to meet his bushy eyebrows somewhere in the middle of his forehead. His nose was wide and looked as if someone had smashed it into his broad face. He had a large mouth that helped to accentuate an even wider, outthrust jaw. No matter how neat and well pressed his uniforms were before he put them on, they soon looked like he'd slept in them. His appearance disappointed Erhardt after all the positive things the squadron commander had to say about Rather, especially after he was told the executive officer was so well respected that they'd even considered making him permanent commanding officer of S-252.

"Diving officer, increase your angle to thirty degrees," Erhardt ordered.

"Aye, sir." The diving officer glanced quickly at Rather out of the corner of his eye. "Increase your angle to thirty degrees," he ordered, his eyes nervously glancing at the depth gauge.

Erhardt turned back to Rather. The slight smile on his face was more curious than anything else. "Then why the hesitation when I just gave the order for ninety meters?"

Erhardt's voice was calm, just loud enough for his executive officer to hear, but Rather saw in his eyes that he was deadly serious.

"Captain, the charts indicate only one hundred seven meters at most in our current position. This is very shallow water. With the currents here, who knows?" Rather shrugged. "It could be deeper . . . maybe shallower. Who knows?" he repeated. "Captain Preminger never dove so . . . so close to the bottom . . ." He was choosing his words very carefully. "And he always employed a shallower angle . . . if he did," the executive officer added, eyeing the depth gauge. The submarine was passing sixty meters.

"Make your angle fifteen degrees," the diving officer ordered the planesman.

"Hold your angle at thirty," Erhardt contradicted, "until I give the order." He moved over beside the diving officer and watched the gauge closely. "Let me show you what I mean." Seventy meters. Eighty meters. "Ten degrees now," Erhardt ordered, "smartly."

S-252 slowed her descent, seeming to level off like an aircraft as her angle changed rapidly.

"Very well." They were close to ninety meters. "Five degrees up angle." The depth gauge read ninety-two, ninety-three, almost ninety-four before decreasing. "Now make your depth ninety meters," Erhardt said to the diving officer. "That's the way I expect we will operate from now on. Crisply. We don't wallow. We fly. Someday it may be the difference between survival or death for all of us." His voice was even and his manner restrained, but each individual in the control room realized that their accepted routines were already changed forever. S-252 had entered a new era.

From that moment on, *Heinz Waller* would fly like a bird. And with each dive, Otto Rather's nerves would become a bit more frayed. His new captain preferred to fly rather than to sail. That was not something that was part of the mystique of Walter Erhardt as he understood it.

What a pair! Francis Waters, *Calm Seas'* captain, couldn't believe they had survived each other for whatever time they'd waited on the dock. The two men, one of them the majority owner, had remained in the shade until all passengers departed *Calm Seas* before coming aboard.

The yacht's owners were Greek, and the one who'd waited on the pier, Mr. Demetrius, was the self-made millionaire. He was short, blocky, and swarthy, and his long curly hair flowed below his shirt collar. Everything not covered by clothing was hairy. Chest hair flooded from his half-open shirt. His arms, even his hands and fingers, were black with hair. And all that fur was set off by gold and precious stones—chains, bracelets, rings. He was a walking ad for a jewelry store, an extremely expensive and successful one. When Waters had first identified him through the binoculars, he was in the process of firing up the largest, blackest cigar in captivity.

Mr. Demetrius gave no indication that he was with a prospective client as he charged up the gangway ahead of the other man. "Francees, baby,"—he pronounced the second word *beebee*—"howsit?" He gave Waters a bear hug and a phony, cigar-laden kiss on either cheek. "Meet a frenomine, Weel Reely." His accent was as thick as his body hair as he turned and clapped the other man on the shoulder, pushing him toward his captain. "Captain *Frenkee* Waters."

Waters was the opposite of his boss. His hair and eyebrows were dark blond and his piercing gray-blue eyes peered out of a tanned, square-jawed, high-cheekboned face. Although his height was average, he was a powerfully built man with broad shoulders. He wore white slacks and a white short-sleeve shirt with black shoulder boards with gold stripes that indicated he was the captain.

"Will Riley," the other corrected, extending his hand. "I'm pleased to make your acquaintance, Captain. Did I understand from Mr. Demetrius that your name is Frankie?" he asked with the hint of a grin at the corners of his mouth.

Waters shook hands with the man who was the antithesis of Mr. Demetrius. He was medium height, with short razor-trimmed red hair, blue eyes, and pale skin. Even though he was wearing a short-sleeve shirt like most men in Haifa as spring approached, he was attired in gray slacks and carried a blue blazer over his arm. Only Americans dressed like that. It was the paisley tie that assured Waters that the man must work for the U.S. government. "I make an effort to go by the name my parents gave me: Francis, if you don't mind."

"Not at all. Francis it will be. I hope we'll be working together for a while."

"Weel may pay for boat for seex monts . . . seex whole monts . . . cash," Mr. Demetrius announced with pleasure.

"I'm pleased to be at your service, Mr. Riley. When would your charter commence?" Waters inquired politely.

"Now, Frenkee, eef he likes our sheep."

Waters frowned. *Calm Seas* was already scheduled for a German industrialist the following week, an Arab sheik for three weeks in March, and the wedding of Demetrius's only daughter the first week of April. "What about the existing charters?" He glanced at Riley as he spoke and saw only that the man was smiling politely.

"Not important, Frenkee. He pay seex monts cash."

Waters frowned curiously. There was no urgent need for cash. *Calm Seas* was a cash cow. Now, quite suddenly, Demetrius was apparently ready to give total control to an unknown American. He and his partners were odd from anyone's point of view, but this was totally unlike them.

"What I really need to do," Riley said politely, "is tour the ship immediately. You know, make sure it's what I think it is, make sure it's capable of serving our purposes without too many alterations. I believe you're the individual who can confirm whether a change is structurally feasible or not."

"Alterations?"

Riley smiled. "If I decide to charter, I can explain in more detail. Mr. Demetrius has agreed to any structural changes we deem necessary." His smile never changed, but there was a hard look around his eyes that told Francis this preppy-looking American was much more than he cared to let on.

Demetrius nodded his concurrence.

"Of course, we'll return it to its original state after we're finished. No problem with that. That's part of our bargain."

Demetrius's head bobbed up and down again in acknowledgment.

Riley glanced at his watch, then smiled apologetically at Waters. "I'm afraid I'm on a tight schedule today. Could we start the tour of the ship now—bow to stern, if that's how you do it?" The smile persisted along with an amusing naiveté that was an obvious put-on.

Waters turned incredulously to his owner. "If this is what you prefer me to do, sir?"

"Eet's best charter yet, Frenkee," Mr. Demetrius replied with a nervous shrug of his shoulders.

Francis Waters's first question after Demetrius's departure was this: "What in the world do you have on Demetrius, Mr. Riley?"

"A lot." The smile was a bit harder, a bit more assertive.

"You don't care to explain?"

"I believe the standard answer is—I'm not at liberty to do so at this time."

"All right." Waters thought he'd gotten away from that kind of bullshit after he got out of the navy. "Seeing that I am this ship's captain, what can you tell me?"

"I'm sure you've already guessed that I'm an American."

"Not too difficult to figure."

"And for a six-month charter, you figured out my boss is pretty well heeled."

"And he's going to make alterations to this ship, which will be at a considerable cost, then change them all back after he's finished."

"Correct. But I'll tell you what. If you consider them improvements, we'll also leave them for you, rather than change them back. Shall we start, Captain?"

"Why not." Waters turned toward the bow. "We'll start up forward, bow to stern, like you said."

Waters opened the watertight hatch farthest forward on the main deck. "Do you really feel you have to see spaces like this chain locker, Mr. Riley?"

"Call me Will, please," Riley interrupted with that practiced smile. "And, yes, every space. I'll want a copy of the engineering design, too, so if I see every single space I'll be better prepared to explain it all to my superiors."

Almost three hours later, the two men sat down for a sandwich in *Calm Seas'* main salon. "Why did you pick *Calm Seas?"* Waters asked. "There are others equally luxurious, some of them even cheaper."

"Because of Mr. Demetrius." Will Riley displayed a knowing grin. "He doesn't dare whisper a word about this to anyone, not even to his wife or his girlfriends . . . and you won't either."

"You're sure of that, aren't you?"

"Quite." Riley displayed a pained expression, the kind that said he hated doing what he had to do. "I'm as sure as I am because you wouldn't want the Feds to learn about a boat trip you once made through the Caribbean to Fort Lauderdale. You were captain of a sixty-five-footer then, and you carried three couples supposedly on vacation. When you brought them in, you landed six very wealthy, very illegal aliens along with almost twelve tons of high-grade cocaine that supported them exactly the way they had lived back in Colombia."

Waters bit his lower lip. That had been twelve years before, and it was the only gamble he'd ever taken. He still woke up at nights scared to death that someone would find out someday.

"It was your only mistake, Francis. Everyone makes a mistake from time to time, and your government is willing to forgive and forget in exchange for your silence . . . your absolute silence . . . just like Mr. Demetrius, who I can assure you makes your little adventure look like a day in the country with your grandmother. We have a marvelous understanding, don't we?"

Francis Waters, unable to find the words to answer, nodded silently. Someone had him by the proverbial short hairs.

CHAPTER THREE

The commanding officer of Submarine Squadron Four had received a phone call less than a week after Captain Hans Preminger's disappearance from the Director-Homicide, Kiel Investigative Bureau. It was just a day after the change-of-command ceremony when Walter Erhardt became captain of *Heinz Waller.*

Dir: Admiral, a fisherman recovered a corpse in his nets earlier today, about two kilometers offshore. I'm afraid it's been chewed up enough that any visual identification is impossible, but we were hoping your people might be willing to loan us Captain Preminger's medical and dental records.

Adm: The navy, of course, wants to cooperate with anything regarding Captain Preminger. But is there anything that might indicate this . . . ah . . . corpse . . . could be Captain Preminger's?

Dir: It's only a guess by our investigators, Admiral. Nothing definite. We currently have half a dozen missing people in our files who are recent enough to fit the condition of this one. Two are female and this one is definitely male. One is an eighty-year-old man suffering from

Alzheimer's. The body of the one we have is too well muscled for anyone that age. One is a local derelict who was six inches shorter than this corpse, and the final one is an Oriental. Our corpse is a tall Caucasian male, probably a bit under forty years old.

Adm: Any indication of the cause of death?

Dir: The top of his head is missing.

Adm: (After a moment's pause) I can't believe one of my captains . . .

Dir: We have no proof this is Captain Preminger, Admiral. It's just that he fits this victim's preliminary ID.

Adm: Is there a reason for the . . . the top of the head . . . ah . . .

Dir: There's enough visual evidence to indicate that a gunshot wound exists beneath the victim's chin. The medical examiner will determine the cause of death before the end of the day. That's why we'd like Preminger's medical records and . . .

Adm: Of course, as I said before, the navy will cooperate. If I might ask a favor of you . . . I hope . . . I mean . . . the newspapers. You understand what I'm driving at?

Dir: Nothing has been released to the media at this stage, sir, because we have no identification of the corpse and no evidence of foul play. But you have to realize that the fisherman who discovered the corpse is not required to . . .

Adm: Of course, sir, I'm not asking that you withhold information from the media. The navy cooperates fully with those . . . ah . . . people at all times. But there are certain boundaries that have to be considered. Mrs. Preminger, of course . . . the whole family for that matter . . . he had . . . has . . . two children. And until the navy can prepare a statement . . .

Dir: The Investigative Bureau never volunteers anything to the newspapers, Admiral. They're entirely capable of doing their own investigative work. Let's put it this way—we have nothing to say to them here until they pin us down if this really is Captain Preminger. If it is, and we can work together on this—you know, cooperate—we'll release a statement approved by you beforehand. Then we'll refer everything to your office. Satisfactory?

Adm: I guess we can't ask for anything better.

The commanding officer of Submarine Squadron Four could have drafted a number of more pleasing scenarios, but there was obviously no way to make everything suit the navy. He didn't like working with civilian organizations. They were so inefficient, so unlike the navy. How did you know when to trust them? His next call was to his immediate superior, the admiral commanding the Submarine Flotilla. Within half an hour, following the time-honored chain of command, the commander of the Northern Naval District and the Inspector of the Navy had been apprised of the situation. He arranged for the Inspector, Personnel to assign a senior captain to handle all communications with the media.

On the same day that the commander of Submarine Squadron Four was contemplating the awful possibility that Hans Preminger might actually have been the first German ship captain to be a victim of foul play since the end of World War Two, the Arab named Michael arrived in Cherbourg. The ancient French port city was at the tip of Cap de la Hague, which extended into the stormy English Channel—a particularly unpleasant place to visit in February.

Although Soraya had insisted he take her with him,

Michael had turned her down cold. Instead, he chose a dark hairy Turk named Ismael, who'd grown up in a fishing village on the Mediterranean coast. The man's complexion had been ravaged by acne, his nose had been broken any number of times, and the teeth that remained in his mouth were twisted and stained by his ever-present, black cigarettes. Ismael was a devout Muslim . . . and a dedicated terrorist. He was also the foremost expert on torpedoes in Hussein's organization.

On one of the few occasions he felt like talking, Ismael explained to Michael that when the body of his oldest brother was returned to their village from Cyprus for burial, he learned the most important lesson of his life. Military reports indicated the casket had been sealed because the corpse was mutilated. A soldier from a nearby village who had accompanied the body hinted importantly to the family that his brother's eyes had been gouged out and his ears cut off, and most insulting of all, he had been castrated—then he had been murdered. *The Greek Cypriots were animals!* And they were also non-Muslims. Ismael's father made him swear on his brother's coffin that he would dedicate himself to killing the infidels who had shamed the family.

It was a somber and profound charge to a small boy, yet Ismael had taken it seriously. He wasn't a bright youth, nor was he attractive or personable, but he became an effective killer because he took to his avocation with a passion. By his late teens, when he arranged an introduction to Michael, he had expanded his goal well beyond Greek Cypriots—any human being who wasn't a dedicated Muslim was a fair target at the proper time. And the proper time was anytime he could kill without a fair chance of getting caught, for to be detained would mean that he could no longer continue his impressive reign of terror.

On that cold February day, their mission was to purchase a boat. It had to be one that was built by fishing people who had faced every type of weather that the Channel and the North Sea could offer. It had to be large enough to sleep at least a dozen people and the galley adequate enough to heartily feed them. They required additional fuel tanks to both allow extended time at sea and to provide fuel to another vessel. And the hold had to be of a size that would accommodate an extensive inventory of supplies, including torpedoes.

Michael considered his last conversation with Hussein, the man he'd never met. It had been abbreviated as always. Hussein contacted him by radio at a prearranged time and place. In a few short sentences, the older man had given him orders to purchase a boat, outlined the minimum requirements for the craft, and even explained that Cherbourg was the place to obtain it. Why Cherbourg? *Far enough away.* That was meaningless to Michael, but he knew better than to question that again. What were they to do with this boat? *Get the boat first, Michael, follow these orders, and then I will tell you more.* The time and the method of their next contact was, as always, prearranged.

To be certain that the craft they selected was perfect for their needs, Michael and Ismael even insisted that the owners take them to sea. The engines were tested exhaustively. The deck crane used for hoisting nets was checked to ensure it could handle its rated weight, for they would have to adapt the equipment to their own needs. When the boat met every requirement, Michael and Ismael made quite certain their trail would disappear in Cherbourg. Ismael cut the owners' throats, then hacked the corpses into pieces that would satisfy the meat-eaters of the ocean. After all, he said, there was no need to have a body turning up in a trawler's net.

Hussein's ensuing orders were simple enough to follow. They sailed it on to the port of Saint-Malo, where they were met by a small crew that had been sent by one of Hussein's associates. Michael remained impatient. "When will I know where to sail it?" *Be patient, Michael, there's work to do.*

When the boat was loaded with adequate supplies to support them for two weeks, contact was made again. *We're ready—now where?*

Hussein patiently explained where Michael should take this craft before establishing contact again. *It's better not to know more than that.*

In the middle of the second night, they painted a new

name on the stern, modified identifying markings, and slipped out of Saint-Malo.

During his first daring, shallow water dive aboard S-252, and then during subsequent evolutions beneath the surface, Captain Erhardt mentally catalogued which of the men appeared adaptable to their new captain's style. It was important to isolate those special talents who might prove irreplaceable. He would be able to keep very few of them. And he needed one officer to spell him in the control room. It would be impossible for him to stand watch on a constant basis.

Erhardt was especially pleased with one of his officers. It was the new lieutenant who had replaced the weapons officer the day before Erhardt took command. In the cluttered confines of his tiny stateroom, on the return to Eckernforde, he asked his executive officer, Otto Rather, about the new man.

"The new weapons officer, Lieutenant Schroeder, what was his previous billet?"

"Shore duty, Captain. He was on the squadron staff. I really don't know much about him. He was in charge of evaluating new torpedo tactics according to the short interview I had with him."

"And our former weapons officer, Lieutenant Messinger, was he due for shore duty?"

"No, sir. It's a strange situation. He'd only been with us for six months. Normal tour, as you know, is two years."

Erhardt turned to his executive officer curiously. "And what did he do so terrible to be relieved so suddenly?"

"Nothing, sir. He was an exemplary officer."

"I'm curious about Schroeder. Would you be kind enough to have Mr. Schroeder report to me now."

There was something about his executive officer that grated on Erhardt's nerves. He was almost too efficient. He tried so hard to please, even when it was obvious that he preferred the way Hans Preminger had handled the boat.

"Yes, Captain, immediately," the executive officer responded. Otto Rather found this new captain at once appealing and disturbing. He would certainly bring a new spirit to *Heinz Waller*. He was also dashing and exciting, whereas Preminger had been conservative and efficient. But Erhardt would also quickly alter the standard procedures that Preminger had instilled to make his crew function so smoothly—not that Preminger's was an exciting system, but Rather had concurred that it was definitely the way a submarine's crew should behave in peacetime. Obviously, this Erhardt was a man who heard his own drummer. *Was it correct to change what had worked so well?* Otto Rather would have to think about that.

Erhardt responded to the sharp knock outside his stateroom. "Come."

Hugo Schroeder was the archetypal traditional German submariner. He could have modeled for a recruiting poster. His blond hair was short and neatly trimmed, his complexion fair, eyes blue, lips full, teeth white and even, and he smiled politely when speaking to his seniors. His uniforms were always neatly pressed and his command presence affected everyone who worked for him. "Captain, Mr. Rather said you wanted to see me."

"Sit down," Erhardt said, gesturing toward the narrow bunk in the tiny stateroom. "I am curious about your assignment to *Heinz Waller,* and perhaps you can help me, Mr. Schroeder. Why were you sent to this submarine from what sounds like appealing shore duty?"

"I've been requesting sea duty for the past six months, Captain. I thought I'd enjoy a few years ashore, and my wife wanted that desperately, but it's no fun standing on the pier and watching others go to sea."

Erhardt was sure that was how he would have answered. "How long were you ashore?"

"About a year."

"Not a normal tour then?"

Schroeder smiled politely and shook his head. "It didn't appeal to me, Captain."

Erhardt showed Schroeder his personnel file, which Otto Rather had not observed on the captain's desk moments earlier. "I see you have an intelligence sub-specialty. Does that have any bearing on your transfer here?"

Schroeder's forehead wrinkled as he answered, "All junior officers are required to develop a sub-specialty now, sir.

After my first tour at sea, I thought that intelligence might be interesting." He shrugged. "It's boring. I'm a sailor first. I hope I never have to get into it again."

"Are you aware of any special reason Messinger was relieved as our weapons officer after just six months aboard?"

"I have no idea, Captain."

"You were attached to the squadron," Erhardt commented, without looking up from Schroeder's personnel file. "Did anyone ever wonder why a perfectly competent officer was relieved in that manner?"

"I'm not aware of the situation, sir."

Erhardt shifted to another topic. "You aren't nervous with shallow water dives." He looked up and smiled. So far, Schroeder's responses made sense. He was a submariner, not a staff fool. "You aren't afraid we might bury our nose in the mud?"

"No, Captain. I'm used to shallow water operations, especially in the Mediterranean. That's where I was qualified on my first submarine." Schroeder found it difficult not to be more enthusiastic. He had been told at squadron headquarters that this was an intelligence assignment and that he would likely be relieved afterward. Yet, in such a short time, he found himself totally enthralled by Captain Erhardt. The man wanted to do everything that Schroeder felt was critical to being a successful submarine officer, one who would go to the top.

"Who was your commanding officer?"

"Captain Sensinger qualified me, sir."

"I should have known. His confidence is written all over your face. Ernst and I qualified together, I'll have you know, and in the Mediterranean just like you." Erhardt smiled broadly. "I'm glad you were transferred aboard *Heinz Waller*. You can help me change some attitudes and prove how important these shallow water tactics are in this so-called era of peace."

There was only one response to his captain's comments. "I'd be privileged to help, sir," Schroeder said. It all sounded too good to be true. It was difficult to swallow what they'd told him at squadron headquarters. Why not make the best of it while he was at sea?

"The other officers, especially Mr. Rather, seemed worried," Erhardt noted with a wry grin. "Why don't we start by making you my officer of the deck during general quarters. I need someone who already understands my methods."

Schroeder nodded his agreement. "I'd enjoy that, Captain. But does Mr. Rather agree? He's the senior watch officer."

"I'm the captain," Erhardt stated bluntly. "I'll explain the situation and I'm sure he'll understand my motives."

The new weapons officer's forehead wrinkled. "Certainly, Captain." Whatever the intelligence people ashore expected, Schroeder decided this was going to be an exciting tour of duty. Erhardt was exactly what the submarine force needed, and Hugo Schroeder determined at that moment to do everything that would please his captain.

Erhardt excused his weapons officer after a few more words. This was a good start. Schroeder's talent was obvious. He would find out quickly whether this was a man he could also control.

Philip Salkin was, like Harry Truman, a man who had been thrust, not unwillingly, but hesitantly, into the White House. But unlike Truman, Salkin was neither a politician nor a man of the soil. He was appalled by the burden that politics placed upon the decision-making process, and too much of his time was spent attempting to return the government to the people. That had been an exercise in frustration, for the bureaucracy wasn't about to surrender its stranglehold. And that was how Phil Salkin determined that his most profound contribution might just be peace—*Pax Islamica* was how he'd put it to Rupert Daniels. "That may sound childish. But no matter how you cut it, Rupert—Christian, Jew, Buddhist, Hindu, or all the other sects put together—close to a billion Muslims spread across three continents have something going for them . . . and perhaps with a little effort we can put it right. Arafat and Rabin set an example for years to come."

But now Rupert Daniels was dead.

The President of the United States studied the young man who sat across from him, nervous, waiting politely for him to speak. "First of all, Will, I'd like you to relax. Please. You're making me nervous. Okay?"

"Yes, sir." But Will Riley's eyes said he was still uncomfortable.

"All right, how about this? I think you'll agree that if no one ever knew who Will Riley was, we'd all be better off. If you check with my appointments secretary when you leave, you'll see that your name isn't even on for today, and you won't be in the future either. Instead, I'm going to let Lou Griffey handle the media when they get wind of our upcoming event—and I'm sure they will." Lou Griffey had been sworn in as Secretary of State just a month earlier.

"He's got a terrific knack with them, sir."

Salkin waved an index finger at his guest. "And you can bet the farm that I'm going to encourage him, too, sort of head them off in another direction. While you're off doing your thing, getting everything ready, we're going to be making a lot of noise about the North Korea situation, and maybe I'll voice doubts about giving up the Canal in a couple of years—you know, anything to get their hackles up." Phil Salkin allowed himself a deep sigh and leaned forward. "There. See. Now you have every reason to relax. Okay?"

Will smiled. "Yes, sir. I feel better."

"Good. Now tell me about your trip, Will. Don't skip a thing."

Will Riley truly liked Salkin. Everything he had learned about the President had come from Rupert Daniels, who had revered his old friend, and Will found he was grateful to be taken into the man's confidence, even to have just been the foil for his humor. Only God alone could understand the strain the man was under.

Riley was young, very young for a man invested with the responsibility Rupert Daniels had placed in him. And now that same trust had been transferred from Daniels to the President of the United States by sheer accident. Will had come off a Kansas farm with a full scholarship to the state university. He was a natural athlete and a superb student. He went directly to law school, but after a year of clerking found himself bored. A law professor suggested applying to the FBI, and one of the happiest periods of Riley's life came during his years as an agent. But his career ended when he was wounded during an exchange of gunfire on a joint investigation with the Drug Enforcement Agency. Even now, he walked with a marked limp.

But if it was true you couldn't take the farm out of the boy, then Riley's red hair, freckles, and mid-America accent told the story of his background. He'd gone back to graduate school at George Washington for international relations, and he attracted the attention of the State Department through his professors' recommendations. He had been a nameless assistant to an assistant secretary in the Middle Eastern department when another assistant secretary, Rupert Daniels, heard about him. From that moment on, he had walked through a dream until now he was sitting across from the President of the United States.

Will Riley continued. "Right after Mr. Daniels's death, I cabled each of the leaders I'd talked to myself, offering to come back and talk with them again if they felt it was necessary. So I will have to go back to Tunis on my next trip. I did visit Amman, Damascus, and Baghdad this time to reiterate that nothing had changed with Mr. Daniels's death. Israel's become an old hand at this. They were most gracious in stating that they required nothing immediate from me as long as it was definite that you would represent the United States personally when the time came. Riyadh had much the same reaction. I'll visit Tehran on my next trip, mostly because they asked me to bring a personal letter from you confirming that, although you will not chair the day-to-day summit, you will be within voice contact at all times and arrive to conclude agreements. Even though the Palestinians are really going to have a homeland, they seem to be as suspicious of the other Arab countries as they are of the Israelis. All in all, I'd say your objective for this meeting outweighs everything else in their list of problems . . . except the demand for absolute secrecy."

"Are you surprised by that, Will?"

"Mr. Daniels explained it to me. I understand the reason that Jerusalem doesn't want it to get out, what with the party splits and the battles in the Likud these days. I went back to the library and studied all the microfiche on the accord with the PLO, and I concur with their approach.

And I know Tehran has maintained such a hard-nosed approach to all the others. But . . ." Will shook his head in wonder. "Even Cairo, who's been to every peace table, and places like Ankara and Tunis who have nothing to lose, they're all adamant . . ."

"Even within their own walls," Salkin finished for him. "Will, I don't really think they're as afraid of what their own opposition might say as they are about the rabid splinter groups. The real threat comes from the terrorist organizations. It isn't anti-Jew or anti-Muslim. All of those leaders, they're all tired of fighting. They want a solution. They saw how much Arafat got when he extended his hand in friendship. They're willing to give and take like no one would have imagined a few years back."

"That's the impression I got. I didn't expect the sincerity I saw."

"Most of them are even willing to agree that they've been at least partially wrong, that there is no black-and-white solution. But there are groups that I don't even think have names who are totally against the concept of all the leaders in one place at the same time. When leaders are brought together, they see that their differences are really minimal compared to what's at stake. Their personal objectives are suddenly so similar that they can finally grasp the need for unity."

"Mr. Daniels told me that was the key to holding their attention."

"That, Will, is the ultimate threat to these splinter factions and special interests. That's why some terrorist group—or any group with a cross to bear—may be willing to undertake anything to stop a summit like this."

Riley had never heard it explained so succinctly. "It's scary, sir."

Salkin sat back in his chair and stretched his arms out, locking his fingers until the knuckles cracked. "I'm scared, too. I'm scared for what I don't know, and you better believe me, Will, I'm scared absolutely shitless—absolutely shitless," he added again with emphasis, "for them and you and me if one of those groups should get wind of this. This summit isn't the final solution. But I'm damn well convinced it can be the inspiration that will end the petty differences and foolish deadlocks."

Will Riley was aware that his mouth was hanging open only after Phil Salkin had ceased speaking. "I was aware . . . I mean Mr. Daniels had explained that part of it . . . but I . . ." He couldn't imagine the man in the White House scared *shitless* about anything.

"Tell me about the boat, Will."

Riley was grateful for the change. "She's called *Calm Seas,* sir. She's Greek owned, but the captain's an American." His youthful face lit up. "I swear I never expected to be aboard anything like that. She's a beauty, like a little QE2. It's hard to imagine that people—private people, I mean—live like that." He gave a quick rundown on *Calm Seas'* specifications.

Salkin listened patiently as Riley detailed his bow-to-stern tour of *Calm Seas* with her captain. "Sounds great, Will. But did you get a copy of her layout?"

Riley opened his briefcase. "Yes, sir. Side view of the ship, cutaway, plus an overhead of each deck." He extracted the folded copies. "I'm sure we can split everybody up in separate suites, fourteen of them, with no problem. They won't be what these people are used to, but they'll be comfortable and private. Of course, with the size of some of the delegations that are going to have to be quartered elsewhere, most of the senior delegates want assurance their people will be nearby."

"We're going to have the *Wasp* attached, probably a couple miles away. She's an amphibious carrier with quarters for three thousand people. Her officers are going to have to double up, but she'll be there to provide hotel space for each nation, and her amphibious group will be around to ride shotgun. But what I'm really worried about is making sure the Israeli isn't sharing a shower with the Iraqi, or the Shiite with the Sunni. You know what I mean."

"I think it can be done, sir. May I lay these out on your conference table?"

Over the next hour, even though he wasn't on the President's schedule of appointments, Will Riley had Philip Salkin's total attention. Together, they penciled in the names of the various heads of state over the projected staterooms. The President relaxed as they tried to figure out how to separate various individuals without anyone thinking they might have a lesser facility than their counterpart.

After Will Riley departed, Phil Salkin felt that perhaps this impossible concept might just work—*as long as there was absolute, unquestioned secrecy until after these leaders had been brought together.*

During the third week of February, a coroner's inquest was held in the second basement level of police headquarters in Kiel. The attendees had been purposely limited at the request of the Inspector of the Navy. One of his reasons was, of course, humanitarian, as he attempted to explain to the wife of the subject of the inquest. There was no reason for the Preminger family to become an object of media attention, he insisted. The late Captain Preminger's wife was well aware that the admiral was more concerned with the media focusing unwanted concern on the navy. Yet she made an effort to show appreciation for the courtesy bestowed upon her by all of her late husband's associates. If the admiral wanted her to believe her concerns were paramount to those of the navy, she was going to go along with the charade. After all, on a confidential basis, she'd already learned that the President of the Republic had approved the Inspector of the Navy's recommendation that the Preminger family receive the captain's full pay and allowances until the childrens' higher education was completed —even if she remarried.

No, she was going to keep her mouth shut. She'd have nothing to say about her husband's sexual proclivities. His roving eye had almost gotten him in trouble in the past. She was well aware he was seeing another woman the past month, but that was secondary to the fact that he was no longer trying to force her to perform some of his weird fantasies.

In addition to Mrs. Preminger's presence, the inquest was attended by the Director-Homicide, Kiel Investigative Bureau, a detective assigned to the case named Herman Gleick; the Inspector of the Navy; the Commander, Northern Naval District; the Commander, Submarine Flotilla; the Commander, Submarine Squadron Four; the Director, Admin/Legal Affairs; and a navy stenographer who was supposed to take notes. The stenographer really wasn't needed because the coroner passed around a succinct report of what he would say during the hearing:

OFFICE OF THE CORONER
City of Kiel
Federal Republic of Germany

Coroner: Wilhelm Braun/Peter Koontz, Assisting
Subject: Captain Hans Preminger, FRG Navy
Purpose: Determination of Cause of Death

Note: Due to the occupation of the subject and the unusual nature of the situation, this report is intended to be a condensed version of the detailed analysis normally prepared for such an inquest for the purpose of a police investigation.

1) A corpse tangled in trawling nets was recovered by fishermen a few miles off the coast. The captain of the fishing boat immediately radioed for assistance and a Kiel Police patrol boat was dispatched. Written report of officers at the scene indicate that the corpse was naked, had been in the water an indeterminate time, and that marine life and normal decomposition in that environment made visual identification impossible. However, it was noted at the time that a missing section of the skull could indicate other than a natural or accidental cause of death.

2) The remains of a Caucasian male between thirty-five and forty-five years of age were delivered to the Kiel Police Morgue within a few hours of recovery and standard methods of preservation were instituted immediately. Assistant Coroner Koontz was on duty at the time and concurred with the initial report of the officers at the recovery scene that the damage to the skull was unnatural and required detailed analysis.

3) The office of the Director-Homicide, Kiel Investigative Bureau, was requested to assist in a missing persons search on that same date. The following day this office requested the medical records of Captain Preminger from the FRG because none of the other currently missing persons fit the basic description of the remains. It should be noted that the navy has been most cooperative.

4) Medical records were compared to data accumulated under standard processes and confirmed the identification of the remains as Captain Hans Preminger, FRG.

5) Standard methods of determining cause of death would normally have been impossible due to the advanced decomposition of the body and concurrent interference of marine life. However, none of the above reasons could account for the shattered condition of the skull. A section measuring approximately 3 centimeters by 3.2 centimeters was missing entirely. Fracture lines radiate fairly evenly around this missing section, indicating that an object exited the skull at high speed. Comparison to records of other damage of a similar nature reinforces our assumption that the exiting object was most likely a high-powered bullet. The exact point of entrance is unknown, but exit characteristics support the contention that the bullet was fired from beneath the chin. Assumption can also be offered that the victim was likely reclining on his back since a shot fired beneath the chin of an upright target is highly unusual.

6) Suicide, while it cannot be ruled out, would be highly unlikely, especially with an individual of Captain Preminger's background and psychological stability. Suicide victims also generally want to be found so there is little reason for someone to position themselves well out to sea before self-inflicting a fatal wound.

7) It is the opinion of this office that Captain Hans Preminger was killed by one shot from a 9mm or larger weapon fired from beneath his chin. Death would have been instantaneous.

8) A detailed report with justifying data has been prepared. That analysis is confidential and copies are retained only by Director-Homicide, Kiel Investigative Bureau, and the City Coroner's Office, Kiel.

Signed (S) Wilhelm Braun, Coroner, City of Kiel

At the conclusion of the formal inquest, Mrs. Preminger wept accordingly and was comforted by the senior naval officers present. She did miss her husband, had loved him even with his sexual problems, and was distraught that her children would not have a father around the house. *But the dirty son of a bitch probably got his brains blown out by some bitch who didn't want to do the things I wouldn't do either.*

A week later, the Director, Admin/Legal Affairs, FRG, convened a court of inquiry into the murder of Captain Hans Preminger. While none of the admirals wanted to bring up the idea with Mrs. Preminger, it occurred to each of them that the cause of death and the coroner's interpretation of how it may have happened were highly unusual for a man in Preminger's sensitive position. If he had been prone when murdered, and likely on his back since the bullet appeared to have entered beneath his chin, was it possible he may have been with a woman? It certainly wasn't proper to involve Mrs. Preminger in such lurid possibilities, nor did they have any idea how they would attempt to ascertain if any improprieties might have been possible.

PART TWO

MARCH

Rehearsal

CHAPTER FOUR

When Michael sailed their Cherbourg boat, which he'd annointed *Baghdad*—even though the name on the stern for obvious reasons was a very simple *Saint Joseph*—through the Strait of Gibraltar into the Mediterranean, he contacted Hussein in accordance with his orders. He was then directed to the Libyan port of Benghazi on the eastern coast of the Gulf of Sidra.

Over the next few weeks, he would be continually amazed by the below-decks transformation to *Baghdad.* A special access trunk to transfer torpedoes was cut through the main deck into the hold. This was followed by the insertion of two reinforced neoprene bladders which were then filled with diesel fuel.

A false deck was installed to conceal their clandestine cargo. This included a separate space for storing both plastic and conventional explosives and detonating devices; .50-caliber machine guns; grenade launchers with fragmentation, smoke, and stun grenades; and a Stinger launcher with its surface-to-air missiles. There were also individual weapons—handguns, automatic rifles, and enough ammunition for twice the number of men selected for the mission. Michael was overwhelmed as Hussein's engineers transformed *Baghdad* into an ammunition ship. Yet to an outside observer, she still remained a fishing boat.

Michael and Ismael had found a fine craft. Under full load, she was slower than they had hoped but rode well in open waters. For anyone curious about this boat with the name *Saint Joseph* on the stern, she looked exactly like the fishing boat she was designed to be, and one heading back to home port with a full load.

Hussein, who was adamant that his leaders not be seen by the younger members of the sect, had sent one of his lieutenants to observe the reconstruction. As always, it was an individual Michael had never met, a man who never offered his name and who knew that Michael knew better than to ask. But he was polite and allowed Michael to lead him through the vessel.

"I can't believe the changes . . . the efficiency . . . the . . ." Michael was speechless. "What will Hussein have me do with her when she's ready for sea?"

The man smiled and shook his head. He had no idea what Hussein expected, nor did he need to know. "You're always too anxious, Michael. Better not to know too much." He chuckled. It was one of the few times he allowed a smile during the few hours he was there, and that was because he had been told that was exactly what Michael would ask him. "When she is ready, you'll receive orders."

When eventually he reported that *Baghdad* was ready, Hussein told him to take the craft back through the Strait of Gibraltar, turn north and parallel the Portuguese coast, then turn east into the Bay of Biscay. He was to sail into a small fishing village on the Spanish coast not too far from Bilbao. But there was no prearranged time to establish contact. *Wait there, Michael. Relax. When I know it is time you will be contacted.*

There were increasing signs of spring blowing off the Baltic Sea by the time the FRG navy and the Kiel police reached an accord satisfactory to both sides on the continuing investigation into Captain Preminger's murder. There were no clues. None of the usual rumors or anonymous phone calls so often associated with such a unique incident were forthcoming. So, in frustration, Herman Gleick, the detective in charge of the case, acquiesced against his better judgment and turned to the navy. It was the only course of action, even though his own department would continue to follow anything new.

He learned that within days after Preminger's disappearance, the Director, Admin/Legal Affairs department, had wisely recommended involving an intelligence specialist, and, in a manner of speaking, the seagoing navy had cooperated. Lieutenant Hugo Schroeder had reported aboard Preminger's former submarine the day before Walter Erhardt assumed command and easily assimilated himself into the wardroom of *Heinz Waller*. In fact, the Legal Affairs office was impressed with how well he appeared to have attracted the new captain's confidence in his first weeks aboard. If there was anything really amiss in the Preminger case, Gleick was told that the navy would locate and root out their own problems. That was why the squadron commander had called the young intelligence officer for a clandestine discussion at his home rather than his headquarters. The admiral felt rather silly meeting that way, but the chief of Kiel's detectives had convinced him of the need for secrecy if there really was a problem. Gleick was allowed to attend the meeting, but only on the condition that he listen and say nothing.

Lieutenant Schroeder glanced up from the coroner's report without lifting his head, and his blue eyes briefly met those of the admiral who relaxed comfortably on his own living-room sofa. Then he reread paragraph number seven: *"It is the opinion of this office that Captain Hans Preminger was killed by one shot from a 9mm or larger weapon fired from beneath his chin."* He could not recall ever being aware that any captain of any German submarine had ever been murdered before. He handed the report back.

"You are the only individual outside my office to read that. Comments?" the squadron commander inquired.

Schroeder wanted to say that he was a naval officer especially qualified to drive submarines, a very unique talent in any country, and not a detective, not by any stretch of his or anyone else's imagination. He also wished he could say that Walter Erhardt had renewed his spirit, made him realize that he was still a warrior rather than a pencil pusher in some boring intelligence section. But that was something he would never do. If there was any blame to be placed for his intelligence sub-specialty, it must fall on his shoulders alone. It wasn't so many years ago when the error of judgment was made, when he was fresh out of officer candidate school, exceedingly patriotic, and set on personally reuniting Germany. The Berlin Wall still divided his nation then, creating a chasm between democracy and tyranny. Schroeder was an avid reader of spy novels in his youth. Therefore, due to some unidentifiable weakness in his makeup, he determined that intelligence would be his contribution to removing that gulf between the two Germanys. But a detective? No! "What do you require of me, Admiral?" he inquired dispassionately.

The only other individual invited, a senior captain from the Director, Admin/Legal Affairs office, responded to the admiral's nod. "You are the one trusted contact we have aboard *Heinz Waller,* Lieutenant Schroeder, or at least the only one we care to reveal this information to. You are also trained to sift out facts and analyze them. Submarines are very closed societies. If this report is to be believed, and we have no choice but to accept it, we need to know what we don't know . . . about Captain Preminger . . . about the other members of the wardroom . . . the enlisted ranks. Only yourself and Captain Erhardt weren't attached to *Waller* and are therefore devoid of suspicion. You've been aboard now for almost a month. You've been accepted. Was there an incident, or incidents, that may offer some information that will aid the investigation? Was there an individual, or perhaps more than one, who may have disagreed with Preminger's methods or been hurt by his method of command? Such information rarely comes ashore. We have agreed to share the results of your work with the Kiel police."

Lieutenant Schroeder said nothing because he wasn't expected to speak yet.

"*Heinz Waller*'s operating schedule has been intensified at Captain Erhardt's request," the admiral noted. "Instead of a maintenance period in April, you will be sent out for two weeks of additional training. As you've learned, Erhardt believes very strongly in shallow water operations and he's convinced us of this to the point that we're going to have him experiment in developing new tactics—that is, in addition to your normal training pattern. This ought to be perfect for your own assessment of the crew. We don't necessarily believe that such problems as hinted at by the director's representative existed aboard S-252, of course, but, as he said, submarines can be closed societies even to a squadron commander. You understand what I mean, of course."

"Certainly, Admiral."

The admiral was studying his fingernails as he expressed reluctant support for something he didn't really care to accept. "I have nothing but the deepest respect and admiration for Captain Preminger and I don't believe there was anything at all we are unaware of that would tarnish his reputation, or that of the navy. But we must consider everything." He raised his head and his eyes went from Schroeder to the military lawyer and back again as he concluded, "I sincerely expect you will find nothing significant. *Heinz Waller* was and continues to remain the finest submarine in my squadron. I have no reason to believe that Captain Preminger's death was anything but an unfortunate event, most likely a case of mistaken identity on the part of his murderer. But I have been asked to provide you with this, Lieutenant." He handed Schroeder a letter written on his personal stationery. Under the gold embossed heading it read as follows:

> Lt. Hugo Schroeder is operating under the special orders of this command in addition to his duties as weapons officer of S-252. Should an incident take place or a situation arise whereby Lt. Schroeder finds that information critical to my personal directive to him must be communicated to this command, then that requirement takes precedence over the orders under which S-252 is operating. If necessary, S-252 should surface and communicate directly with this command over circuit Whiskey Alfa, which will be guarded on a twenty-four-hour basis.

Schroeder knew it was time to respond. "I will do everything within my capabilities, Admiral." He placed his hands on the arms of the chair as he was about to stand up.

The admiral raised a hand and shook his head. "Not quite yet, Lieutenant."

Schroeder allowed himself to drop back into the chair.

"Perhaps there really is a problem," the admiral began cautiously. "Perhaps there is someone dangerous on board. And perhaps," he continued with a sigh, "there is the chance that a radio may malfunction at an inopportune time." He pushed a compact, rectangular plastic object across the desk in Schroeder's direction. "Take that with you, Mr. Schroeder."

Schroeder picked it up and turned it over in his hands. There was nothing to indicate what it was. A single button was evident on one side. He looked up curiously.

"That is an extremely high-powered transmitting device developed by one of our civilian departments. As long as you are outside the hull, push that button, but don't touch it now," he cautioned, "and you activate a receiver in one of our communications satellites, which, in turn, transmits a signal to one of our ground receiving stations. And that automatically rings the phone right here until either I or the duty officer answers."

"That's all?"

"That's all. But since you are the only one to possess that particular device, receipt of that signal will signify that Lieutenant Hugo Schroeder exists even though he can't talk to us by radio. I don't believe you will ever need to employ it, and I don't know what we will do if you activate it. But at least we'll know you have a . . ." The admiral was uncertain how to finish. "You do understand?"

"Yes, sir."

Once again Hugo Schroeder was the recruiting-poster model as he realized that they expected no further comments from him. Even though he was in the admiral's house, he rose to his feet, snapped to attention, saluted, about-faced, and left the room wondering how a young man who had once envisioned bringing the two Germanys together could end up as a quasi-detective investigating a murder. It was quite suddenly possible that the murderer might even be aboard S-252 and that learning about this investigation might hazard his own life. Or even Captain Erhardt's? He resolved at that moment to appoint himself as his captain's protector.

* * *

Will Riley reviewed a CIA-prepared list of facilities capable of completing the alterations to *Calm Seas* by April 1 before selecting Monte Carlo. It was the most logical choice because the tiny wealthy principality of Monaco was a place where few questions would be asked about such an opulent yacht. Details were coordinated directly through the palace by the ambassador. Then Will wired Francis Waters to pick him up in Naples so he might sail aboard the vessel on the final leg of the journey to the repair facility. While the hook had already been set in the yacht's captain, it was now necessary to prepare him for the radical changes to the ship and to his life.

They were in the pilot house of *Calm Seas,* sailing northwest through the Tyrrhenian Sea on a brilliantly sunny day. Waters had already pointed out the mountain peaks rising out of the sea above Porto-Vecchio on the island of Corsica. It was so clear for that time of year, he'd explained, that spring would be early.

"Tell me, Mr. Riley . . ." Waters began.

"Will."

"All right. Tell me, Will, what guarantee do I have that our government forgets what you told me in Haifa . . . about my . . ." It was so difficult to dredge it up after twelve years. "About my childish indiscretion that you mentioned?" His dark blond hair was curly, longer than he would have gotten away with when he was in the navy, but it fit well with his deep tan and clear blue eyes. He looked the part of a captain in his starched whites, at least the way a woman would envision a man like Francis Waters. But he didn't sound like a captain at the moment. His voice was as uncertain as a man in his position could sound, and he wasn't looking at Riley as he spoke.

"You have my word." Riley's tone of voice conveyed the fact that his word was all that was necessary.

"I don't know you. I don't even know what you do for a living. What is it? You attached to the Drug Enforcement Agency? CIA? FBI?" Waters was a man whose past had come back to haunt him.

"None of the above." Riley let his own silence serve as an exclamation point. He wanted his captain to understand the power he was willing to exert. How often does a man's past come back to haunt him like this, especially a man who'd made only one mistake and had been convinced it was behind him? This captain was scared. He was as scared as a man who was ashamed of himself and wanted to stay honest could be. Will watched as Waters stared straight ahead toward mountain peaks that still could only be seen with the boat's powerful binoculars. Finally, the captain moved out to the port wing of the bridge and leaned on the railing with both arms, staring moodily down at the passing sea.

He doesn't know whether to test me or not, Will mused.

Finally, Waters returned to the pilot house, noted their course on the compass repeater, and glared at Riley. He was about to speak, but checked himself. Staring directly ahead, he asked, "You going to tell me why you're busting my stones, all over something you say I don't want to know?"

"I'm buying your silence, your total cooperation, and your soul if you so much as whisper a word about me or about anything that takes place until we're finished."

"I told you that first time in Haifa I wouldn't say anything." Waters looked sideways at Riley. "Look at yourself goddamn it, Will. I know you work for the government—nobody dresses like you around the Med—but in polite society this would be called blackmail." He was choosing his words carefully. "Don't you think it would be nice on your part if you gave me something in writing . . . something that promised me a clean slate? I mean you started this whole thing by twisting my arm, rather than asking if I'd like to be patriotic and help out Uncle Sam . . ." He looked away nervously, then turned back to Riley. "I mean, what you laid on me about that boat trip twelve years ago involves a lot of years of hard time. I've been a nice guy since then. That was my one and only mistake." He had a full broad mouth, but his lips were a narrow line now, and his jaw was set in a stubborn manner.

Will Riley took an envelope from his breast pocket and handed it to Waters. It bore the embossed symbol of the Secretary of State. "Read it."

Waters extracted the letter inside and read it. There was a single paragraph, but it said all he needed to know. If he cooperated totally with Will Riley—and the extent of that cooperation was explicit—then Francis Waters's indiscretion would be fully pardoned. "This guy—Louis Griffey—he's the one who replaced the guy who was killed by that bomb in Washington?"

"That's correct. Rupert Daniels was my boss and had already received approval from the President of the United States to write exactly what that letter states. Louis Griffey is my new boss and he concurred with me that we would owe you this, at least."

"This is like being back in the navy. Shit," he said emphatically, "I was really enjoying the civilian life. You can't imagine how hard I've worked to get all this." He looked ruefully at Riley. "Now along you come and before I know it someone owns me again. Considering that pardon, I don't have much of a choice, do I?"

"If I thought you'd do anything but work with me, you would have been fired last month in Haifa and we would have had to hire someone more reliable but less satisfactory in this environment. Your background has been turned inside out in the past couple of months, and you're the perfect person for this job." Riley smiled pleasantly for the first time. He disliked bullying people. "I won the argument back in Washington about how a navy officer would stand out like a sore thumb if we replaced you. You've been in the Med for so long that every port director and bartender knows who you are. You make a perfect front for me, my friend."

Waters carefully folded the Secretary of State's letter and placed it in his wallet. "I suppose you still can't tell me what's behind all this."

"You're better off not knowing."

"Do I have to like you?"

"No. But I expect my charm will grow on you because we're stuck with each other."

Before they arrived in Monte Carlo, Will Riley and Francis Waters had gone over the plans for every square foot of *Calm Seas.* Although he was never told why alterations were being made, he was consulted on the feasibility of each change. Where suites had adjoining doors, a solid bulkhead would replace them. A storage area on the same deck but well forward of the galley would be converted into another galley. Riley said nothing about it becoming a kosher kitchen. New, easier-to-climb stairs would be installed. Riley said nothing about the necessity of avoiding the chance of heads of state encountering each other at inopportune moments. The main salon would be enlarged, although there was no need to mention the effort that would be made to satisfy the delegates from fourteen nations. The stern would be reinforced from below. Riley was forced to acknowledge that that was to accommodate larger helicopters, but he said nothing about their making the run back and forth from the *Wasp* with foreign staff members. But on the outside, *Calm Seas* would remain the ultimate luxury yacht.

On the following day, satisfied that Francis Waters would ensure absolute compliance with these alterations, Will Riley left Monte Carlo for Ankara on the first leg of his journey to reassure heads of state that, even after the tragic loss of Rupert Daniels, President Salkin remained firm in his goal of engaging them all in a meaningful summit meeting. He was willing to go to any lengths to bring about a peaceful solution to generations of hatred and misunderstanding.

Commencing the final week of March, *Heinz Waller*'s two-week at-sea operations schedule called for every exercise the commander of Submarine Squadron Four could possibly require of each of his four submarine captains. He intended to push Walter Erhardt to prove to himself that the man was really as superior as he appeared.

The Type-212 submarine was brand-new—a small, highly sophisticated undersea craft that was a significant improvement on the Type-206A that Erhardt had previously sailed. Quieter under electric power than a nuclear submarine, they were capable of sudden, short bursts of underwater speed that would leave a surface craft wondering what they had encountered. Most navy tacticians, whose experience was limited to highly technical equipment designed for deep, open ocean searches, would admit that there were few opportunities to find or track a Type-212 in the shallower waters that were its natural home.

After evaluating Erhardt's ideas on shallow water

procedures, the admiral directed his staff operations officer to outline parameters for a series of drills unique to that class of submarine. In the final analysis, almost all of the experimental directives were based on tactics S-252's new captain deemed critical to his own personal mission.

Although his crew had generally learned to expect the unexpected during their short time with Erhardt, he surprised them by conducting a series of small boat drills in the North Sea soon after leaving port. These included the unpleasant task of launching inflatable boats from a violently rolling submarine into cold heavy seas and—even though they were wearing survival suits and were attached to safety lines—practicing live man-overboard drills. Walter Erhardt had as much to learn as they did, and he would not have the luxury of learning later on.

Another surprise was that their captain, rather than employing the designated small boat crew according to the executive officer's standard station bill, insisted on trying three senior petty officers as boat coxswains and, at the same time, varying the crews. There were but twenty-six men assigned to *Waller,* and it became a contest between crews. Although this was different and Erhardt made the contests fun, they had no idea of what they were competing for. After all, S-252 was a submarine, not a frigate or destroyer.

Walter Erhardt was already determining who could be easily managed and who were the most independent . . . for the latter would be disposed of first.

The men were exhausted before the end of the first day, yet exhilarated by the oddities of their captain. He was pushing them to a level beyond the other submarines in the squadron. There had never been a professional military man who didn't like to boast that he was a member of a unique unit, and Erhardt left no doubt he was pushing them in that direction.

Passing through the crowded English Channel, while *Waller* was both surfaced and snorkeling, they employed their surface search radar to track and attempt to identify each type of contact on their screen before it came into sight. This was unusual because submarines normally preferred not to use their radar. Walter Erhardt, however, intended to find out exactly how his radar functioned with each type of contact. There should be no surprises later on.

For Otto Rather, these changes were unsettling. *Heinz Waller* was a submarine, not a surface ship, and he wondered at the reaction of any ship's captain who might have noted a submarine changing course in their direction. Of even more concern would be the sight of a snorkel cutting through the water toward them. Preminger had followed the book and *Heinz Waller* had still been the finest submarine in the squadron. Life with him had been so much more comfortable . . . predictable. But Rather said nothing. It was all he could do to please Erhardt.

Before departing the Channel, S-252 made one of Erhardt's "critical angle dives," as he called them, in shallow waters off the Channel Islands. The crew had learned by then to reach for any solid object when their captain gave the order to dive. Their submarine maneuvered like a seabird, diving at steep angles, employing the maneuvering planes like wings to slow their descent, using the propeller and rudder as if the sub were an eagle diving on a rabbit. It was unnerving because their former captain had been a conservative submariner who concentrated more on their natural stealth than these flights of fancy. But Walter Erhardt was learning all he could about the limits of his new command.

As they moved into deeper waters, S-252 sometimes maneuvered in this manner for more than an hour. It was a never-ending roller-coaster ride and Erhardt announced he would continue until he was sure which men were most skilled at operating the bow planes and rudder. The response was one of enthusiasm. Their captain was demanding the absolute best from each of them. Eventually, he would know which of them understood S-252's unique maneuvering characteristics better than the others.

And as soon as Hugo Schroeder became adept enough to oversee these maneuvers on his own, Erhardt left the control room to observe how the rest of his crew operated in each individual space.

The open water operating area for *Heinz Waller* was in the shallow Celtic Sea off the Irish coast in the general vicinity of fifty degrees north and ten degrees west. That is where they rendezvoused with the destroyer that would alternate with them as target and attacker. For three days, the two craft chased each other around a sector two hundred kilometers southwest of Ireland. S-252's crew and the destroyer's antisubmarine team found themselves employed in the most realistic dog fights they'd ever encountered. This was not training-as-usual. Erhardt explained to everyone on both vessels that he intended to be the last craft afloat in the next war.

Then they moved five degrees west to deeper water. The exercises continued until the seas gradually became so rough that the surface ship could not keep pace with the sub. Although the weather was of no concern to Erhardt or his crew in the black environment that was a submarine's home, Erhardt knew how difficult it was for the destroyer. This was much more than he'd planned for—the weather was making his plan look more plausible.

He sent a terse message over his sonar releasing the destroyer, explaining that he didn't want to endanger the surface ship and that he was breaking off further exercises and going his own way independently. Without waiting for a response from the destroyer's skipper, Erhardt broke contact and announced to his crew that for the next twenty-four hours he expected only the watch section to be awake. "You are the finest submariners afloat. You are to do nothing but eat and sleep—nothing else!" It was his reward to them for superior achievement. Walter Erhardt's men were growing to revere their demanding captain.

Within hours of *Heinz Waller*'s leaving the destroyer, Otto Rather was a deeply troubled man. He'd taken the time to complete some paperwork at his desk, and then, being conscientious, he'd stopped in the control room to chat with the watch. It was a practice that, as senior watch officer, allowed him to evaluate his watch standers more carefully. The executive officer's habits were no different from anyone else who passed through the control room—that individual's eyes casually swept the dials and indicators for depth, course, and speed. And that's when he saw their course . . . *145 degrees!*

"Mr. Wippler," he said to the officer of the deck, "who

gave you permission to alter your course to one four-five?" After their operations with the destroyer were completed, they were supposed to be headed back through the Channel, reprovision at Wilhelmshaven, and return to sea with two staff officers who would observe Erhardt's shallow water tactics. Instinctively, Rather knew the course should be about 105.

"Captain Erhardt, sir. His orders for my relief are to remain on this course also." There was a look of uncertainty in his eyes, but he wasn't about to express his feelings. In such a small submarine, with only twenty-six officers and men, everyone knew the ship's schedule. But it was also a foregone conclusion that Erhardt was a genius, and their faith in him, even though he'd been aboard such a short time, was unquestioned.

Rather moved over to the chart table. The course laid out by the quartermaster was indeed 145, and, rather than a track into the English Channel, S-252 was proceeding southeast. There was even a chart for the Bay of Biscay lying to one side. He called over the quartermaster of the watch. "Did the captain order you to lay out this course?"

"Yes, sir." The man looked quickly at Rather, then down at the chart as if that would explain everything to both of them.

"Does he have a destination?" Rather snapped, both angry and embarrassed that crew members would know that their executive officer had not been involved with *Heinz Waller*'s change in operating schedule.

"If he does, he didn't mention it to me, sir. He just said to lay out a course to a point midway between Llanes and Santander on the Spanish coast. I . . . I don't believe it's my place to ask Captain Erhardt his intentions, Mr. Rather."

The executive officer picked out Llanes and Santander on the chart. They were approximately seventy-five kilometers apart on Spain's northern coast facing the Bay of Biscay. There appeared nothing of any size between them, just desolate, barren coast. Rather picked up the phone and punched the button for the radio shack. "Have we sent a message, or do we have a message ready to send, reporting a change in our operational schedule?"

The response was negative. No message had been sent. None were pending. Actually, the captain had told radio to stand easy—which meant the duty man could nap in the radio shack—and left word with the control room to waken the duty radioman when the antenna was poked above the surface at scheduled times. Radio's only responsibility was to listen on the appropriate frequency at the correct time for any messages directed to S-252.

Otto Rather was second in command. That position demanded that he be included in all decisions affecting *Heinz Waller.* He'd felt over the past couple of weeks that Erhardt was achieving total control of the ship, beyond the standard German command structure, but he had determined to gain the captain's respect by working even harder. He'd had to obtain Hans Preminger's respect when he assumed command and he'd been determined to do the same with Walter Erhardt. After all, that was part of the burden of serving as executive officer—to prove that you deserved to be promoted to a command of your own. But what was now taking place could be considered an insult to him, and there were already members of the crew aware of that. Otto Rather had been sensitive to what he considered personal slights all his life, and this was one more that must be confronted in his struggle to prove himself.

He returned to his stateroom and shaved, even though he'd already shaved once that day. Then he put on a clean shirt and freshly pressed pants, buffed the toes of his shoes, and walked the few steps to Erhardt's stateroom. There was no door, just a curtain. He rapped sharply on the bulkhead.

"Come." Erhardt's voice was sharp, as if he knew his executive officer stood outside the curtain.

Rather gently slipped the curtain to one side and took a step inside. "Captain, I'd like to talk with you for a few moments."

Erhardt took in his executive officer's fresh appearance. He could see that the uniform was clean and pressed, and he could smell a light touch of aftershave lotion. But nothing could hide the man's unruly hair or his homely features. It was unfortunate. He reminded Erhardt of the ugly Arab who worked closely with Michael, the one called Ismael, who rarely spoke. He'd met Ismael once and found him distasteful. But his executive officer was trying hard to please him and there was no reason to upset him or create suspicion. Better to take advantage of his capabilities for as long as possible. Erhardt smiled cordially. "What is it then, Otto?"

Rather's effort at self-control was impressive, his voice moderate, his tone calm. Obviously, the captain was unaware that his executive officer was upset. It was his responsibility to do whatever was necessary to work with his captain. "Captain, I was just in the control room. I noticed our course has been changed to one four-five. The quartermaster has a course laid out that takes us into the Bay of Biscay. I wasn't aware—"

"Of course," Erhardt interrupted. He ran a hand through his hair and shook his head apologetically. "Of course," he repeated again. "I was so tired. How foolish of me."

"Why—?" Once again Rather was cut off.

"Shallow water exercises." Erhardt spread his hands out, palms up, as if to say, *How could I?*

Rather licked his lips. "We did that very well for a couple of days . . . in the Celtic Sea. I assumed we might be finished since the destroyer is no longer with us." He became more uncomfortable as Erhardt's concerned expression seemed to change to one of chagrin. *The man really is sorry he overlooked including me. It was a slip!* "Well, sir, I recommend we should radio squadron headquarters if you really do plan to alter our orders. I'd be happy to . . ."

Erhardt spoke up. "I am aware of that. Please don't worry—not after my foolish mistake. I will take care of it eventually." The captain folded his arms and tilted his head slightly to the side as if he was thinking about how to apologize. But he said nothing. His narrow lips had disappeared into an aspect of deep thought. He glanced up as if he expected his executive officer would chastise him. His deep-set blue eyes seemed to penetrate into Rather's very soul, as if to ask forgiveness.

That disturbed Rather even more. "Would you care to have me prepare the message, Captain? Normally, that would be my responsibility."

"No. I'll do it. And please, Otto, understand that I'm going to make an extra effort to avoid anything so embarrassing again. It was totally unintentional and I would have reacted just like you back when I was an executive officer." He turned abruptly in his chair and returned to the papers on his desk, looking up guiltily to say, "I do have a great deal to take care of here."

Now was the time to show that a good executive officer could cover for his captain. "If I may say so, Captain, squadron directive requires us to request permission to alter our assignment . . . rather than report such a change at a later date. So I'd be happy to prepare two messages for you, Captain . . . I mean as a way to avoid any later repercussions from squadron headquarters."

"I'll take care of it, Otto." When he looked up this time, Erhardt's sad features had become more assertive, and his voice indicated there would be no more discussion. "As commanding officer, I still have to make the decisions—and accept any consequences for overlooking regulations—and I will in this case take care of the necessary communications. Is there anything else?"

Otto Rather drew himself erect in his best military manner and saluted vigorously. There remained a distance between them that he couldn't fathom. He didn't want that to grow. They must work together, but it would obviously be on Erhardt's terms. "Certainly, Captain." He desperately wanted to say more, but it was so difficult to measure this man. Better to take things slowly, culture their relationship. That was also part of being a good executive officer. He slid the curtain back in place as he departed and returned to his own stateroom, unaware that he was as disturbed at their unannounced change in operations as before until prone on his own bunk.

A raw wind blew into the Bay of Biscay from the northwest as *Baghdad* slipped away from her pier. It was slightly after midnight and the boat responded almost immediately to the chop, even though she rode low in the water under a full load.

In addition to Michael, Soraya, and Ismael, there were

ten others, all male, all in their twenties and thirties, all with varying degrees of Arab blood running in their veins. They came from such diverse countries as Brazil, India, Turkey, and Peru. There was even one from South Korea whose features were more Far Eastern than Middle Eastern. But they shared much in common—they were all Muslim and each man had served aboard Type-209 submarines in his former country's navy. The third and most important item was that their countries' 209s had been built in Germany and these men had all been trained in the German submarine school. As a result, they possessed a reasonable knowledge of the German language and were expert with much of the equipment installed in both the 209 and 212 classes of submarine.

It had taken almost seven months, shortly after Hussein had first learned of the conference from a high-level contact in Damascus, to locate them and bring them together. He had personally selected these ten devoted Muslim fundamentalists as ideal for his purpose. By the time their training was complete, they would look forward to the day they would ascend to heaven forever as martyrs for their cause.

Their course was northwest, directly into five-foot swells, and Michael had allowed for a slower passage. They were headed for a point in the Bay of Biscay, forty-five degrees north, five degrees west. It was approximately 150 kilometers from their point of departure. It would take about thirty hours and they would be on station before sunup the following morning, a few hours before Walter Erhardt anticipated surfacing.

Michael snapped off the light over the chart table and turned back to look for Ismael. In the past month, Michael had absorbed more about the sea from the Turk than he ever imagined was possible. When they had first acquired *Baghdad,* Ismael, out of necessity, had assumed responsibility for handling the craft. But Hussein had said it was vital that at least two of them be able to sail the vessel because a time would come when Ismael would have to concentrate solely on his torpedoes. The Turk, an efficient, if unenthusiastic, teacher, was standing out near the stern, barely visible in the darkness except for the red glow from his ever-present black cigarette. Michael moved out beside him. The wind whistled around the two whip antennas installed in Benghazi. Occasional gusts howled like a distant siren.

Ismael noted Michael's presence with a nod and lit a new cigarette from the old before releasing that one to the wind. They stood together silently, legs spread apart as they moved with the motion of the boat. Tiny phosphorescent particles in the water sparkled down either side and disappeared into their wake. After a few minutes, Soraya appeared from below, lurched unsteadily to the railing, and was violently seasick. When she was able to look up from the sea and saw that they'd been watching her, they both laughed. Soraya made an obscene gesture and moved unhappily to the opposite side.

"A little more than twenty-four hours and we should contact that submarine," Michael shouted above the gusts.

Ismael nodded and sucked deeply on the cigarette. The boat's bow rose slowly, then descended a bit more quickly down the opposite side of a swell, burying its nose in green water.

"Will that make a believer out of you?"

Ismael took another puff and inhaled deeply before answering, "Only one thing will make me a believer."

The boat shuddered slightly as the bow rose up once again, shaking off the weight of the water. Michael nodded in agreement. Ismael was indeed correct.

The operations officer of Submarine Squadron Four (SUBRON FOUR) in Eckernforde flipped through the previous day's messages on the daily communications board. Occasionally, he would stop to read one, but only if it appeared that it might affect him. Most of them were administrative in nature and the squadron was included more for information purposes than anything else.

But there was one that attracted his attention instantly. Once again, SUBRON FOUR had been included only for informational purposes. In retrospect, perhaps this was why communications people racked their brains to add additional information addressees. It was the navy way, but it also covered asses. This one was from the destroyer that had been exercising with *Heinz Waller,* and it was informing its own squadron commander that training had been canceled due to excessively rough weather at the request of the commanding officer of S-252. *Why the hell didn't someone tell me what Erhardt was doing?*

The operations officer leafed through the remaining messages, couldn't find what he was looking for, and went back through the entire stack again. Nothing. He called over to the chief radioman. "Chief, where's the message changing *Waller*'s operational status?"

The chief looked at him curiously. "Message, sir?"

"Message, Chief," the ops officer mimicked. "You know the kind—when a submarine changes status, the one they always send whenever they complete an evolution—especially if it changes *their status,"* he commented with emphasis. He ripped the destroyer's message off the board and waved it in the chief's direction.

The chief wrinkled his forehead with concern. "We haven't gotten a thing from *Waller,* sir. May I see what you have there?" He read the proffered message before looking up at the ops officer with a worried expression. "Nothing, sir. Nothing at all."

The two men stared silently at each other for a moment without speaking.

"I'll get out an urgent right away, sir." The last words came over the chief's shoulder as he headed for the communications room.

The operations officer was already headed in the other direction, toward the admiral's office. According to that message, it had been almost thirty-six hours since the destroyer broke contact with *Heinz Waller.* No submarine, especially in Submarine Squadron Four, ever operated independently without informing their immediate superior.

That was how they became lost.

FEDERAL REPUBLIC OF GERMANY

FLASH—FLASH—FLASH

CLASSIFICATION: TOP SECRET

FROM: COMMANDER, SUBMARINE SQUADRON FOUR

TO: INSPECTOR OF THE NAVY/COMMANDER, NORTHERN NAVAL DISTRICT/COMMANDER, SUBMARINE FLOTILLA
INFO: ALL FRG SHIPS IN SECTORS BC12/BC23/ CD12/23/DE12/DE23

1) HEINZ WALLER (SS), S-252 UNREPORTED FOR THIRTY-SIX HOURS.
2) LAST REPORTED POSITION APPROXIMATELY 15W 50N DURING EXERCISES WITH DESTROYER GOTTINGEN.
3) EXERCISES TERMINATED DUE TO WEATHER CONDITIONS.
4) REPEATED EFFORTS TO ESTABLISH CONTACT DURING SCHEDULED COMMUNICATIONS PERIOD UNSUCCESSFUL.
5) ALL SHIPS ABOVE SECTORS ARE REQUESTED TO ATTEMPT CONTACT BY VISUAL, RADIO, SONAR.
6) COMSUBRON FOUR GUARDING CIRCUIT WHISKEY ALFA TWENTY-FOUR HOURS.

The commodore's cabin for the commander of Amphibious Squadron Four aboard the helicopter carrier U.S.S. *Wasp* (LPH-4) was not elegant in the manner of the luxurious suites aboard a cruise ship. But it was comfortable and sumptuous in comparison to the stateroom Lieutenant Commander Jake Steele sometimes shared with his junior officers. The admiral's aide had called Jake at 0730 and told him to appear in the admiral's quarters at 0800 sharp. As soon as he stepped past the marine sentry who held open the door for him, Jake caught the smell of fresh doughnuts and coffee. There hadn't been doughnuts in either the ship's wardroom or the commodore's that morning. The admiral had been raiding the crew's galley again.

Rear Admiral John Harrison Turner, the commander of Amphibious Squadron Four (PHIBRON FOUR), figured he'd earned the comfortable facilities after twenty-seven years in the navy. His quarters, situated beneath the flight deck, consisted of a separate, reasonably sized bedroom with private toilet facilities off a large main room. The main area consisted of a lounge section with a sofa and comfortable chairs. These were all gray metal frame, covered with standard navy-green Naugahyde, and attached to the deck. The sofa was also bolted to the bulkhead. Above it were various fighting-unit plaques and photos of ships, the only decorations in addition to the mandatory photograph of President Salkin.

There was also a table that could be converted for dining if Rear Admiral Turner preferred not to use his staff wardroom. On the far side was the admiral's desk, which was vacant more often than it was in use because the admiral preferred to spend his time on *Wasp*'s bridge or in flag plot where his staff controlled Amphibious Squadron Four. The desk was neat, an in-out basket to one side, a telephone on the other, unencumbered space in the middle to sign letters prepared by his staff in the outer office. The bulkhead behind the admiral's desk was decorated with plaques and photos of his other commands and ships he'd served aboard. There were also personal pictures of the admiral posing with more senior officers and VIPs.

Steele's eyes made a final trip around the admiral's spaces. These were the kind of quarters that made Jake think that maybe it was all worthwhile to bust his ass and stay put in the navy and aspire to higher things. *No, no way. They don't make a habit of turning SEALs into admirals, especially "mustang" SEALs who had begun their careers as enlisted men.* How many SEALs with admiral's stars? Never more than one or two. That was all the navy could handle at one time.

"Commander Steele, are you with us?" the admiral's chief staff officer, Captain Black, inquired. Black's own quarters were across the passageway from the admiral's, but much of his time was spent with Turner.

Jake's head snapped around to the neat, efficient officer who was studying him with a bemused look. "Yes, sir." Then his gaze traveled toward the admiral, as a steward placed a cup of coffee in front of the man. Turner was actually grinning.

"Care to switch jobs for a day, Commander?" Rear Admiral Turner, who was known to smile more than most admirals and had acquired the name of "Happy Jack," might have been thirty years old or sixty. His blue eyes sparkled mischievously. His short, neatly trimmed hair was pure white and had been for as long as anyone could remember. But his face was lean and without a crease and he might have been younger than Jake. There were a few close friends who were comfortable in teasing the handsome admiral with the small bow mouth—they said he looked more like Elvis Presley than a navy admiral. "It's kind of fun on the bridge, Jake. You get a comfy chair and a great view." He chuckled at his own humor.

Steele was mortified. *What a hell of a way to start the day.* "I'm sorry, sir. I didn't mean to be staring." He'd been aft in flag plot and up on the bridge any number of times at sea, and he'd spent a lot of time working with Rear Admiral Turner and his staff. He knew the commodore's sense of humor, but it was always more fun when he was kidding someone else.

"Shall I begin, Admiral?" Captain Black asked humorlessly.

"Let Jake look at the intelligence analysis first. He reads. No point in reading it to him. Munch on a couple of those doughnuts, Jake, while you read that stuff."

Steele accepted the two-page synopsis prepared by Lieutenant Peter Germond, the PHIBRON FOUR intelligence officer, from the COMSIXTHFLEET intelligence report and those he'd received from other units. These analyses were prepared in detail by the intelligence specialists attached to each command, then circulated widely. Each command then sifted through these reports and extracted the items they deemed of value to their own people. Lieutenant Germond had culled out and considerably shortened reports of the movements of known terrorists around Europe and the Middle East; the latest security arrangements for industrial, political, and military purposes; and certain political events over the previous forty-eight hours that he considered worthy of note to Rear Admiral Turner. One section, outlined with red ink, appraised a recent report from Cherbourg authorities concerning a missing fishing boat; the boat had been listed for sale, and reports from individuals in the dock area indicated that the owners had taken some prospective buyers (possibly

Arabs) to sea for a day in February; neither the boat nor the owners had been seen since then. A second note reported rumors that a fishing boat named *Baghdad* had loaded weapons at a Libyan port a few weeks before; the rumors had yet to be confirmed by reliable sources and there had been no sighting of any small craft named *Baghdad.* However, Lieutenant Germond noted, COMSIXTHFLEET intelligence took every report of Libyan weapons seriously. There was a handwritten comment in red: *any relationship here?* Someone else had noted: *doubtful!* Germond's handwriting was obvious with this notation: *Need to keep an eye on this—descriptions are similar and Libya under our responsibility.*

On a separate page, there was a copy of a message from German navy headquarters to NATO headquarters noting that an FRG submarine (S-252) had gone unreported for thirty-six hours; a comment beneath the message, obviously from COMSIXTHFLEET intelligence again, included the fact that the former captain of that submarine had disappeared under mysterious circumstances in February and the FRG navy appeared to be sweeping the situation under the table. This, too, had been outlined in red. *I thought the German navy kept track of the COs of these boats 24 hours/day* was Germond's handwritten comment.

Steele handed the analysis back to Captain Black. "Something special in those red ink notes?" he asked. It was all he could see in the report to justify showing him.

"Who can say for sure?" answered Black. "The only one that concerns us is the Libyan thing since we're operating in the Med." PHIBRON FOUR was the United States' first response team. They were in the Mediterranean to react to situations similar to the Iraqi invasion of Kuwait and they were also the American navy's answer to any military problems on land. In addition to the marine group aboard *Wasp,* the amphibious ships sailing with the squadron carried their own complement of marines and could land them from sea by air-cushion craft or vertically envelop the enemy by helicopter.

"It's a shot in the dark, Jake," Turner said. "Anything remotely to do with Libya makes a lot of people jittery. Soon as that name begins to appear in messages, I start getting other messages asking what I'm doing about the Libyan situation. If you're like me, you may be asking what Libyan situation they're talking about." Admiral Turner leaned forward and flashed one of his famous grins. "So, we're going to make believe a fishing boat that no one's seen is running around the Med loaded to the gunwales with weapons—or drugs maybe? But since we're then assuming that she's capable of blowing up the world, you're going to devise the exercises to combat the problem."

"Sounds interesting." What else could he say? It did sound interesting. It was becoming more boring each day to plan the same old beach feasibility studies and surface observation exercises even though he tried to insert changes to challenge his men. It was more fun to train with another country's special forces team for a few days, but that often meant they would have to play charity soccer or softball games afterward in front of people who didn't speak a word of English. This could be different.

Jake Steele was the N7 on Admiral Turner's staff, which meant he was the SEAL/MARG (Marine Amphibious Ready Group) liaison officer for the commodore. A marine colonel commanded the marine unit, but Jake was officer-in-charge of a special operations unit composed of two platoons of navy SEALs and four Small Boat Unit crews and their boats. The naval title for this was Maritime Special Purpose Force Commander which was a fancy way of saying he was the senior SEAL officer. Steele's orders to report to PHIBRON FOUR had only been issued in early February, and he'd reported for duty without having worked closely with the men. There'd been less than a week to train together before they boarded *Wasp* for deployment to the Mediterranean.

"Sounds like fun, even if nothing comes of it," Jake added when he found the other two still watching him. "What about that German submarine? The notation on that was outlined in red just like that supposed fishing boat. Any relationship to the terrorists in Libya or is that too much of a long shot?"

"I don't know." Turner frowned. "Who marked this in red?" he asked his chief staff officer.

"I think Peter said that was done at Sixth Fleet, Admiral.

This summary came from them on the courier flight. It's probably that Captain Davis, their senior intelligence officer. They say he's notorious with a red pen."

"Probably doesn't mean a thing, but it's a good idea to check back on that," Turner noted. "Never hurts to ask since we can't read minds out here."

"I'll get Lieutenant Germond on it," Black answered.

Rear Admiral Turner looked at his watch. "Why don't you play with this, Jake. Say we did learn there was a fishing boat loaded with weapons, and maybe a crew that knew how to use them. We can't go blowing them out of the water without proof or all the lefties will raise hell. We probably have to capture some of the terrorists to prove they exist and we definitely have to have some captured weapons to display. Let's start with a tabletop situation exercise. Since you look like you'd like to move into my quarters, come on back here at 1200 sharp and have lunch with me and we'll talk about it." His smile seemed to be a yard wide.

"I'd enjoy that, sir."

After Jake had left, Turner commented to his chief of staff, "There's something I like about Jake. I've only known him for a couple of weeks, but he looks like he's supposed to look for the job he does."

Jake Steele was medium height, but he was structured like a football player. He had a thick powerful neck on wide muscular shoulders. His chest appeared broad enough for a man twice his size, yet his waist was narrow and there wasn't an ounce of fat on his body. Muscular arms and legs balanced out his frame. His complexion was dark, his eyes hazel, and his black hair was beginning to thin.

Jake returned to his stateroom on the same deck forward of the commodore's wardroom. It wasn't large but it had been designed for two men. Jake had it to himself because his wet suits, diving gear, body armor, flight suits, boarding equipment, and occasionally some of his weapons and demolition equipment, when there was no time to return them to the armory, were stored there. There was barely room for his work and dress uniforms.

Rear Admiral Turner had given him a formidable problem, one he would enjoy working out on his own before he passed it on to his platoon leaders to see how they would handle it. Jake Steele folded the front of his desk out of the bulkhead and sat down to experiment with ideas on how you managed to capture a fishing boat full of terrorists and weapons without blowing it out of the water or getting yourself and your own men killed.

CHAPTER FIVE

The homicide detective in charge of the Preminger investigation, Herman Gleick, was a short, balding, nondescript man who would admit at times that he had a naturally dirty mind. The human condition revolved around sex—everyone required it in some form—and every individual had something in their background they would prefer to keep to themselves. Whenever he worked on this theory and conducted his investigations with that assumption, more often than not he turned up something in the victim's sexual behavior that contributed to their death, even with his latest case. Hans Preminger had been so "squeaky clean," he told one of his assistants, that "eventually his dick would turn against him."

But each day of the investigation seemed to prove Gleick wrong. Preminger's associates considered him the perfect family man. German intelligence had conducted background investigations both when he applied for submarine school and when he was selected for command, and each time he qualified as the perfect altar boy. The detective decided Preminger was so pure that it was indeed a miracle that he had married or fathered children. For the first time in his career, he was about to be proven wrong. Perhaps this man would be the first he'd ever encountered "whose dick had a conscience."

Eventually, there was only one solution left. Gleick went

to the individual who knew Hans Preminger, and his penis, better than any other person—his wife.

Mrs. Preminger was an attractive woman and she dressed to enhance her appealing figure. Gleick had been told by the squadron commander that she was a perfect complement to any naval officer. This was the third time he'd interviewed her. The other times had been in late February and early March, and each time she had been well in control of her emotions, almost too well he had decided. "You must be getting tired of seeing my face," he said conversationally as he added a spoonful of sugar to the coffee she'd offered him.

"Someday, I'd like to put this all beyond me, for the children if for nothing else," she answered. "But I understand your job is to find out exactly what happened to my husband."

Gleick reviewed what he'd done since he last talked with her, whom he'd seen, what they'd offered to his questions. "Your husband seems to have been a perfect human being."

"That seems to have been the conclusion," she answered.

But there it was . . . wasn't it? Was that a touch of sarcasm? Hadn't her eyes turned toward the ceiling for just an instant, as if to hint that she'd heard that comment once too often? "Would you disagree with that comment, Mrs. Preminger?" He was on dangerous ground. If the navy learned of his approach, there'd be hell to pay. "I'm only asking you that because it's part of my job, believe me. I've run out of everything else. If there's anything you want to say off the record, it won't go beyond me. If I'm out of line, please say so."

She appraised Gleick, holding his gaze for a moment. No, he wasn't being forward. Nothing in his bland features indicated that he tended toward the lewd. She folded her arms, licked her lips deliberately, and took a deep breath. "Hans Preminger was so perfect he would have screwed your wife, perhaps even your dear old mother, if he had a chance." Her eyes flashed angrily.

"Go on."

"He was as good at hiding his women as he was at fooling everyone in the navy. He misled me for a long time. All those people who were so amazed with his goodness made fools out of themselves hopping into bed with anyone who'd have them. I guess it had something to do with pride—how many notches you had on your penis," she said, her eyes darting about the room nervously. "They boasted about their little conquests while my husband apparently went about it quietly. I suppose that's why Hans seemed so goddamn pure to them . . . why he got command so early. He never said—they never knew. Oh, he was so cool about it all. He was so cool about all that . . ." Her eyes came back to the detective's. "That only a wife would find out. When we were in Hamburg, when he was overseeing construction on those new closed power plants, that's when I found out."

"Did you confront him?"

"Confront him? Confront Jesus Christ?" she asked bitterly. "I knew. It was all little things. I couldn't prove it. I couldn't find out who it was, or when it was going to happen, but I knew. And he lied." She shook an accusing finger at the detective. "He was the most perfect liar ever created. That's why he had them all fooled."

Gleick let her talk until she had it out of her system. "I'm sorry, Mrs. Preminger. It was all I had left to follow up. Maybe it will help us. I know it hurts to admit it to anyone."

She nodded. There had been no tears as she spoke. "I hope something will come of it because . . . because I still love the dirty son of a bitch." That's when the tears flowed. But the woman Gleick comforted professionally was not the distraught wife one would have expected. She was angry—angry because she had been made a fool of in her own mind. Hans Preminger probably never realized what a lucky man he was.

Gleick pondered the situation as he drove through the streets of Kiel. Why was he right every time about people's sexual leanings? He thought back to one of the reports he'd reviewed just the other day. The night manager of the Bodo Cabaret had seen what might have been a body being carried down the back stairs across the alley from his establishment on the night Preminger disappeared. Gleick had already been to the Bodo, interviewed that manager, then gone to the building in question, which turned out to be apartments. All the tenants had been uninteresting to Gleick, except one, and he'd made a mental note about that particular one for himself.

Now there was an even better reason to follow up on the Arab woman who had rented that apartment, yet had been in residence for a much shorter time than her lease. The name she'd given the landlord must have been a phony, but this was reinforcement to his theory that somehow there might be a break here. The landlord had said she was an extremely appealing woman. How did he say it? "The type that would make you lie to your wife." One that Preminger would lie to his wife about? It would take some digging, but just maybe it would be worthwhile. Nothing seemed to be related, but to Gleick it was better than anything else he had—a horny submariner, a possible corpse, a mysterious woman? Maybe.

Hugo Schroeder had come to the conclusion that he would share his background with the executive officer. The squadron commander had suggested that he find one officer he trusted implicitly and explain that—just in case something happened to Schroeder—another person must be aware of the Whiskey Alfa radio circuit. He felt he could trust this man and he was convinced that an officer as loyal as Rather could never be involved in the murder of his captain.

"I won't keep you long, Mr. Rather." He extracted the letter given him by the squadron commander and handed it to the executive officer without a word.

Rather scanned the simple paragraph written by the squadron commander designating Schroeder's special orders. Then his bushy eyebrows rose until they seemed to join with his hairline, and he reread the words carefully a second time. He handed it back. "So . . ." he murmured, "So everyone ashore seems to know more than the executive officer of the *Heinz Waller* . . . even the weapons officer who came aboard under mysterious conditions. So . . ." he repeated softly. He stroked his chin with a great deal of care as he pondered the admiral's terse letter.

"Mr. Rather . . ." Schroeder's primary responsibility was to the squadron commander and he knew how troubled Rather was—and why.

"Am I to remain in the dark on whatever this means also,

or are you going to tell me what this *personal directive* of the admiral's is all about?"

"Hans Preminger was murdered."

Rather's wide mouth fell open. Even his tongue seemed too large for his body.

"I was ordered aboard as an investigating officer in February after Captain Preminger disappeared. My orders were to determine if there was anyone who might have been involved with Captain Preminger or may have had information concerning Captain Preminger's death. It's not something I asked for. I was ordered to do this."

Rather found his voice. "And you think I might know something?" The expression on his face was one of astonishment.

Schroeder shook his head and managed a smile. "No, of course not. I haven't found a thing, nothing at all. I wanted you to see that letter for a specific reason. You are the only one who knows about it."

"Have you shown this to the captain?" Rather asked.

"No."

"I know this submarine better than anyone aboard," Rather said, "and I can assure you no one was involved, no matter what happened to Captain Preminger."

"I thought that's what you would probably say," Schroeder commented.

Rather reached out and clapped Schroeder on the shoulder. He could think of no other response. An executive officer was in such a difficult position, so withdrawn from everyone beneath him, a buffer between captain and crew. "I do appreciate this, Lieutenant Schroeder, and I won't forget." He appeared thoughtful for an instant. His smile was genuine now, and he extended his hand toward the letter Schroeder was still holding. "But may I look at that again."

Schroeder handed it to him.

Rather read it over quickly and returned it. "Squadron is guarding Whiskey Alfa on a twenty-four-hour basis." He shrugged nonchalantly. "I don't know. Who knows what will happen?" He thought about his brief audience with Erhardt before he was dismissed. "If that circuit must eventually be used, you won't be compromised, Mr.

Schroeder. You keep on with what you have to do, whether or not you like it, and I will keep on with what I have to do . . . whether or not I like it."

Soraya could see light intensifying through the single porthole above her bunk. Day was breaking. She was not one to pray for such minor personal triumphs, but she had indeed survived a horrible night—Allah be praised. Rising on an elbow, she could also see whitecaps through that porthole, when it wasn't covered by rushing water, as *Baghdad* slid down another swell and buried her nose into green water. In her heart, Soraya could not thank Allah for that. Maybe Allah . . . after all, Allah couldn't be everywhere at the same time. He couldn't smooth the seas but he'd allowed her to see another day, even though she'd been so seasick she was sure she would die. Soraya felt so miserable that she was certain Allah would understand and allow this moment of skepticism.

The light snapped on over her bunk and she blinked against the sudden brightness. She had turned it off because it was easier if she couldn't see things swaying in the little cabin she and Michael had intended to share. But there had been no sharing, not with his travels the last few weeks and their hours of work, and certainly not on this most horrible of nights. "Turn it off!" she shrieked.

Michael sat down on her bunk and snickered mirthlessly. "My apologies, my queen of the sea, but it is close to morning. We have work to do today."

Yes, they had work. Today was the day. And Soraya felt worse than miserable. "I'll do anything in the future. I'll cross the minefields. I'll drive car bombs . . ."

"Here." He lay a damp cloth on her head. "I have pity for you. See, I'm not so bad now, am I?"

The cloth did feel good. It was damp and cool and soothing. "But you were laughing at me, you and that silent . . ." She searched for a derogatory word that would adequately cover Ismael.

"You should be pleased that he reacted. Normally, Ismael doesn't smile or laugh or cry or anything. You pleased him."

Soraya groaned. "I need something in my stomach. I wish . . ."

Michael produced a box of soda crackers. "Ismael said to eat these. Just these and some water—not too much water. He said they'll expand in your stomach and make you feel better."

She accepted a handful of crackers and took a tiny bite to test this theory. "How does someone like him know this?" She'd heard Ismael's simplistic philosophy of life too many times—either you remained alive to kill infidels or you were better off dead. He never considered sex! It was the blunt credo of someone who killed for pleasure without understanding the other pleasures of life. But the cracker tasted good and she stuffed the rest of it in her mouth.

"He was brought up in a fishing village. Remember how much he's taught me since the day we acquired *Baghdad.* He said they always had bread or crackers on their boats for the rough weather."

"So he actually took pity on me."

"Not exactly." Michael grinned at her. "He said if you weren't capable of fighting, then there was no room for you on this boat."

"The asshole," she snarled. She knew he was unbalanced enough to have thrown her overboard for exactly that reason. He might have done it even if he was aware of her particular orders.

"Now, now." He ran his hand up under her sweat shirt. "That doesn't sound like the woman who can charm any man on earth." He found her left breast and squeezed it before she could react. "I thought that since sex has always been your cure for everything, that maybe I can help you . . ."

Soraya's hand lashed out.

Michael ducked and her cupped hand barely touched his curly hair. His grin turned into a nasty chuckle. "See, you're feeling better already." But he'd already yanked his hand from under her sweat shirt.

"You're an asshole, too," she raged, sitting upright and throwing the cloth on the floor.

Michael jumped up from her bunk and took a couple of steps backward. "What a miraculous cure. Crackers and sex."

Soraya threw the remaining crackers she had in her other hand at him. Her face contorted in anger.

"Now Ismael will be happy. You are a fighter again." He pointed at the box of crackers that had fallen to the deck. "Don't throw any more, my love. Eat them. They'll give you strength. Maybe you'll be able to throw up on the German sailors."

Soraya gave him a hateful look and bent down to pick up the box. She was feeling better, or was it just anger that had made her forget what a miserable night it had been. "How soon do we expect them to surface?"

"It's a little after six now. Sometime between six and seven, Walter said. We agreed that it had to be light. Erhardt can't tell what the weather is like here on the surface, but if he has to wait an extra hour or so, it won't hurt him." He looked at his watch. "I'll start sending the signal at seven."

Heinz Waller's last known position—called a *datum* in naval terminology—had been 14/54 west, 49/41 north, which was approximately 415 kilometers west-southwest of Ireland's Fastnet Rock. Within hours of the first message from the FRG, the patrol aircraft came from England and France and Norway to join the Germans in their search for S-252. They scoured the North Sea, the English Channel, and the Celtic Sea, where the submarine should have been transiting. The Americans directed their carrier, *Abraham Lincoln,* which had been participating in joint exercises in the Norwegian Sea, to search the seas west of Ireland. Search patterns were coordinated by each unit through their individual commands and faxed to Fleet Command in Flensburg to ensure that not a square mile of ocean where *Heinz Waller* might be was overlooked.

But there was no sign of *Heinz Waller*—no radio message to break the tension, no telltale foam from a snorkel, no oil slick from ruptured fuel tanks, not even an empty life jacket bobbing on the whitecapped surface to signify her gravesite. She had disappeared into thin air or, more likely, the murky abyss of the Atlantic Ocean.

The men who operated in the U.S. Navy's Special Boat Units (SBUs) bore little resemblance to the vast majority of sailors in the surface navy. They were independent to the point of sometimes being considered eccentric, and they were totally absorbed in themselves and their own very special niche. Even Jake Steele, who'd operated with the SBUs for years, found them unique. These small-boat sailors, who inserted the SEALs into hostile territory and often supported them with covering fire when there was trouble, might not have been as physically tough as SEALs, but they were just as tough mentally. Their knowledge of small-boat operations were what often got the SEALs in position to complete their mission and many times appeared at the crucial moment to extract them. The SBU guys were different—but they were so good at what they did!

Jake Steele had concluded within moments after his initial meeting with Rear Admiral Turner that there was only one way to get near a fishing boat bristling with well-armed Arab terrorists—with the small boats called RIBS (Rigid Inflatable Boats) that his SBUs maintained so lovingly aboard the *Ashland,* a dock landing ship (LSD) steaming with PHIBRON FOUR.

A fishing boat was too small and difficult to approach by parachute, day or night, not to mention the profusion of ground tackle that would make a landing just about impossible. That would also make fast-roping from a helicopter difficult, too. No, the best way was a high-speed approach, preferably at night. The RIBs could do thirty-five knots plus, and their radar profile was almost nonexistent. If they were sighted, suppressing fire from helicopters would cover them during their approach.

Jake had gone over preliminary plans with Rear Admiral Turner, Captain Black, and Peter Germond, the staff intelligence officer, and they basically agreed that was the likely scenario. But Captain Black brought up the critical factor: what kind of firepower might they be facing if this fishing boat wasn't just a fanciful rumor? The available data weren't based on hard American intelligence. There were no photos from aircraft or satellite recon. More than likely, someone had been selling intelligence and there was no way for the purchaser to guarantee that it was absolute. The Arabs were experts at manufacturing false leads. No one knew whether this fishing boat really existed, and there was no hint at its mission.

"Jake's done as much as he can, I think," Peter Germond commented, after they'd analyzed some of the scenarios that Sixth Fleet intelligence had scripted. "If this boat really exists, Jake's going to have to take it from there." Lieutenant Germond fixed Steele with an innocent grin. "Isn't that why some twisted person invented SEALs?"

Now, half an hour after leaving Rear Admiral Turner's cabin, Jake Steele found himself imitating Peter's comment when he sat down in his stateroom with the master chief petty officer in charge of the two special boat units. The chief had come over to *Wasp* from *Ashland* by helo. "And I suppose that's why they invented SBUs. We needed someone crazy enough to get us there." Jake shrugged his shoulders. "That's as much as I can tell you, Master Chief. No one knows any more than that."

Chief Bewick looked amused. "I suppose that's why I'm a chief and that old guy back in flag plot is an admiral." He had bad feelings about an operation like this—too little hard intelligence. "Shit, I'd just take a missile and blow this bad guy out of the water. I never saw a bad guy worth the food he gobbled up. Let's kick butt like we used to do in Vietnam." He remembered when they used to deliver SEALs to a jump-off point and wait for them to come back with prisoners for interrogation. Sometimes the SEALs returned drawing heavy fire and Bewick remembered cranking away with the fifty-cal machine gun. "Those firefights kept us on our toes."

Doug Bewick had been an enlisted river rat in Vietnam, operating the small craft that raced through brown jungle waters over twenty-five years before. After years of high-speed firefights and hard-drinking liberty ashore, he had a face like a road map, a cast-iron stomach, and hands like a vise grip. His talent for keeping small-boat engines functioning long after others had given up was legend among the special operations people.

He lived for engines and rode for excitement. When he didn't have a RIB engine screaming at top speed, he was racing a Harley on the mainland. His garage at home was full of boat and motorcycle parts—just in case they're needed, he explained. His fingernails were split and dirty. His hands and arms were covered with scabs. And his working khakis proudly displayed the grease that signified his profession. Chief Bewick was a sailor, but he looked like a motorcycle mechanic.

"I tend to agree with your one well-placed missile, Chief, but the intelligence people always like to take some prisoners, someone to justify their existence. So, we're all going to earn our paychecks if this fishing boat really exists."

"They gonna let us drive our boats beforehand for a little practice?"

"You got it, Chief. We'll start with dry runs on the flight deck to get seating and positions. And I want my guys to do some climbing on the inside of the well deck, maybe to the second or third level. We'll have SBU guys supporting the climbers, passing equipment and weapons, unsecuring rigging, the usual training stuff."

Bewick nodded. "My guys can do it in their sleep, so we'll bring yours up to speed." His face remained devoid of expression.

Steele grinned. "Right, Chief. I'm told there's a bunch of VIPs coming aboard over the next few days and Admiral Turner's not keen about anything that could possibly make them nervous. So he said we have to start playing tonight. Tomorrow, we'll work on approaches for boarding, evasion if we come under attack, standing off to provide cover, then practice boarding one of our own landing craft, and finish up with emergency extraction."

"We need some night work anyway, sir, in close-in maneuvering and signaling by radio and chem light. My men have been messing around with that in the well deck, but it's a hell of a lot different when you're in a RIB bouncing over the waves at thirty-five knots."

Steele was jotting down some notes. "Good enough. Who knows what the sea state's going to be if this thing ever goes down? It's probably just a wild goose chase, but what the hell. We haven't had that much time to work. The boys need to play together or they'll get dull."

Lou Griffey learned early in life that the more complex a situation, the more he enjoyed it. Boredom was his greatest enemy. When he was in college, he was certain that he wanted to join the Foreign Service. He remained convinced of that until he actually had the opportunity to work in the State Department after graduation. Eighteen months in Washington persuaded him that the bureaucracy would drive him insane, so he entered medical school on the assumption that a medical practice would provide a continuing challenge. A flourishing partnership at a medical center provided enough money to allow him the opportunity to do volunteer work in poor countries, and that was how he came to the attention of Rupert Daniels.

Daniels did have the patience to work his way up through the State Department. He obtained increasingly more responsible positions overseas until he became ambassador to an island nation purely on his native ability. He and Lou Griffey met at a formal function on that island and hit it off immediately. When Daniels returned to Washington, he had induced Lou to work with him. They intended to convince Congress of the need to provide more medical assistance to Third World nations in lieu of the cash grants that always seemed to disappear into deep pockets.

In the ensuing years, Lou Griffey gradually acquired a "Dr. Tom Dooley"–type of reputation, although all his time was spent administering medical assistance programs rather than actually practicing his profession. He became a celebrity within a small circle in Washington because he was able to employ his intelligence, rather than political influence, to accomplish his goals. Yet he was also gaining the political clout that he had once assumed would never come his way.

When his trusted friend, Rupert Daniels, was killed, it seemed only natural to Phil Salkin that he appoint Daniels's closest associate. Lou Griffey had been working behind the scenes with Daniels to bring the Middle Eastern leaders to a realistic summit. He looked upon this historic meeting from a humanitarian, rather than a political, perspective. Lou Griffey achieved what he had dreamed of in college, but he had come to it in the most roundabout manner of any new Secretary of State.

Griffey had no compunctions about telling the President what he honestly believed. It had been dicey when Rabin and Arafat had come together in Washington. They weren't about to be coerced into shaking hands by anyone's baby-faced president. If any of the leaders felt themselves being pushed toward an agreement, which was a distinct possibility if Phil Salkin was constantly at the table, the summit could collapse. Rupert Daniels had fully believed, and Lou Griffey agreed, that no peaceful settlement could be reached if it came from anywhere other than these diverse leaders themselves. A peace proposed by an American president would be just what the Arabs had been rejecting since 1917—an American, not a Middle Eastern agreement. It would collapse like an eggshell at the first hint of pressure. The PLO had wanted a homeland. These people had to be guided into achieving their own settlement, *and it must be their own.* "I honestly believe, Mr. President, that your presence early in the talks would be more of a hindrance than anything else."

Salkin nodded his agreement. His dark eyes moved rapidly from Griffey to the abbreviated schedule for the summit that lay on his desk. Although he was over seventy, there was never a hint of age in his features, his voice, or his reactions. His mind moved at a more rapid pace than most men's. His questions were always well thought out and penetrating. He had a way of getting to the core of a problem that would take others an agonizingly long time to comprehend. And his humor, a continuous flow of puns and one-liners, was legendary. But the humor was also a means of getting to the crux of a situation and bringing those less capable with him. "I would think no more than five days for this summit—max. What do you say, Lou, five days maximum to get as far as possible?"

Griffey nodded his agreement. "My tentative schedule is five days. Any more than that and I suspect the Arabs would feel the Jews were intractable as always, and vice versa, I might add. Each Muslim nation has something different in mind." Griffey was a short, round-faced, rosy-cheeked man who appeared younger than his years. "All I can do is keep you informed on a steady basis. This is the first time anyone's ever gotten all these people in a place they can't just walk away from, unless, of course, they're exceptional swimmers."

"This yacht, *Calm Seas,* looks like one hell of a floating

palace." Salkin ran his hand through his remaining hair. "What I wouldn't give for a couple of days aboard that—just me and Marian, no phones, no Secret Service, no appointments, no functions, no newspapers. Imagine that, Lou. Just sunning out on the deck, sipping a little Chivas whenever I wanted, a couple of good cigars every day, stop for a swim when we got the urge." His eyes rose from the photo of *Calm Seas* to look wistfully at Griffey. "I know. It's a dream. But what a hell of a dream."

"Hey, why not? If you ever pull this off, they ought to give you that yacht for a gift. I understand from Will Riley she's got one hell of a captain. The guy pulled off the impossible in Monte Carlo. Got all the alterations done in record time, then made sure she looked like a million bucks. The Jewish delegate has her own stateroom, kosher kitchen, and wines." He laid out some photos that had just come over the fax. "The Muslims have the rest of the spaces, but the Iraqis and the Iranians can't get near each other. The Turks, Kuwaitis, and Saudis will only see the Iraqis at the conference table. The Egyptians will have the same situation with the Western Arabs who are buddies of the Libyans." He spread his hands in an all-encompassing gesture. "All these leaders showing up and the security is still perfect. Not one of our intelligence sources has heard the slightest word about the summit, not even a word between the Arabs. Rupert Daniels and Will Riley did such a superb job on a personal basis that these people are coming with only one thing in mind—peace. They want to get on with bringing their own countries into the next century without wars that leave them destitute. They honestly believe in this concept," he said fervently.

Salkin rose to shake hands with his new Secretary of State. "And if we don't have it by the fifth day, I guess I'll never see that yacht," he added wistfully.

"You'll see it, Mr. President."

[illegible]

[illegible]

[illegible]

[illegible]

PART THREE

APRIL

Under Way

CHAPTER SIX

Calm Seas was ready to get under way from Monte Carlo on the morning following the meeting between President Salkin and Secretary of State Griffey. A brilliant spring day and a warm sun quickly dried the morning dew on her wooden decks. Francis Waters was outfitted in starched whites, the perfect picture of a man in command of a ship. Will Riley stood on the wing of the bridge, waiting for Waters to give the orders that would separate the yacht from the land. He would never have admitted to anyone that he felt like a kid off on a grand adventure.

The crew members, on deck in their white pants and white monogrammed *Calm Seas* shirts, consisted of two distinct groups. The first were older hands who had been aboard for a few years and understood the intricacies and vagaries of *Calm Seas.* They were unaware of the fact that successful in-depth background investigations were the only reason they were still aboard. The second, and by far the majority of the largest crew *Calm Seas* had ever carried, were American sailors selected from the racial and religious backgrounds of the Middle East. Each member of the crew had also been approved by the intelligence chiefs of the nations attending.

Waters had taken in all but the last bow line and he was backing down slowly. *Calm Seas'* stern swung out from the dock. "Take in the bow line," Waters ordered.

The last line was lifted rapidly over the top of the cleat on the dock and thrown in the water. The deck hands on the bow hauled it quickly aboard as the yacht backed into the open waters of Monte Carlo's harbor. Waters put his rudder over and ordered the engines ahead slow. There was a slight shudder as the twin propellers reversed direction and dug into the swirling waters off her stern. *Calm Seas* moved forward, her bow swinging toward the harbor mouth.

Waters glanced at the gyrocompass and checked his course to open water. "Steer course one seven five," he ordered as he stepped back out on the wing with Riley. "There you have it, Mr. Riley. Simple as pie. We're under way. In about eighteen minutes, we'll be out of the mouth of the harbor. Then I've got to set a new course or we'll run into Corsica before sunset. Care to tell me where we're headed?"

"I'll tell you what, Francis. I'm going to call you by the name your parents gave you. Not Frank or Frankie or the *Frenkee* your owner called you. Just Francis, because I like you and I like the work you did for me and I think we'd better stop treating each other so formally." The smile was bright, the eyes indifferent. "And, once again, I want you to call me Will. How about that?"

"Terrific, Will. That makes us buddies," Waters answered humorlessly, hoping he might mirror Riley's cold smile. "I hope we get along like buddies are supposed to. Where are we headed?"

"I'm going to tell you that before we hit Corsica," Riley answered with a slight grin, "because we're buddies." He then turned away to stare out toward the open sea. He was certain his selection of Waters was correct. But security was paramount. Perhaps he could explain later. There was no reason to set a course until they were out of range of prying eyes.

On shore, the short, dark, mustachioed man who had thrown off the last line watched until *Calm Seas* passed through the harbor's mouth. The other line handlers drifted off until he was the last man on the dock. Then he headed for the nearest phone to call the number assigned to him. He had no idea whom he was calling, nor did he know what would result from his call. He was simply following orders that a Muslim brother assured him would further their cause. What he had been told was that his report would eventually reach a very important man who needed to know that *Calm Seas* had departed Monte Carlo.

The nights were still chilly in the Lebanese mountains, even in early April, but the days warmed quickly. Hussein, who had just removed an ancient, woolen shawl that had been passed down through his family for generations, received the messenger's report without change of expression. The high-frequency radios they used for long-range communication could have been brought to his camp, but Hussein preferred to receive the news as his ancestors had done—by word of mouth. This was admittedly a time-consuming and inefficient method if ever an instant decision was required. But Hussein believed from the bottom of his heart that if he followed the old methods, preserved traditions that so many were sure had been lost from their heritage, then his people's devotion and willingness to die for their cause would be strengthened. He would break with the past only if he sensed approaching disaster.

Hussein's face, weathered by years in the sun and traced by years of pain, was as stark as the land that had been stolen and given to the Jews. It rightfully belonged to his people, some of it even to his own family. It didn't matter that the region had been barren and unproductive compared to what the Jews had done for it. That was the way his people had lived on their native soil for centuries and that was how they'd preferred it—barren, apparently lifeless. Yet it had once been full of life, as his kinsmen knew it. That had been a long time ago and there was hardly a soul alive who could remember the contentment that had belonged to their forebears.

"No word on where she sails to?" he asked the man who had brought the news of *Calm Seas'* departure to the mountain camp.

"That is all I have been told," the messenger replied solemnly.

Hussein closed his eyes and kept them shut. It was a habit which unnerved the others because some said he could still see them quite clearly. "None of those who are supposed to attend this grand meeting have left their capitals yet?"

"I was told only of the Americans and their ship," the man answered softly. There was fear in his voice. He'd heard terrifying tales of what happened to men who angered Hussein. Had he done something wrong?

"There has never been any doubt in my mind that they will all meet aboard that ship." Hussein's eyes remained shut, but his face swung from person to person as he spoke, as if he really did see them. "The young man who did so much work with Daniels, the American Secretary of State . . . what was his name?"

"Riley," one of the others volunteered.

"This Riley wouldn't remain involved otherwise." If ever Hussein had misjudged something, it was the resolve of the leaders involved. He admitted now that the assassination of Rupert Daniels had accomplished nothing. It had been foolish. If anything, it had drawn the participants closer and drawn the wrath of the American President. He'd gone along with the recommendations of the elders, who would never understand what motivated these outsiders. He would not accede to them in the future. The meeting arranged by Daniels would still go on, regardless of Daniels's death. His eyes snapped open and settled on the messenger. "When you return, you will explain that I want to know where that yacht is at all times. And I want to speak directly to Michael by radio once he is ready. I'll take the chance and come to the base camp then." He would use the photographs from the French satellite. Reluctant sometimes to acknowledge the modern world, Hussein had no illusions when it came to employing modern technology to succeed in a mission.

Otto Rather pushed aside the paperwork on his desk and tilted his chair back on two legs against the bunk frame. Then he shifted his weight until he and the chair achieved the proper balance. The coffee was still warm in the heavy mug with his XO's stamp on the side. He sipped at it thoughtfully, as if it were still boiling hot, and even managed to smile wistfully to himself.

After leaving Lieutenant Schroeder in the torpedo room, Rather had stopped by the tiny wardroom to pick up a mug of coffee. The pot had just been fresh-brewed and its rich bouquet combined nicely with the aroma of baking rolls that the cook said would be ready shortly. The executive officer rarely had more than coffee for breakfast, because that was the one meal he could avoid in the constant battle to keep his weight even.

What the hell. It wasn't quite 0700. *The paperwork can wait another few hours. Fill your ugly belly with some of those fresh rolls and . . .*

The ship's public-address system clicked on and the duty quartermaster's voice announced that breakfast would not be served at the normal time. They would surface in five minutes.

The remaining coffee in Otto Rather's mug splashed across the papers on his desk as the chair slammed down on all four legs and he propelled himself into the passageway toward the control room. *Damn him . . . damn him . . . in any other submarine in the world, the captain would inform the executive officer of his intentions.*

Erhardt saw Rather out of the corner of his eye as he entered the control room, and Rather noticed this, but the captain never said a word. He acknowledged his executive officer with a quick nod, then made a show of monitoring the process of preparing to surface. One of the lookouts, who would follow Erhardt through the hatch to the conning tower as they broke the surface, handed the captain foul-weather gear and then donned his own.

Rather was mystified. The Type-212 submarine was self-sustaining and capable of remaining at depth for so much longer. What earthly reason could there be to surface, especially now when the crew was preparing to eat after the long rest the captain had allowed them? How many of the men in the control room were aware that the captain hadn't kept his executive officer informed? All of them perhaps? He was barely able to contain his anger. "Captain, could you tell me the purpose of surfacing right now?" Rather asked calmly and evenly. What was so critical that the crew's breakfast must be postponed?

Erhardt glanced quickly at his XO before acknowledging the reports that came to him as *Heinz Waller*'s up angle increased in their ascent to the surface. Then he looked back at Rather as if he had just noticed him. "The weather, Otto. I wanted to see what the weather is like up there." He grinned as if it were all a great joke. "If it is calm, perhaps we will conduct some surface drills."

Was the man joking with him, or insulting him? Why didn't he stop using his first name in front of the ratings?

To Otto Rather, his captain had reached the height of absurdity, or the son of a bitch was making fun of him. "Will the crew be able to have their morning meal before exercises commence, Captain?"

"We'll see." Erhardt pulled on the foul-weather gear as they passed forty meters. As always, the control room was alive with anticipation as they prepared to surface. It was an efficient, impressive evolution that required clockwork precision, and Erhardt listened to each report, acknowledging some, issuing commands as they were anticipated.

Then he was scampering up the ladder, spinning the hatch wheel, and slamming the hatch cover back into its grips. *Heinz Waller* had been rolling from the surface effect before she broke the surface. Now her round hull reacted to the chop, and the men below could sense that the Bay of Biscay was not calm.

Erhardt ordered a speed of five knots and brought the submarine to a more comfortable course.

Otto Rather grabbed a nearby foul-weather jacket and climbed the ladder. When he could be heard, he requested permission to join Erhardt on the tiny open bridge.

"Granted." Erhardt's voice might have disappeared into the wind if Rather wasn't already halfway through the hatch. But he also heard the captain instruct the lookouts, "Keep a sharp eye out for fishing boats. I understand these are fertile fishing grounds."

Where the hell had he ever heard that?

It was one of those gray mornings where the whitecapped surface of the sea and the sky seemed to join without any reference points. There was no horizon, just gray foam sliding off gray waves to merge with gray clouds. *Heinz Waller*'s great round nose rose easily with the swells, sliding down the opposite sides into green water that rolled back along her deck almost to the sail before falling back into the sea. She rolled slowly and easily, just enough motion to feel down below, not enough to make anyone seasick.

Erhardt called down to the control room. "Find out what circuits radio is guarding."

The response was called up to him within moments—only the squadron frequency.

"Why aren't they guarding the distress frequency?" All ships at sea were supposed to guard that circuit, including surfaced submarines.

The answer was that there was only so much equipment and that Captain Preminger's standing order had only required guarding that circuit during extended periods on the surface. Did the captain plan to remain on the top long enough to shift to the distress frequency?

Erhardt's response was an angry bellow. "Tell them my commands always guard the distress frequency, and they can start right now."

Otto Rather waited for a few more moments while Erhardt continued to scan the horizon through his binoculars. It was almost as if he expected to see something. When he finally relaxed, Rather spoke up. "Captain, can I authorize feeding the crew before we begin our training? It would allow everything to run more smoothly, I'm sure."

Erhardt's head snapped around. "Is this submarine in the German navy, Otto? Do our sailors travel on their stomachs like the infantry?"

The look on his face was difficult to fathom. *Is he angry, or perhaps continuing his joking?* They rolled heavily. *Joking? Out here?* Rather wondered.

"Oh, go ahead. Feed them. I just hope they're not such babies if they're ever in a war." Erhardt turned back to his binoculars and began to scan the horizon off their bow.

"Thank you, Captain," Rather remarked. He returned to the ladder and stepped down.

The last words he heard as his head passed through the hatch were Erhardt's: "Lookouts, keep your eyes peeled for fishing boats. There's got to be some out here." And as he passed through the control room, he heard Erhardt's voice come over the intercom: "Radar, keep a sharp eye out for fishing boats. Remember our experiment on the way out. They won't paint well on your screen today and I don't want to be embarrassed by sneaking up on one."

"Fishing boats," Rather muttered to himself as he headed forward to the galley. "Why the hell is he so interested in fishing boats?"

"Is your radar operating normally?" Michael asked his electronics specialist for perhaps the fifth time. And then, realizing how silly the question sounded when the answer had been affirmative so many times, he added, "Are you sure it's peaked for small contacts? You must . . ."

"Michael," the man answered patiently, "I've already explained how difficult it is to pick up a submarine at any distance in this sea. When it's on top of a swell, we'll paint it if it's not too far distant. But if only the sail is above the surface, we're going to have trouble picking it up until we're in visual range. There's a good chance you might see it with your binoculars before my radar provides an accurate contact."

"Why don't you use the distress signal then?" Soraya asked. "We could waste hours running circles around each other." The soda crackers had settled her stomach, but they had done nothing to improve her temperament. "Besides, Walter told me once—and I'm sure you were there—that it made more sense for a warship to come directly to another craft in distress rather than go looking for a fishing boat that may have a problem."

Michael turned to the man on the radar who also was in charge of the radio. "She's right," he agreed. "Send the distress signal."

"For how long? If we keep sending, every ship within range will come running, and someone will inform the Spanish rescue service."

"Ten seconds? Does that seem right?" He had learned so much about the sea from Ismael, but these electronics mystified him.

"I'll try that—A weak signal, though. If he's nearby, and guarding that circuit, he ought to hear us. If it doesn't work, then we'll do something else."

Michael looked back to the after deck. The trawl nets were neatly rolled. The crane and ground tackle for hauling full nets—and heavy torpedoes—had been lubricated and tested once again. His crew lounged on the deck, their backs against the nets, looking for all the world like fishermen. Those who were smoking had affected the ugly black cigarettes that Ismael enjoyed. The silent, ugly Turk had become a cult hero among them. But their weapons remained out of sight and they were otherwise the picture of innocence.

Ismael looked up from his place on the deck, which was apart from the others. "Nothing?"

"We're using the radar, and a weak ten-second distress signal." This was the part Michael didn't like, the waiting, the uncertainty. He'd learned in his early training that time was sometimes a greater enemy. *The longer one waits, the more dangerous each second becomes.* Action was what he loved. He hated the all-knowing smirk on Ismael's face as the Turk rose to his feet. "Do you have a better idea?"

Ismael moved over to the barrel he had prepared near the stern. He held the flame from his cigarette lighter to an oily rag, and when it was burning well, he tossed it into the barrel. Within seconds, black, greasy smoke rose into the gray sky. "That's what will do the job," Ismael said, as he lit another of his black cigarettes. "Smoke at sea. Every sailor understands that."

Detective Gleick sat in the visitor's chair across the desk from the commander of Submarine Squadron Four and listened politely to the admiral's lecture. The oration was delivered with equal courtesy, since he was once again expounding on the thoroughness of the background investigations undertaken before any officer was accepted into the submarine force.

". . . and, of course," the admiral continued, "before we complete the selection process for command, our best and brightest are vetted once again." It was important to demonstrate to civilians that the navy took neither character nor integrity for granted when it came to the men who were ordered to command their submarines. Those on the outside simply weren't exposed to such demanding standards. But no matter how he explained it, this civilian detective simply didn't understand.

"I never dreamed your investigations could be so detailed. It's sometimes difficult on the civilian side to comprehend that," Gleick commented politely.

The admiral beamed. "So you see it's totally impossible for Captain Preminger to have had anything to do with such people." He wondered why the Bremerhaven police wasted their time chasing down such foolishness. *Arabs—ridiculous!* Hans Preminger had been devoted to two things—his navy and his family. As a submarine commander, he had time for nothing else. As a matter of fact, the wives—Preminger's included—often protested that their husbands never had enough time for their families. But in this case, the admiral knew personally that Preminger was like a choir boy, almost to the point that he could be a boring person when anything other than submarines was a topic of conversation. But, then, he'd already mentioned that to the detective.

"Normally, I might have to agree with you, Admiral. But in my business, we are more often surprised by what we least expect." Because he was familiar with the admiral's "show me" attitude, he carefully reviewed the testimony of the night manager of the Bodo. He was the one who was sure he'd seen a body wrapped in a blanket carried down a fire escape on the night Hans Preminger had disappeared, and that represented one of their earliest solid clues. No, they hadn't the slightest proof that it was Preminger, but every lead, no matter how remote, has to be tracked down. Gleick had explained to the admiral that it had taken some time for his investigators to interview each of the individuals who rented the apartments facing the alley behind the Bodo nightclub. They had finally decided, after carefully analyzing each of the tenants, that there was only one who merited suspicions—an Arab woman—and that was because she'd vacated immediately after Preminger's disappearance.

"Where is this all leading to?" the admiral asked. "I don't see your point."

"There's nothing absolute yet, believe me. If I mislead you, sir, let me apologize. We don't know where this all leads to. That's why I'm here. We thought there might be something that would ring a bell with you, something we might have found that reminds you of something we all may have overlooked. You see, all the other occupants of that building are clean. No way they could be involved here." It wasn't quite time to mention his conversation with Mrs. Preminger, not after the lecture that had just taken place. Let the admiral relax for a while. Why did the navy think it was so perfect?

The admiral waited patiently, his "show me" expression a mask to any other feeling he may have had.

Gleick decided to continue cautiously. "We're still trying to follow up on this Arab woman because we don't even have a solid name to go on. The references she gave the building manager are phony. The checks she used to pay the rent were written on a bank account that's been closed, and the name on that account turned out to be phony—fooled the bank completely, too, because she opened her account with traveler's checks. The flat was empty when the manager went up there in early March."

"What made him go then?" the admiral asked.

"Because he hadn't been paid. Apparently, there'd been a lot of interior alterations there—against the owner's rules and in violation of fire laws, by the way—but that had all been ripped out when he got there. Unfortunately, the manager wanted to rent it as quickly as possible and had begun a cleanup, before we displayed interest. So there wasn't much we could find for ourselves—clues, I mean. The flat had been sanitized." His eyes settled on the admiral. "Except for one thing."

The admiral leaned forward.

Gleick could see he had the admiral's interest and continued. "We dug a nine-millimeter bullet out of the wall. The hole had been covered over with plaster, but it wasn't a perfect job. The bullet's being analyzed now. Maybe we'll be able to trace it, maybe we won't."

The admiral was puzzled. "But what is the point?" he asked impatiently.

"That's just it, sir. The best lead we have is that someone made an effort to conceal something. That wouldn't happen unless there was something illegal going on, would it? So far, everything we've constructed around Captain Preminger's death is circumstantial, but there's enough to tell us that he could have been involved with something . . . shall we say . . . ah . . . less than pleasant. If you'll remember, the coroner's report assumed a nine-millimeter bullet killed him."

The intractability of the military was mirrored in the admiral's reaction. "Not Preminger . . ." he began defiantly.

Gleick now found it necessary to become firm, if only to match the other's disbelief. "Until we can establish otherwise, we have to work on the theory that the body observed by the Bodo's night manager was indeed Captain Preminger. We have to assume that somehow he was involved with a woman."

"No, not Hans Preminger. If you will excuse me, he's pure. I think the expression is—'pure as the driven snow'," the admiral said with a wave of his hand to show that Gleick's assumption was impossible. "No, not Hans. With all due respect to Mrs. Preminger, he wouldn't know where to stick it." As if to end the discussion, he added with a chuckle, "We always used to wonder where the children came from."

Gleick sighed. Now he had no choice but to relate his conversation with Mrs. Preminger. As he did, he found the changing expression on the admiral's face fascinating. He wasn't sure if he'd ever seen a man's face reflect the shattering of absolute beliefs so quickly. Not only was Preminger's character now suspect, but also a system of guaranteeing a man's character—his country's own intelligence system—had crumbled in minutes.

Gleick decided it was time. "In my experience, when a crime of this magnitude has taken place, one may determine that such reasons as sex, money, jealousy—any of the standard causes for murder—can be dismissed."

"Go on." The admiral's eyebrows were knitted into a "show me" attitude. It was obvious he didn't care for civilian interference into what he considered a military problem.

"Have you considered that this woman may have been part of an underground organization?"

"Underground?"

"Which my department would normally consider as terrorist?"

"Not Preminger," the admiral retorted.

"It may have been someone else, but this Arab woman is the most likely for now," Gleick continued. "We do know from the building manager's description that she was extremely attractive. The depth of Preminger's involvement is . . ."

The admiral finally found his voice. "I would assume you are not going to release this to the media." He imagined the havoc it would create in the naval establishment. And sooner or later—much later he hoped—the naval establishment would have to announce that *Heinz Waller*, Preminger's former command, was late in reporting. *Won't they have a wonderful time with that?* He supposed he should tell Gleick.

"There's no reason to at this stage of the investigation." But Gleick was positive of what he'd suspected up to now. The navy's cooperation was obtained in small steps, and those steps were lengthened only when the navy found itself cornered. "However, I'd like your permission to talk again with some of Preminger's associates . . . about more personal aspects of his life, if you will. And, for the navy's piece of mind, I'd like you to make whatever arrangements you deem necessary to insure the privacy and confidentiality of these interviews. If you concur, I'd like to talk with your people one at a time, and perhaps you could have some influence insuring that they don't discuss their conversations with each other. Would that be agreeable?"

The admiral knew when his choices were down to zero. Yet he even found himself liking the way this detective had maneuvered him. If he could manipulate Gleick in the same manner, perhaps the navy could save some face in the end. "Your points are well taken, sir. Let me assure you that I will pass your suspicions on to our intelligence section and let you know of anything we find. How's that?" The admiral stood to indicate the meeting was over.

"I'd appreciate that, Admiral." Herman Gleick had been thinking much the same thing—that intelligence operatives should be involved. But he knew the military would pay him little heed. He would get in touch with the people he knew in the civilian sector whom he trusted.

FEDERAL REPUBLIC OF GERMANY

FLASH

CLASSIFICATION—TOP SECRET

FROM: COMMANDER, SUBMARINE SQUADRON FOUR
TO: ALL COMMANDS, WALLER RESCUE OPERATION

1) USN COMMAND HOLY LOCH HAS RELEASED SUBMARINE RESCUE VESSEL (DSRV) THIS DATE TO THIS COMMAND. DSRV NOW PROCEEDING TO DATUM AND WILL REPORT TO ON-SCENE COMMANDER UPON ARRIVAL.
2) IT IS ASSUMED THAT WALLER HAS EXPERIENCED ELECTRONIC CASUALTY AND IS UNABLE TO RESPOND TO RADIO QUERY.
3) ALL COMMANDS ARE TO CONTINUE UNDERWATER VOICE INTERROGATION ON A REGULAR BASIS. REQUEST WALLER FIRE RED FLARES TO MARK POSITION. THEN REPORT CLEAR TO SURFACE AND ORDER WALLER TO SURFACE PER ORDERS THIS COMMAND.
4) UPON SIGHTING WALLER, DETERMINE EXTENT OF EQUIPMENT AND/OR PERSONNEL CASUALTIES AND REPORT DIRECTLY TO ON-SCENE COMMANDER, INFO THIS COMMAND.
5) MESSAGE FOLLOWS SEPARATELY WITH DATA FROM DSRV TO BE TRANSMITTED TO WALLER IN PREPARATION FOR RESCUE OPERATION IF SITUATION DEMANDS.

"Captain!" An urgent voice from the control room was booming out on S-252's open bridge. "Captain, radio just intercepted a weak distress signal from a ship apparently near our position."

Erhardt pressed down the speak button. "What kind of ship? Any name? What else?" *It has to be Michael.*

"All we got was that they have a fire. It was very weak."

"You heard that," Erhardt shouted at the lookouts. "It's near us. Look for smoke on the horizon." He pressed the button again. "Did you get a bearing on the frequency?"

"No, sir."

"Well, interrogate," he snapped angrily. "Send that we are nearby. Tell them to keep broadcasting so we can get a bearing." His voice increased in pitch. "What's wrong down there? Doesn't anyone understand what that distress frequency is for?"

Otto Rather looked up from the control room toward the bridge as if he could see through the decks and the miles of wiring and piping. Nothing was wrong below. What was wrong up there? What was going on with this man? One minute he's bellowing about guarding the distress frequency, and the next minute there's a distress signal. It was almost too coincidental.

"Captain, I have smoke—"

Erhardt's head snapped around toward the starboard lookout. "Bearing?" he interrupted before the man could finish. Without waiting for an answer, he raised his binoculars toward *Waller*'s starboard beam in the same general direction as the lookout.

"Just forward of the beam, Captain. Steady black smoke on the horizon. I'm sure it wasn't there a few minutes ago."

Erhardt shouted orders to the control room, changing his course toward the smoke. "Tell radio to inform the vessel sending the distress signal that we hold them visually and are preparing for rescue operations. Also tell them they no longer need to employ that frequency. We will coordinate communications to the shore for them."

"Captain," Otto Rather called up to the bridge, "I will prepare the rescue and assistance party for the rescue operation." The executive officer was in charge of preparing for any rescue and was supposed to command any operation away from the submarine.

"Negative, Mr. Rather. I want you to remain in charge here. I'll be going over with the rescue boat."

CHAPTER SEVEN

Wasp, her well deck partially flooded, was down slightly by the stern. The commodore's barge, the navy's version of a private yacht for entertaining dignitaries, was afloat, rocking erratically with the internal waves that swept back and forth against the high wooden-ribbed sides. Eerie dashes of sunlight danced off blue Mediterranean waves beyond *Wasp's* stern, rebounding through the cavernous interior. They reflected inside against the gray metal sides of the well deck, beckoning the shiny black boat to come out and play with Chief Bewick's precious toys that were just now being lifted from *Ashland's* flight deck a mile astern.

A sailor, Mickey Mouse ears covering the sides of his head, repeated the message just passed down from the bridge. "Permission granted to get underway," he said. The words were drowned out by the rumble of the high-powered diesel. Lines were heaved across to the sailors on the barge's deck and she backed down, turned her nose toward the welcoming open sea, and cruised into the bright sunlight. Once she was clear, the coxswain turned and pushed his throttle forward, moving two thousand yards ahead of *Wasp* before cutting back his speed to match the carrier's.

Jake Steele, his legs spread for balance, had been watching through binoculars from the barge's stern as two of the Special Boat Unit's RIBs were lowered by crane beside *Ashland.* He saw the RIBs' crews disengage from the LSD's tethers, then grinned to himself as Chief Bewick pumped his arm twice. He knew their Volvo Penta engines had just rumbled into life. Then Bewick twirled his index finger in the air and pointed toward the barge moving ahead of *Wasp*.

Jake could imagine the sound as the coxswain pushed the throttle forward and the turbo-charged engines growled with power. The RIBs seemed to rear back for an instant, then a flood of white water surged in their wake as they rocketed toward him. The four SEALs crouched forward in each craft were barely visible above the inflated gunnels. The RIBs' wakes were barely visible as they literally skipped across the water's surface. Foam sheared back from their sterns as the small craft shot by the barge on either side, executed perfect outward turns, and settled back to match the barge's speed fifty yards off either beam.

High on *Wasp*'s flag bridge, Rear Admiral Turner's binoculars had switched from one RIB to the other as they chased by after his barge. He would have loved to be riding with them. The coxswains who drove the RIBs were the ones he really envied. He nodded his head in appreciation as they turned at exactly the same second on Bewick's orders, one in a sharp right turn, the other to the left, both appearing to stand on their tubular rubber gunwales as they whipped around in a tight circle and settled on either side of the barge. "Makes you wish you were a kid again," he murmured softly to himself.

"Imagine if some kid ever got hold of one of those," his chief staff officer responded. The ever-efficient Captain Black had appeared quietly by his admiral's chair. "Probably try to water ski," he added.

"I would have taken a shot at it," Turner answered, "if I was sixteen and full of beans and trying to impress some cute little blonde." Bewick's men had the RIBs so well tuned they might hit forty knots in a reasonably flat sea. "And I'd hope to hell I didn't take a spill off those skis, because there wouldn't be anything left of my crotch for that little honey when they hauled me out of the water."

Wasp was operating east of the toe of the Italian boot on this brilliant April morning. Her escorting frigates were in the distance on either beam, and a cruiser and a destroyer were on the horizon ahead and astern.

"Can we patch their radio circuit up here?" Turner asked.

"Sure can, Admiral. I'll call down to the communications officer . . ." Black began.

"No. Scratch that. I'd much rather watch them without knowing what they're going to do. Sort of like watching two prizefighters."

Turner recognized the telltale foam astern of his barge as the coxswain brought her up to full speed. The RIBs seemed to merge, one behind the other, two miles ahead of the carrier. But, in a second, the forward one darted ahead and swung off to starboard at full speed, slowing only when it was approximately three miles distant. The other followed like a shadow, at first moving at high speed, then slowing and easing off on the other's starboard quarter.

Both men watched through their binoculars with the envy that older men have for youthful games as the RIBs danced over the light chop. The next hour reminded Rear Admiral Turner of water bugs skittering across a pond. Steele had the barge slow, speed up, turn in different directions, reverse course, and even turn into the RIBs as they made their approaches.

The SEALs who rode the RIBs studied each tactic closely also, turning over in their own minds what the other boat chose do on each approach. They were the ones who would have to board a hostile boat that would be maneuvering exactly like the barge. But any boarding effort would be after dark. Night would at least improve their odds.

Before the exercises were over, Rear Admiral Turner had already adjourned one deck below the flight deck to flag plot. He studied the chart of the central Mediterranean for a moment, before running an index finger down from *Wasp's* current position to the Libyan coastline. His finger stopped almost on top of the port city of Surt and he held it there and murmured to no one in particular, "If we headed due south right now, that's where we'd end up—Surt—right between Tripoli and Benghazi. I wonder if that fishing boat's still around?" There had been no further intelligence reports concerning the mysterious boat or any other craft loading out in Libya for that matter. He wondered if perhaps they were chasing a shadow.

Since Turner often spoke out loud when he was thinking, there was no response from his staff.

"I wonder," he continued, "if any Americans have ever been in Surt since the revolution . . . or given a shit whether it existed."

Then he turned and his eyes skipped from Captain Black to the other staff members on duty, and he asked directly, "Got anything else on that fishing boat that was supposed to be loading that bad stuff in Benghazi? Anything on her whereabouts?"

"Nothing, sir," said his intelligence officer, Lieutenant Peter Germond, the youngest member of his staff. "It just seems to have disappeared into thin air."

"How about anything from Sixth Fleet intelligence on what she loaded?" Turner persisted.

"Not a word on that either, sir."

"And they don't know what that boat's name is either, do they?" he concluded.

"That's correct, sir."

"But they want me to keep an eye out and go after it if I happen to see it coming my way." His gaze took in each man in the small compartment as he spoke his next words in a carefully measured tone. "We got all these VIPs coming aboard soon and these brilliant intelligence specialists have their minds on a fishing boat that they can't tell us anything else about. Tell me, have they even intimated that maybe this super fishing boat has something to do with our impending guests? Or is it a decoy? What would they want to use a decoy for?" he said, answering his own question. "If we don't have the dope on why we've got guests coming aboard, why should anyone else know?"

His question was met with silence.

Then Lieutenant Germond spoke up. "I've been thinking the same thing, Admiral. But . . ." He shrugged. "I couldn't come up with anything."

"Well, Peter, there are intelligence staffs at Naval Forces Europe, Spec Ops Europe, Sixth Fleet, SHAPE . . . hell, how many more? I think we ought to recommend to those intelligence geniuses that they get their spook network oiled up. Maybe they ought to cover the Med with search aircraft.

We can't do that. Otherwise, I think Jake's job is just about impossible."

Detective Herman Gleick acknowledged politely that he would accept one of the heavy mugs of coffee from the tray held by the pretty American secretary. The seal of the United States of America was emblazoned on the side of the mug that faced him. While she bent slightly from the waist to make his task easier, Gleick turned the coffee a light beige with heavy cream and then sweetened it with almost three teaspoons of sugar. "I make my coffee into milkshakes, like your McDonald's," he said, smiling apologetically at her. "Warm milkshakes."

She looked down at the diminutive German now stirring his coffee with the precision of an engineer and decided that there was something appealing about the mousy little man, even if there was nothing attractive about his features. They were nondescript, his face small and round, his paleness emphasized by his baldness and the remaining blond fringe of hair that had grown too long around his ears. Yet the gray eyes behind the rimless glasses were sharp and intelligent and they twinkled with humor when he made pleasant fun of himself for his coffee milkshakes. She placed the other mug of black coffee before her boss and quietly left the room, pulling the door shut behind her.

"Pretty girl," Gleick offered, as he took a large swallow of his tepid coffee.

Roland Lyford smiled happily. "That's my gift to myself for staying on an extra year." Officially, Lyford's title was Assistant Director of Communications for the American Embassy in Berlin. "I was supposed to have two years in Langley before I retired, but they asked me to stay one more year to help your people chase down some of your bad guys from the East who're still underground." In actuality, Lyford operated as the undercover CIA liaison in Berlin. "I finally agreed, if I could hire her."

"She is attractive," Gleick responded politely.

Lyford's wandering eye began to wander on its own accord. He guffawed and fixed Gleick with a friendly smile. "Life does have its rewards, doesn't it?"

Gleick smiled back, totally confused now about which of

the American's eyes he should be concentrating on. Instead, he looked into his coffee mug and took another large swallow. "Yes, you are correct, Mr. Lyford," he said, employing his precise English by avoiding addressing him as *herr.* "I think perhaps if I am ever in the same position, I might initiate the same type of request." He already liked this American CIA agent. So often, he'd been told, or perhaps he'd read in too many suspense novels, how humorless they were with their sharp jaws and steely looks. This one was not what Gleick expected. What remained of Lyford's curly black hair was gray-fringed. Besides the wandering eye, he was chunky, and his heavy dark whiskers appeared to require shaving two or three times a day if he were to meet the traditional image of the American intelligence agent.

Lyford picked up the half-glasses on his desk and looked at Gleick's card again. "Detective . . . Kiel . . . up north, isn't it?"

"That is correct, near the Baltic Sea, a navy town."

"And my old buddy, Oppenheimer, sent you to me. Did you get in touch with Oppie up in your town, or down here in Berlin?"

Oppie? "I contacted Herr Oppenheimer as a backup to naval intelligence in Kiel." Gleick gulped the remainder of his coffee and looked for a place to put down the mug.

"On the desk. That's fine. That'll just be another reason for Jaqui, my secretary, to come back in here." He grinned again and pressed a button on the inter-office intercom. "So tell me about you and Oppie."

"I am in charge of the investigation into the murder of one of our naval officers—"

"Yeah," Lyford interrupted. "I heard something about that. Wasn't that guy in submarines?"

"That is correct. He was the captain of the *Heinz Waller.*" Herman Gleick began to explain. He was interrupted by a rap on the door.

"Come on in, Jaqui," Lyford called out.

Jaqui entered with her tray and picked up Gleick's mug. "Are you finished with your coffee, Mr. Lyford?"

"Sure." He took another sip before reaching out in her direction with his mug.

She bent at the waist to reach across the desk to accept the mug. "Anything else I can do for you, sir?"

"We're all set now, thanks. I'll ring if there's anything else." His smile as she left was one of pure joy.

"If you will permit me a few moments," Gleick continued, amused with the little game played out by Lyford and his secretary, "let me explain my situation." The detective related as precisely as possible the details surrounding the Preminger case, as he had understood them. His explanation was so fascinating that the American listened quietly while Gleick brought him up to the present on his recent interviews with Mrs. Preminger, the ensuing one with the unbelieving commander of Preminger's submarine squadron, and his reason for going on his own to Oppenheimer.

"You've got to be kidding," Lyford said. "This guy Preminger was dicking everything in sight and the only one who ever figured it out was his wife? A veritable swordsman," he said, guffawing in admiration. Then his face turned suddenly sober. "A guy like that could be dangerous—I mean all those broads could make him a security risk. Just as much potential for bribery as a fag."

"That is my opinion precisely," Gleick agreed with a nod, certain that he interpreted Lyford's response correctly. Such relationships were equally security risks. "That is why I bypassed our naval intelligence. I wanted to find out from someone else why they guaranteed that he was such a choir boy when he was, in fact, as you explained it, as much a security risk as a . . . homosexual," he finished, unable to remember the exact term Lyford had just used. "Naval intelligence is most protective of their investigative procedures. Am I correct in believing that Herr Oppenheimer functions in a manner similar to your own?"

Lyford couldn't help grinning. "I'll tell you what. Whatever Oppie said about me, I'll go along with. But tell me why he sent you to me."

"Arabs. He explained to me that you know more about the Arabs in Germany than anyone in German intelligence."

"I might not have put it that way." Lyford frowned slightly. "But that's why I'm still here instead of working banker's hours back in Langley." He leaned forward and placed his arms on his desk, a serious expression on his face. "Mr. Gleick, my initial reaction as you were telling me your story was exactly the same as your conclusion. When an Arab female starts messing with any submarine officer, I'd be automatically suspicious." He wrinkled his forehead and asked, "You really can't find any of this guy's fellow officers who knew he was screwing around?"

"A choir boy, Mr. Lyford. He had them all fooled. And I think you will agree his wife wasn't particularly concerned about the nationality of her husband's female friends. It was the perfect scenario for someone to compromise him." Gleick removed his glasses and rubbed the lenses against his suit jacket. "I know nothing of Arab women." He peered with gray intense eyes at the American. "May I tell you what little I know about the one I think was involved and ask that you assist me in trying to determine who she is?"

"You certainly may," Lyford responded in an equally polite manner. "And maybe I'll get something out of this exercise, too. Maybe you can add a new twist to some Arab operations in your own country that I'm unaware of. And," Lyford continued, stroking his chin thoughtfully, "maybe you can tell me why neither of us has used the word *terrorist* yet." He employed the word as if he'd just found a hair on his tongue. "Considering that we've used the words security and compromise, I expect we're both thinking the same thing, aren't we?"

Gleick nodded. "I appreciate your assistance, Mr. Lyford."

"Let's start with her name."

"I have three," Gleick answered. "I'm sure none of them is her given name."

"And I'm sure that she probably had a passport for each name." But Lyford's expression was confident. "That's how we begin to narrow them down. They think they have perfect cover. We let them think so. Just the fact that they may travel under a number of different aliases gives us a chance to put together a computer profile."

"I'm impressed."

"Don't be, not until we pin down your lady. Now, let me show you how we're going to go about this."

Gleick was impressed. Perhaps his investigation of Hans Preminger's murder had just reached another plateau.

"Michael," the sailor manning *Baghdad's* radio shouted excitedly, "they've seen our smoke. The submarine's seen our smoke."

"Which direction?" The binoculars around Michael's neck banged against his chest as he climbed to the roof of the pilot house. The trawler was heaving badly and he was forced to wrap one arm around a support cable anchored to a nearby stanchion. There had been so many days when he wondered how such a complex plan could actually work. What could possibly have made Hussein believe that it could all come together like this?

"Didn't say . . . just that they sighted smoke . . ." the radioman shouted up to the pilot-house roof. The rest of his words were lost in the wind that whistled through the trawler's rigging.

"Stop sending signals." Ismael's sharp voice could be heard above the wind and waves and the crackling of flames from the fire in the barrel on the stern. This was followed by a shout from below and then the sound of something heavy impacting on another object. Angry words ensued.

Then Ismael emerged from beneath the roof of the pilot house and looked up at Michael. "The radio!" he shouted, shaking his upraised fist. "That fool was trying to contact the submarine again. We won't need it again anyway."

The man who'd been operating the radio appeared next to Ismael. "He smashed the radio, Michael. It's useless."

"That's all right," Michael shouted against the noise. Thank goodness that Ismael didn't harm the radio operator. "He did the right thing." He brought the binoculars back up to his eyes again and was attempting to scan the horizon while maintaining his balance. It was impossible.

Oily smoke from an errant gust of wind blew across the deck, enveloping them for a moment. Then, just as quickly, everything was once again clear.

"You're not going to see anything yet," Ismael called up to Michael, "not with these seas." Even with the heavy cargo below, the fishing boat was rolling in great arcs.

Ismael was correct, as always, when anything had to do with the sea.

Soraya had appeared on deck moments before. There was a grin on her face for the first time since they'd gotten underway. "Ismael's right, you know. Why don't you come down here before you get thrown off there?"

Michael nodded. He could tell from her expression that the seasickness was no longer a problem for her. An Uzi hung from a sling around her neck and rested comfortably across her midsection. Maybe that was a reason for her change in attitude. She adored violence. Perhaps she could smell it in the air. That part of her personality made Soraya a perfect complement to Ismael no matter how much she disliked the Turk.

As Michael climbed down to the deck, putting out a hand to Soraya, he saw Ismael, a black cigarette stub between his teeth, testing the blade of a knife against his cheek. He was staring with anticipation toward the horizon where the submarine would soon appear.

Well over a hundred kilometers from *Baghdad,* a French navy frigate, the *Pierre Retard,* heading for a weekend visit to La Rochelle, picked up a vague distress signal. The radioman on watch had been unable to identify the source of the signal or the location, and there was no response to his queries. He reported the signal to his communications officer, who, in turn, notified the ship's captain. The latter, realizing there was no possibility of offering assistance to a craft with no name and no known position, which also failed to respond to their queries, resolved to report the incident as soon as he arrived in La Rochelle. It was quite possible that, through a quirk in signal propagation, the origin of the call could be a great distance away. He would be alongside the pier there by ten in the morning, and civilian authorities could decide what to do.

Erhardt had increased *Heinz Waller*'s speed to ten knots, which, since they were taking the seas on their beam, caused the submarine to roll heavily with a corkscrew effect. Whenever they were on the top of a swell, he could see a plume of black smoke hanging over the sea ahead of them, but it was impossible to make out the fishing boat.

"Can you see the boat yet?!" he shouted to the lookouts above the sound of waves crashing across the hull.

"I think . . . no . . . no, now I'm not sure," one of them responded.

Erhardt turned in his direction in anticipation of a visual confirmation, but the sailor never noticed. One of his arms was wrapped around the bridge railing in a viselike grip, while his other hand struggled to hold his wet binoculars to his eyes.

"I thought I saw a mast . . . or something poking into the air . . . but now it's gone."

"Radar," Erhardt bellowed into the intercom, "anything?"

"Too much surface return, Captain," came a voice.

"Add two more knots," Erhardt ordered.

Two knots! Otto Rather had found a handhold in the control room, just like every other man on *Heinz Waller,* and he was not about to let go. Obviously, the captain cared nothing about what was happening below decks, more or less how the crew could possibly get something into their stomachs. Rather had been in the conning tower so many times in heavy seas, and he knew the men up there could anticipate each violent motion of the submarine. But below, each of *Waller*'s movements was a surprise.

The rounded hull of a submarine was designed for silent running beneath the seas, anything but the turbulence of the surface. When she slid down the front of a swell, there was none of that sleek compensating design of a destroyer or cruiser to ease the process, no keel, no stabilizers. A submarine, especially a small diesel type like *Waller,* just plunged until its own buoyancy arrested its descent. At the same time, the rounded hull would roll sharply to one side, then snap over in the other direction, producing the spiraling effect that could send a man's stomach to his throat in an instant.

Hugo Schroeder, who'd come to the control room preparatory to relieving the watch, timed the submarine's crazed motion and stumbled over beside Rather during the instant before they rolled in the opposite direction. He grabbed for the same handhold that the executive officer gripped, so that they were face to face. "What's so important about this fishing boat, sir? If those people are in real danger, they can go over the side and we'll pick them up."

Rather glanced for a moment at Schroeder who was much bigger and seemed so close that he might hug him. "I have the same curiosity, as I'm sure every member of the crew does, Mr. Schroeder." It would have been so easy to question Erhardt's reasoning. "However, it appears we are learning yet another side to our captain. He has a special concern for fellow sailors in danger." Then he did his best to shrug as if it was of little concern to him, but a sudden motion of the submarine threw him against the other.

"Mr. Rather"—Erhardt's voice came over the control-room intercom in a barely controlled bellow—"is my new rescue and assistance team ready to launch an inflatable raft as soon as we're in range of the burning fishing boat?"

Rather struggled across the rubber-matted deck, grasping whatever was available to him until he could depress the button on the intercom. "Negative, Captain. Everyone down here is holding on. I think it could be dangerous until we turn downwind. We'll be more stable then, less chance for injuries."

The response was an explosive roar from Erhardt. "This is a warship. The men aboard are sailors, not ballerinas. There may not be any time later. Make all preparations now, instantly. Is that clear?"

Rather understood there was nothing else to say but this: "At once, Captain."

"I intend to come about in the lee of this fishing boat at a range of about five hundred yards. Since there could be compressed gases in tanks and the possibility of an explosion, I don't want to bring us too close."

In the background, as Erhardt's voice tailed off, one of the lookouts could also be heard: "I see it, Captain. Two high cranes for hauling trawls. Now she's below the swells . . . but it's a big fisherman . . ."

Erhardt's finger was still depressing the intercom button. "We have it in sight . . . maybe five or six kilometers distant . . . heavy black smoke . . ."

Why didn't the captain inquire with flashing light if the

trawler's radio was inoperative? That was standard procedure in this situation. "I recommend we try to communicate by light, Captain."

Erhardt paid no attention to him. "We will launch an inflatable immediately through the forward trunk. I expect my 'alfa crew' to take me over."

Otto Rather was already moving through the control room toward the forward compartment. As he did so, he was barking orders, switching men on watch with others in order to muster the crew that the captain insisted upon. *If the fishing boat was in such trouble, why didn't they just abandon ship into their own small boats and row them over to us?*

Will Riley had left word that Waters should awaken him when *Calm Seas* was near the northern entrance to the two-mile-wide Strait of Messina. Soon after the phone in his stateroom had rung, he'd climbed sleepily to the bridge. The sight that greeted him was stunning. The sun was brightening the peaks that cluttered the toe of Italy on their port beam with a brilliant orange glow. Sicily was off the starboard bow and still in shadow but for the village windows that faced east and reflected the apricot-colored sunrise.

"It's going to be a perfect day," Waters remarked.

"How can you tell?" Riley asked. "The sun's not up yet."

"You can smell it in the air." Waters took a deep breath. "Definitely going to be a beauty. Go ahead, try it. Breathe through your nose. Nice and deep now."

Riley was taken in by the beauty of the early morning, and he inhaled deeply. He shrugged. "What am I supposed to notice?"

"I can see you need a little training, Will. Too much city in your makeup." He gestured toward the mountains rising above the Italian toe. "Look at the air. The sun's just poking over that mountain now. See how sharp and clear the air is?"

"It's pretty," Riley agreed, "but what does that mean?"

"It's pretty because it's clear. Low humidity. No clouds. Hell, if you'd come up here half an hour earlier, you would have seen stars like you wouldn't believe. When it's like this so early in the morning, you're going to have a great day. Warm, too. But spring warm, not summer hot, when you have the damp air, then increasing humidity, and then thunderstorms."

"So all that means it's going to be a nice day, huh? I'll buy that, Francis, but I would have bought it even if I'd slept an hour longer." He rubbed the sleep from his eyes with the heels of his hands. "What are the chances of a cup of coffee?"

"The chances for the captain getting a cup, along with some fresh croissants they were baking in the galley when I came up here, are fantastic. Mine should be here any minute."

Riley failed to rise to the bait. "Sounds so good I think I'll go back below and get some for myself," Riley said, turning toward the ladder at the rear of the bridge.

"Hey, Will, stay. I was yanking your chain. You said you wanted to be up here for this, so I ordered for you, too. Really, I'm a very nice person. Life aboard can be very pleasant if you know the captain."

"I guess I'm just a lucky fella," Riley said. He could see that Waters was preparing again to grill him about their destination, but this time he was prepared. He'd talked with Lou Griffey last night over the scrambler installed in his quarters and the Secretary of State had reported there still appeared to be no leaks concerning *Calm Seas*. Washington's intelligence network had been working overtime and there was absolutely no indication that their mission had been compromised.

Riley pointed ahead to where it seemed that the Italian mainland and Sicily were joined. "Narrow passage. I never would have imagined it was that tight."

Waters took him over to the chart table and showed him the north and south shipping channels through the strait. During coffee and croissants, he explained the navigational fixes they used in addition to the radar to insure they remained on the correct track.

As the sun climbed higher in the sky, and local boats came out to conduct their day's business, the traffic increased in the strait. When the shores on either side grew more distant, it was hard to believe that an hour and a half had passed.

After the city of Reggio di Calabria, mainland Italy's southernmost city, dwindled into the distance, Waters turned to Will Riley and said, "Well, we've passed through the Strait of Messina and we're headed due south. If I take her up to cruising speed, I figure we'd run into the Libyan coast in less than two days . . . give or take a couple of hours." He folded his arms in exasperation. "So what do we do now? I've shown you a beautiful sunrise. I've shown you how to navigate. I've even had your breakfast brought to you. What do you say, Will?"

"We should turn left." Riley smiled a curious little-boy smile. This time, his eyes were involved, too.

"Funny. Of course, if we turned to starboard, we'd run into Sicily. Come on, Will. I've gone along with everything you asked. How about including me?"

"Okay. We're going to be looking for an amphibious carrier. U.S.S. *Wasp,* to be exact." He extracted a slip of paper from his pocket. "This is where we're supposed to meet it. I don't think we have to go a long way to get there. Gives us time to prepare."

"Prepare," Waters stated precisely. "Prepare for what?"

Riley handed him another slip of paper. "The people listed there are going to be our guests . . . for a summit meeting . . . for peace between the Arab world and Israel . . . hell, between all of us."

Waters looked up from the list of names. "I thought that agreement between the PLO and the Jews took care of the problem."

"That was just a beginning. There's never been anything like this, Francis, and the fact that we could put it together was a miracle in itself. The only way we could get them all to agree to this was to meet in neutral territory. That's why we redesigned the interior of *Calm Seas.* We didn't want them sharing accommodations."

Waters whistled to himself. "Security . . . how . . ."

"That's exactly why we chose *Calm Seas.* They will be on nobody's land. This crew, including those we retained from your former crew, have been cleared. Each one of those delegates is a captive audience—nothing to do but pound out an agreement. It's safe for each of them. And best of all, no one—good guys or bad guys—knows they're aboard here."

Francis Waters stared out at the water. "I'd think you'd want them to be surrounded with so much firepower that . . ." His voice trailed off.

"That's just it, Francis. They will be. *Wasp* and her squadron provide an outer ring of security. It's so safe that there's actually a chance to reach a peace accord."

PART FOUR

APRIL

HUSSEIN'S NAVY:
THE APPROACH

CHAPTER EIGHT

DAY ONE

Phil Salkin's eyes snapped open before he knew he was awake. He turned his head automatically to the right, toward the bright red numbers on the digital clock by his bedside—four minutes after four, and it was still dark outside the White House. *Go back to sleep.* He closed his eyes. Seconds later, they popped open again. Still four minutes after four . . . then the far right digit blinked and it was five minutes after four.

There would be no going back to sleep. His mind had already outrun his body and shifted into gear before the message demanding more sleep could take effect. It was time to start the day—and what an important day it was going to be.

Marian would be most unhappy if he awakened her as he slipped out of bed. So, very quietly, he pulled back the covers. He lay still until he'd counted to twenty. Then he swung his legs off the bed and sat up with his feet on the floor, again counting to twenty. Let the heart get used to the idea of motion. It's not twenty years old. Very gingerly, so as not to rock the bed, he stood up, sliding his feet into his slippers as he did so. Success! She was still asleep.

He padded over to the nearby chair where his bathrobe lay, and he pulled it on, counting once again. When he reached twenty, he headed for the bathroom, careful to tread as lightly as possible. He decided he would not turn on the light until the door was shut behind him.

"You're very quiet, Phil, but I read you too well." Marian's voice was clear, without the throaty murmur of sleep.

He turned with his hand still touching the knob on the bathroom door. "I'm sorry," he said apologetically. "I really tried to be like a mouse, a very small, very stealthy mouse."

"You were, dear, and a very lovable mouse, too." She propped herself up on an elbow and turned on the bedside light, her eyes squinting at the sudden brightness. She was also smiling. "But you were radiating all sorts of nervous energy last night. I could tell as soon as you lit your cigar after we got back from that dinner."

"Signal, huh?"

"You gave off lots of signals. When you and Lou Griffey had that little tête-á-tête for a minute . . ."

"It couldn't have taken that long."

"It was and you should have seen all the heads turn. Poor Bill Herbert's phone's going to be ringing all morning." Bill Herbert was Salkin's communications director, a man who manipulated the press like chess pieces. "He's going to be angry with you unless you've let him in on what's going on." Marian never asked to be involved in matters of state. She was happy to point out any number of times that she hadn't run for office. Her first and only responsibility was to deliver a healthy, functioning President to the people. "And if you keep it all bound up inside," she scolded, "you're going to end up with an ulcer."

"Lou and I really looked that intense?" he asked unhappily.

"It couldn't have been a dirty joke, Phil. Neither of you laughed."

"It's big, Marian. And it's surrounded by the best security I've ever seen." He wished he could explain it all. "That's what Lou was explaining to me—that it's all going off like clockwork." He spread his hands out, palms up. "I can't believe it. I really can't."

His wife fluffed a couple of pillows and lay her head back against them. "If it's going so well, then you should get a night's sleep, Phil. No . . . wait . . . forget I said that. I don't want to nag. I could tell last night with that late-night cigar."

He grinned sheepishly. "Signals?"

"Signals," she answered with a grin. She reached over and turned out the light. "I'm going to try to get enough sleep for both of us. Have a good day, dear. Love and kisses."

Heinz Waller was as close to the fishing boat as Walter Erhardt intended to come. He had no idea how realistic the situation aboard the trawler appeared, and there was no reason to allow a chance look through binoculars that would create suspicion.

He'd maneuvered the submarine until her port quarter was to windward, so that the swells coming from that direction alternated between washing over her stern and sliding underneath. But her motion was lessened considerably because she was no longer running directly into them at twelve knots. The trawler was visible whenever one of them rose on a swell, but it would be almost impossible to view the activity on her deck.

Lieutenant Hugo Schroeder had been called to the conning tower by Erhardt and given definitive instructions: "You should keep the seas off the port quarter, and I want you to maintain this distance from the fishing boat. As soon as the inflatable is away, I want the forward trunk secured and all exterior hatches to remain shut. No one, absolutely no one, on deck for any reason. It's much too dangerous. And no one up here but you and the lookouts, and I mean no one. When I go below for my gear, I will explain these instructions to Mr. Rather. He will, of course, assume interim command while I am away but will remain in the control room."

Erhardt clapped each of the lookouts on the shoulder to make sure they were also paying attention to him. "I know you are curious about this rescue effort, but you lookouts should be scanning the sky and your own surface sectors in case any other ship or aircraft reacts to the distress signal. You still bear a great deal of responsibility for the safety of your shipmates." Then he disappeared down the ladder to the control room.

Schroeder found it strange that the executive officer was to remain in the control room, but said nothing. Less than thirty seconds later, he heard Erhardt's voice again and turned to see the captain's eyes peering up at him through the hatch.

"Mr. Schroeder, I will keep in close contact with you over this radio." Erhardt extended his arm, and Schroeder bent down to take a small portable transceiver. "It's already set for circuit number two. I do not intend to use another frequency even if we find the trawler's radio operable. It might possibly confuse ships in the immediate area. You may keep Mr. Rather informed over the intercom of any communications between you and myself. Since there may be seriously injured people, my orders may be counter to what you anticipate. Strange things happen during sea rescues, and sometimes standard procedures must be altered."

"I understand, Captain." Schroeder slipped the radio into the pocket of his slicker and went back to the job of holding *Heinz Waller*'s position, as the boat crew struggled to prepare their equipment on the forward deck. This was a new side of Walter Erhardt. It was unheard of that a commanding officer would physically leave his ship. But there was also no time to ponder his reasoning during a rescue operation where men's lives were in danger.

The bow hatch remained open as gear was passed up to the captain's personally selected boat crew. Each man was outfitted in yellow foul-weather gear and was attached by a lifeline to a chock on the hatch. Although the swells did not sweep over the forward section as long as the submarine held position, footing was still difficult.

There was no rain. Yet everything appeared gray—the sky, the water, the foamy wave tops, even the chill air in the Bay of Biscay. The rubber boat, inflated by a high-pressure air system, bumped against the hull as the submarine wallowed in the swell. Then Erhardt emerged from the hatch, and just as quickly as he'd appeared on deck, he, his crew, and all their equipment were in the inflatable, the engine was started, and it was pulling away from *Waller*.

Schroeder raised his binoculars and looked quickly

astern. The fishing boat's position was punctuated by oily clouds of black smoke billowing angrily into the air. The kingposts that supported the heavy trawling gear were generally visible even when the deck house of the burning craft fell beneath the swells. It was hard to assess the damage at that distance, but he was almost certain that the fire seemed to be restricted to the stern. That seemed unusual considering the time that had passed since the distress signal.

If the fishing boat was in so much distress, why hadn't they launched one of the dorys that were visible on either side forward of the pilot house? But that was a problem for Captain Erhardt to confront.

"They've pulled away from the submarine," Michael announced. He was perched on the section in front of the pilot house. "I count six men in the boat."

"Weapons?" Ismael questioned.

"Too far to make that out. Why should they be armed for a rescue operation?"

"Why should a fishing boat be armed?" Ismael snapped back. "Never take anything for granted, Michael. You'll end up just as dead as so many of our brothers if you let your guard down just once. That's why something like this should be for men only." He moved among the men, shooing all but one of them to a place behind the deck housing where they wouldn't be visible. The lone man he sent below decks.

"Where is Hamari going?" Soraya asked warily. She didn't care for Ismael's remark about men only and she didn't like him giving orders without all three of them agreeing beforehand. It was accepted within the organization that those who were asked to work together must trust each other. The Turk neither trusted nor cared for anyone. Yet their orders had been clear—Hussein considered Ismael's role a critical one to their mission for he was the torpedo expert. And no one would ever question the purpose behind Hussein's orders.

Ismael remained silent, his face a mask, until he saw that Michael had overheard her and was also waiting for an answer. "I sent him down to the bilges. I told him that if there is a problem and we are in danger from the submarine, that I will let him know. He'll detonate the explosives. At least, the Germans will die with us," he concluded passionately.

"Nothing's going to happen," Michael chided. He brought the binoculars to his eyes again and, as the inflatable crested on a wave, recognized Erhardt staring back at him. "Good. There's Walter. He's one of the six. That's just five we have to worry about."

"He said he'd pick men who wouldn't be . . ." Soraya began.

"Shit," Ismael said, snarling. "They are German sailors and they have no faith. When they see us, they'll be just as dangerous as any other infidel." He gestured toward the approaching boat with his Uzi. "They're dead men the minute they set foot on deck."

Michael's binoculars fell to his chest as he jumped down to the deck. In an instant, he was standing before Ismael, his face inches from the other man's. It was the first time he'd ever confronted the Turk and he hoped his uncertainty was masked. But he couldn't let Ismael's emotions damage their mission. "Hussein appointed me captain of *Baghdad.* You don't fire a gun, you don't do anything on your own, not until I give the orders." And just as quickly as his fury had risen, his expression became placid. "We follow orders for a purpose. None of us can act on our own. We're all equal, Ismael."

Michael looked over his shoulder. The boat from the German submarine was closing rapidly, no more than 150 meters away. He turned away before Ismael could respond and began to wave his arms excitedly. "Look excited," he said to the other two, "like we're thankful. We're about to be rescued."

"Those people aren't wearing life jackets, Captain," one of Erhardt's men said, "but they're sure glad to see us." There was no need for binoculars to recognize the obvious excitement aboard the fishing boat.

"I only see three people," Erhardt reported to Schroeder

over the radio. "Perhaps there are injured. As soon as I'm aboard, I'll assess the situation and be in contact again."

"Isn't that a woman?" another of the sailors remarked curiously.

"Yes," Erhardt responded. "There seem to be two men and one woman. Come alongside forward, near the deck house. We don't know how badly the aft end is damaged by fire."

"Captain," a sailor named Koster exclaimed, "look at that fire . . . that barrel?" He looked strangely at Erhardt and the others in the inflatable.

"Stand by," Erhardt bellowed, as they bumped the fishing boat's hull. "Get a line over." Koster was the only remaining member of the original rescue and assistance crew, and obviously it was a mistake to have included him. "Koster, I want you to go up first and secure the lines for me."

The inflatable swung around near the bow of the fishing boat and came down the port side in the lee of the waves. The deck was about a meter above the waterline, and the low railing another meter above that. Koster stretched up with the first line in one hand and it was immediately taken from him. As the engine on the inflatable backed down and the trawler rolled in their direction, Koster grabbed a hand and scrambled up and over the side of the fishing boat carrying a second line.

Erhardt searched out Michael immediately and gave a sign with his eyes indicating Koster. Then, before any of his men made a move, he reached up in the same place Koster had just disappeared. A hand grasped his, and as the inflatable rose on a swell, he was heaving himself over the side.

As his feet touched the deck, he saw that a dark ugly-looking fisherman was assisting Koster with the line—Ismael! They were both squatting, and as they finished, a knife appeared in Ismael's hand. Erhardt saw Koster open his mouth and perhaps he attempted to rise, but before he could make a sound he was suddenly facedown on the deck, still out of sight of the others in the boat.

"Your other men . . ." Michael began, gesturing toward the inflatable bobbing alongside.

Erhardt cut him short, indicating Koster's limp form. "Get him away, quickly," he hissed. Then his eyes fell on Ismael. "And if that asshole tries anything else like that in the open, we're going to lose it all."

The inflatable was too low in the water to see over the side of the fishing boat, but one of the men called out, "Captain, is everything all right?"

Erhardt went to the side and smiled down. "Yes, we need you aboard. We must help them evacuate. The hold is flooded. Koster has gone below to check on the injured. Just a minute . . ." He turned around and saw that Koster's body had disappeared.

Michael came to the railing beside him. His face betrayed a mixture of fear and relief as he called down to the German sailors, "Please, come aboard, quickly. We'll give you a boost up. We need your assistance. My mate will help you." Ismael, his face expressionless, materialized beside him.

As each of Erhardt's remaining men were hoisted over the side, they were faced with Soraya, kneeling so she couldn't be seen from the sub, covering them with an Uzi. At first glance, their captain seemed helpless, his hands hanging useless at his sides.

Michael was the only one to speak. "If you make any move, your captain will be the first to die. We intend to put our boats over the side and unload our cargo into them. As long as you assist us, you will not be harmed. Ismael here will tell you what to do. He is not the kind you should disobey." He turned to Erhardt. "And, Captain, I'm sure you are in radio contact with your ship. If you come with me, I will tell you what to report back."

Astern, out of earshot, Erhardt spoke into his radio to Schroeder. "The fire appears under control here, but the hold is flooded and they have injured who need medical attention. The engine in one of their dorys is inoperative, so I am allowing the captain to load their valuables and portable equipment in our inflatable and their other dory. I want you to send over the other inflatable to assist in evacuating. I need the eight men on the list I left with the XO to assist me here."

There was a pause before Schroeder's voice came back to them. "The XO is concerned about so many men away from the ship, Captain. That's more than half the crew."

"Explain to the XO that my orders stand," Erhardt snapped. He shoved the transmitter back in the pocket of his foul-weather gear. The tension of the moment was clearly evident in his face. So far, everything was actually working as planned. "Besides myself, my executive officer, the watch officer in the conning tower, and the two lookouts up there with him, that will leave nine men below decks," he said to Michael. They would be the most difficult. "They will all be manning a watch station. As long as I am with you, there should be no trouble." *As long as Schroeder continues to follow his orders without question.*

While they waited for the second inflatable boat from *Heinz Waller,* five of Michael's men switched into the clothes that had been worn by Erhardt's men. They would be ready to greet the Germans when they came alongside.

FEDERAL REPUBLIC OF GERMANY

FLASH

CLASSIFICATION—TOP SECRET

FROM: COMMANDER SUBMARINE SQUADRON FOUR
TO: ALL COMMANDS, WALLER RESCUE OPERATION

1) AS OF 0600Z THIS DATE, THERE HAS BEEN NO INDICATION OF WALLER WITHIN DESIGNATED SEARCH AREA.
2) AT 1200Z, PERIPHERY WILL EXPAND 250 KILOMETERS SOUTH OF CURRENT AREA AND EAST TO 5W.
3) AIR AND SURFACE COMMANDERS WILL COORDINATE SEARCH SECTORS WITH UNITS INVOLVED AND REPORT AREAS OF RESPONSIBILITY TO THIS COMMAND.
4) ALL UNITS WILL CONTINUE TO EMPLOY SEARCH AND IDENTIFICATION METHODS OUTLINED IN PREVIOUS MESSAGES.

5) THIS COMMAND CONTINUES TO REQUIRE USE OF SPECIALLY ASSIGNED FREQUENCIES FOR SECURITY PURPOSES.

Herman Gleick was still not sure which of the CIA agent's eyes he should be following and he was becoming embarrassed by his own curiosity. He wanted to explain that it was of no concern to him, and he wanted Lyford to know that. But, quite obviously, it was of little concern to the American.

"It has to be one of these three." Lyford placed three women's photographs—each one taken head-on, passport style—flat on his desk, turned so they faced Gleick. "Each of them were in Germany at the time your man was murdered. This one"—he tapped the photo of the oldest one with his finger—"was definitely in Berlin for a few days before and after the date of death, plus the organization she works for is all noise and no action. The other two were a little harder to keep in contact with—damn hard actually. Either one could have been in Bremerhaven on the date of Preminger's death."

"You allow them to remain free, even if . . ." Gleick began.

"Current policy," Lyford responded. "We hope they'll lead us to some bigger fish."

Gleick picked up one of the photos and studied it. He turned it so that Lyford could also see the face. "The others aren't very appealing, but this one is most attractive. . . ."

Lyford nodded and waited for Gleick to continue.

"If I happened to be the great lover that Captain Preminger apparently was, I think it would be natural for me to select the prettier one as my next conquest. And if there was a reason to seduce Preminger, she is"—he shrugged—"a natural."

The CIA man grinned knowingly. "You're into the mind of the master cocksman."

Gleick frowned. "Excuse me?"

"An Americanism. Your boy, Preminger—you said he was a real swordsman, a great lover. Also known in the States as a *cocksman*—someone who makes a habit out of screwing lots of women."

"I understand. Yes . . . I was driving at the same thing." After a moment's thought, Gleick smiled knowingly also. He found the term amusing. "Wouldn't you agree then that he'd select this one. She looks very lovely."

"Same one I was thinking of. And she has three aliases she's been using in her travels recently, almost so you'd think she was triplets. The last names are all impossible to pronounce. The first names are a little easier: Goriyeh, Soraya, and one that's more Spanish-sounding, Marta. You take your pick, you get the same girl. Unfortunately," he said with a sigh, "we lost her trail."

"How long would it take to run a complete printout on everything in your computer on this one?" Gleick inquired. "I mean everything, your own files, anything you can find from any other agencies in your network."

"By noon, no later. I can have everything available here for you by then."

Gleick gave a sigh of relief. "Wonderful. Our own sources are nowhere as efficient, and time . . ." Then he nodded his head as if answering his own silent question and pursed his lips. "I can be in Bremerhaven before the end of the day with your material. Perhaps I can even have a confirmation on this woman by the owner of the building where we believe the murder took place." He stood up and held out his hand. "I don't know how to thank you."

"Simple. She's known to be attached to a known terrorist group, but they're so well organized we don't know who the upper-level people are. We don't even have a firm name for the organization. You get something—I want to help." There was no reason to say more at this time. With the conference at sea and the President making an appearance, this was one group they desperately wanted to learn more about. Maybe, just maybe, Gleick would turn up something here. Time was as important to him as it was to Gleick—more so. But he couldn't tell the German about the summit or the President's appearance.

"Agreed." Gleick hesitated, then decided there would never be a better time to ask. "Mr. Lyford, I don't mean to embarrass you—and I must admit I'm embarrassed to say so—but I like to look a man in the eye when I speak to him and . . ." Suddenly, he wasn't sure how to say it.

It was Lyford's turn to smile warmly. "I know. I know. It's confusing, isn't it? And so many people don't know how to ask." Lyford had come from behind his desk and had walked to the office door with Gleick. "You know what I tell them? I give some people who I don't care for very much the wrong eye. Then I can study them when they think I'm looking away."

"Very interesting," Gleick commented, wondering what Lyford's final answer would be.

"And then sometimes I act dumb and tell others I don't understand what they're driving at, and that gets them flustered. I kind of like to keep some people on edge. It gives me an advantage."

"I can imagine." Gleick could see that the agent wasn't finished with his story. He was thoroughly enjoying himself.

"But with my friends, I tell them my good eye is my left eye." They were in the outer office now, and he added, "Isn't that right, Jaqui?"

Jaqui looked up with a dubious expression on her face. "Yes, sir. That's correct." It was obvious she was among that vast number who were unable to remember but, like those others, wasn't about to admit it.

Gleick could see as well as Lyford that she wasn't sure. "I'll remember that," he said to the CIA man.

"Oh, you'd be surprised how many people forget." Lyford laughed good-naturedly. "They never ask a second time, but I can tell they're not sure and they're damned if they're going to ask again."

Gleick's expression was serious as he shook Lyford's hand again before he departed, making sure to look him in the left eye.

Before he went back into his office, Lyford leaned over his secretary's desk momentarily. "I'm glad that at least you remember which is the good eye, Jaqui. I can always count on you."

She looked directly into his left eye and smiled politely. "Of course I do, Mr. Lyford," she answered, completely unaware that his right eye was enjoying the view down the front of her dress.

Once seated back at his desk, CIA agent Lyford reflected on the fact that his wandering eye was almost better than two of the standard eyes. It allowed him to appreciate Jaqui's charms that much more, and one had to be extra careful about enjoying a co-worker's attributes in this politically correct world.

And that eye did give him a decided advantage over others. Perhaps he'd apologize to Herman Gleick when he returned at noon and tell him that his good eye really was the right one. He rather liked the little German detective. The man was persistent, a digger, and it sounded to Lyford like they might just have something to work with.

The captain and executive officer of the French frigate, *Pierre Retard,* paid the customary courtesy visits to the officials of La Rochelle before allowing the crew liberty. Shore patrol headquarters were set up in a separate room at the local police station. Emergency medical arrangements were established at a nearby clinic. Trash pickup and pierside facilities were coordinated. The ship would provide an honor guard for Sunday services in memory of Allied war dead from World War Two. The officers would attend a dinner that evening to meet local officials. And, finally, visiting hours were established for local citizens to receive tours of the ship.

The standard arrival details were so time-consuming that the captain almost overlooked the one item he had promised himself to take care of immediately upon coming ashore. He asked both the harbormaster and the coast guard officer-in-charge if they had received any reports of a distress signal similar to the weak one they'd intercepted as they were nearing La Rochelle.

They hadn't. There were no vessels from La Rochelle, nor were they aware of any from other ports in the vicinity, that were overdue. They all noted that, while the seas were up the past day or so, there had been no storms.

They all wondered whether it could have been a freak of nature that caused the radio signal to be picked up by *Pierre Retard.* But, because the distress signal had reported a fire on board, they agreed that a general message should be issued to all marine interests. Since this was the weekend that reserve air crews were practicing search and rescue techniques, they would be assigned to search for the source of the mysterious signal. It would be a worthwhile exercise for them.

The second inflatable raft from *Heinz Waller* made its approach to the fishing boat in the same manner as the first. The men aboard could see Captain Erhardt standing by the railing, along with a man and a woman. On occasion, when the boat rolled, they recognized the uniforms of their fellow crewmen from the submarine.

"Make another line fast to our other boat," Erhardt called down, as the inflatable's forward line was secured to the fishing boat by the man next to him. *Waller's* operations officer was in the boat, and Erhardt said, "Mr. Wippler, let me give you a hand. I can use your help."

He assisted Wippler up over the side, shouting down to the others, "Quickly now, we may not have much time. She's still taking on water." Then he put an arm around his operations officer's shoulder and led him toward the opposite side of the trawler. "I have a list of things for you to check for me . . ." he began, and stopped only when he felt Wippler shudder in surprise as he saw Soraya's Uzi.

In a little more than a minute, the other seven men were aboard. They, like the first group, found themselves helpless as they were herded below decks. There, incredulous, they, too, were forced to remove their clothes and watch as the remaining members of the trawler's crew donned the uniforms that fit them.

"Mr. Schroeder," Erhardt called over his short-range radio, "Our portable pumps are limiting the flooding here, and the fire has been isolated to the aft section. But she's still in danger of sinking. I'm preparing to transfer some men with burns back with us, along with some of their valuable personal items. I'll return in the first boat. Mr. Wippler and the rest of our men will remain aboard here to assist in keeping her afloat a little longer." Erhardt could sense the adrenaline infusing his system as Michael's men, in *Waller* uniforms, prepared to head for the submarine.

With Lieutenant Schroeder and two lookouts in the conning tower and the executive officer in the control room, the remaining nine crew members of *Heinz Waller* were spread throughout the submarine. Otto Rather would be in the control room with two other watch standers. Erhardt had asked the engineering officer to perform some maintenance while they held their position near the trawler, so he and his two remaining men would be aft in the engineering spaces. That left just four other men spread thinly, perhaps in radio, sonar, the torpedo room, or involved with food preparation in the galley.

Soraya was impatient now. She hated the trawler. Ismael continued to act as if she didn't exist. Even Michael had paid little attention to her since Erhardt had come aboard. "May I assume I will be allowed to go over to the submarine with Walter?" she asked acidly. "You don't seem to need me. And Ismael seems happy preparing the lambs for the slaughter."

Michael had found himself uncomfortable with Erhardt seemingly assuming command. *Heinz Waller* was Erhardt's submarine, but *Baghdad* belonged to Michael. "You'll be going back now?" he asked Erhardt.

Erhardt nodded. "I'm the one to handle my executive officer. Why not let her come with me?" A woman aboard a submarine might prove an interesting diversion if he needed one. "She can probably attract some attention. And she's as good with a gun as any of you."

Waller's inflatables were the first to pull away from the trawler. The first contained Erhardt, Soraya, and three of Michael's men wearing German outfits. The second carried five more, two of whom appeared to be injured crew from the trawler, along with a few crates. Everything appeared just as Erhardt had reported.

"Mr. Rather," Schroeder called down on the intercom, "the two inflatables are returning now. The captain is aboard the first one. I expect him alongside in a few minutes." The sea was subsiding slightly, but it was difficult for him to keep binoculars centered on rising and falling boats from the conning tower of a rolling submarine. He called down below for the forward hatch to be opened.

The first boat bumped against the submarine, and a sailor scrambled up on the hull with a line, securing it to a chock by the forward hatch. The next off was Erhardt, who gave Schroeder a friendly wave.

The combination of wind and the wash of the waves around the hull created too much noise for Erhardt to shout up to the conning tower, so he used his radio. "Mr. Schroeder, I am going below for a minute. I'll explain to Mr. Rather what we will be doing until we have transferred everyone from the trawler. They will be using their own dories for the next transfer. We will leave the inflatables where they are because there is a possibility the trawler may need more assistance."

Schroeder slipped the radio back into the pocket of his foul-weather gear and watched as Erhardt disappeared through the forward hatch. The individual who followed was a woman from the trawler. Two *Waller* crewmen followed. Then he watched as the injured men from the trawler were helped down through the hatch. It would have been so much more interesting to have been in the control room to learn just what had happened aboard the fishing boat.

Schroeder turned back briefly to look at the trawler through his binoculars. The smoke had lessened now, and it was still difficult to make out much with the two vessels rolling in the swell. But he could see men passing up crates that were being stacked on the fishing boat's deck. Someone else was preparing to swing one of the dories out over the side. *What was so important about the cargo?*

CHAPTER NINE

"Good morning, Commodore."

"Hmmm?" Rear Admiral Turner, his concentration interrupted, turned quickly to his left without lowering his binoculars. "Oh, Jake. You surprised me."

"Sorry about that, sir." Steele smiled easily. He was still dressed in the fatigues he'd worn on Turner's barge and could just as easily have been one of the marines doing PT on the flight deck below. Lines remained etched on his dark face by the protective goggles he'd worn during their high-speed maneuvering. "Just as soon as we were secure below, I got the word to report to the admiral on the double. Always willing to please, sir," he said with a disconcerting grin.

"You're bullshitting me again, Jake. Don't you like admirals?" This was a game he and Jake had come to enjoy since Steele reported aboard. Jake Steele wasn't really a permanent member of the admiral's staff and he made no bones about his disappointment at being thrown into something he'd had no time to prepare for. Rear Admiral Turner had needed a liaison officer for the SEALs and Marine Recon when *Wasp* deployed to the Mediterranean, and Steele was the man they'd sent him at the last minute. Considering they'd never worked together before, their relationship had matured quickly. Turner had learned long ago that if you treated SEALs like the professionals they were rather than military hit men, they returned your loyalty many times over.

"Admirals? Yes, sir. Always wanted to be one myself. Hope you'll put in a good word for me." Jake's grin widened. "Will I have to wear a tie all the time?"

"Commander Steele, you don't want to be an admiral. You're better off doing what you do." Turner extended the binoculars to Jake. "Take a look through these and tell me what you think of that barge off our port bow."

Steele moved the binoculars back and forth until he picked up the vessel on the horizon. Then he adjusted the focus slightly. "Barge?"

"The white one. You got it yet?"

"I've got it, Admiral." He whistled softly. "You fooled me on this one, sir. I was still thinking admiral's barge." Steele was focused on a graceful, white motor vessel that was considerably larger than the navy's newest minesweepers or patrol craft. "I know people travel that way, but it's still hard to imagine. I wonder where she's headed."

"She's headed with us."

Steele lowered the binoculars and glanced out of the corner of his eye at Turner. "You mean she's going to be steaming with us, like an escort?"

"Not an escort, but she'll tag along like a baby duck, just like she was one of the task group. If you want to be accurate, I guess you could say we're her escort. That's the part I couldn't tell you until now. We have a new set of orders—super classified—in effect as of twelve hundred today. I'm sorry I couldn't say anything before now. But if certain things didn't come together, and I guess there were a lot of good reasons they wouldn't, no one would have known about this."

"She's even got a helicopter pad aft," Jake noted as he handed the binoculars back to the admiral.

"Right you are. Our helicopters are going to be using that flight deck a lot. While you were out there playing bumper pool, I received a message that everything in an operation order I was briefed on before we departed Little Creek is a go. There's going to be a lot of high-powered people coming and going here on *Wasp,* some of them living aboard. That floating palace you saw just a moment ago is going to be headquarters for a summit conference. I'm not aware of all the details myself, just what I need to know, I guess. But it's important enough that we're going to have a lot of bigwigs passing through. We're security cover for that yacht. What do you think of that?"

"So that's why I got those orders aboard here at the last minute."

"I imagine so, Jake. I promise I didn't have anything to do with it. But now that you're here, I need your help."

"It's nice to feel wanted, Commodore." Steele leaned his back against the railing in front of Turner, so that he was facing the admiral, and folded his arms. "This fishing boat that was loading in Libya, the one Sixth Fleet intelligence picked up on—are we supposed to think there's a possible connection?" Jake had a habit of raising his eyebrows and wrinkling his forehead when he asked a question.

"The security on this has been so tight I can't imagine it had anything to do with this summit. But you never know," he added carefully.

"That makes my job a little different." Steele's eyebrows were still raised. The only part of his job that ever scared him was lack of intelligence. "Now I see why you were questioning a slow fishing trawler as a threat. Too obvious?"

"I guess you could say that, Jake. Come on down to my cabin. I'd like you to see this op order. It might just curl your toes."

Heinz Waller's chief torpedoman was working on the number-three tube when Erhardt dropped down through the forward hatch. He continued tightening the flange on a pressure gauge, but said pleasantly, "Can we be of any assistance, Captain?" He and another rating were the only ones in the torpedo room.

Erhardt nodded pleasantly as he stepped back and waited for Soraya to reach the bottom of the ladder. "I think we've got everything under control, but you can never tell. If you can just move back for a moment to make room for our guests." He pointed up at a form backing down the ladder.

Two men in German submariners' gear with *Waller* stenciled on the back followed. The chief's eyes widened as he recognized that they were complete strangers. Then those same eyes seemed to pop as he saw the handguns pointed in his direction.

"Cooperate, Chief," Erhardt stated calmly. "It may just save your neck." Then he watched as the chief and his rating were forced to face the bulkhead. Their hands were pulled behind them and secured tightly.

Soraya had come aboard with a large shoulder bag. Without a word, she opened it and removed a hypodermic syringe and a small vial. She then drew the vial's liquid through the needle into the syringe and looked questioningly to Erhardt.

While the last of the men from the inflatable came down through the hatch, Erhardt pointed at the chief torpedoman and nodded his head once. He'd insisted months before that there should be no shooting. One shot inside the submarine could be their first mistake, their only mistake. A single bullet, poorly aimed or a richochet, could destroy a critical instrument, and the element of total surprise was crucial.

One of the gunmen moved quickly forward and hissed in the chief's ear, "Don't move," as he encircled the man from behind in a bear hug.

Soraya's hand moved almost as quickly, injecting the chief in the upper arm with the hypodermic.

The old torpedoman's head snapped around angrily. "Captain, what the hell . . ." But whatever thoughts of struggle passed through his mind seemed to dissolve.

"Relax," Soraya interrupted soothingly, "you're only going to fall asleep until we're settled in."

Even before she finished speaking, the muscles in the chief's face grew limp. His mouth dropped open in an attempt to speak. His lower lip quivered, then fell slack as he tried to draw in air. His eyes blinked rapidly a few times before his knees buckled.

The man who'd been holding him eased the body to the deck and dragged it behind the ladder.

The remaining torpedoman found himself trembling uncontrollably. Then he felt unseen hands gripping his shoulders. He closed his eyes as they turned him around. He was face to face with his captain.

Erhardt looked him squarely in the eye. "I don't think you need to sleep, Neuner. The chief might have made some things difficult for these people. I don't think you will. Am I right, Neuner?"

Neuner looked over at his chief's crumpled body behind the ladder. "Yes . . . sir."

"Wonderful. I've been pleased with your work, Neuner. You know this torpedo room as if it was your own room back home. And you know these torpedo tubes better than the toys you played with as a child. I think I can depend on you." Both his hands were squeezing Neuner's shoulders. "I can—can't I?"

Neuner had no idea whether his chief was sleeping or dead, but he knew his prospects for the moment sounded much better with his captain. "Yes, Captain." His voice was barely audible. "You can depend on me."

Erhardt clapped his hands sharply beneath the man's chin. "Good, Neuner. I'm proud of you. Our cruise is just beginning. I'm sorry your hands must remain bound, but you will eventually be released once our crew is intact again. One of these men will remain with you for now."

No more than three minutes had passed since Erhardt had scrambled up onto *Waller*'s hull, but to him time seemed to have stopped. The men from the second inflatable were now coming through the hatch. "Come," Erhardt said to Soraya and the others, "this has to be done swiftly."

The next space they came to was the galley. The cook was equally shocked when unfamiliar faces in *Waller* gear appeared at the entrance with handguns. As with the torpedoman, Erhardt spoke briefly and encouragingly. "This man is a cook, an excellent one. We can use him. Take him to the torpedo room," he said to one of Michael's men, "and keep him with the other."

Now Erhardt turned to Soraya. "We've been over the design of this submarine. The radio room and sonar are on either side of the passageway just before the control room. There may or may not be a man on duty in each one. The radio watch may have been shifted to the control room. You will handle them while I go ahead. I must appear first in the control room on my own."

Soraya's mouth opened but Erhardt never gave her a chance to speak.

"I didn't have an opportunity to select my own executive officer," he continued. "This one will be a problem. You see, he is a good officer and wise enough not to like me. Give me exactly sixty seconds from now."

Soraya looked at her watch.

"You"—he jabbed a finger into her chest to make it clear that he, not Michael, was in charge of U-252—"may follow then. But after you, only men in my ship's uniforms. The surprise must be instant. Remember, no commotion, no shooting. There must be no indication to either engineering or the conning tower that something has taken place." Then he turned on his heel for the control room.

Seconds later, the duty sonarman found himself in a bear hug and experienced the quick sting of Soraya's needle. He was left on the deck. His misfortune, like that of the chief torpedoman, was that Michael's men had been selected because they, too, were experts at these trades. There was no one in the tiny radio shack.

Soraya studied her watch intently. She sensed her whole body shaking with tension and excitement, just as it did when she killed an enemy. The sensation brought a smile to her face. It was all happening just as Erhardt said it could. He was acting with confidence, as if nothing unusual was taking place. *Strange.* She'd found Walter extremely unappealing once she understood she couldn't seduce him. Now she found herself wanting him—wanting to control him. *What a cold bastard he'd turned into. What a challenge he'd become.*

"Otto, you've done a superb job in my absence." Erhardt entered the control room with a broad smile. "We are bringing all the trawler's crew over here now. The fire has been controlled, but the damage is extensive. It started with a lube oil pump." He was moving about the small control room as he spoke, his eyes shifting from the diving officer to the planesman, before coming back to Rather. "I don't know how the flooding occurred, but they unfortunately couldn't control it, and our own portable pumps were insufficient. So," he said with a wave of his hands, "we will have guests on our tiny submarine until we can obtain assistance."

"I'll prepare a message right now . . ." Rather began.

"That won't be necessary, Otto. We're close enough to the

Spanish coast that I think we can take them into port ourselves."

Soraya came through the forward hatch, followed by men in *Waller* foul-weather gear.

"Come over," Erhardt called to her. "This is the man I told you about, the one in command while I was gone."

Soraya came across the deck, pushing back the hood of the foul-weather coat she wore. She shook out her long black hair, and her engaging smile temporarily held Otto Rather's attention. Even the planesman, who glanced quickly over his shoulder when he heard her voice, found himself smiling with her.

Rather, totally distracted by her presence, held out his hand to the woman they had saved. It was only when she didn't extend her hand in turn that he saw the 9mm Beretta pointed at his belly. His surprise faded quickly into shock as he saw that the men in *Waller's* foul-weather gear were not only strangers but also armed. Without hesitation, they moved beside the diving officer and the planesman.

Erhardt's voice was soft and even and firm as he spoke. "One word, even the slightest movement, and I am sure these people will kill you. Believe me, I have been pleading for your lives and with God's grace we may all be spared. But, please, don't give them reason to shoot."

Soraya was fascinated with this version of Walter Erhardt. *He'd fuck his mother and make her like it!*

The planesman was removed from his seat and replaced by one of Michael's men, as was the diving officer. They, along with Rather, were then herded over to the bulkhead by the after hatch.

Erhardt depressed the button on the intercom. "Mr. Schroeder, have the dories gotten under way from the trawler yet?"

"They've both been lowered into the water, Captain. One appears to be pulling away now."

"Fine. We're operating on borrowed time. Mr. Rather and I are going back to engineering to see how the maintenance is progressing. If you need me, call me on the intercom back there, please."

Then he turned to Soraya. "These are all good men," he said grandly. "I want the executive officer and that planesman to remain here. Take this other man forward to the torpedo room and treat him just as the others have been. I'm going aft by myself to determine how much longer my engineering officer will have his machinery opened up."

In La Rochelle, the local coast guard commander called the quarterdeck of the *Pierre Retard* to see if the captain was available. He'd decided it would be a courtesy, not to mention an opportunity, to make his own service look good. The captain came to the phone.

"Captain, I wanted to inform you that your valuable information about that distress call is being acted upon. One of our search and rescue aircraft has been released from other duties to search the Bay of Biscay until the reserve crews can assume responsibility. Perhaps something will come of it." Who could tell? Perhaps even the reserves would be the ones to solve the mystery of that lost sub.

"I don't even like being near those things," Francis Waters commented to Will Riley as he studied *Wasp* through his binoculars. "That thing could run right over us and keep on going."

"Well, we're not going to get that close to it. My boss says to keep our distance until the *Wasp* signals differently."

"Why?" Waters wanted answers to everything. He'd decided that the government had him by the short hairs, but he still wasn't going to grab his ankles without knowing why. If they could get him out of trouble with the flourish of a pen, why couldn't they dump him right back in the middle of it with an equivalent lack of effort?

"I wish I had all the answers, Francis. These guests of ours don't seem to mind that we're bringing them together. We've given them an opportunity to come to the table without any of them appearing to have lost face. But they don't want to see Americans hanging over their shoulders. That's why we'll keep our distance from *Wasp*. We're going to use her as a hotel since only two members of each delegation can stay aboard here. But we'll still remain a couple of miles away from her."

"What if they want me to maneuver with this formation? I don't know how to do that."

"Then I suppose," Riley answered with a twisted grin at Waters's uncertain expression, "that maybe they'll *keel haul* us."

"I don't think that's funny."

"It's probably better than doing hard time, Francis." And when there was no response, he added, "You can be sure someone will come aboard to explain everything to you."

"Can you wrap it up quickly, Junker?" Walter Erhardt was squatting on the deck plates with his engineering officer. The cover plate was off the Siemens electric motor next to them. One of the ratings was in the process of replacing a unit within the motor and only the bottom two thirds of his body was visible. Another man was working on the innards of one of the diesels.

Junker leaned over to the man who seemed to be disappearing into the electric motor. "How much more time?"

"The last unit's installed," the man answered. "Just need a few minutes to clean it up and run a test."

"Weber," the engineer called down to the man on the diesel. "How close are you to being done?"

"About to wrap it up, sir. She was clean inside. Not as much to do as we thought. The exhaust absorber's fine. I can't see any reason for opening up anything else."

Junker turned to Erhardt. "That's it, Captain. Give me another ten minutes. The whole plant's in great shape. We really don't need to worry too much about anything until we're back in port again." Junker still wasn't clear on why the captain has insisted on one more inspection of the power plant—but, then, who argued with the captain?

"That's what I was hoping to hear." It was too bad he couldn't retain the engineering officer, but the man couldn't be trusted to cooperate. His presence would have left too much to chance. But it was nice to have such reassurance on the engineering plant. "Join me in the control room when everything's wrapped up here. No need to change out of your working gear," he added, indicating the engineer's dirty coveralls. "I want to go over a couple of items with all officers before we get underway."

He depressed the intercom button for the conning tower. "Mr. Schroeder, status report on the trawler please."

"The first dory from the trawler is alongside and offloading crates on our forward deck. The other one appears to be waiting until this one is finished. It's remaining well off our beam. And something else, Captain. There're some men who seem to be rigging the trawling gear. Aren't they all supposed to be abandoning, sir?"

"To my knowledge, yes. I wouldn't be concerned, Mr. Schroeder. Their master is still aboard and it may be for something they want to transfer to us. I wouldn't be concerned. I'll be up with you shortly."

Erhardt had decided to retain the diesel technician and the man who knew the electric motor so well. So far, that made a total of six he'd decided to keep. Controlling them wouldn't be difficult when it was explained what would happen to their families ashore if they failed to cooperate. There was no necessity to feed the two lookouts in the conning tower—they were the newest members of the crew and really had very little to offer. And then there was Schroeder. Erhardt was already tired and his efficiency would decrease without sleep. He knew that another conning officer was necessary to relieve him from time to time.

But Walter Erhardt wondered about his executive officer. What was it about the man that he'd been unable to make a decision a few minutes before? The man disliked him, and he had made no secret of his distaste for his executive officer. It was only common sense that Rather's body should already be among those in the torpedo room. Why did he hesitate? Did he want to flaunt this in the man's face before he died? *You are being foolish, Walter—dispose of him now!*

Otto Rather was confident that he would be dead soon and was surprised that he was much less concerned with his fate than he might have expected. A submariner's outlook on life and death were different from that of most people. Because each man depended on the next, one mistake by a single individual could likely doom every man aboard. So it was only natural that the possibility of death would be considered from a different light. If one were apt to dwell on it, he didn't belong on a submarine.

The situation with his captain was much more disturbing

to Rather than whatever fate he faced. Walter Erhardt was one of the most talented officers in the submarine force, and Rather had gone out of his way to adapt and be an excellent executive officer for him. Yet, no matter how much he tried, Erhardt continually rejected him. *And now this!*

The humiliation of being a crew member of a submarine actually taken over by a terrorist group was exceeded only by the fact that he'd failed to exercise better judgment. He remembered the terse letter from the commodore of Submarine Squadron Four that Schroeder showed him, almost as if he was reading it again. The radio circuit they were guarding at squadron headquarters in Bremerhaven was . . . was . . . he closed his eyes.

Whiskey Alfa! Whiskey Alfa! It was a special circuit assigned to the squadron and programmed into each submarine's primary radio so that it could be accessed by the touch of a switch.

"Are you all right? Mr. Rather!" A rough hand on his shoulder was shaking him. He could feel the warm, slightly fetid breath of the speaker washing over his face.

Rather opened his eyes. "I'm fine . . ." Erhardt's face almost touched his own, but he could not bring himself to say "sir." The man was a traitor.

"I was worried, Otto. Your eyes were closed and you were rocking back and forth as if you might collapse. I thought that fright may have taken control . . ."

"I'm not afraid," Rather retorted. "I was thinking."

Erhardt's face was still only inches away. "About what will transpire with you?"

"No. I was trying to determine how this could possibly happen in a German submarine."

"It is something I find difficult to conceive of myself, Otto." And it was. The only members of his crew in the control room were Rather and the planesman he'd selected to remain. Erhardt knew that the others were all dead now, their bodies in the torpedo room until they could be disposed of. "It is very difficult to . . ." He turned quickly at the sound of someone coming through the hatch behind him.

"Captain . . ." It was the only word the engineering

officer spoke. His eyes had instantly fallen on the strange faces manning the various watch stations. Then he noted the woman with an Uzi slung from her neck standing near his captain.

"I'm sorry, Mr. Junker." Erhardt sounded almost apologetic. "But I assure you that you will be well taken care of." He turned to Soraya and said, "Would you please escort Mr. Junker to the torpedo room?" He smiled cordially at his engineering officer. "Don't worry about your men, Mr. Junker. They'll be well taken care of."

Schroeder's voice came over the intercom. "Captain, the second dory's alongside and preparing to offload. And they're still doing something with their trawling gear as though they planned to operate it."

"Mr. Schroeder, give me two more minutes and I will be up there with you to see what those people on the trawler are actually doing." He turned back to Rather. "Well, Otto, you have a lot to consider here, don't you? I'm indeed curious how your mind works after these difficult weeks we've experienced together. I have to go aft for a moment, then up to talk with Mr. Schroeder. But when I return, I'd like to know what you're thinking. Really, I would." Erhardt was savoring this opportunity to make the final moments of Rather's life as unpleasant as possible.

It required less than two minutes in the engineering compartment to convince the two remaining ratings that they should cooperate with Michael's engineering officer. Then Erhardt climbed up to the bridge.

Hugo Schroeder's countenance was apprehensive as he greeted his captain. His eyes reflected great anxiety. "There's no longer any smoke from the trawler, Captain. She's not listing from flooding either." His eyes were troubled as he looked at Walter Erhardt. "Most of our men are back aboard. They came back on our own inflatables, and some on the dories. Yet there are still men aboard that trawler."

Erhardt fixed his binoculars on the fishing boat. He could see that Ismael, the ugly Turkish fisherman, had just about completed rigging the trawling gear to transfer the torpedoes and heavier crates of explosives.

"Mr. Schroeder, you have been on duty up here much too long. You've had nothing to eat this morning and you deserve a break. There's fresh coffee and pastries in the galley." He pressed the button for the control room and said, "Mr. Rather, I'm relieving Mr. Schroeder and taking the conn up here. He and the lookouts deserve a break and I'm sending them below now." His voice rang with sincerity. "I'd appreciate it if the two lookouts could be taken up to the torpedo room after their break to assist the others."

The weather hadn't been a major consideration when final plans were being devised, but Erhardt had indicated that clouds, rain, fog, windy surface conditions, or anything that limited visibility was preferable. A surfaced submarine, particularly one near a vessel that was smoking, would provoke suspicion.

This morning had begun perfectly. But now the wind was abating considerably, and as a result, the swells were also decreasing. Erhardt studied the cloud formations above him and decided that the front that had passed through was weakening rapidly. Visibility would once again be sharp for any nearby aircraft, and he didn't want to be spotted on the surface. This rendezvous point had been selected because it was outside air-traffic patterns, but there was no point in chancing a random sighting.

Erhardt depressed the switch for engineering. "I'm about to go alongside the trawler. Are watch stations manned and ready?"

"Engineering is ready." It was Michael's man who answered.

Erhardt switched to control. "Control room, ready to go alongside?"

"You have experienced submariners manning all positions in control, Walter." Soraya's voice carried a trace of irritation. "Believe me, these men are ready."

"Very well."

Otto Rather listened to Erhardt's words as they came over the intercom, unable to accept what he was hearing. *Heinz Waller* was no longer under German command, and the man in the conning tower was no longer a German as far as Rather was concerned. He had served as executive officer under three captains now and he refused to believe that the finest submarine in the German navy had reached such an ignominious plight. Why these people—Erhardt especially—had allowed him to survive this long was beyond him, but he was sure his remaining hours, maybe minutes, were severely limited.

But there were two words that continued to course through Otto Rather's brain—*Whiskey Alfa*—one of the basic squadron circuits programmed into the communications system. Rather had never operated the equipment, but he'd watched the radioman out of curiosity when messages were being sent. He was certain that the designation of each circuit was listed over the appropriate button. All you had to do was push that button and the transmitter cycled to that circuit. Then you transmitted your message.

He looked to his side. *Waller*'s planesman was terrified. He sat on the deck staring dejectedly at his feet. Lieutenant Schroeder, a few meters away, still appeared overwhelmed by the presence of the guns that had greeted him as he came down the ladder into the control room. There was no reason to involve anyone else. Another person would probably just make it that much more difficult to accomplish what had to be done.

Otto Rather made his decision as *Heinz Waller* began to maneuver toward the trawler. The familiar purr of the silenced diesels came to his ears. He felt the slight shudder as the propeller dug into the ocean water. The deck tilted slightly as they began to turn.

Casually, as if he'd seen something out of place and thought maybe he'd investigate it, Rather eased toward the forward hatch. He even moved some items aside on top of the chart table as he stopped by it momentarily. Erhardt's maneuvering orders were coming quickly. The new crew seemed mesmerized by their ability to take over so smoothly.

It was no more than ten short steps to the forward hatch, but each step was an eternity. Then, as if he'd been struck by lightning, Rather dove through the opening. Bouncing to his feet, he yanked the heavy metal door from its clip and, as Soraya's Uzi whipped around in his direction, slammed it. He spun the dogging wheel as tight as possible, knowing he had only seconds to get to the radio shack.

The curtain was back as he lunged through the entrance to the tiny space. A radioman's chair was in front of the panel that Rather remembered studying intently one day. His eyes seemed to blur as they scanned the panel. *Where the hell . . . ?*

There! He saw the circuit designations that had been neatly typed by the radioman. They were covered with Scotch tape and ran vertically down beside the switches. His index finger ran down the list . . . searching. *Where the hell is it?*

There it is. Whiskey Alfa!

He flipped the switch. A red light came on next to the Whiskey Alfa designation. He heard the wheel spinning on the hatch from the control room. *Hurry, Otto . . . do your duty . . . do your duty . . .*

Was he saying that out loud or just thinking it? He fumbled for the microphone lying on the desk, picked it up, and depressed the speaking button. "This is . . ." Nothing. He wasn't transmitting.

His hand ran down the wire . . . not plugged in. He jammed the plug into the transmitter receptacle. There was a crash outside as the hatch was flung open and slammed back into its clip. Voices . . . shouting . . .

"This is *Heinz Waller* . . ." He could hear his voice. He was transmitting. "On the surface . . ."

Soraya held the Uzi's trigger down. The radio shack exploded with violent sound.

Otto Rather felt the world crash into his back as he was hurled forward. "Help . . ."

Heinz Waller's executive officer smashed face first into the panel, then was hurled sideways as the Uzi's bullets tore into him. Soraya, angry with both Rather and herself, was beyond control. She held the trigger down until the clip was expended.

The Uzi's din was followed by absolute silence. The submarine's communications equipment was shattered. The radio shack was spattered with blood and pieces of flesh. Otto Rather was unrecognizable.

"I need men on deck to handle lines," Erhardt called

down on the intercom. "We're about to come alongside the trawler."

There was no confirmation.

"Control room!" Erhardt's voice was sharp and commanding. "This is still a military vessel. I expect a response to each of my orders."

Erhardt knew someone in control was pressing the intercom switch because he could hear background noise. That was followed by some garbled phrases in Arabic.

Then Soraya's voice came through. "Walter . . . your executive officer . . . he got to the radio. . . ."

"What?" His roar of anger leapt across the water to *Baghdad,* but it could not be heard in the control room because Soraya was still speaking.

". . . don't know how your radios work. I'm not sure whether he was able to send anything."

"How long was he out of your control?" Erhardt held his breath as he waited for her response.

"Twenty seconds maybe. Maybe a little more."

Hardly enough time to accomplish anything. "And what is his current status?"

"Dead."

"Good. Let him serve as an example to the others."

FEDERAL REPUBLIC OF GERMANY

FLASH

CLASSIFICATION—TOP SECRET

FROM: COMMANDER SUBMARINE SQUADRON FOUR
TO: ALL COMMANDS, WALLER RESCUE OPERATION

1) GARBLED VOICE RADIO MESSAGE RECEIVED FROM SOURCE SAID TO IDENTIFY ITSELF AS HEINZ WALLER AT 1121Z OVER SUBRONFOUR CIRCUIT WHISKEY ALFA.
2) WALLER SAID TO BE ON SURFACE. HELP REQUESTED.
3) NO POSITION REPORTED. NO OPPORTUNITY TO DIRECTION FIND.

4) ALL UNITS ARE DIRECTED TO MAINTAIN A GUARD ON SUBRON FOUR CIRCUIT WHISKEY ALFA.
5) ALL UNITS UTILIZE ECM LOCKED ON CIRCUIT WHISKEY ALFA FOR DIRECTION FINDING PURPOSES.

Baghdad carried two torpedoes that had been specially designed for the mission. The process of transferring torpedoes at sea during absolutely calm weather is, at best, hazardous. For the trawler, swinging the two torpedoes out over the submarine and positioning them above the loading slide to the torpedo room was the easy part. *Heinz Waller* and *Baghdad* were lashed together as securely as possible. The intention was that they would move in tandem with the sea. But lowering a torpedo at the proper angle to enable it to slip down the shoot into the torpedo room was a challenge.

Neuner, the torpedo rating that Erhardt had chosen to survive, was told that his chances of living were as good as anyone else's if he cooperated. Soraya escorted him on deck to show him the man on the trawler whom he would be forced to work with. She even explained Ismael's temperament. Neuner was also reminded that failure to follow orders would cause a message to be sent to terrorists ashore who would then eliminate his family. While the trawler's men had all come from submarines with similar equipment, this was a new vessel and they depended on the frightened German torpedoman who knew the intricacies of *Waller*'s gear. The result was that Neuner worked as hard as any of Michael's Arab people to insure the operation moved smoothly.

The first torpedo required almost an hour to secure. The second took only twenty-five minutes. During that period, while the submarine's fuel tanks were being topped off from the trawler, Walter Erhardt generally divided his time between haranguing and encouraging the men and worrying over being sighted by an aircraft. And as the second torpedo was released from *Baghdad*'s winch into the custody of the submarine's work force, he was badgering Michael to complete his final duties aboard the trawler. The remaining

German seamen aboard the trawler had been forced to assist them. Now they were no longer necessary—and *Baghdad* had served her purpose. Everything had been removed, except for a life jacket with the S-252 designation stamped on it. It was meant to mark the grave of *Heinz Waller*.

As soon as the forward hatch was watertight, and even before the second torpedo had been reported secured, S-252 submerged. Though that was totally contrary to the safety habits that Erhardt constantly preached, he felt like the rabbit who had just scampered down his burrow to escape the dogs chasing him. He and *Heinz Waller* were back in their natural habitat.

The search and rescue aircraft from La Rochelle had been flying an east-to-west pattern, gradually working south from a line that had been arbitrarily established at the latitude of Saint-Nazaire. A little more than two hours into their search, as their plane banked around to the south, both pilot and copilot saw a brilliant flash on the horizon. They flew directly to the source.

"La Rochelle Control, this is SAR One Zero. Over."

"This is La Rochelle. Go ahead One Zero."

The plane gave its coordinates. "We are currently flying over unidentified wreckage. We were attracted by what we assume was an explosion. Small oil fires are still burning themselves out on the surface, but there is too little wreckage available to determine what kind of vessel was here. No life rafts. No life preservers. No sign of life. Suggest surface craft be dispatched to area ASAP to evaluate wreckage. That's going to be the only way we'll have a chance of identifying what was out here."

"Well, Mr. Schroeder, it's time we talk." The two men faced each other in the control room.

Hugo Schroeder said nothing. He'd remained in approximately the same position since the executive officer's fruitless dash from the control room. He'd considered his options and concluded that he was now the only individual aboard who could possibly give a warning about the submarine's fate. He still possessed the signaling device given to him in the squadron headquarters. He could choose not to cooperate, which would hasten his death. Or, if given the chance, he could go along with Erhardt.

"I can see you've developed a dislike for me." Erhardt smiled pleasantly. "I feel badly about that because you are truly the finest submarine officer I've encountered in quite a while." He raised his eyebrows in question. "Come now, Mr. Schroeder, aren't you going to say something pleasant about those kind words? *Thank you* would be adequate."

"Thank you, Captain. I appreciate your trust." *Was there a chance?*

"I'm sure you do, even though you still don't care for me." He gave Schroeder a comradely pat on the shoulder. "You'd be a poor officer if you weren't concerned for your ship, wouldn't you? I'm sorry I can't tell you more. The past few hours have indeed been strange and I don't expect you to approve of what's happened. What I would like you to do is accept the fact that we're now on a special mission, a very special one. When it is over, I'm sure you will realize that the loss of your fellow crewmen was a necessity, a sad but necessary one."

"Can you explain, Captain?" It was important to be compliant if he was to remain alive long enough to send his signal, perhaps even to help someone to locate *Waller.*

"I'm afraid I don't have all the details myself, Mr. Schroeder. And even if I did, I probably couldn't reveal them. If you will accept the fact that our mission will be for the betterment of Germany, that will be enough for now." He chewed on his lower lip before continuing. "Since I don't know how many days we will remain at sea, I need someone to relieve me, someone I can trust. I selected you soon after we went to sea because you exhibited all the positive traits of a fine German submariner, and that is why I'm offering you this opportunity. I'll need sleep over the coming days. I can't keep the conn forever. If I allow you to relieve me, will you promise to cooperate and follow my orders even though I can't tell you more at this time?" He held up an index finger and smiled oddly. "Of course, I can't leave you alone, so you don't have to worry about being unfaithful to your captain. There will always be someone here watching you. But this is a gift of life. Now, what do you say to that?"

Hugo Schroeder studied Erhardt carefully before closing his eyes and taking a deep breath. This was his only chance.

"I'll recommend you for command upon our return," Erhardt added as an inducement.

Of course there would be no return, but Schroeder said, "Certainly, Captain. I prefer to remain alive. You have my word."

Hussein came down late that day from his mountain retreat. From the moment the armored vehicle that carried him left the security of his camp, a system of lookouts covered every mile that Hussein traveled. The distance wasn't great, but the safety measures were so extensive that it was dark by the time he arrived at the communication center.

When Michael established contact on the radio he'd transferred from *Baghdad, Heinz Waller* was surfaced off Cape Ortegal on the northwest coast of Spain.

"How long will it take you to arrive at Gibraltar?" Hussein asked.

"Forty-eight hours," Michael answered after consulting with Erhardt. "May I have my orders now?"

As always, Hussein smiled a smile that Michael could not see and would not have understood. "Pass through Gibraltar. Once you have done that, contact me again. Forty-eight hours—I'll be waiting."

CHAPTER TEN

DAY TWO

Captain Tom Davis, staff intelligence officer in Sixth Fleet headquarters, had been following the disappearance of the German submarine *Heinz Waller* with special interest since the initial report that she was missing. Submarine incidents were rare, but when they occurred, they attracted attention because an entire ship's crew was at stake.

Davis found the current situation especially unusual because the *Waller*'s previous commanding officer had disappeared under odd circumstances. That the German navy refused to comment on that initial incident, in fact attempted to sweep it under the rug, now piqued his curiosity even more. He was a man consumed by detail, the trait that had made him a superb intelligence specialist.

Successful military intelligence practitioners understand that their trade is not restricted to purely military affairs. Nor do those who operate within this unique arena limit themselves specifically to concerns or activities involving military intrigue. There are many who would claim that military intelligence thrives because of military distrust of civilian intelligence activities. A thorough staff intelligence officer, especially one on duty overseas, will have his people sifting through every military, political, industrial, police, and media source available to them. Like their civilian counterparts, they will develop a coterie of sources on a professional and social basis who can furnish tidbits that expand their comprehension of a particular subject.

That was how Tom Davis had directed the attention of his staff toward *Heinz Waller* in the first place. Much earlier than the German navy would have appreciated, his sources reported the disappearance of Hans Preminger, the recovery of his body, and the forensic determination that he had been murdered. The investigation coordinated by Herman Gleick and the reluctance of the German navy to accept the detective's findings piqued his curiosity. And word of Gleick's eventual visit to the resident CIA agent at the U.S. Embassy in Berlin attracted Davis's attention even more. He knew Lyford only by reputation, but he'd talked with him many times by phone.

Originally, Davis had left what appeared to be an unfortunate incident to his subordinates to investigate. Any murder of a senior military officer might have a greater meaning than civilian authorities could understand. Such incidents, unfortunately, occurred. But what happened in February became more important in early April with the disappearance of the submarine that the murdered officer had once commanded. Then there was the mysterious, abbreviated voice message ostensibly from *Waller*. When CIA agent Lyford happened to mention during a phone call that the case also included a woman suspected of being an Arab terrorist, Davis's personal attention became paramount. That was why he journeyed to Kiel, on Lyford's advice, to meet with Detective Gleick.

"My curiosity has unfortunately attracted more attention than I anticipated or, I must admit, care for, Captain Davis." Herman Gleick removed his rimless glasses and began polishing them meticulously with his handkerchief. "I'm an investigator, you see, and we like to conduct our efforts quietly without others knowing what we're actually hoping to accomplish."

Tom Davis's face softened appreciably and he made his best effort at smiling benignly. "I can't agree more, Mr. Gleick. You will note that I'm not in uniform. I rarely wear it off American military premises." The intelligence officer was short, about Gleick's size, but his features were much more pronounced. Where the German was mostly bald with a blond fringe that hung over his ears, Davis was thinning, but his hair was still black and precisely trimmed. His eyes were black, complexion dark, teeth extremely white when he smiled, and the observant Gleick would have assumed he was of Spanish descent if not for his name. Davis would have appreciated being told that he radiated precision.

Gleick blinked without revealing whether the uniform made any difference to him. "Having Americans associated with me could limit my investigation. I prefer being obscure. Americans don't tend toward obscurity."

Again, the precise smile. "And I, too, embrace anonymity when I'm working. Please believe me when I say that our conversation will remain between the two of us, and I'll be the first to inform you if my responsibilities involve others, including those within my own community."

"Why are you so interested in Hans Preminger, Captain?"

"I'm not interested in him at all. I'm interested in the investigation because outside parties could be involved, specifically a terrorist element. My particular area of responsibility requires that I ensure that situations like the one you're investigating don't affect the U.S. One never knows." His teeth flashed precisely.

"You've been talking with Mr. Lyford."

"He's part of my network. We work together when something appears to demand a joint effort." Captain Davis was an expert at his job because he was meticulous to a fault. "Have any of your navy sources told you that a possible attempt was made by *Heinz Waller* to communicate over a special radio circuit?"

Gleick held his glasses up to the light and rubbed at something on one of the lenses that he'd apparently overlooked moments before. *Why didn't they inform me right away? After all* . . . "No, they haven't. But I do appreciate your sharing that bit of intelligence with me." He lifted a pad of yellow paper which had been covering an enlarged photograph. "This is the photo that Mr. Lyford and I selected as someone Hans Preminger might have been attracted to. Pretty girl, isn't she?"

"Very."

"And very easy to remember. There's no absolute proof, but I don't think there's any doubt that she was involved in Preminger's murder. Yesterday, as soon as I arrived back here from Berlin, I showed this photo to the manager of the building where we believe Captain Preminger was killed. There was no hesitation on his part. He identified this woman as the one who rented the apartment where we dug the spent 9mm bullet out of the wall. And please remember that your own CIA confirms that she is a member of a terrorist organization. They don't even know the name or who the leaders are, just that there is some sort of organization and that she is part of it." *And now* Heinz Waller *may not have sunk as reported.*

"You don't normally picture someone in her line of work as appealing. But I must say she's not bad." Davis considered Gleick's self-satisfied manner for a moment, then said, "You really don't have any doubts, do you?"

"Do you make such absolute statements when you harbor doubts, Captain?" *Are these American navy people as bull-headed as our own?*

"No."

"Neither do I," Gleick agreed.

"May I assume you are wondering whether these terrorists may have had a hand in the disappearance—or reappearance—of *Heinz Waller?"*

"You may."

Phil Salkin was unable to suppress pangs of remorse as he talked privately with his new Secretary of State. It was their final meeting before the latter's departure, and the President's mind drifted back to that first time when the concept of this historical summit was conceived. This should have been the dawn of Rupert Daniels's finest hour. Instead, the attainment, and most likely the historical credit, would fall to Lou Griffey. But that moment of nostalgia passed. Lou had worked in tandem with Rupert on this Middle Eastern summit. If it was indeed a success, then its success should be credited to the man who ushered those nations into a new era.

"It would be wonderful to be going with you, Lou. But I know when I'm not wanted."

"Not now anyway. Later, I hope." Griffey understood the emotions that lay just beneath the surface of Salkin's calm exterior, but there was no way to comfort a President. He and Salkin had become friends as well as professional associates, much in the manner of Harry Truman and Dean Acheson. But Rupert Daniels and Phil Salkin had been like brothers, so close over the years that those in-the-know in Washington knew how foreign policy would evolve before either man spoke on a subject. "Believe me, I understand how hard this is for you . . . how much it meant."

"It means a great deal, Lou. But remember, even Rupert and I had different objectives. I was . . . I am looking for a benchmark for this administration, something I can beat my chest over and say, 'look what we did.' Rupert Daniels had a passion, a desire to see a Middle Eastern peace that would stand because it was a compromise, rather than a triumph, for each country. Everyone would give a little, take a little . . . and the rest of the world would learn by example. My desires are a little more simplistic. You and Rupert were out of the same mold."

"I'll be on the scrambler every day at the end of each session." He noticed Salkin studying his fingertips, touching his thumb to them one at a time. The President needed to hear more than that. "There won't be any bullshit. If it's going bad, I'll tell you. Near the end of the week, if it looks to me like you should pack your bags, you better believe I'll be like a kid on his first date when you step out onto the *Wasp's* deck."

Phil Salkin's eyes twinkled. "Terrific." He winked at Griffey mischievously. "And when I step onto that deck, I'll think with that accent of yours that I'm being greeted by the Canadian foreign minister."

Griffey picked up the bait. No one ever tired of kidding him about his accent. "I keep telling you it was very cold where I grew up in upstate New York. Certain parts of the anatomy tighten up in that weather." Griffey's round face was lit with a cherubic grin.

"And I suppose that accent always holds everybody's attention because you don't quite sound like one of us." Salkin stood up and reached across his desk to shake Griffey's hand. "I know you're confident. I know you can handle these people. But take care of yourself, Lou. These people have made a tradition out of killing each other, and there's no telling how many others would like to see all of them turned into shark bait."

"The security's as good as if you were going to be right there with me."

Francis Waters had just steadied *Calm Seas* to bring the relative wind about ten degrees off her starboard bow. That was exactly how the approaching helicopter wanted it, and Will Riley had explained that they were to observe each pilot's wishes. An air controller sent over from *Wasp* had transmitted approach data to the pilot from the wing of *Calm Seas'* bridge as the aircraft grew from a speck in the sky to a large noisy helicopter. Now, he, too, watched as the helicopter descended toward the landing platform on the stern.

"Aren't our first VIPs showing up just a little bit early?" Waters asked.

"Nope. Inspection team," Riley answered.

"Not another. What are these guys inspecting . . . the heads?"

"Wrong again, Francis. Us. *Calm Seas.* Everything. Everybody. They're going to know this ship like your mama knew your shiny pink bottom."

"Has the whole world gone paranoid, Will?" Waters's expression was one of resignation. "How often has this got to happen? Our own people have done the same thing. The Israelis were here yesterday. Then the Turks. Then the Saudis. The Iranians this morning."

Riley gestured toward the helicopter which was settling gently on the landing platform. "Well now you get to say hello to the Libyans. They don't trust anybody, not Jews, not other Arabs, and definitely not us. I don't even think they trust each other."

It would be one more inspection team receiving an escorted tour through *Calm Seas.* They would see the quarters for each nation to ensure that none was larger or better appointed than their own. They would search their own quarters electronically for any foreign devices, anything out of the ordinary that might preclude their own representatives from coming aboard by the end of that day.

Then they would leave a person in those quarters until their representative arrived. Included in the tour would be the galleys and dining facilities, the engineering and storage areas, and the administrative and electronic spaces. They would also ask to see the records of each crew member, even though the background investigations of each individual had been forwarded earlier. And once they were grudgingly satisfied, they would depart with a warning that any hint of change would terminate their own country's involvement in the proceedings.

"Doesn't all this stuff frost your ass, Will?"

"No. I'm used to it."

"How can anyone get used to this shit?"

"Back home in Foggy Bottom, Francis, there would be innumerable bureaucrats creating innumerable checkoff lists, forms, absolutes . . ." He shook his head to emphasize his own disbelief. "More bullshit than you can conceive of in order to justify their jobs and cover their own asses within their own little field of responsibility. And it would all be to protect President Salkin or my boss, Lou Griffey. If I happened to be in their position, I suppose I'd do it all, too. So that's what these people are doing."

"I'm getting tired of having my chain yanked, Will. What is your real job?"

"Just another bureaucrat, Francis. It's just that I don't spend as much time at a desk as the others."

Riley was full of shit, but there was no point in antagonizing him now. "There's nothing those bureaucrats are going to come up with."

"Don't you believe that for a moment. They'll find something. They have to. Their middle name is persistence. As a matter of fact, did you know you're a very suspicious character?" Riley shook an index finger in Waters's direction as the engines on the Libyan helicopter were shut down. "You can't believe how many of these people have asked me why I have you aboard as my captain."

"Me?" Waters pursed his lips. "What do you mean, me?"

"You have a reputation, Francis. If some of them wanted to run some contraband, they might likely choose you because you have some background. I keep having to explain why I think you're a good guy."

Francis Waters looked disturbed. "I thought we'd gotten that out of the way."

"We have, but not all these others have. Let that be a lesson to you, Francis," Riley chided with an amused expression. "You thought it was all behind you. Just one mistake—one tiny little fuck up—and no one ever forgets it. Life can indeed be cruel. Security is paramount. Nothing is overlooked by anyone."

"You can't imagine how glad I'm going to be when this is over."

"By the end of today, we'll have everyone aboard. Then, like the lady said, Francis—'relax and enjoy it because it's going to be over before you know it.'"

A numb Hugo Schroeder sat at the wardroom table pushing his food from one side of his plate to the other. It had been twenty-four hours since *Heinz Waller* dove after taking aboard the last of the trawler's cargo. He hadn't expected to survive this long, yet here he was sharing the wardroom table with these people. His only chance to send a warning was the transmitting device, but there had been no opportunity to send his signal. Only the radio antenna had broken the surface when the one called Michael had used the communications equipment he'd brought on board.

Schroeder had decided that if an opportunity presented itself with what he considered a fifty-fifty chance of success, it was worth risking it. They were going to kill him eventually anyway. No one ever imagines they will actually be in a situation where they will choose death, but that had become an acceptable alternative now that *Waller* was in someone else's hands. Death would not be welcome, and he would be the only one to know it was honorable. There would be no statue memorializing Hugo Schroeder, but heroes never saw or knew statues had been erected in their honor. Yet he felt comfortable with his decision.

"Mr. Schroeder, starving yourself won't solve a thing," Captain Erhardt said jovially. "While you are not here by your own choice, I think this certainly is better than the alternative."

Schroeder didn't look up from his plate. Regardless of his

incredible situation, he knew he was one of only seven survivors of *Waller's* crew, including Erhardt. None of the other officers were alive. He'd been told by the torpedoman, Neuner, that the men brought forward to the torpedo room were all dead. Even though the crew had been told they were just being put to sleep until the capture of *Waller* was a reality, none of them were alive. Their corpses had been loaded in sealed, weighted bags and dumped over the side right after the torpedoes had been transferred from the trawler. He was still in the control room when the explosions aboard that vessel came across the water, and he'd heard the description of the effect of the blasts as Erhardt watched through the periscope.

The terrorists, Michael and Soraya, were at the table also, and like the rest of the Arabs who had come aboard, they were always armed. The thought passed through his mind that they didn't really trust Erhardt either. But their constant scrutiny was effective. Even when he'd awakened once during the night from a fitful sleep, he could make out someone fully awake watching over him. Neuner had whispered as they squeezed past each other in the passageway that it was no different for the five ratings—never for a moment were they alone, whether they were on watch, eating, sleeping, even using the head. It seemed these Arabs needed no rest.

"He's frightened, Walter," Michael commented.

"No, he's angry," Soraya said.

Schroeder looked up at her from his plate. Try as he could, he was certain his tired eyes radiated frustration and hatred. As long as Erhardt needed him, he saw no reason to make any effort with them.

"He wants to see us all dead," she concluded with an engaging smile in his direction. "And he's frustrated because there is no opportunity."

"I suppose she's right, Mr. Schroeder," Erhardt noted. "And I guess there's no reason I should have expected anything different. But you proved to be certainly the most valuable officer aboard in a very short time and I know I shall require your talents at certain moments."

"Everyone you've brought aboard seems to know this submarine quite well." It was the first time Schroeder had spoken directly to Erhardt since sitting down at the wardroom table. "It's beyond me what purpose there is in keeping any of us."

"There were arguments for doing away with all of you, believe me," Erhardt said cheerfully. "That Turk named Ismael would be just as happy to kill you all off. I believe he'd even dispose of me if the opportunity presented itself. But his friends here," he said, indicating Michael and Soraya, "know me well enough to acknowledge there are good reasons for everything I do. Their sailors are all graduates of our submarine school, and they've been trained in almost all the equipment aboard *Waller*. But their at-sea experience is with the Type-209s from their own countries. They're adapting quickly however," he acknowledged with a wry smile.

"Other than myself, no one knows how to handle this submarine as well as you. You're a natural, Mr. Schroeder. We make a good team. And I decided I needed someone expert at reloading the torpedo tubes, like Neuner. The rest, an extra planesman and some experts back in engineering, sort of supplement these other people. And we couldn't do without a cook."

"He's not impressed, Walter," Soraya commented. "He's going to make us forcefeed him."

Erhardt stuck a forkful of food in his mouth and continued to speak as he chewed. "Now, come on, Mr. Schroeder, eat. Your options are nil. There's nothing you can do about your situation. I assure you that our mission is short enough that you'll never be able to starve yourself in that time."

It was Soraya who spoke up again. She was smiling strangely as she reached out and patted Schroeder's hand. "I'd be disappointed if you didn't hate us, but I'll be even more upset if you make life unpleasant for yourself." She turned to Michael and said, "I don't know what it is about these blond German men. I'm finding myself strangely attracted to them."

Michael's lips narrowed. His eyes moved from Soraya to a mystified Schroeder, then back to Soraya again. There were times when sex and killing seemed far more important to her than their cause—yet he also knew she was implicitly trusted by Hussein. No matter how long their relationship lasted, it would remain impossible for him to understand why she said things like that. "Forget it, Soraya. You won't have the opportunity."

She found instant pleasure in the anger that sparked in Michael's dark eyes and her smile, one that seemed to include everyone in the tiny wardroom, expanded as her fingers closed around Schroeder's hand. She held on tightly when the German tried to pull away.

"Keep your hands to yourself, Soraya." Michael looked away from her in an effort to control himself.

When Schroeder again attempted to pull back, she grasped his hand in both of hers, digging her nails into his wrist. "If it becomes necessary, Schroeder, I suppose I could even force-feed you." She turned brightly to Michael. "Objections?"

Michael's gaze settled back on Soraya, but now his expression had changed from anger to blankness. She was crazy and he wasn't about to let her drag him into one of her silly games that normally ended in wild sex. There was no time. No place. "There's not nearly enough time for him to starve himself to death. The hell with him."

Soraya pouted and gradually relaxed her grip. Michael wouldn't play.

Schroeder folded his hands beneath the table and made an effort to center his attention on Erhardt. "Where are we now? Where are we going?" he asked.

"I'm happy to tell you everything, Mr. Schroeder, within reason," Erhardt answered pleasantly. "I intend to share as much as I know with you, although I'm not yet allowed to explain why we were selected for this mission." That seemed the best way to approach Schroeder. "We're about midway down the coast of Portugal. We'll pass Lisbon to port shortly after eighteen hundred this evening. At about this time tomorrow, I'm planning to be about fifty kilometers west of Gibraltar. After we enter the Mediterranean, I can honestly say I don't know where we're going from there. Even Michael has no idea. Isn't that right, Michael?" Anything was better than the tension between Michael and Soraya.

"You may handle him any way you care to, Walter," Michael responded truculently. "That's up to you. I really have nothing to say to him, and . . ."

Angry shouts across the passageway, one in German, both high-pitched, were followed by a cry of agony. Michael was closest to the door and bolted into the passageway where he came up abruptly against an enraged Ismael. Angry words in Arabic followed. Then they floundered into the wardroom, Ismael pushing Michael backward.

Michael regained his balance and, barking sharply at Ismael in Arabic, grasped him firmly by the shoulders. Then he said to Erhardt, "Your people, Walter, apparently do not understand that they are prisoners or that they are alive only because of us."

Schroeder stared in wonder. Erhardt was actually being threatened. What was his real relationship with these people?

Ismael shook free and pushed past him in Erhardt's direction, restrained only by Michael's grip on his belt. He waved a fist in Erhardt's face and shouted in broken German, "Either you tell German swine they do what I tell, or I kill you next." His swarthy face was as flushed as it would likely ever be. He waved an index finger close to Erhardt's nose. "I don't care who you are. You shit, too," he exclaimed. "Killing you just pleasure as any others."

"It seems we are going to have to cook for ourselves now," Michael said. He had one arm around Ismael's chest and was gradually easing him away from Erhardt. "Your cook apparently could not rid himself of some of his bad habits. He lifted a knife in Ismael's direction when he took some food from a platter."

Hugo Schroeder realized at that moment how vital cooperation with Erhardt really was if he were to live long enough to use that transmitter. Erhardt had not only given him life, he was a protector. Without him, Schroeder knew that that madman would kill him. It became even more important, therefore, to make Erhardt believe that he would cooperate completely with him. Schroeder knew that was the only means he possessed if he was ever to climb the submarine's sail to open air.

"So Ismael killed him," Erhardt stated, "for a bite of

food." He'd remained calm through Ismael's rage. Now he glanced up at Ismael with evident distaste. "We are on a mission, a military mission, Ismael. Regardless of the situation, people on a submarine must conduct themselves in an absolutely military manner or both the ship and the mission are in danger." Erhardt's voice and manner were calm, as if he were reasoning with a child. "Submarines do not function like cruisers or aircraft carriers or destroyers, and especially not like Arab trawlers. And they do not operate with animals or low-grade morons as crew members." His eyes never left Ismael's, and he spoke slowly and precisely expecting that the man would understand his German.

Ismael knew enough of the language, and he understood by Erhardt's countenance the gist of what was being said. The revulsion in the German's eyes as he looked Ismael up and down required no translation.

"He is dead man, Michael." Ismael spat out the words. He stared into Erhardt's eyes with hatred as he spoke. "When I have chance, I will cut out his heart."

Michael grasped Ismael by the shirt, turning him slowly around. "You'll do nothing of the sort," he said in Arabic. "We cannot function without him . . ."

"I don't know what you are saying to him, Michael," Erhardt interrupted, "and I don't particularly care. You know as well as anyone that I remain in command of this submarine, and my word is law. There is no room for animals on this ship, and that man is an animal. We are on a mission more important than Ismael will ever be able to comprehend. Understand right now that I hold you responsible for his actions. Any failure in this mission will be entirely on your shoulders. There is no room for questions, no explanations, no nothing. Is that clear?"

Ismael had understood Erhardt's words well enough, and now his eyes, burning with hatred, turned to Michael.

"I understand, Walter. Ismael understands also." Very gently, Michael's fingers touched the Turk's cheek and turned his head until Ismael's face was opposite Michael's and their noses seemed to touch. "You do understand, don't you Ismael? Captain Erhardt will bring us to wherever we are to complete our mission. Only he can do that. Then we will be depending on you. Your torpedoes will be critical." His voice was soft and reassuring. "You understand that the mission is more important than anything we will ever do again in our lives . . . don't you?" he finished in a whisper.

Ismael's eyes were blank when he turned them toward Erhardt. "I understand."

Erhardt's expression never changed. "I will conduct my first drills with this crew this afternoon. There are now twenty of us. I began this cruise with six additional men. I expect this smaller crew to function exactly as a full complement. I can't afford to lose another individual. Each man I chose from my original crew was selected because I considered them vital. I expect no further confrontations." He dismissed Ismael with a wave of his hand. "You remain responsible for him, Michael."

A second transport helicopter settled gently onto *Wasp*'s flight deck, rocking slightly on its shocks as the rotors began to slow. It was parked in an area designated especially for those helicopters conveying the staffs for each delegation.

Rear Admiral Turner watched from the bridge as the doors slid open. Seven people—five men and two women, members of the Israeli delegation—stepped down onto *Wasp*'s flight deck. Their reaction was no different from others arriving for the first time. Whether civilians landed on a giant, nuclear attack carrier or a smaller amphibious type, their curiosity would win out. Their gaze would sweep gradually from one end to the other, always fascinated at the extent of the flight deck. Then, shading their eyes against the sun, they'd study the carrier's island rising above them and wonder why the ship wasn't listing to that side. A few would inch over to the edge of the flight deck and peer down at the ocean rushing by so far below.

Carriers, Rear Admiral Turner knew, inspired awe in newcomers. Each time he arrived aboard one, even though he'd commanded a carrier before becoming commodore of this amphibious group, they still managed to amaze him.

Seven people had also alighted from the first helo to land. That one had carried the Egyptian delegation. Each country was limited to seven individuals, including each nation's ambassador to this summit meeting. Since that figure also included translators, a tremendous amount of responsibility was placed on each individual, a requirement that the late Rupert Daniels had insisted upon. If fourteen nations were going to come to a meeting of the minds, no one country could appear with more delegates than another. While they could decide the makeup of their own group, seven members each made them equal.

Turner had read Lou Griffey's organization plan three times. Each time he found it remarkable how much the success of this summit rested on human interaction and psychological factors as opposed to face-to-face negotiations. The emphasis on equality was evident at every stage. That concept had been clarified from the first day the summit had been proposed to those countries involved.

Each nation had been allocated a suite aboard *Calm Seas.* No suite was larger or more luxurious than another. Each suite was composed of a small office/living space and two tiny bedrooms and a shared toilet. The second bedroom was for whomever the senior delegate chose, whether it was a security guard, translator, mistress, secretary, special chef, or selected government official. The remaining five members of each delegation would occupy private quarters aboard *Wasp* and they, too, would find absolutely equal treatment.

The kosher galley aboard *Calm Seas* had been planned by Rupert Daniels before he ever contacted a soul, and he'd made it clear to each diplomat that the United States considered it a courtesy rather than a privilege. It was proportionately smaller and had been stocked earlier that day by the Israeli security team that arrived to inspect every inch of their host ship. Each senior Islamic delegate was asked beforehand if there was an equivalent courtesy they would appreciate.

The galley for the Arab participants had been rebuilt on a modular basis to accommodate the needs of each nation. Individual refrigerators and cooking facilities were available, allowing them to separate themselves or share if they so desired. The galley was under the management of *Calm Seas'* chef, who had arrived on a temporary assignment from the QE2's five-star galley the day before they departed Monte Carlo. He would prepare gourmet meals for the main dining room and assist with special diets for those ambassadors who preferred to avoid shared tables. A steward was assigned to each suite to respond to individual needs and serve meals to those who preferred privacy.

It had been anticipated that the fourteen ambassadors would eventually gravitate to the main dining salon as the summit progressed. Rupert Daniels had noted in his first personal letter to each delegate that he hoped men and women of reason, seeking to find a common ground, would come together as much over the cordiality and fellowship of the dining table as a conference table. Lou Griffey and Will Riley had reinforced his wishes.

Rear Admiral Turner marveled at what he considered a touch of genius in bringing these people together in this manner as he browsed through the organization plan for the last time.

A speck on the horizon was growing into a third helicopter carrying the Iraqi delegation when Jake Steele appeared on the flag bridge beside Turner.

"Afternoon, Commodore," he said, saluting. "Look who's coming to dinner." He indicated the approaching helicopter. "Yesterday's bad guys."

"Today, they're all gentlemen and ladies, Jake." He recognized a message on a clipboard tucked under Steele's arm. "Got something interesting for me?"

Jake handed Turner the clipboard. "Could be. A second opinion would be nice though."

Rear Admiral Turner scanned the message, then read it more closely the second time. It was the initial report from the French SAR headquarters in La Rochelle concerning a blast at sea that had been so powerful there was little left to identify. His forehead wrinkled. He stroked his chin thoughtfully. Then he glanced at Steele out of the corner of his eye curiously and saw that the other man was intent on watching the next helicopter drop down to its marked spot on the flight deck. "Since the explosion was so powerful, do you think this might be the same fishing boat that they traced to Benghazi, the one they wanted us to worry about? What was the name—*Baghdad?*"

"I thought about that, yes." Steele watched the helicopter's portside wheels touch the deck first, then settle down on the starboard side. The roar of its engines died at a signal from the flight-deck coordinator. "I'd like to wait for an analysis, but it seems to me that the few pieces of wreckage French search and rescue have picked up are so small that there must have been high explosives involved. No civilian ship would carry stuff like that."

"And . . ." Turner prompted.

"If the burns on the pieces they do pick up are just diesel fuel, I wouldn't know what to say." Like all SEALs, Jake Steele was highly trained and skilled with explosives. "On the other hand, those intelligence reports that got our RIBs revved up said that *Baghdad* was loading weapons. If they find traces of plastic or something else just as sophisticated, perhaps we have some ragheads that screwed up and blew themselves into tiny pieces."

"But what were they doing in the Bay of Biscay if intelligence thought we should worry about them here in the Med?" Rear Admiral Turner studied the Iraqi delegation alighting from the third helicopter and decided they displayed a combination of both awe and arrogance. Would they know anything about a fishing boat loading suspicious cargo in Benghazi or one that had disappeared mysteriously in the Bay of Biscay?

"I suppose I should raise Sixth Fleet intelligence on the scrambler and see what a little prying can do."

"Why don't you do that, Jake. And while you're at it, why don't you ask them for me about that German submarine that's missing."

Steele appeared curious. "No sign of it yet?"

"Not a thing. There's a search operation going on in the Atlantic. One of our carriers is involved up on the northern fringe. I wouldn't have known any more about it except for the daily intelligence reports Sixth Fleet puts out for all major commands." He glanced at Steele. "I don't like submarines. They're sneaky."

CHAPTER ELEVEN

DAY THREE

FEDERAL REPUBLIC OF GERMANY

OPERATIONAL IMMEDIATE

CLASSIFICATION—TOP SECRET

FROM: COMMANDER SUBMARINE SQUADRON FOUR
TO: ALL COMMANDS, WALLER RESCUE OPERATION

REF: FOLLOW-UP REPORT FROM LA ROCHELLE SAR UNITS CONCERNING YESTERDAY'S EXPLOSION VICINITY 5W45N.

1) SAR PERSONNEL NOW REPORT RECOVERY OF S-252 LIFE JACKET, LITTLE WRECKAGE, NO SURVIVORS.
2) SURFACE UNITS CURRENTLY APPROACHING SITE TO INVESTIGATE.
3) ALL UNITS ARE DIRECTED TO CONTINUE SEARCH IN ACCORDANCE WITH ESTABLISHED PROCEDURES UNTIL ON-SITE SAR CONFIRMS FINAL ANALYSIS OF SURFACE DEBRIS.

Type-212 submarines can remain submerged for extended periods of time due to their sophisticated closed-cycle, air-independent propulsion (AIP) system. Oxygen-hydrogen fuel cells and life-support systems similar to those of nuclear submarines allow them to become true submersibles, although their time beneath the surface is limited by their size. With their submerged displacement close to 1800 tons, they are but a quarter of the volume of an American nuclear attack submarine. This reduced space for machinery, weapons, living space, and food limits the staying power of the crew. Yet there are benefits to being small. They can also be even quieter and more elusive than their more highly touted nuclear-powered sisters, and nearly undetectable in shallow waters or beneath thermal layers, caused by sharp changes in water temperature, that deflect sound. Under electric power, they become next to invisible.

Heinz Waller remained beneath the surface during the daylight hours as she followed a south-southwesterly course well off the Portuguese coast. Erhardt had decided to come to the surface that night to dispose of the cook's body. When she surfaced just after midnight after her second full day at sea, the glare of Lisbon's lights loomed to the northeast.

"Lookouts, surface sector reports." Walter Erhardt had been the first to scramble onto the submarine's sail and was already scanning the sky on his own.

"Nothing," came a voice to Erhardt's right.

"Same here. Nothing," echoed another to his left.

Erhardt was calm and steady as he responded. This was the first time for Michael's men on his bridge. "This is still a German submarine and it will continue to function as one. Both of you were trained in German submarine schools and you learned exactly how a lookout reports. I don't care how you reported in your own navy. Our mission is critical and we will function in a military manner at all times. Once again now. Lookouts, surface sector reports."

"Starboard lookout, sir. I have no surface contacts in my sector."

"Port lookout, sir. I have no surface contacts in my sector."

"Very well. That is exactly as it should be done. Commence air sector survey." He pressed a switch on the interior communications system. "Radar, report."

Walter Erhardt's voice boomed from the speaker in the control room. A cursory sweep from snorkel depth had indicated there was nothing on the surface within five miles.

"Four contacts within ten miles. One directly off the bow appears to be headed due west. Three astern appear to follow us."

"Aye," Erhardt grunted. The voice from radar was heavily accented, probably Spanish or Portuguese, he guessed. And the method of reporting was anything but military. The one reported as heading due west had probably come out of Gibraltar and was more likely swinging toward the northerly shipping lanes. The ones behind could be coming down to the Strait also. "Mr. Schroeder, get on the radar and train that operator in tracking and reporting procedures."

"Permission to come to the bridge?" It was Michael's voice calling through the hatch.

"Permission granted," Erhardt answered. He must have asked Schroeder what to do before he started up the ladder.

"The air smells good up here," Michael remarked as he squeezed through the hatch. "Quite a change down there, too."

"Nothing the matter with our air below," Erhardt answered. "Ask one of my engineers, if that crazy Turk of yours hasn't already killed them all off. Our air is scrubbed. Carbon dioxide removed. Farts, armpits, food, any foreign smell is purified." Michael hadn't been wearing the red night lenses before he came up and his eyes weren't accustomed to the darkness. Erhardt could see Michael much better than the other could see him. "You and your men have become too accustomed to that trawler. Fishing boats are dirty and they stink," he said distastefully.

"My men are submariners also," Michael countered. "I thought all of them lived like that . . ."

"Not in the German navy!" It was the first time Erhardt had come close to losing his composure. He had read the records of each individual Michael had brought aboard. They were indeed a talented lot. All of them had been trained at the German submarine school as required by the contract each of their countries signed before purchasing a submarine. Only one of them, from South Korea, had graduated below the top-ten percent of his class, but it appeared that even he was a natural at handling the planes.

Michael remained silent.

"There is no submarine force equal to our own. These men allowed their discipline to slip in the other navies. I will see that change in the next few days."

"A word of warning, Walter. Please be careful. These men are all Muslim. Their most recent training emphasized that they're on the path to paradise." He lowered his voice to be sure the lookouts wouldn't overhear what he was saying. "If a man can be molded into a fanatic, these men are a prime example. They're trained to hate infidels like yourself."

Erhardt grasped Michael by the arm, squeezing the upper muscle until Michael tried to pull away. "Until this mission, whatever it may eventually become, is successfully completed, there are no differences between us. My goal is the same as their goal, and it will only be accomplished if we all become one aboard this submarine. We will unite according to the demands of the commanding officer. Without me, you and all your men are helpless. The mission will fail. No eternal heaven for anyone. Allah will never greet any of you. Instead, you and all your men will face eternal damnation," he concluded nastily.

"They wouldn't believe that could happen."

Erhardt relaxed his grip. "So be it. But that is why I remain in command. That is why you will control that animal, Ismael, and that is why you will explain to these men why they will follow my training. The mission, Michael . . . the mission . . . the mission. Don't ever let that escape them."

They were interrupted by a voice coming over the bridge speaker. "Bridge, this is Radar. I have a contact bearing one eight five. It is on a course of three four five and it will pass us at a range of three miles. Each of the contacts astern are all opening ranges now. Mr. Schroeder says they appear to be heading into Lisbon."

"Bridge, aye." The accent was still heavy, but it was apparent that Schroeder had explained exactly what Erhardt expected. "You see, Michael, that wasn't difficult for your radar operator to relearn. All your men were trained in Bremerhaven, same school, mostly the same instructors. They can be retrained quickly. Now, tonight the ocean is calm." Their first night had been rough and *Waller* had not surfaced. "I intend to have the men come out on deck in two sections. They should get some fresh air. I want them to bathe, first with saltwater because our fresh water is limited. Then I will have a freshwater hose hooked up so they can rinse off quickly. Cleanliness was also taught in Bremerhaven."

"Is this to be done each night?"

"No, not at all. I think this will be the only time. Tomorrow evening we pass through Gibraltar, so we won't surface again. I want them to start out fresh, so that no one will have a reason to complain. No one will be different from the next." He gripped Michael's arm again. "Except for Soraya. Women are poison aboard ships, especially submarines. Now that we are out here, can you tell me why she is included?"

Michael could feel the fingers once again digging into his muscle. He made an effort to flex and tried to jerk away, but Erhardt's grip grew firmer.

"Out here, I am in command, Michael. Life is very different at sea." His voice lowered until he could barely be heard. "People die at sea and no one ever knows how or why. There are no bodies. You could disappear as easily as Soraya, or that animal, and no one would ever know. Why is she here, Michael?"

"Because she kills so easily."

"Be honest. They all do. All those men. Ismael lives to kill." He squeezed until Michael let out a grunt of pain. Then he eased up. "Tell me."

"None of them, not even Ismael, will kill you, Walter. They have been promised eternal damnation if they do. You should be pleased about that. And I don't think they would kill me either, unless it was a matter of survival for them. But Soraya would kill either of us if she judged it was necessary."

Erhardt released his grip.

"I've known her for a long time. But I don't know who she is close to or why she's been chosen. She doesn't say. She never will. Maybe she doesn't even take orders from Hussein. Maybe there's someone higher than him."

"And if there is, none of you know that?"

"That's why we're strong, Walter. Even if she does report to Hussein, I'm sure that when I make contact with him after we are on the other side of Gibraltar, Soraya wouldn't know any more than I do. None of us ever do. I'm sure whoever has placed her with us expects her to kill you or me, or even Ismael, if any of us ever consider jeopardizing the final mission."

"Tinker . . . tailor . . . soldier . . . spy . . ."

"What is that, Walter? I don't understand."

"That is exactly what your leader has ordained, Michael. Neither do Ismael or Soraya or any of our crew really understand. Nor do I really. We are at sea on a ship of despair . . ." His words drifted off into the night. "Go below, Michael. Explain to our crew of lost souls what their captain intends. Tonight we enjoy the fresh air, we cleanse our bodies, perhaps even our souls for the last time."

"Their souls are perfectly happy. They have been promised."

Erhardt paid no attention to him. "When we dive before sunrise, they are going to relearn everything they were taught in our wonderful German schools. We will soon have a mission which we shall complete. I have kept the best planesman in the navy to teach your best. My torpedoman is also the best. Schroeder can drive this boat like a race car. And my remaining engineers—all they need is backup in case there is an accident. Go on, Michael. Go below and tell them what their captain intends to do . . . so they might pass through to heaven," he added with a grimace.

An hour later, Erhardt called Schroeder to take his place on the bridge while he studied the charts in the control room. It was a test of sorts. Erhardt would instantly know if a contrary order was issued.

But he couldn't watch Schroeder's every move.

Hugo Schroeder's struggle to contain himself was internal. To allow his hands to shake, to display any of the emotion surging through his chest, anything at all suspicious, would shatter his chances. This opportunity seemed too good to be true. Erhardt was actually going to leave him on the bridge. Even if he had only thirty seconds, that would be more than adequate. Then the shock of a bullet shattering his skull would be a sweet release as long as he'd been able to activate his signal.

Moments after his captain dropped through the hatch into the control room and Schroeder had ordered the lookouts to complete visual sector air searches, a silent signal from *Heinz Waller* had been relayed by satellite to Submarine Squadron Four headquarters. S-252 was very much in existence.

And Hugo Schroeder remained very much alive. That was when he realized the human desire for survival was so powerful. Now, if he could only manage to do it one more time to reveal *Waller*'s track. . . .

Roland Lyford sipped the sparkling water tentatively, swirled it around in his mouth like wine, then swallowed it. "Nice."

Tom Davis beamed. "I've become very attached to the Italian waters. They beat the hell out of Perrier any day."

Lyford had suggested lunch at his favorite *gasthaus* when Davis called him the previous day from Bremerhaven. He made it a point to avoid this type of meeting in the U.S. Embassy to satisfy State Department protocol and the current ambassador's distaste for the CIA. "They have great homemade sausage here," Lyford said after the waitress left menus. "Nice sauerbraten, too."

"I think I've eaten everything in Europe. Just look at that." Davis patted his stomach affectionately. "My waistline is a notable example. Living in Italy with all that great pasta has done nothing but fill me out like a panda."

The CIA agent patted his own ample belly. "I can say the same for the local food here. Hell, if I drank beer, they'd have to roll me into the office. My employer doesn't look kindly on fat agents."

Never having met face to face before, they were going through the time-honored process of feeling each other out. They exchanged information on duty stations, specialties, and acquaintances that the other might have encountered.

Davis had mentioned his meeting with Detective Herman Gleick when he'd phoned to set a meeting with the CIA agent. Lyford finally asked, "How is my friend Gleick doing on that murder case of his, the one with the randy submarine captain? I'm assuming that's why you felt we ought to meet each other." Of course it was.

"I found him a very interesting man," Davis answered. "He's taken the information you gave him and constructed an interesting scenario. As he obviously told you, he learned from Preminger's wife that the good captain couldn't keep it in his pants. And from Preminger's associates, it became evident that the man led two entirely different lives."

"He did have a kinky side, didn't he?" Lyford snickered. "The sweetest ones always seem to be the horniest."

"Gleick talked with a shrink who explained that there are some men who see the women they're attracted to as sexual challenges, never as individuals. There is apparently a compulsion to prove their manhood again and again via sexual contact."

"I'm familiar with Preminger's compulsion. Gleick explained that. But the shrink angle is interesting, isn't it?"

"Compulsion," Davis acknowledged. "That's what Gleick decided. This shrink gave him a lecture about all the different levels and habits that make up compulsive behavior. There's a hell of a lot more guys than you'd imagine who just can't keep their dick out of the wrong places. But usually it involves very unstable types, not someone capable of commanding a submarine."

"I'd agree with that."

"So now Gleick's research gets a little more complicated. We have this Arab woman, extremely attractive, and Preminger has yet another challenge on his hands. But"—Davis tapped one index finger with the other—"you've confirmed for Gleick through your own sources that she's also attached to an unnamed organization whose goals not only are indefinite but we don't even know who they are or where they operate from."

"And I don't know any more than when Gleick visited me either," Lyford admitted. "None of my usual sources have come up with anything more yet."

Davis nodded. "So we seem to have an organization we know nothing about that very badly wants something from this German submarine captain. Did they get what they want? Why did they kill him?"

"Gleick's sure they were the ones who pulled the trigger?" Lyford asked.

"Gleick has no doubt this woman did Preminger in, even though he can't prove it. And you provided him with the only background anyone has on her. He has to go with that. What were they after? He doesn't know." He finished the bottle of sparkling water and said, "Let's order lunch and we'll sample a different label. Each one is unique, you know, once you get your head into these waters, especially the Italian ones."

Lyford sipped the water from the new bottle as if he were again sampling wine. He held it in his mouth, appeared to gargle, closed his eyes, and pronounced, "Nice. Very nice. I'll remember this." He picked up the bottle to study the label.

Tom Davis beamed.

Then Lyford returned to the subject. They'd been circling, waiting to see which one would confirm the other's suspicions. "I have to assume your interest is heightened because the submarine Preminger had been captain of is suddenly missing at sea . . . or supposedly missing."

Davis frowned. "You weren't informed the Germans received a signal via a communications satellite early this morning that supposedly came from the *Waller?*"

Lyford smiled. "My own source called me just before I left my office to meet you. He also said that the signal came from a position southwest of Lisbon." He shrugged as if to say he wasn't sure he trusted the information.

"You seem skeptical."

"Why not?" Lyford responded. "They've been trying to cover their asses since it all started. Plus, they've stated they'll follow it up on their own. My people don't know enough about who might have sent it or what's behind it all. If the signal is for real, did it come from an intelligence specialist the German navy put on board? And if they did, why'd they do it?"

Davis nodded. "Gleick should have mentioned that to you."

"I haven't talked with him today."

"He told me the guy was put on *Waller* to investigate Preminger's murder. That would make things a little heavier." Davis folded his arms and grinned. "How about if I toss out the concept of a kidnapped submarine. What would you say?"

"Pretty far-fetched . . . but I like it. Sounds like a movie I saw a few years ago. But who do you think might have stolen it?"

"Gleick's into Arabs." Davis shrugged. "Terrorists. Might as well make it a real movie."

"Well, I suppose I know a little more about those types," Lyford offered. "That's why Gleick contacted me in the first place."

"Where does the CIA see Arab terrorists fitting into this?" Davis asked.

"I don't know. I can't figure out what these Arabs might be after, especially out there in the Atlantic. My contacts haven't come up with anything yet and they say all the usual sources are dry."

Davis nodded. "I haven't the vaguest idea either. But this is one of those weeks where if something ugly happens, guys like us get blamed. How about making a deal?"

"You one of those nice people who trusts the CIA?" Lyford said with a grin.

"Never. But we have this international peace conference going on in the Med, and supposedly we may have the President putting in an appearance at the end of the week. So far, security's tight as a drum. Since we're both supposed to be working toward the same goal, and since we're both intuitive geniuses, how about if I spend my people's time trying to figure out where that submarine might be or if it even exists. And why don't you get your sources humping on this supposed terrorist organization. You picked out the girl, so you already have a handle on something. Gleick promised to call you at the end of each day with anything he'd come up with in Kiel."

"I'll buy that," Lyford agreed. "I don't want to look like an asshole with the President showing up on our turf."

"Me, too. I think I'm going to put in a call to the

intelligence officer on the *Wasp.* I trained him. Now I'll see how good he is."

"Twenty-four-hour weather report, Captain." The sailor brought his right hand smartly to a position just above his right eye, his message board extended toward Francis Waters. He waited for a return salute.

"Francis . . ." Will Riley said softly. He nodded in the direction of the radio messenger, a uniformed sailor transferred from *Wasp,* who was still holding his salute. "You're his captain."

"Oh . . ." Waters looked from the messenger to Riley and back to the messenger. "Shit . . . I forgot." Waters made an effort to return the salute, but it appeared more that he was shading his eyes against the morning glare.

Waters studied the weather report and handed it to Riley. "Nothing but blue skies," he quipped, "and calm seas."

"Perfect," Will acknowledged, glancing at the weather report.

"Am I going to have to go through that horseshit every day?" Waters asked with exasperation. "For Christ's sake, Will, if I want the weather I can go down to the radio room and read it myself. Better yet, it's usually more accurate if I step out on the bridge wing there and look at the sky. Color of the sunset's a pretty good guarantee of what's next. Sunrise, too. Lowering clouds mean rain. Lifting, thinning clouds mean a change. Want me to go on?"

"You know, I wasn't kidding about being a part of the task group. It's not my doing, but I think for the duration of our assignment you can officially be considered a naval vessel. That's why we've got live fresh-caught sailors aboard. President Salkin intends to make this look official. Makes the delegates more comfortable. Probably even gives them more of a feeling of security."

"Security? Look around you, Will." Waters covered the horizon with a sweep of his hand. In addition to *Wasp,* there were two LSDs, three LSTs, a fast combat support ship, two frigates, a cruiser, and a destroyer visible. "All those ships around us are what's called security. A mosquito couldn't make it through to us without a passport. Isn't this like waving a red flag?"

"As far as the crews of those ships are concerned, they're involved in a very complicated amphibious exercise. The Pentagon's even prepared a series of informational messages so that other countries' intelligence services are under that impression also. They've even worked with the Italian government to prepare an amphibious landing site in Sicily. We just hope we can fool everyone until the summit's complete."

"Is this everything?" Waters indicated the spread of surface ships.

"And three nukes cruising beneath the surface somewhere in the Med, Francis. Yes, that is definitely security, but with President Salkin and Lou Griffey involved, the Secret Service is more security-conscious than you can imagine. They spent months coordinating a plan with both military and civilian intelligence people. You can't imagine the staffs in the Pentagon who spent months preparing the operation order for this supposed landing, and actually believed it was going to take place. I can't even conceive of how many aircraft are above us right now, but I'm willing to bet there're a bunch of fighters playing tag with each other."

"I thought they couldn't fly anything like that off *Wasp.*"

"They can't. I suppose some of them are from the *Teddy Roosevelt,* and likely some land-based aircraft, too. *Roosevelt's* southeast of us, down toward Libya. And, of course, there have to be Hawkeyes out on the perimeter tracking every aircraft that's on a course that'll bring them within two hundred miles of us."

"I'll believe your story about perfect security when this is all over."

"Trust me," Riley replied firmly.

Waters looked at Riley curiously. "So what do I need real sailors for right here?"

"You have to realize that these delegates only feel comfortable with what they see. And they appreciate those starched white uniforms. Even the ones who still hate us understand that these sailors are symbolic. *Calm Seas* is a safe haven."

A red light on the ship's intercom in front of Waters flicked on. "Bridge, this is Radio. Voice transmission from *Wasp* as follows: We have a bird airborne to deliver a package to you. Be prepared to receive Doc Jock in approximately three minutes. Over."

Waters was puzzled. "Who the hell's Doc Jock?" he asked Riley.

Will smiled. "My boss. Lou Griffey. That's his official call sign. It's employed for security reasons to avoid using his actual name over voice radio. No one will ever figure out the U.S. Secretary of State is called Doc Jock."

Riley was looking through the binoculars at a helicopter coming toward them from *Wasp.* "Let's get back aft, Francis. Time for you to meet my boss."

Calm Seas' flight deck had been installed one level above the main deck and covered the narrow stern like a tent, overlapping on both sides. Other than a winch to haul a helicopter in safely during rough weather, the flight deck was bare. A navy air controller, who had come aboard with the first helo from *Wasp* the day before, was now talking the pilot in.

Waters and Riley watched from the main deck as the pilot approached *Calm Seas.* He eased his helo lower until he was about level with the height of the bridge and had matched the forward speed of the ship. Then the helicopter dropped the last few feet, landing with an audible thump.

When the engines had stopped and the door slid back, Lou Griffey hopped easily down to the deck. Griffey appeared the perfect bureaucrat, dressed in a dark pin-striped suit, white shirt, and burgundy-colored paisley tie. He carried a thick briefcase in one hand, with his crash helmet under his other arm. A sailor escorted him down to the main deck.

Will moved forward to shake hands with his boss, then introduced Waters.

"Glad to meet you," Griffey said, shaking Waters's hand. Then he turned back to Will and handed him the crash helmet. "Try it on for size."

Riley looked at him curiously. "What?"

"It's all yours, Will. The helo's waiting for you. You're on your way back to the *Wasp.* Lieutenant Germond, Admiral Turner's intelligence officer, will meet you on the flight deck."

"But . . . can't you tell me what . . . ?"

"Sure. There's some things coming into the admiral from Sixth Fleet that may alter our security plan somewhat. I said you were in charge of coordinating the decisions with the navy." He smiled and tapped an index finger on the helmet. "Go on, Will, suit up. Can't keep the navy waiting."

Griffey's first words after the helo had lifted off were: "She's gorgeous," indicating *Calm Seas* with a sweep of his hand. "You ought to see her from the air."

"I'd like to sometime." He reached for Griffey's briefcase. "Let me take that and show you your quarters. You'll be bunking in the captain's cabin."

They were moving forward on the main deck, and Griffey asked, "Did I evict you from your bed?"

"Not exactly. It was my choice. Will had you in a stateroom toward the stern. Since it looks like I'll be spending most of my time on the bridge while all our guests are aboard, I figured you might prefer to be separate from the delegates. You'll also be right by our radio room. Will tells me you'll be using that a lot."

"So where are you going to hang your hat while I'm using your cabin?"

They'd gone up a second ladder, and Waters held a watertight door open. "I have a roommate, or rather Will has won me as a roommate. There's plenty of space in his cabin for the small amount of time I'll be in there."

Griffey stepped through the door into the captain's cabin. "Hey, not bad. Are the quarters for the delegates as nice as this?"

"No complaints from their front men yet," Waters answered. "I haven't been told when the actual occupants will be coming aboard, but every nation has had someone here to check out living space, food-preparation areas, main conference room, and whatever else interested them."

"And we passed the test?"

"So far. They all agree each facility is equal to the next. The Iraqis and the Syrians had a couple of questions about the kosher galley, but they all felt better after they saw their own main galley." Waters perched himself on the corner of his desk. "When can we expect our guests to arrive, Mr.

Griffey? The schedule lists your first organizational meeting tomorrow morning at ten. They can't all show up at once, can they?"

"My preference would be for them to arrive from now on at their own convenience." Lou Griffey smiled wanly. "Unfortunately, if they did that, the first to arrive would be considered too anxious and thus ready to give in easily. All the others would consider the last one aboard to be treating them with disdain."

"A pecking order," Waters remarked.

"Exactly. So what you would see about nine thirty tomorrow morning if you were aboard *Wasp* would be fourteen adults on the flight deck being assigned to three helicopters by Admiral Turner. They'll allow the admiral to do that because then none of them appear more important than the next."

"Is it always this way for a conference?"

"Not necessarily. But here you've got Jews and Arabs. Volatile mix. Then among the Arabs, you have conservative fundamentalists, liberal Muslims who are trying to escape Third World status and join the rest of the world, and Arabs who have fought each other for centuries for deserts and waterholes and slaves. Of the two men who were able to accomplish the impossible and bring these diverse people together, Rupert Daniels is dead and Phil Salkin remains in the White House because he realizes that his presence would give the world the impression that the goal is an American peace. That is incorrect. These people were brought together by Rupert Daniels and Will Riley on the premise that we would moderate but would not influence the talks."

"Then why are you here?" Waters asked bluntly.

Griffey's expression was as serious now as it had been relaxed before. "I'm an ombudsman or interlocutor or moderator or whatever they want to call me. I'll open the initial meeting so that no one delegate will appear to have more power than the other. Then I'll act as an unofficial chair until they're ready to elect their own. I'll offer ideas only if requested and that request is then approved by a vote of all delegates. I have no vote. Will Riley will be at my side keeping track of notes, votes, and iced-tea orders."

"And you feel absolutely secure out here," Waters commented, as he rose to his feet and set his captain's hat back on his head.

"Mr. Waters," Griffey said with a broad smile, "If we were to forfeit the lives of these people, the world order would never be the same again. We're supposed to be cloaked in an invisible shield. Now if you believe that, I think I ought to find someone else as captain because I'd figure you must be a closet drinker. I just sent Will back to the carrier because there are people in the intelligence network who aren't quite as positive about our security over the past twelve hours. Other than that, I can't tell you anything else. We'll see what Will has to say when he gets back."

"Mr. Griffey, who is Will Riley? He keeps telling me he's just a desk man who's had a few lucky breaks. I don't buy that."

"He does put on a good show, doesn't he? Has he told you that he's just a simple farm boy, too?"

"He's not, huh?"

"Oh he came off a farm all right. But that's not where he got that limp. He was with the FBI. There's still a bullet lodged near his spine that he picked up when he was working on a combined FBI/DEA action in Latin America. He went to the State Department afterward. Rupert Daniels grabbed him from a desk." Lou Griffey gave Francis a knowing grin. "He's a tough son of a bitch, isn't he?"

"Not exactly outgoing," Waters admitted. "Now I think I know how he knew so much about me."

"He likes you, Francis. He told me that. If President Salkin trusts him, I think you can, too."

The air was cooling and the sun casting long shadows when a man in a business suit was escorted into Hussein's headquarters. The building had been selected because it would be difficult to identify from the air. The four walls had been constructed from mud bricks. The roof was canvas because its camouflage design allowed it to blend with its surroundings, even if a helicopter were to hover overhead at a few hundred feet. When Hussein was away, the canvas was removed so that it would appear deserted to whomever might pass by. With no water or electricity it was Spartan living, but it was exactly what Hussein and his followers preferred. There were too many curious people in the Lebanese mountains these days.

Hussein was seated in a folding chair behind a folding aluminum table that served as a desk. There was little else in the room. Two guards with holstered automatics stood to either side of their leader. Hussein gestured to one of them to bring his guest a folding chair.

The man in the suit was frightened. A nervous tick caused his cheek to jump as if he were trying to wink at Hussein. Nothing had been said to him since he was picked up at the checkpoint at the base of the mountains except: "Don't speak until you are spoken to." He accepted the chair and thanked the guard for it. Then he said, "Thank you," to Hussein.

"You were told not to speak until you were spoken to," Hussein said softly.

The man blanched and nodded. His cheek jumped spasmodically. A sheen of perspiration appeared on his forehead. He folded his hands in an effort to hide their trembling. He knew what happened too often when people were summoned in this manner.

"How many others have you told about the torpedoes?" Hussein inquired calmly.

"No one. No one at all. I agreed to that."

"Yes, you did. You promised me. I also told you then that if you ever discussed the weapon with another person you would die."

The man's composure was rapidly escaping him. "Not a soul knows about the torpedoes. Believe me, I keep my promises." Beads of sweat from his bald head ran down his cheeks. "I have been in this business too long. I keep my promises," he repeated. His eye blinked uncontrollably.

"Another organization we sometimes work with, in Syria, wants a torpedo like the ones you built for us."

"They . . . they didn't hear about that from me. I swear. I made them just for you. I burned the design afterward. Your man, the one named Ismael, saw me burn it."

"Do you mean this design?" Hussein extracted a paper from inside his shirt. He unfolded it slowly and smoothed it on the table until it was perfectly flat. "One of my people managed to obtain this from that other organization. I have been told this is an exact copy of that design."

The man appeared stricken as he accepted the paper that Hussein held out for him. The paper shook violently as he studied it. "No, this isn't mine. Look at this." He forced a smile of confidence. "The detonator is different, quite different. If I had my original design I could show you that—"

"No!" Hussein interrupted angrily. "You couldn't. What you are looking at comes from Damascus. The change you see in that detonator was drawn in at the last minute by one of my people who worked in the defense ministry headquarters in Damascus. After he modified the design, he was able to make this copy. He was forced to compromise himself within a few hours of passing this copy to one of my men. He went before a firing squad shortly afterward. We sincerely hope that they don't know that he redrew that detonator. If they do find out, then we have left a trail to be followed."

The man stared wordlessly at Hussein, who had risen to his feet. He opened his mouth to speak but found that he could only blink back the tears he could feel forming at the corners of his eyes. The quiver of his cheeks masked the tick. He knew he was going to die and his only hope was that death would come quickly.

"You were well paid for those torpedoes."

The man nodded.

"But you were greedy. Love of money was more important than keeping your word. No man among us is allowed to survive such a gross error."

"No . . ." It was the only word he could manage.

Hussein turned his head toward one of his guards. "Take him to the top of the mountain."

"No . . ." The man broke into deep sobs.

"Stake him out."

When the guard moved to the man's side and motioned for him to stand up, there was no movement. Try as he could to get to his feet, control of his muscles had abandoned him. There would be no merciful bullet, no knife, not even the relief that would come as his own weight at the end of a rope snapped his neck. Instead, they were going to leave him staked out naked in the hot sun and the chill night. That was the worst torture imaginable. He sincerely hoped he would be dead before the birds pecked out his eyes or the animals began to gnaw at his belly. Death couldn't come quickly enough.

Hussein had nothing more to say. Staking was a fine example for anyone who might ever consider crossing him. He sat back down at the folding table and looked at the torpedo design more closely. It was a standard twenty-one-inch weapon, chemical propulsion, wire guided or acoustic homing at longer ranges, and extremely difficult to evade once it located its target.

The only major change to this particular torpedo was the incendiary warhead, and that was why a special one-of-a-kind detonator had been designed. This torpedo wasn't intended to break the back of a ship because the time between hitting a target and actual sinking would more than likely allow passengers to escape. Instead, this one was designed to strike near the surface, exploding up and outward so that its incendiary materials would turn its target into a flaming pyre.

Hussein stepped outside the building and turned his face to the last warm rays of the sun. The heat was comforting. It would not be so for the traitor at the top of the mountain.

Soon it would be time to begin the trek down to the village where the radio was now located. Hussein had ordered that the location of the communications center be changed daily. There were too many opportunities for error if they became complacent.

Hussein shuddered to think of what might have happened if . . . if his man in Damascus hadn't found that torpedo design. It would have been entirely possible that a traitorous Syrian—none of the Syrians could be trusted—might have sold it to an American spy, or even someone who also might pass it on for money. All it took was one mistake, one simple error, and a single foolish clue could end up in the hands of the wrong people. Then, through a series of coincidences, their entire operation might have been compromised. There was less than a week left. What—maybe four days? Five days until Michael was in position?

"What is the time?" he asked one of the guards.

"A few minutes past five, sir."

Hussein studied the long shadows cast by the peaks that surrounded him. Soon the sun would drop below the horizon and there would be a sudden chill in the air. Was it like that out on the Mediterranean? He must remember to ask Soraya when she returned. If anyone would survive she would. And if Michael or Ismael did also? Well, she'd dispose of them. She'd been sworn to do so.

When he next spoke to Michael, the submarine would have entered the Mediterranean. Until he had received the design of that torpedo from Damascus, he was positive that not one aspect of his plan had been compromised. He doubted there would be any further troubles. The weapons expert was not one of his own. Hussein was confident that none of his people would ever turn against him.

CHAPTER TWELVE

Herman Gleick's office in the Kiel Central Police Station was more of a work space. It consisted of two movable, plastic room dividers to separate him from the desks on either side. There was nothing private. Everyone's phone conversations could easily be heard, but their department head often pointed out that crime was everybody's business in that room.

Only Gleick's immediate superior, the director of the homicide division, actually possessed an office with solid walls and a windowless door. His name was emblazoned in white on a black plastic plaque—NEUMANN, H. E. in large letters, DIRECTOR-HOMICIDE beneath in smaller letters. The director's office also contained a water cooler and a coffee maker. When the door was shut, no one in the large outer office, where all the other detectives and their assistants worked, could overhear either his phone conversations or his interviews.

The chief investigator often lent his office to his men when they were interviewing people under special circumstances. He also left them alone to conduct their work because he sympathized with their lack of privacy and the fact that a good detective often derived more through establishing a personal rapport during an interview. He was particularly considerate of Herman Gleick, whom he considered by far the finest detective in his department.

Gleick sensed that the small man sitting across Neumann's desk from him was impressed with the director's office. Mr. Paddha appeared to be enjoying his coffee, which was half milk and half coffee, as he sipped at it thoughtfully. When Gleick first ushered him in and closed the door, the man's eyes had immediately spotted the framed photographs decorating the walls. They were mostly of Neumann shaking hands with important personages from Kiel and Bonn and Berlin. He also appreciated the glass display case lined with classic handguns, explaining that he had a relative who was a collector.

Gleick appreciated the fact that his guest was nervous and had been willing to go along with the light conversation that usually relaxed someone. But he grew instantly more curious about this gentleman when Mr. Paddha pointed out the photo of Neumann on the deck of a submarine shaking hands with an admiral. Gleick could be seen slightly behind the director. Paddha asked Gleick if he was familiar with submarines. "No, that was the only time I was ever on board one. The admiral was hosting the department that day." He redirected the conversation. "I take it you decided on your own to contact me, Mr. Paddha. You did say you wanted to talk only with me, I believe?"

Paddha nodded. He removed his gold-rimmed glasses and polished them nervously as he spoke. "Yes, Mr. Gleick. It was right after the announcement in the paper the other day that S-252 was overdue that I made the decision myself to talk with someone in your department." He settled his glasses back in place with both hands, very carefully balancing them on his nose.

"I'm afraid I have nothing to do with that, Mr. Paddha. That's entirely a navy problem."

"Yes." Paddha was short, small-boned, his features delicate, and his manner careful and precise. Gleick assumed from his accent and the spelling of his name that he was Middle Eastern, although his German was excellent. "But it seemed to me, since you have been involved in a separate investigation involving S-252 and her former captain, that you might know something in addition to the fact that the submarine is missing."

Now that investigation had never been public knowledge. Gleick made a concerted effort to control his irritation. "I beg your pardon?" He wrinkled his forehead. "There is no public investigation involving S-252. Perhaps you are mistaken, Mr. Paddha, and—"

"Please, Mr. Gleick," Paddha interrupted, lifting his hand slightly, "you must see that this is extremely difficult for me." His brown eyes blinked rapidly. The gleam of perspiration was evident on his forehead. "If you will accept the fact that I am aware there is another investigation without our wasting precious time discussing how I know, perhaps I can be of some help to you." He crossed his right leg over his left and cradled his right elbow in his left hand, as if he had rehearsed the position beforehand. He was trying desperately to appear relaxed. But his right foot bounced continually and his right hand stroked his chin feverishly.

"Certainly, Mr. Paddha. Perhaps you could explain your interest in this matter."

"I have a niece . . ." He blinked rapidly. "Rather, I had a niece, a beautiful young lady. She was the youngest child of my oldest brother. Her name was Darra." He stared down at the bouncing foot and seemed to will it to stop. "She had an affair many years ago with a German naval officer named Walter Erhardt." He looked away and blinked even more rapidly, as if he was about to weep.

"Are you familiar today with Commander Erhardt?" Gleick asked.

"Oh, yes. I was the only one in the family who lived outside the country. I came to Germany when the Shah was still in power."

"From Iran?"

"Yes. From Tehran. I emigrated. I'm a naturalized German citizen."

"Mr. Paddha, I appreciate your coming to me." Gleick sensed that he may have just been struck by lightning. This man had appeared to him completely out of the blue. Was there a link that he'd overlooked? "Perhaps you'd be kind enough to explain a little more of your background and what you know about your niece's relationship to Captain Erhardt."

Paddha explained how his niece had met Erhardt on a holiday in Malta, about the tragedy that followed, and how the Paddha family had arranged for Erhardt to sneak into Tehran for Darra's funeral. "Some family members even considered killing him for destroying Darra, but it became evident how deep their love had been. None of us ever saw him again, Mr. Gleick. My single brief conversation with him was a strange one. Certainly he was distraught, but he was also an angry man. I saw another man inside when I looked into his eyes. It was so tragic. He said he would avenge my niece's death, and I believed him."

"Did he say that to anyone else?"

"Yes, to my brother, Darra's father. Unfortunately, my brother is dead now. On the few occasions we saw each other after that, we talked about Erhardt, and we both agreed that he was a strange young man . . . even a frightening one," he concluded.

"He's been extremely successful."

"I've followed his career in the military press. I was excited when I read that he was posted to command S-252. Perhaps, I said to myself, the young man learned over the years to control his emotions."

"You had your doubts? I mean after his threat to avenge your niece's death."

"Oh, yes. Military commanders should be individuals who have a firm control of their emotions. It pleased me that Erhardt had learned to control his and had done so well in a very brief career." Once again, Paddha began meticulously polishing his glasses. "It took me a while to realize why S-252 resided in my memory. Then I remembered there was an investigation into the death of the man who had been captain before Erhardt."

"Captain Preminger?" How did Paddha know there was an investigation? There'd never been any public notice.

"Exactly." Paddha placed his glasses back on his nose and leaned forward, his nervousness apparently gone. Both feet were on the floor. His arms were folded as precisely as he spoke.

"You seem confident of your information, Mr. Paddha." Gleick knew he must be cautious in his approach. The man obviously possessed some excellent sources.

"I'm a newspaperman of sorts. My official employer in Berlin publishes what most people call scandal sheets—all the dirt and unpleasantness that accompanies celebrities. You've heard of the *Spotlighter?*"

"Yes." Scandal sheet was a more polite term than some of the others Gleick had heard.

"I also have a secondary position with a lesser-known organization that researches and arranges the release of information promoting Middle Eastern people in Germany."

"Public relations?"

"Precisely. We publish nothing. We make an effort to have our material appear in newspapers and magazines where it will do the most to improve understanding of our people. You can appreciate, Mr. Gleick, that I am in a position to learn a great deal both positive and negative about what people from my part of the world do in Germany."

Gleick sensed that Mr. Paddha was getting close to his point. "Would you care for some more coffee, Mr. Paddha?"

"Please. Just as before, thank you. It's very fine coffee."

Gleick wondered if Paddha realized how much he'd already revealed that Gleick himself hadn't known. There was nothing in Erhardt's service record about being in Iran. Nothing in his psychological profile indicated the possibility of personality defects that Paddha had mentioned. But it was obvious this man had more to say before he got to his point.

Paddha sipped his coffee. "Very good coffee. Very good." He indicated the photos on the wall of Chief Investigator Neumann and the well-known people he met in the line of duty. "I have met most of those people also. However, I am not on the same pleasant terms. Some of them have been the subjects of articles I have written."

Gleick did not read the *Spotlighter*, but he was familiar with the uncomplimentary stories from that publication that seeped over into the daily newspapers. It was difficult to imagine Paddha—such a tiny, quiet individual—muckraking for a living. "Do you have many enemies, Mr. Paddha?"

"No, I don't believe so. But I'm sure a number of people I've written about would go to extremes to avoid me.

However, I see what you are driving at. Am I getting even with someone? No. I'm just troubled about Walter Erhardt. I felt his pain at Darra's death. I feared that his anger would become his worst enemy. And I was pleased to learn that he had overcome any problems when he was posted to command a submarine. Then I realized it was the same one . . . the one whose captain had died under mysterious circumstances. Do you know exactly what happened to Captain Preminger?"

"None of us does," Gleick answered. *But here it comes.*

"There is an underground group, Mr. Gleick. Terrorists. Preminger was lured into it—with sexual favors—by an Arab woman."

"I've gotten that far," Gleick responded.

"I don't mean to insult you, Mr. Gleick. I don't know who *they* are any more than you do. No one really does. But rumors have a way of repeating themselves until you have to accept them after a while. You see, I have heard through my contacts that his murder was planned over a long period of time. Once I began to think about it, I wondered if perhaps Walter Erhardt might have had something to do with Captain Preminger's death."

Gleick smiled slightly. "That was one of the early ideas I toyed with. However, Captain Erhardt was at sea at the time, serving aboard another submarine. He'd rarely come in contact with Preminger. Preminger's wife had never met him. He was scheduled to succeed to the next command that became available, and there would be an opening everyone knew about, so there was no reason for him to be involved." He was perplexed. "So, you see, I have my doubts about your theory, Mr. Paddha. Are you trying to gain some information from me that I don't quite follow?"

Paddha was instantly animated. His back straightened. A hurt look spread across his face. "I am here to be of assistance. You have misunderstood my intentions."

"I must admit I'm having trouble following you. Just what are you insinuating, Mr. Paddha?"

"I'm a German citizen. I want to help my adopted country." He leaned forward, his hand on the front of the desk. "Don't you find it odd that both the past and the current commanding officers of S-252 were involved in one way or another with Middle Eastern women, even though the circumstances were decidedly different?"

"Yes."

"Were you aware of Erhardt's involvement?"

"No."

"And now that submarine is missing under unusual circumstances. Mr. Gleick, the reason I got in touch with you is that I thought perhaps I might assist your investigation. Maybe nothing will come of it, but some of my contacts, particularly in the Arab community, feel the same way many others of our faith do. The fanatics are damaging a religion that is the heart and soul of a people who believe in peace. Muslims like myself who call Germany their home are decent people. We like the freedom, the opportunity we have been allowed, the money we have earned. Perhaps we can return a favor. Perhaps we can find what you can't—perhaps learn if there is a connection of some kind." Paddha almost seemed to be pleading as he spoke. "And my niece, Darra—I would do anything in her memory."

"I believe what you're saying." Gleick looked at his watch. "It's lunchtime. Would you join me?"

"It would be a pleasure." There was a look of relief in Paddha's eyes, almost as if he were carrying the weight of the Muslim people on his back, Gleick thought.

There were two points Paddha made during lunch that particularly impressed the detective. Of all the recognized organizations and splinter groups that could be considered authentic terrorists by their actual deeds, all of them directed their aggression against the Jewish state or those who actively supported Israel. Only two, both in Lebanon, were known to actively vent their hatred against any Muslim efforts to promote some form of settlement with the Jews. Because they were literally at war with their own people, their leaders had effectively disappeared and their members were rarely known to the Arab world. There were yet-to-be-substantiated rumors that they might have united.

"Their standards are brutal, Mr. Gleick. When someone becomes a threat to their security, a traitor actually, even if there is but a hint or rumor, that individual normally is dead within twenty-four hours. Their trademark, if such barbarism could be considered a trademark, is to remove the victim's heart, much like the Aztec ritual sacrifice to the gods."

"That is barbaric." Gleick shuddered at the thought.

"In the world of Islam, there are still those who consider such an act in the realm of the eye-for-an-eye practice. A bit excessive for the Christian world, but I assure you it's most effective in limiting the number of traitors to a cause. That's why no one knows the name of this mysterious organization or who its members may be."

"What's to prevent them from killing you?"

"Nothing, I suppose. But I don't know names, names of individuals, I mean."

"Do you know the names of organizations?"

"There are a few I remember. You know, of course, about Black September—that came from Al Fatah's intelligence wing. And others like Al Takfir and As-Sa'iqa and Ahmad Jebril. But if they're still in business"—he wrinkled his forehead doubtfully—"I'd be surprised. No, I don't think I can help you there."

Paddha leaned forward and spoke softly. "All I know is that they are rumored to be somewhere in the mountains east of Beirut. They move around a great deal. Because they have money from an unknown source, they are very sophisticated—electronics, modern weapons, that sort of thing."

"Even though they tear the hearts out of their victims," Gleick mused. "Civilization has made tremendous advances in the latter part of the twentieth century, hasn't it?" He winked mischievously at Paddha, then his expression grew serious. "I realize you are a German citizen, and I'm pleased that you want to accomplish something for your adopted country. But I still don't understand, even if you don't have names, why you would talk to me about this if these people are so vicious."

Paddha thought for a moment. "I was going to say that perhaps this is my way of repaying my adopted country for allowing me to succeed. But even to me that sounds silly. I am a Muslim. I believe in my faith. I believe that people can live together."

"Most people would call you an idealist."

"I am an idealist. And I'm also too soft-hearted. I guess

it's also because I found that I liked Walter Erhardt for giving my niece something special before her death and . . ." He thought for a moment, and when he spoke again Gleick saw fear in his eyes. "He was also so brilliant and venal at the same time that he terrified me. There was something about that man . . ." Paddha seemed to be searching for the proper words. Finally, he shook his head sadly. "Something I find I can't put into words. Perhaps this will lead nowhere," he concluded sadly.

Gleick saw that, even though Paddha's eyes seemed fixed on him, the man wasn't really looking at him.

"There is one other item that may or may not be worth following. I heard a rumor that an unknown group—terrorists was the rumor—outfitted a fishing boat in Libya with weapons. Other than that, I know nothing about the individuals involved, the boat, its cargo, or where it was destined. But I will begin to check with my sources this afternoon."

After lunch, Gleick brought Paddha back to his office, introduced him to Director Neumann, and showed him the photograph of Soraya. It was the photo that the owner of the building where Captain Preminger had been murdered had identified as the woman who rented his apartment. Paddha did not recognize the woman. When they parted, Gleick made a point of asking Paddha to call him with any ideas he might have, no matter how insignificant they might be.

Shortly after Paddha left, Gleick called Roland Lyford, the CIA man in Berlin, to tell him of the meeting with Paddha.

Lyford's response was immediate. "Now that I think about it, I have a couple of sources who've talked from time to time about some terrorist group in the Lebanese mountains that even the Arabs are scared of. And I remember the Sixth Fleet intelligence people had something on a boat loading weapons in Benghazi not so long ago. Goddamn boat disappeared. Lousy weather, I guess. Satellites couldn't track it."

Gleick frowned to himself. "Captain Davis didn't mention that boat when he talked to me."

"Hell, he probably didn't even think about it. That was ancient history by the time you talked to him. It disappeared. I'll tell you what. Get Mr. Paddha back in your office first thing tomorrow morning. Call me when you have him there. Let's both talk to him."

"Come up to look at the stars?" Francis Waters could barely make out Will Riley's face in the dim light from the pilot house.

"Screw the stars," Riley responded softly.

"Screw the stars," Waters echoed. "Just like that. Screw the stars. Someone say something to offend you over on the carrier?" Riley had just returned to *Calm Seas* by helicopter.

"You know, Francis, every time I think I've finally got you under control, you say something wise."

"It's in my nature."

"Remember our conversation about submarines?"

"I do." Waters remembered that Riley didn't take his comments about submarines very seriously.

"There are some intelligence people who are trying to make my life more difficult by intimating that a German submarine that's been reported missing and presumed lost just may not be lost at all. They're toying with all sorts of interesting theories, all of which would be preposterous at any other time."

"Is it the Med?"

"No." Riley weighed his words carefully. "Outside in the Atlantic. But in my business, you worry about everything. Everyone else is discounting this sub, except for some CIA guy in Berlin who's about to retire and a naval intelligence type in Naples. And they don't really know why I should be worried."

"Should I worry?"

"Francis, I'll tell you when to worry."

Heinz Waller came to periscope depth. She was making bare steerageway. The ocean above was relatively calm and the motion of the boat was gentle.

"Radar report," Walter Erhardt called out from his position at the periscope.

"Heavy concentration of shipping to the north. Too many to designate. Should be the Gibraltar shipping lanes."

"Designate anything that appears to be coming within five miles of us. ESM report." A wandering military aircraft on a training mission was more of a threat to *Waller* than anything on the surface. The ESM gear would pick up and identify any airborne radar.

"Scanning . . ."

Waller's control room was silent. The crew had been training hard the past two days and they were tired. The only sound came from the planesman whose controls determined the submarine's course and depth. That required a deft hand at such a slow speed, and he had a habit of talking quietly to himself as he maintained *Waller*'s position.

Ismael seemed to find the control room a perfect location to display his own brand of hyperactivity. He'd adapted poorly to life beneath the sea, sleeping little, constantly on the move. The German sailors who remained were deathly afraid of him. Michael's men were a hardened lot, afraid of nothing. They laughed at Ismael's discomfort, irritating him even more. Now he paced in the tiny control room like a caged lion, his eyes seeking out anyone who dared to look at him.

"Still scanning . . ."

"What are we waiting for?" Ismael snarled. "No one knows we're here. They all think the German submarine sank three days ago. Let's get on with it."

They were north of Tangier, a city on the northwest coast of Morocco near the entrance to the Strait of Gibraltar. Thirty kilometers northeast on the opposite side of the strait was Spanish Tarifa. There was more than enough room for a quiet submarine to dive and probably ease through the strait unnoticed. But Walter Erhardt, aware that the British at Gibraltar were in the habit of monitoring the traffic that passed through the strait both above and below the surface, was more cautious. Since being found meant mission failure, this bore no resemblance to a training exercise.

Ismael, angry that no one had responded to his question instantly, shouted, "What are you all scared of?!"

"Talk to him, Michael." Soraya wasn't afraid of Ismael, but she also wanted nothing to do with him. Michael was as close to him as anyone. He could take care of him. "We don't know how many more days we have underwater. Do you want him to wipe out your crew?"

Soraya's voice startled Michael. It wasn't familiar to him. It was the voice of authority. His attention had been focused on Erhardt's cautious approach to the Strait of Gibraltar, and it came as a surprise when he looked up and saw that Soraya's comment had prompted others to turn their attention on him. They were all waiting for him to respond.

The ESM man broke the silence. "Lock on . . . weak signal . . . low frequency . . . looks like a British ninety-seven . . ."

"Dive. Fifty meters," Erhardt barked. "Speed five."

"Fifty meters, aye," the diving officer answered. The snorkel was secured as he gave his orders. There was a slight rumble as water rushed into the forward ballast tanks. The bow dipped.

Erhardt noticed Lieutenant Schroeder's blue eyes studying him intently. "If that was a British ninety-seven our operator picked up, Mr. Schroeder, it was probably aboard a helicopter on patrol out of Gibraltar. Most countries file movement reports for their warships passing through the strait, but these Brits like to keep everyone honest. I believe they also have passive listening devices on the floor of the strait."

"I see." Schroeder said nothing more. Since that one brief moment on the bridge, he had been forced to remain below. Now they were about to enter the Mediterranean, and he was certain the search for *Waller* would never be considered there.

"Mr. Schroeder, since you are the next senior officer aboard, it's my responsibility to qualify you for command." Erhardt spoke as if nothing special had occurred since their departure from Bremerhaven. "Tell me, how would you take us through the strait without being detected?"

"Level at fifty meters, Captain," the diving officer called out with a heavy accent.

Schroeder's eyes moved briefly to the diving officer, then back to Erhardt. "I suppose I would take her down near maximum depth and maintain as much silence as possible."

"That, too, Mr. Schroeder. But there is so much more to

evasion. Come over here," Erhardt said, gesturing toward the chart table. "Look at this." He pointed to a relief map that had been folded and placed above the regular chart to match the Strait of Gibraltar. It displayed in sharp artistic relief a deep cavern running through the strait. Then he pointed to the regular chart that showed depths in meters. "To me, that cavern shows much more than the fact that earthquakes or shifting plates created the strait. There are constant tides and currents in our oceans. It seems only natural that a current must run through the strait. Correct?"

Schroeder nodded.

"Good." Erhardt was animated. "That means the water temperatures change. And that means that sound is affected by strange natural occurrences in this strait. Since there are so many ships passing through at all times, there are an abundance of sounds all affected by the laws of physics. So, we take advantage of that. We situate ourselves beneath the shipping lanes with all the surface traffic and we constantly measure the water temperature. Now why do that? And I would appreciate an answer," he added with a frown.

"Whatever sound we are making reflects off the temperature gradients above and whatever sound escapes blends with all the others." Schroeder reasoned that cooperation would be the sole means of ever appearing on the bridge again.

"Mr. Schroeder, you are about to understand why I have gone out of my way to make sure you remain with me. I'm going to let you maneuver through the strait just to show you what a fine submarine commander you're going to be someday."

It required a greater effort for Hugo Schroeder to maintain his composure each time Erhardt made comments like that. He was never going to be a submarine commander and the only "someday" he could expect was the day of his death, which he knew was imminent. But it was necessary to continue the charade, to go along with whatever Erhardt said, and to appear as normal as possible. Perhaps . . . just perhaps, if he was allowed to conn *Waller,* he might have a chance to sabotage . . .

"Walter . . ." Michael's voice contained a sense of urgency.

Erhardt turned. "You're worried about Schroeder doing the driving, of course. But I assure you there's no reason to be concerned. He is a qualified submarine officer who responds to challenges. Believe me, he has nothing to gain by causing trouble. He may not appreciate this situation, but he's not going to endanger himself as long as he believes there may be a chance for survival. Plus, I need his expertise." He glanced around the control room and then asked, "Where's Ismael? Does the thought scare him?"

"I sent Ismael forward to clean weapons. That has a calming effect on him." Michael indicated Schroeder. "And, yes, I am concerned and I think it's dangerous to allow him to take control."

"Not if I'm right beside him to assist, and I plan to be at Mr. Schroeder's shoulder to encourage his talents."

Michael frowned.

"What seems to escape all of you is that I'm not superhuman," Erhardt explained. "I still require sleep. Since we don't know how many more days we'll be together, he must take my place at certain times. When he does, your diving officer will be right there with him. He knows this ship almost as well as we do."

Half an hour later, their periscope again broke the surface. To the west, Erhardt studied a waning sunset for a moment. Then he turned to the east where the running lights of the ships entering and leaving the Mediterranean in the assigned shipping lanes stood out against the dark sky. Schroeder suggested that perhaps it would be a good idea to surface after dark to give the crew some fresh air, but Erhardt simply smiled and declined, reiterating his concern with aircraft. They reversed course and spent the next couple of hours running slowly back and forth in a small box. Erhardt insisted it was preferable to pass through later at night.

When Erhardt determined the time was right, he coached Hugo Schroeder into a position beneath the east-bound shipping lane. They matched the speed of the surface ships, then varied their depth until they encountered a definite temperature layer.

At the narrowest section of the strait, the African and European continents were less than fifteen kilometers apart.

When the British fortress of Gibraltar was due north, the gap had widened to over twenty kilometers, and soon after they were in the Mediterranean. The tension that had been building in the control room evaporated. Erhardt, forever the master of manipulation, congratulated each of the men who had contributed to their harrowing passage with a personal comment.

"Not so difficult, was it?" Erhardt said to Schroeder with a broad smile. "I'll bet deep down you enjoyed that."

It had indeed been an experience Hugo Schroeder found fascinating. It had taken them almost four and a half hours to travel forty-five kilometers under trying conditions. Now that they were in the Mediterranean, he must find a way to signal again via the satellite.

Erhardt beamed. "I told you in my stateroom weeks ago, Mr. Schroeder, that you had the talent. Stick by me and I'll give you the chance to be the finest officer in the entire fleet." He clapped Schroeder on the back. "You look tired. Get a few hours of sleep. There's so much I want to teach you."

Walter Erhardt knew the best time to draw a man to your side was when he thought he had no future. Fear remained the most effective teacher. In a matter of time, he was certain he would be able to control Schroeder.

Erhardt finally concluded that it was safe to poke the antenna above the surface more than two hours past the time Michael had expected to contact Hussein.

"I apologize," Michael began. "Erhardt made a change to his plans for coming through the strait."

"Apologize only if you fail," Hussein cautioned. "Were you in danger of being discovered?"

"No. Erhardt is careful."

"You are confident in your crew, Michael?"

"The crew is functioning superbly."

"Good. Where will you be in forty-eight hours at normal cruising speed if you follow the African coastline? Talk to Erhardt. I will wait."

Michael watched Erhardt as he inserted a series of courses along the southern Mediterranean coast into the computer. Then he marked his progress in six-hour periods on the display until his pencil marked an *X* to indicate the end of their fifth day.

"Off the Tunisian coast," Michael reported. "Near Bizerte."

"Good. I couldn't hope for more. I believe that our timing will be perfect."

"Our timing for . . . ?" Michael began.

But Hussein gave him no chance to finish. "You're young and you're anxious, Michael. I like that. Contact me again in forty-eight hours. And don't concern yourself if you're a few hours off schedule."

"How . . ." Michael's voice faltered slightly before he said, "How much longer?"

"Is there a problem?"

Michael thought about Ismael and his barely controlled violence. "No, none."

CHAPTER THIRTEEN

DAY FOUR

Paddha failed to appear in Gleick's office the next morning as he had agreed. "I'm surprised. He seemed to be a very precise person," Gleick said. "I'll call him again, but I can't understand why he'd fail to keep this appointment after coming to me on his own yesterday."

"Maybe he's scared," Lyford offered.

"No. He wasn't yesterday. He shouldn't be today."

There was no answer in Paddha's room, but the hotel desk confirmed that he was still registered. Because Gleick's naturally suspicious mind issued an instant warning that all might not be right, he decided to go to Paddha's hotel and wait for him. It was something in the back of his mind—something that Paddha had mentioned about how those splinter groups often reacted instantly and rashly to a perceived problem—that bothered him. Could they have somehow found out about Mr. Paddha?

When the bell captain opened the door to Paddha's room, he was greeted by the sight of the little man's naked corpse sprawled between the bed and the door. The body was covered with blood. It had been so badly mutilated, and blood had flown so freely, that it was impossible to determine the exact cause of death.

Later that afternoon the preliminary coroner's report indicated that a heavy knife had actually slashed through the man's rib cage, slicing through the bone. Then the ribs had apparently been pulled back by hand and the heart torn out, rather than cut out. It could not be determined if the man was dead before the invasion of his chest cavity occurred. Finally, it was noted that Mr. Paddha's tongue, which had been cut out of his throat, had been stuffed into his chest cavity.

Will Riley briefly enjoyed a warm feeling of pride as he studied the assemblage in *Calm Seas'* main salon. True, the delegates were still going out of their way to be polite to one another, but they were no longer tentative. Was it new-found sincerity, more than likely modified by generations of distrust, that made them appear almost childlike in their approach to individuals they might just as soon have killed a year before? Whatever it might be, Riley knew the day couldn't be more perfect.

"Mr. Riley . . . Mr. Riley . . ."

He turned toward the voice softly calling his name. One of *Calm Seas'* sailors, in dress whites, beckoned to him through the open door.

Riley stepped out onto the deck, his eyebrows raised in question.

"You're wanted in the radio shack, Mr. Riley. Call from shore, sir."

"Unless it's coded as a red call, I'd prefer to wait until this session is complete."

"Sorry, sir. It's on the scrambler and the other party claims it's a brilliant red."

Riley took the call in a small soundproof room accessible only through *Calm Seas'* radio shack.

"This is Roland Lyford, Mr. Riley, CIA desk in Berlin. I'm sorry to say we haven't had the pleasure of meeting each other."

"Are we going to?" Riley inquired warily.

"Probably. Not today though. Let me get right into it, Mr. Riley. I was given your name by some acquaintances of mine back in Washington. I chose you because I didn't want to bother the Secretary of State, plus your background's a lot like mine—except they call me an old fart now."

"Who the hell is this?"

"They didn't tell me your memory was bad, Mr. Riley. Let me try again—Roland Lyford here. And let me give you just the code names of the people who think I should talk with you—Spider, Orgy, Crash." There was a pause. "There, doesn't that make you feel more comfortable that we run in the same circles?"

"Meaning?" Those code names would forever remain in the recesses of his mind. They'd been employed during the joint operation with the DEA . . . back when he'd taken that slug in the back that had almost crippled him. They'd saved his life!

"Meaning you qualify for the contact I need. The military deals in a military way, if you know what I mean. And I think they're doing a pretty good job with security for your little party out there. But there's something going down that's not military at all, something I don't understand that may have a lot to do with your operation."

Riley found this last comment odd. "Maybe you can tell me where this is leading."

"First you need to trust me, Mr. Riley. I'm now directly involved in your operation. I came in through the back door. We need a little face-to-face time."

"Mr. Lyford, I need to know a little more about . . ."

"Mr. Riley, there is no point in using this means of communication. My information has everything to do with your conference out there. The fact that President Salkin is going to be there concerns me even more. I'm not getting far with people here, Mr. Riley. There's a lot of denial since I wasn't directly involved with this from the start. Tomorrow. We need to get together tomorrow."

"I'll see what the military can do."

"Already done, Mr. Riley. I said my contacts were good. *Wasp* will take care of your transportation. It just means you don't get to sleep much, but neither do I."

Berlin is an international capital and as cosmopolitan as any city can be in Germany. But it is not a place where foreigners would feel comfortable building their own unique houses of worship. The country's Muslim population, people who settled there over the years for any number of reasons, were generally satisfied to practice their beliefs privately. They were a minority. They had no desire to build mosques that would call attention to themselves. When they gathered for religious or cultural purposes, they did so without fanfare. But there was a common bond that brought them together at times for mutual support.

The leader of the faith resided in Berlin in a place that also served as a cultural and religious center. Anything that affected the faith eventually found its way there. That was the reason that the package containing Mr. Paddha's heart was delivered there. The package contained a note that had also been sent to the weekly paper that served the Islamic community in Germany.

Within hours, any Muslim in Germany who had the slightest knowledge of the various terrorist organizations knew what was in that package. They also understood the message conveyed, for it contained tens of generations of Islamic tradition.

Silence, it demanded. And silence was exactly what it accomplished.

Francis Waters turned when he heard footsteps coming up the metal stairs on the port side of *Calm Seas'* bridge. Will Riley's face appeared above the top step. As the upper half of Will's body came into view, Waters saw that he was wearing a dark suit with a conservative tie. "Coming from a funeral, or headed for one?"

"You wear a uniform. So do I. It just happens that the State Department's dress code is rather unimaginative. You don't know how thankful I am that Mr. Griffey said the hell with vests. If we weren't out on your bounding main, I really would look like a funeral director."

"Or maybe the customer," Waters muttered without enthusiasm.

"Hey, Francis, soften up. You're just as tight as you were yesterday. It's another lovely day."

Waters's face cracked into an unenthusiastic smile, which lasted scant seconds. "This isn't my idea of excitement, Will. Why don't you ask me where we are today?"

"Okay, where are we today?"

"Same place we were yesterday at about this time. Our noon navigational fix, which I have faithfully transmitted to Washington in accordance with my orders, even though I'm sure *Wasp* does the same thing, placed us at approximately thirty-seven degrees north latitude, seventeen degrees east longitude. For the uninitiated, that means we're about one hundred eighty kilometers east of Siracusa, which is an ancient city on the east coast of Sicily."

Riley leaned on the bridge railing beside Waters. "I'm a better man for knowing that, Francis. But what does it matter where we are or where we're headed? You knew we weren't going any place exciting anyway."

"I got tired of looking at those navy ships through the binoculars the first day," Waters said. "About the only kick is the helos running back and forth or those speedy little inflatables that bounce around the outside of the screen occasionally. Other than that, I've got this part of the Med memorized."

"Would it make you feel any better to know you're making history?" Will Riley turned his head toward Waters and nodded when *Calm Seas'* captain raised his eyebrows. "Yup. And you are there. Someday, history books will note that Captain Francis Waters's ship was the place where world peace finally gained a foothold."

"No shit, Will," he commented indifferently. He lifted his white hat and ran his fingers through his thinning curly hair.

"Look down there." Will pointed toward the bow. "See those two guys in the bow by the anchor windlass. Don't they look like they're enjoying their cruise?"

"Yeah. So who are they?"

"One of those gentlemen is the delegate from Iraq and the other is the delegate from Saudi Arabia. Not so many years ago, if you care to remember, they were at each other's throats. And look at that. See that woman moving up the starboard side to join them?"

Waters glanced at Riley and raised his eyebrows. "I thought women were second-class citizens with these Arabs."

"Not the distinguished delegate from Beirut. Her name is Isabel Mehari, and she's a combination of Margaret Thatcher, Indira Gandhi, and Mother Teresa. She gave a little speech this morning about her own country and how absolutely nothing had been accomplished after years of Lebanon tearing itself to shreds. She's the only one in her family left alive. Two brothers were killed in an ambush. Her husband was murdered because he tried to mediate a settlement. Her oldest son died in the fighting and she doesn't even know where he was buried. Her mother and her two other children were killed when a mortar shell landed in their apartment. She's a very talented woman, and when Mr. Griffey saw what she was doing, he just sort of disappeared into the background. He figured she accomplished more than a full day of organized discussions."

Waters watched as the Iraqi and the Saudi stepped back and deferred to the woman who had joined them. "I suppose it would be nice if people like that got along with each other," he commented wistfully. "How are the Jews handling all this mutual sweetness?"

"The Israeli delegate has decided to host small intimate luncheons for the next three days. Different group each day until they've all had a chance to schmooze together. He was going to try cocktails at the end of the day, but Mr. Griffey reminded him that wasn't quite the way to make teetotalers comfortable."

Waters smiled at that. "I'd just about kill for a cold beer right now, but I guess I can wait." He lifted his binoculars in the direction of the carrier. "That's it." He glanced at his watch. "Right on time." He shouted orders into the pilot house and almost immediately *Calm Seas'* bow began to swing.

"The formation's a little different today," Waters ventured, as they steadied up on the reverse course.

"Yes, it is."

"The ships on the outer edge are closer to us."

"That's what I'm told."

"Why?"

"Antisubmarine screen. I don't know much about it, so don't ask. It's what Admiral Turner decided after our meeting yesterday. I'm told it's a little odd for an amphibious formation."

"Submarines," Francis murmured.

"They didn't do it because of you," Riley retorted. "Believe me."

Waters let his binoculars bump against his chest. Then he leaned against the railing, his hands deep in his pockets.

"Ten years from now, if this all works, do you think anyone will remember who was driving *Calm Seas* when the world was changed?"

"Why wouldn't they, Francis?"

"Read your history. They only remember the captain when he goes down with the ship."

Lieutenant Peter Germond, the PHIBRON FOUR intelligence officer, finished attaching the eight-by-ten photos to the bulletin board with push pins. There were twenty-six black-and-white photos, many of which overlapped each other. Each one contained a separate photo of a fishing boat. The perspective was from above since all of the photographs had been taken by satellite.

Jake Steele pushed open the door to Rear Admiral Turner's briefing room, just off flag plot, and stepped inside. "Hope I'm not late."

"Right on time, Jake," Turner responded. "Peter's set up a little beauty contest for us. How do they look to you?"

Steele moved closer to the bulletin board. "Good thing we can't smell 'em, Commodore."

Captain Black waved toward an empty chair. "Take a seat, Commander. Mr. Germond is going to provide us with an intelligence briefing. All you ever wanted to know about trawlers."

Lieutenant Germond was standing to the side of the bulletin board. "Does that mean I'm on?" He was tall and husky and blond, and, like Steele, he looked like an athlete. His blue eyes were always wide open as if it were an effort to keep awake.

"You're on, young man," the admiral said. "What do you think you've got for us?"

"Frankly, I don't think I have anything, Commodore." As the staff intelligence officer, Germond was responsible for filtering the intelligence that might have a bearing on PHIBRON FOUR out of the masses of information that came via the intel staffs of Sixth Fleet and the European naval and combined commands. And when Rear Admiral Turner decided something could pertain to his operations, it was Germond's job to gather all available information on that subject and present it for analysis. "We've been trying to catalog every fishing boat in the Med that might be near the size of the one reported in Benghazi a few months back. Believe me, there must be one attached to every fishing village."

"How many, would you judge?" Captain Black inquired.

Germond's eyes widened. "Thousands. And it's just like trying to keep up with water bugs. Most of them have nothing to interest us at all. The photos here were relayed by satellite a couple of hours ago."

Turner pointed at the bulletin board. "If there's a maverick out here running around with a load of weapons, I don't want to wait until he finds us. Could be something there those shore-based intelligence people don't recognize with all their fancy education. Come on." He got to his feet and sidled over to the bulletin board. "Each of us is going to decide for ourselves if all these boats smell like Jake says they should."

For the next ten minutes, the four men studied each of the photos on the bulletin board. A few of the boats were relatively new. Most of them were older and looked as if they'd been too many years away from a repair facility. Those that didn't have gear in the water displayed netting and net buoys on their decks. Some had actually been photographed in the act of hauling their nets aboard, and the decks were awash with fish. None of them gave any indication that they were anything other than fishing boats.

"They all look like they smell the same," Steele concluded. "I wouldn't want to take my nice clean SEALs aboard any of those."

Rear Admiral Turner chuckled. "How about some of those delights who drive your RIBs? They look like they've been in grease pits all day."

"Grease, yes—fish? I don't think so, Admiral," Jake answered. "That's another world in those fishing boats. And looking at those, I'm beginning to think we're chasing a dead issue."

"I concur," Turner said. "Peter, what have you got that we don't already know about the people in each of the delegate's parties?"

Lieutenant Germond gave a short laugh, and his blue eyes widened with amusement. "It's a regular rogue's gallery,

Commodore. I don't know if they fooled each other, but nothing is what it appears. The second delegate to the Israeli group is one of the senior officers of the Mossad. But the Iraqis and the Syrians have their own here who are equal to him. If they're intelligence experts, they're into counterterrorism or special operations, too."

"Troublemakers?" Turner wondered.

"Capable of it, but they all seem relatively calm so far, according to Mr. Riley," Germond answered. "Probably they're here more as bodyguards. But I've still never seen so many heavies in one small place. Captain Davis, the Sixth Fleet intelligence officer, said we ought to ask for a group picture when this is all over, especially if everyone goes away happy."

"We've got at least three more days to find out," Rear Admiral Turner commented. "What do you make of that report from Captain Davis yesterday, Peter. Could that satellite signal the Germans received really mean that Type-212 sub of theirs is loose? Or was that just a freak of nature?"

"From what Captain Davis says about the system, it would be pretty hard to imitate, Admiral. The Germans in their inimitable fashion are not cooperating—probably because they, like everyone else, have no idea what's going on out there. When Davis gets a bug up, I always pay attention. I think tightening up the antisubmarine screen makes sense until we hear otherwise. That's what I told Mr. Riley."

Desperately needed sleep for Walter Erhardt was fitful at best. Sounds, real and imagined, jolted him into a consciousness somewhere between sleep and a semiaware lethargy. Strange dreams punctuated welcome moments of unconsciousness when his mind was completely at rest. Again and again, Darra's face appeared, as beautiful as the last moment they were together. Yet this was not a wholly unusual experience for him. He had been as weary in the past because a career beneath the sea often demanded more of a man than the mind and body were accustomed to giving. It was his memory of Darra that gave him strength to continue, strength to bring him to that golden moment when he would gain revenge for her death.

But this time anxiety was as much a cause of his exhaustion as lack of sleep. Erhardt never doubted that he was now on his final mission in life. But he was certain that Darra's murder would be avenged, and with that would come a peace he was unable to attain in life. Not being a religious man, he'd never anticipated life after death or a reunion with Darra in another time and place. Rather, he would welcome death as a respite from what he considered an eternal hell as long as he remained alive. Revenge—revenge would bring him that final peace.

His exhaustion also came from an inner need to make sure that his mission was accomplished regardless of the odd assortment of people he must depend on. If he'd possessed the physical ability to remain awake until the end, he would gladly have welcomed it. Sleep was a necessary intruder in Walter Erhardt's consciousness, and he allowed it only as a means of preparing himself for this final mission.

"Walter . . ." The voice was barely above a whisper intruding in his subconscious. "Walter . . ." His mind conjured up leaves fluttering on trees. The trees became quivering human faces. The faces became . . . who? He couldn't make them out.

"Please, Walter. I must talk with you." This time the voice was louder, distinctly feminine. The faces became female. Was one of them Darra . . . or . . .?

He felt something . . . touch . . . something touching him. His hand fluttered involuntarily in an effort to ward it off. The faces that were almost in focus began to blur. "Come on, Walter. I know you're awake." His leg. That's where the touch was. There was a hand on his leg. "Come on. Your eyes are open."

Erhardt sensed his eyes wide open. But everything appeared gray, unreal. Where . . . ? The hand on his leg was real. It moved to his crotch. "Maybe this will bring you around." The voice was still soft, but very female. "Why, I'll be damned!"

He had an erection and a hand was gripping it.

"You can do it, Walter! I was beginning to think you didn't have one. Look!"

His eyes focused on Soraya bending over him, her long black hair swaying on either side of his face. She was so close that he was sure there were gold flecks in her black eyes.

"It's hard, Walter. Look at that."

He experienced a sensation of helplessness as her hand grasped his penis through his pants and moved up and down rhythmically.

"The thing's as hard as a rock. I didn't know you had it in you." Her face slowly lowered until her breath enveloped him. Then her lips covered his. Her hand moved up and down his erection. He gasped for air as her tongue searched his mouth.

Darra . . . she had been the only one.

Walter Erhardt heaved upward with all the strength he could summon. Soraya's teeth dug into his chin as she was hurled backward. She fell back across his knees, her mouth open, her eyes wide with surprise.

"Asshole!" she snapped. She patted her upper lip and looked at her fingers to see if there was blood. "Queer!" There was no blood, but her lips were twisted in rage.

Erhardt perched on his right elbow. He ran the back of his left hand across his chin and saw that it was covered with blood. "Bitch," he retorted. He reached into his back pocket and took out a handkerchief, which he held over his chin. It hurt.

Soraya sat up on the edge of his bunk and patted at her lip again, surprised that it wasn't bleeding. She was breathing deeply. "What kind of man are you? You were excited. I was just helping . . ."

"I was asleep . . . it happens . . ." Erhardt waved his hand with the bloody handkerchief at her. "Get off my bunk." He pointed at the single straight chair a couple of feet away in the corner. "There," he growled. "What do you want?"

"I needed to talk to you."

"Talk."

Soraya took some more breaths, then licked her lips, her eyes tightly shut. "Michael won't listen to me about

Ismael." She opened her eyes and glared at him. It was a tack she hadn't anticipated. But before this mission ever began, she had been charged with holding the leadership together. Hussein's unerring success was due to his consistently assigning an individual known only to him and a trusted lieutenant to watch over the others. Her contact understood the volatility of the individuals—Michael, Ismael, Erhardt—and he'd chosen her to make sure there was a balance that would see them through to the end.

"What about him?"

"Ismael's dangerous," she replied. "You've said that yourself. He's getting worse. I'm afraid he could destroy our mission before . . ."

Erhardt interrupted her, snapping, "He's psychotic and could kill us all before we even have a mission to accomplish."

Soraya frowned. "Have you ever had an idea what our mission will be?"

"We're going to sink a ship," he retorted. "That's what a submarine and torpedoes are for." Erhardt looked at the bloody handkerchief and refolded it. "So how am I going to explain this? Just tell Michael that I hurt myself sleeping?"

"Michael?" She sneered. "Michael is the type who could have watched and laughed, or at another time he might have killed us both. He's made me watch him with other women before."

Another reason to despise them both. "Do any of you really care whom you kill?" he asked. Then he couldn't resist adding, "Michael told me you're here to kill either of us if you feel it's necessary."

"Michael loves to tell people shit just to see how they react. He doesn't know that for sure," she said with disdain. But her expression appeared to say the opposite. "We're all here because we were ordered to be here, Walter. Each of us has something to contribute or else they wouldn't have sent us."

"Who wouldn't have sent you, Soraya? Do you have a name?"

She shrugged. "Okay. I'll tell you. His name is Yassim. I met him once in Jubay."

"What about the one Michael contacts on the radio?"

She shrugged again. "Hussein? I never met him. Neither has Michael. I don't know where he is. I don't even know if Yassim is still in Jubay. I haven't seen him for a year."

"Then how do you know whether or not he would want you to kill one of us now?"

Soraya glared at him. "I'll know when someone is no longer useful. But you don't have to worry, Walter. And neither does Michael. Right now, we all have to be more worried about Ismael. He's been on the edge since before we passed through the Strait of Gibraltar. It's being underwater. It's driving him crazier than he already is. Michael has him barely under control. When I talked to him about Ismael, he laughed and said that Ismael was keeping everybody aboard honest. Your people, our people, everyone's scared of him."

"Then why don't you kill him?" he taunted. "If you're so bloodthirsty, why do you have to limit yourself to keeping an eye on Michael and me? We're critical to the mission."

"Michael lies to frighten you. He likes to do things like that. And it apparently works." She sneered. "It would be insane to kill the captain of this submarine, wouldn't it? You surprise me, Walter, believing something like that." Her smile was both seductive and evil. "Look at what I was going to do for you just now. And you pushed me away."

Erhardt shook his head and wondered briefly how anyone could survive long around people like this. "You didn't answer me before. If you're so worried about Ismael, why don't you do the job yourself?"

"The man never sleeps. Besides, Walter, he is the expert on the torpedoes we have aboard."

"What's so special about those torpedoes?" he asked curiously. All he'd ever been told was that additional weapons would be transferred at sea. They'd had to sink two of their regular inventory in order to store the two that were brought aboard from the trawler. Both of those were now in the forward tubes.

"I don't know about the torpedoes. They aren't my business." Soraya stood abruptly. "Go back to sleep, Walter. I can see that you will do nothing with Ismael." She shook a finger at Erhardt as she stepped toward the door.

"And don't believe everything that Michael tells you about me. If you'd just relax, you'd find out I'm the kind of woman you could enjoy," she said coyly. "I know I would enjoy you." She flicked her tongue at him, enjoying the distaste on his face, before backing through the curtain that hung over his doorway.

Erhardt fell back, his head on the pillow. He pulled away the handkerchief and saw that the bleeding had lessened. But his lower lip was swollen and it hurt. Michael would be contacting Hussein again in less than twenty-four hours. Perhaps then they would be near the end of their mission and soon he could be finished with them.

Walter Erhardt closed his eyes. He shifted positions. But sleep wouldn't come back to him.

"Captain Davis here." Tom Davis's voice was so clear he might have been in the next room rather than his office in Naples.

"Tom, good. Lyford here. Gleick's on, too." Roland Lyford was in his Berlin office. "Conference call. It's also a secure line."

"Good morning, Captain," came Herman Gleick's even, slightly accented English from Kiel.

"Good morning to you, sir."

"My network's come up with a solid ID on that woman, the one we suspect was in the apartment with Captain Preminger last February," Lyford explained. "It cost more than I ever put down before, but at least it's something I'd go on. And it's not pretty. Her name's Soraya. That's all anyone seems to know her by. She may be Lebanese, but my informant isn't absolutely sure. And she's nuts, absolutely fucking mad."

"Excuse me?" It was Gleick's voice.

"Insane. Before she ever got involved with any terrorist group, she was in an institution for the criminally insane somewhere outside of Beirut. She murders men. Apparently has sex with them, then cuts their peckers off as far as I can gather."

"I thought the Arabs took care of people like that themselves," Davis said. "You know—the eye-for-an-eye thing."

"I don't know about that," Lyford answered. "I'm told she was sent to this asylum in Beirut, released to someone, although no one seems to know why, and she was last seen late last year in Jubay, a coastal city north of Beirut."

"And we don't know how she got to Kiel," Herman Gleick seemed to be saying more to himself. "That says wonders for our German immigration people, doesn't it?"

"I wouldn't blame them," Lyford answered. "This organization she belongs to is more highly sophisticated than any we've encountered. Any trail we pick up goes dry fast. They're too good. I haven't found any of my sources who can give me anything solid on the name of the group or who runs it. Apparently, she was supposedly seen once in Germany with an Arab who operates under the name Michael."

"Where in Germany?" Gleick asked.

"That source is dead, I'm afraid. Just Germany. Other than those two, the trail's cold. If we could find a reason for killing Preminger, maybe we'd have an angle."

"What do you think about Preminger's submarine?" Davis asked. "Sunk like we're supposed to believe? Captured by these people? After all, there was that so-called mysterious signal that the German navy's making more mysterious by keeping mum about it."

"I don't know what to think," Lyford answered. "One more of those mysterious transmissions and I'd go along with the latter."

Davis looked over his shoulder at a map of Europe. "I plotted the position where the *Waller* was reported to have gone down—in the Bay of Biscay. And then where that satellite signal was supposed to originate. If that sub's on the move, it's moving fast."

"Does the German navy give any indication of cooperating?"

"Not a word. They're scared shitless about this incident. They hate to admit anything. You know, security of weapons systems, all that crap. But I also know there's been a major search of that area southwest of Lisbon where that transmission supposedly originated, and no one's come up with a thing."

"You've got a bug up your ass, don't you?" Lyford commented.

"Far enough up to increase surveillance on all Sixth Fleet units until I hear something that'll make me feel better."

Hugo Schroeder had just accomplished what he'd intended. Ismael, the man Michael said was the expert on the torpedoes they'd brought aboard—Ismael, the madman, the most dangerous individual aboard *Heinz Waller*—now intended to kill him. And he would certainly do so in the next few seconds if Schroeder's plan didn't work. But if he was lucky, if Ismael did as Hugo Schroeder hoped, then a vital link would be removed from the terrorists' plans. It would most likely mean his death—but they would kill him eventually anyway.

No one in S-252's control room had dared to move when Hugo Schroeder lunged for the general quarters switch. Instead, as the alarm echoed through every compartment in S-252, their eyes followed Ismael, who was advancing resolutely toward the German officer. He moved slowly, the knife in his right hand held away from his body as he approached Schroeder, who had moved behind the chart table.

Ismael's narrowed eyes never left Schroeder's. The Turk moved sideways across the tiny space until the table was no longer between them. Why the German seemed to have cornered himself puzzled the Turk momentarily, but Ismael didn't bother to consider it further. The fact that Schroeder was trapped was all that mattered.

Schroeder's gaze shifted around the control room. Could he expect anyone to help? He was met with blank expressions. Then he looked back into Ismael's eyes and recognized the look he'd anticipated, the look of a killer. Schroeder knew there was little time left to make his move. Ismael was advancing with slow, short, measured steps.

Schroeder glanced quickly to his right and his eyes fell on the reason he had backed into the corner behind the chart table—the fire extinguisher set in a clip on the bulkhead to his right. He yanked it out, his fingers searching wildly for the trigger.

The Turk stopped momentarily, his eyes darting from Schroeder to the fire extinguisher, then back to Schroeder. Whatever had gone through Ismael's mind evidently wasn't about to deter him. An eerie smile spread across his face as he took another step toward the German officer. He was concentrating on Schroeder's eyes, no longer concerned about the fire extinguisher.

The general-quarters alarm continued to ring. How much time had passed since he hit the alarm? It was important that Michael and Erhardt should see Ismael attack if Schroeder was to save his own neck.

Ismael shifted his knife to the other hand as he picked up a long plastic ruler from the chart table. Then, with his arms extended to either side, the knife and the ruler bobbing up and down, he moved again toward Schroeder with sure short steps.

Hugo Schroeder, aware of pounding feet and voices as others responded to the alarm, realized that one more step would bring Ismael within striking distance. He pulled the safety pin on the fire extinguisher. There was no more time to wait. As Schroeder's finger closed on the trigger, Erhardt burst into the control room.

Ismael made his move, lunging at Schroeder.

A loud hollow noise drowned out every other sound as chemicals under pressure erupted from the nozzle. Schroeder, darting to one side, waved the extinguisher wildly, aiming it in the Turk's face as the knife chopped the air just inches away. White foam saturated Ismael. An animallike howl of pain and anger arose as the foam filled his eyes and nose and mouth.

Schroeder, ducking as Ismael swung the knife blindly in his direction, fell to his knees and began to crawl for his life. He was just beneath the blind slashes of the Turk's knife when Michael came through the hatch behind them. Without pausing, Michael launched himself at Ismael, wrapping his arms around the man's legs. The two of them crashed to the deck. Schroeder, his heart pounding, skittered away on his hands and knees.

Michael never stopped. Both his hands grasped Ismael's wrist and twisted until the knife was released. They rolled against the chart table where Michael pinned the other, shouting in his ear until finally Ismael went limp. But a soft moan of pain issued from his lips as he shook his head from side to side.

"Give me a towel!" Michael shouted. "He's in agony." Michael wiped at the carbon-based foam that covered the Turk's face with a rag from the chart table. For a moment, no one in the control room moved.

Michael, still intent on keeping Ismael calm, looked up. "Don't you understand?!" he cried. "That turns to acid when it's wet. His eyes are burning." His voice rose to a scream. "I need his eyes! I need his eyes!" He'd been told that Ismael was the only one who fully understood the detonators for the two torpedoes in the forward tubes.

Soraya was the first one to react. She, too, knew why Ismael was aboard. In seconds, she was back from the galley with another towel.

While Michael lay on top of Ismael, keeping his hands and arms pinned, Soraya daubed carefully at Ismael's eyes with the wet towel, wiping away the remnants of the foam. As she did so, Michael whispered constantly in Ismael's ear. The Turk's soft cries of pain were replaced by occasional moans.

Michael raised a hand to stop Soraya. He smoothed hair back from Ismael's forehead and stroked his cheek gently. "Open your eyes slowly." He shaded the man's eyes with his hand. "What do you see?"

"Don't know," Ismael grunted.

"Light," Michael prompted.

"Yes."

"Can you see my fingers moving?"

Ismael took a deep breath. "I guess so."

"But you do see something moving?"

"Yes."

"I'm going to get up, Ismael. But I don't want you to move. Your eyes are still in danger. If you do move, I'm going to have to tie you down and I don't want to do that." He spoke to Ismael as if he were talking to a child. "Soraya is going to help you. It will save your sight. Do you understand me?"

"Yes."

"Promise you won't move until I come back with something to make your eyes better?"

"Yes."

Michael rolled off Ismael and got to his feet. He looked around the control room. Schroeder had gotten to his feet and was watching from a distance. Walter Erhardt's hands were clasped behind his back as he considered the scene from the diving officer's position. None of the others in the control room appeared to have moved.

"You have a first-aid kit?" Michael asked Erhardt.

"Right there." Erhardt indicated a canvas bag clipped to the bulkhead above Schroeder. "There should be something in there for his eyes."

Michael went over and lifted the kit from its clip. He fumbled through the contents until he found a salve, nodded his head as he read the label, and hung the kit back in place. Then he indicated Schroeder. "Walter, you told me you needed this man." He poked Schroeder in the chest. "I need Ismael."

"And?"

"Your man may have blinded him."

Erhardt's eyes grew hard. "Ismael was going to kill him," he replied through clenched teeth. "I saw it myself. Schroeder was protecting himself."

"Why were they fighting?" Michael asked.

"I have no idea. Maybe someone else can tell you." Erhardt looked down at Ismael with contempt. "He doesn't seem to need a reason."

Michael shook the tube of salve in Erhardt's direction as he crossed over to Ismael. "If he is blind, your man is a dead man." Michael sank to his knees behind Ismael and gently lifted the Turk's head, resting it on his own thighs. He handed the tube to Soraya. "Listen, Ismael, I'm going to hold your head so you can't move it. Soraya is going to put this salve in each eye. Don't move your head. She's going to be very gentle because she feels badly for you. I don't want this to hurt you, so you have to blink and work it into your eyes yourself. Do you understand?"

"Yes," Ismael grunted.

"Go ahead," Michael said to Soraya.

Once the salve was in his eyes, Ismael allowed it to work in very carefully. When Michael asked how he was feeling, Ismael said there was very little pain but he was tired. They led him forward to the torpedo room, made sure he took an extra dose of pain pills, and strapped him in one of the drop bunks.

Back in the control room, Michael moved over beside Erhardt. "I've secured Ismael in his bunk. I explained to him it was for his own good in case there was more pain and I said I would check him regularly. He can't get out until I release him."

"Nothing's ever stopped him before," Erhardt said.

"With the drugs I made him take, he'll probably sleep until sometime tomorrow. If Ismael still can't see, I'm worried about those torpedoes. I hope your man, Neuner . . ." He stopped in midsentence and turned to point an accusing finger at Schroeder. "Maybe I'll kill him now."

Hugo Schroeder waited calmly, unsure of his fate. He'd taken a chance and it had worked. Since he'd never considered himself a brave man, the past moments had surprised him. Had he succeeded in preventing . . . what? *I don't even know what's going to happen.*

"As long as I'm captain of this submarine, I won't allow . . ." Erhardt began angrily.

Michael interrupted by clapping his hands loudly twice. "You won't have anything to say about it, Walter."

Jake Steele hopped easily down from the helicopter onto *Ashland*'s flight deck and scurried across to the walkway overlooking the LSD's well deck. Chief Bewick was leaning casually against the railing, a friendly easy smile lighting his smudged face. The chief's work clothes displayed an uneven coating of grease. A torn blue baseball cap sat backwards on his head.

"Master Chief," Jake said as he was beckoned to follow Bewick, "are you going to tell me one of your oil filters exploded while you were working on it?"

"Not a chance. Not on my boats. They're tuned to kiss

your ass if you ask nicely enough." As they rounded the corner and came into the area where the RIBs were stored, Bewick slowed to glance back over his shoulder at Jake. He lowered his head so that he was looking over the tops of his glasses. "You've tried that on me before, Mr. Jake. You also asked me twice before where I hid the motorcycle, and also if I shrank myself and climbed inside the engine. You got to think faster if you want to outthink a master chief."

Steele grinned as he circled one of the RIBs. "Looks fine to me. Looks like the boat survived the ordeal and the chief lost. So tell me, Master Chief, what happens with you if someone calls a surprise inspection?"

Bewick removed his glasses and rubbed an eye with a clean section of his wrist. "I tell 'em that it's all the fault of Admiral Turner's N-7." He replaced his glasses and squinted at Steele. "How come you didn't fly me over to your ship again? I like to ride on helicopters. Great views from up there. So tell me, did you just come over to hand an old guy a lot of shit?"

"Not this time. I came over to supervise some target practice for you and your men because Happy Jack Turner's worried about my motorcycle repairmen getting hurt if something goes down."

Bewick snorted. "You're kidding. Tell me you're yanking my chain."

"No I'm not, Master Chief. I've spent so much time telling the admiral how vital you guys are to world peace that now he's worried about you."

Chief Bewick frowned. "We're as good with those guns as we are with the engines. Talk to me, Mr. Jake. Someone's worried about something. My boys like to hear it straight."

"It's just a chance, but we might need you and your boys giving us more backup than we planned if there's an evil fishing trawler out there," he said with a grin. "This is more like covering all the bases than anything else," Jake cautioned. "If we run into any trouble with a well-armed trawler, we want to make sure the firepower's on our side."

"That's sort of what we've been playing games for out here." Bewick sat down on one of the inflatable rubber gunwales on a RIB and patted a spot beside him. "Plenty of room for two here. Let's see now. You said there might be a trawler. So we trained like we were going after one."

Steele sat down beside him. "That's right."

"And we made sure the helos gave us cover when we were playing out there the last couple of days. So what's changed?"

"Admiral Turner worries about missiles blowing helicopters out of the air."

"You serious, Mr. Jake? You think there's a missile-armed trawler out there?"

"I don't know myself. It's probably being overly cautious, but you know how the brass worry when they're not sure what they're worrying over. There's not even a fishing boat out there that looks threatening. Intelligence hasn't got anything for us to go on other than they're worrying their butts off about some highly sophisticated terrorist group they don't know anything about."

"My boys are already experts with small arms," Bewick said defensively.

"I know they are. Mine are, too." Steele's expression grew more serious as he explained, "It's what the brass like to call refamiliarization. All of us are going to play at it, SEALs included. And my boys are real experts. But sometimes we need backup from pros like you."

Bewick had worked with Jake Steele for years and could tell when the kidding was over. "I take it that we need a little briefing to bring my boys up to date."

"I don't know what we're expecting," Jake answered. "But intelligence seems to think there could be some very nasty people out there, even though they don't know who, what, where, why. . . ." He shrugged.

"Okay, Mr. Jake. Doesn't sound like anything we haven't handled before. I'm ready to bury nasty people. When are we going to begin this target practice?"

"I radioed ahead. My platoon leaders are in the armory now, breaking out the hardware. They're going to work closely with your guys this time."

"You don't mind if I do my imitation of an intelligence expert, do you, Mr. Jake?"

"What's on your mind?"

"There's always a grapevine. What's this I hear about submarines?"

"Nothing to worry about yet. Sixth Fleet's got a bug up about some German submarine that's been missing—and then the Germans think maybe they heard from it in an entirely different location. Believe me, Master Chief, there's nothing firm to go on."

"Okay, Mr. Jake. It's a surface threat for now."

Rear Admiral Jack Turner watched through his binoculars as the SEALs and the sailors who manned the RIBs went through two hours of live fire exercises. They stayed well away from the other ships as they practiced at high speed with every weapon they had. They fired .50-caliber machine guns mounted on a metal plate on the bow of their RIBs as well as automatic rifles, light side arms, and grenade launchers. They fired at targets floating in the water and targets towed at high speeds. They fired until all their ammunition had been expended.

As they were waiting for the deck cranes to lift the RIBs back aboard *Ashland,* Chief Bewick asked Steele, "My boys look as good to you as I claimed?"

"Terrific." There was a playful smile on Steele's face. "My platoon leaders say they'd let your boys rescue them from any whorehouse in the Med."

Chief Bewick ran a greasy hand through his sparse hair and looked over his glasses again. "That's what I call real sailors, Mr. Jake."

Francis Waters had quickly become accustomed to the navy's operations around *Calm Seas.* Helicopters flitting back and forth no longer caught his eye. Even the small boats lowered from *Ashland* that afternoon failed to hold his attention. He was tired. Being awakened and coming to the bridge half a dozen times each night was something new to him, and the end of this week couldn't come soon enough.

When *Calm Seas* was on charter, nights were either spent on the calmest course possible or secure at some dock while his passengers played ashore. Everything was different with *Wasp.* She changed course often at night and broadcast warnings of every approaching ship that might pass through their screen. Each time, Francis had to be on the bridge. His passengers were too critical to take any chances.

So Waters had broken out a folding couch behind the bridge that afternoon, spread it almost flat, and gratefully stretched out in the shade. Gentle swells barely rocked *Calm Seas,* and a light breeze played across the deck. He was sound asleep in a very short time.

He was awakened by something that he hadn't heard for years. It was a troubling sound, one that had given him nightmares for years. But like most things in life, he'd been able to push it into the back of his mind until it gradually disappeared.

Automatic weapons . . . live firing . . .

It had never been so bad when it was distant, but somehow it had always seemed to get closer rather than subside.

. . . fifty-caliber could chop a thick jungle tree in half . . .

Waters went from sound sleep to wide awake in seconds. He sat bolt upright swinging his feet onto the deck. The firing was in the distance, so far away that he was amazed that it had disturbed his sleep. But as he listened, he could tell instantly that he was hearing fifty-caliber—and that was a sound that had always awakened him.

Back on the bridge, he scanned the horizon through his binoculars until he found the source. He saw the RIBs racing across the horizon, recognized the tracers seeking their quarry, and once he even saw a towed target disintegrate.

The moment Will Riley appeared on the bridge at the end of the day's meetings, Waters cornered him. "What's going on that I don't know about, Will? There was some pretty serious live firing exercise out there this afternoon."

Riley was puzzled. "We were in a closed, air-conditioned room all afternoon. Didn't hear a thing." He shrugged. "I suppose the navy needs to keep their people busy. . . ."

"I don't have a nervous stomach, Will, but I suppose I could get one. You tightened up the screen for submarines, now you're back to chasing things on the surface. These were the little boats we've seen before. This time they were busy. No one was playing tag. This was live ammo. Looks like someone else is nervous."

"I haven't heard any more than you have, Francis. I'll ask Mr. Griffey when I get a chance."

The release of all units involved in the search for S-252 was short and unique in its simplicity.

FEDERAL REPUBLIC OF GERMANY

OPERATIONAL IMMEDIATE

CLASSIFICATION - UNCLAS

FROM: COMMANDER SUBMARINE SQUADRON FOUR
TO: ALL COMMANDS, WALLER RESCUE OPERATION

1) UPON RECEIPT OF THIS MESSAGE, ALL UNITS PARTICIPATING IN S-252 SEARCH ARE RELEASED FROM TEMPORARY DUTY WITH THIS COMMAND.
2) UNLESS OTHERWISE ORDERED BY SEPARATE MESSAGE, YOU ARE TO REPORT YOUR CHANGE IN OPERATIONAL STATUS TO YOUR ADMINISTRATIVE COMMAND AND RETURN TO ORIGINALLY SCHEDULED DUTIES.
3) ANY MEDIA EFFORTS TO OBTAIN INFORMATION ARE TO BE DIRECTED TO THIS COMMAND.
4) UPON COMPLETION OF INVESTIGATION OF LOSS OF S-252, THIS COMMAND WILL FORWARD A DETAILED ANALYSIS OF SEARCH AND RESCUE EFFORTS BY INDIVIDUAL AND COMBINED UNITS TO UPDATE YOUR FUTURE SAR EMERGENCY OPERATIONS' DOCTRINE.
5) COMSUBRON FOUR CONVEYS TO EVERY UNIT AND INDIVIDUAL INVOLVED IN THIS COMBINED EFFORT THE PERSONAL APPRECIATION OF THIS COMMAND AND THE FRG NAVY FOR YOUR UNCEASING EFFORTS TO RENDER ASSISTANCE.

There was no mention of the signal received via satellite indicating that Lieutenant Hugo Schroeder and *Heinz Wal-*

ler might have been on the surface at a position southwest of Lisbon.

Neither the announcement that his communications director was there to meet with him as scheduled nor the fact that Bill Herbert had actually crossed the floor and was standing before his desk registered immediately with Phil Salkin. He had followed the disappearance of the *Heinz Waller* with the same empathy he would have had if she had been an American ship, and he had also been informed of the receipt of Schroeder's signal. His morning intelligence briefing, however, included the investigation of possible terrorist involvement. That meant that the German sailors' lives might still be forfeit. Now Salkin was experiencing one of those moments that he rarely had time for in his demanding schedule—a time to bond for a moment with the survivors who would surely be scarred forever.

In the three years that he had been President, his affection for the men and women who served in the military had intensified tremendously. As he toured military bases and ships in his capacity as Commander in Chief, he'd found the human element that had previously escaped him. When he sat down to eat in messes and wardrooms and galleys, he was able to communicate freely with individuals who wished for the same things for themselves and their families as those who strolled past each day on the Pennsylvania Avenue mall. But these military people he met were working for him, and they were willingly sacrificing more in their daily lives than the vast majority who passed the White House.

He was sure the men aboard that German submarine had been no different, and his heart went out to the German people who suffered this tragedy that very moment.

"Mr. President . . ."

Salkin blinked his eyes rapidly and looked up. Had he been dozing?

"Mr. President . . ." Bill Herbert said again. "I thought that you were expecting—"

"Bill!" Phil Salkin interrupted whatever was about to be said. "Don't be concerned. You were announced. I guess I said to send you in." He sat up straight in his chair and noticed the memo on his desk. *Those poor goddamn German sailors.* "My eyes weren't shut, were they?"

"No. Your head was down but your eyes were open. Are you feeling all right?" Herbert asked with concern.

"All right? Hell, Bill, I feel fine. I guess I was thinking about those poor German sailors on that submarine, whatever's taken place." He pursed his lips and said, "No, I guess it wasn't them I was thinking about so much as their families. The last time those sailors walked out their front doors, they were expected to come back through those same doors when that submarine returned home. The only people coming through those doors the next couple of days will be people coming to say how sorry they are." Salkin shook his head sadly. "See, I got carried away, Bill." He looked at his watch. "Late. After six. Cocktail time." He rose from his chair. "I hope you'll join me in a drink."

"I'd like that."

Salkin walked over to a bookcase behind his desk and opened the cabinet beneath. "What'll it be, Bill? You know everything I got down here." Once he'd made it clear he wanted his own bar and didn't want anyone mixing drinks for him, the staff stocked everything that had ever been bottled.

"I guess I'll have whatever you're having."

"Chivas. They always make sure there's a couple of extra jugs down here. Hell, the seals on most of the other stuff have never been cracked." He took out a bottle and poured a couple of ounces in each glass.

"Does that mean everyone likes Scotch?"

Salkin took ice cubes from the bucket on the bookcase's first shelf and dropped them in each glass. "Hell, Bill, I think it's more that everyone's scared to ask for what they want when I'm the one mixing drinks." He swirled the ice around in each glass with his index finger. "I know you don't take anything else in it." He handed one of the glasses to Herbert.

Herbert grinned. "It wouldn't make much difference if I did, would it? The first drink I ever had in here—when Rupert Daniels brought me in the first time—I remembered you said no one ever ruined good Scotch by diluting it."

Salkin beamed. "You're right. Your memory's better than mine. But now I remember that." He strolled over by the tall window facing out on the gardens and studied the wonders of an especially brilliant sunset. Spring flowers nodding in the light evening breeze were enriched by its orange-gold tint.

Herbert came over beside him. "Cheers." He held up his glass.

"Cheers." The President took a sip of his drink, followed by a larger swallow. He turned sad eyes to Herbert. "And here's to the flower of German youth who won't be returning home."

They both sipped their drinks and stared out into the garden.

"I feel so helpless when something like that happens, Bill. I'm so thankful it wasn't American boys, but you always know deep inside that something else will happen that will kill some of our own, too. I wish I could do something . . . say something . . . that would let their families know how I feel." He turned to look at the other man. "Do you know what I mean? Everything said officially is so hollow."

"It is hard to put something like that into words."

"Sit down, Bill. You didn't come in here to listen to me be maudlin. I believe my schedule has the director of communications discussing the peace conference with me."

"Everything there still coming up roses?"

"Better than we could ever have hoped for. I just got off the phone with Lou Griffey. He's ecstatic. They're talking to each other, actually communicating."

"That's wonderful, sir."

"Lou says they're going to meet each other more than halfway. But it's even more than Arabs and Jews. It's Arabs and Arabs. Sunni and Shiite. They're away from everything they normally identify with, the centuries of tribal warfare, the border disputes, the religious leaders who've fomented so much of the hatred. They're on a boat in the middle of the Mediterranean, where Lou has made it clear that no single individual is more important than the next. They're not looking out a window at the oasis claimed by their ancestors or the oasis that's belonged to the ancestors of the person sitting next to them."

"Are we going to see new borders coming out of this?" Herbert asked.

"Not at all. That wasn't Rupert Daniels's purpose. It's not ours. It's still a peace conference. Those people are going to produce and sign a protocol of their own, which Lou will help them with, but only if they ask for his help. It's going to be both a nonaggression pact and a mutual defense treaty, an extension in a way of that first agreement between the Israelis and the PLO, but much, much more."

Herbert frowned. "I can't quite believe it will work, sir. Some of those countries have made a tradition of fighting with each other. It's in their nature."

"Rupert Daniels was a student of that part of the world. Just before he was killed, he told me if that pact wasn't concluded soon, those nations would tear themselves apart and take the rest of the world with them. It's selfish in a way because it's also our means of keeping away from a potential world war that would start off the next century."

Herbert looked into his glass, tipping it one way and then another to catch the glint of the ice cubes. When he looked up, his face displayed a resolution that hadn't been evident before. "It's obviously of historic proportions, and that's where we get into my end of this business of politics. I expect you'll be there to announce to the world what you've done," he said evenly. "There's a lot of good that can come of this with the election a year away."

Salkin smiled and shook his head slowly. "When the time comes, Bill, I'll need your help to do it right. But that's not the way I want to have it when they sign. I'll just be a witness to the history those people are making. We'll make it clear we underwrote the conference, but we'll also emphasize the fact that those nations were the ones who made it happen. When it comes time to campaign, I think you'll be able to make something of it then."

Herbert frowned into his glass and sipped the last of his drink.

"You look like you could use another couple of fingers, Bill."

Herbert stood up and extended his hand toward the President's glass. "Since you're making my job tougher, I guess I could use another. But let me do the honors this time. You've got a heavy hand and I have a dinner to attend tonight."

Salkin looked over his shoulder as Herbert dropped ice cubes in each glass. "Would you do things differently?"

"To be honest, I pictured bringing you in just under God in this one, sort of a Woodrow Wilson, but one who succeeds." He poured Scotch into each glass and returned to his chair across from the President. "Are you still leaving for Europe as scheduled?"

"Day after tomorrow. Lou says the timing looks good."

"What about this terrorist thing? Your security people aren't going to let you in there if they think you may be a target."

Salkin frowned. "I suppose you're right. The Secret Service is fretting over what the CIA has been worrying themselves about in Berlin. But that seems to me to be a German problem. I can't quite see how it's going to affect the conference." He spun the ice cubes around the glass with his finger. "I want you to be there with me and Lou to see this happen, Bill."

CHAPTER FOURTEEN

DAY FIVE

Shortly after midnight, *Waller*'s periscope edged above the Mediterranean's surface. The satellite navigational fix confirmed the inertial navigation system's position. They were just northeast of Bizerte, about thirty kilometers off the Tunisian coast.

Soraya now found it difficult to read Michael's shifting moods. At times, he was churlish, worried about Ismael's eyes, angry at himself for not paying enough attention to Ismael's outbursts, frustrated because Erhardt had shown no sympathy for his problem. And he could not explain how critical Ismael might be at a later time because he did not know himself. Yet he was animated as he attempted to establish contact with Hussein and enthusiastic when he finally did.

Hussein had no interest in conversation. Once their position was verified, his next words were: "I would like to include Erhardt now. I want to hear his voice."

A moment later, Hussein heard, "This is Captain Erhardt."

Hussein spoke slowly in poorly accented German, as if he were reading a speech. "Good evening, Captain Erhardt. A pleasure to speak again with you. My German, as you are aware, is poor. Michael will translate for us." Then he lapsed back into his own language. "But I want to hear your responses in your own language before Michael does, so I will be sure by the tone of your voice that you comprehend. Do you understand? Explain, Michael."

Michael translated.

"Yes. I understand," Erhardt responded. He felt a chill course down his spine and seem to swell as it centered in his groin. They must be so close to . . . to his final mission . . . to . . . to what?

"You must have an accurate depth chart of the eastern Mediterranean. Will you get it out, please?" Hussein's method of speaking gave no clue to the man.

"Yes. Please wait a moment." Erhardt ordered Schroeder to remove it from the chart-table drawer as Michael translated.

Hussein continued. "We will be in contact only one more time. While your former command has declared you lost at sea, there are many military ships capable of locating a submarine in the Mediterranean quite by chance. I want you to remain as close to your maximum depth as possible to avoid that possibility. You will pass to the east of Cape Bon off Tunisia, then I want you to turn to the south. Do you see on your chart where the sea mountains rise east of there?"

Erhardt could see the trenches and mountains beneath the Mediterranean's surface. "Yes."

"There are British destroyers training with a submarine in that area right now. Their orders keep them above thirty-six degrees north. You will select a course that will keep you west of that shallower water and south from them. You can't take the chance of being heard. When you are satisfied, you may turn east on a course that will take you south of Malta."

Malta! That was another word that Walter Erhardt recognized instantly. Had Hussein planned it that way? Malta—where he and Darra had lived their dream. "I can see a place to turn east and then north along the trenches," Erhardt replied. He could already see the path he would take into the Malta Trough. Once again, that sensation settled into his loins like cold steel. "I can use the bottom topography to mask our sound."

"Estimate how long it will take you to reach a position fifteen degrees directly east of Malta. Take your time in doing so because we will not speak again until you are there."

"Mr. Schroeder, do the calculations." Erhardt was old school. He insisted on human backup to a computer; a good submariner could correct for human error before it was too late. As Erhardt selected each leg of their projected course and programmed it into the automated surface display, he called out the distances. Schroeder inserted each one into the calculator.

"What do you make it, Mr. Schroeder?"

Schroeder divided the total distance by their intended average speed on the calculator. "It could be done in thirty hours . . ." He hesitated. "Better thirty-six though."

"Tell him thirty-six," Erhardt said to Michael.

"It can't be longer than that." It was the first time there'd been any sign of concern since the initial contact off the coast of Spain.

Erhardt felt that tingle again. They were getting so close. . . . "Maybe thirty . . . with luck . . ."

"Thirty hours then. As long as you are able to avoid detection."

Michael knew better than to ask anything more of Hussein. *Thirty hours from now we will have a target.*

Before radio contact, Hugo Schroeder had casually suggested surfacing to bring fresh air into the submarine. Now he struggled to control his disappointment. If only he'd been able to employ the signaling device one more time, just to let squadron headquarters know that S-252 not only existed but was now in the Mediterranean. *We're alive—we're dangerous!*

Herman Gleick waited patiently, the phone precariously balanced between shoulder and ear while he carefully polished his rimless glasses. Whoever had answered the phone at the U.S. Embassy in Berlin had rushed off to find Lyford before Gleick could volunteer to leave a message. Were Americans always as rude when they heard a German accent? The lady on the other end hadn't bothered to hide her exasperation. Or was it that she, too, resented CIA agents in their midst? Lyford had mentioned that he wasn't exactly revered by the State Department people.

Gleick glanced up at the ancient clock on the far side of the office as he placed his glasses carefully back on his nose. He watched as the largest hand clicked forward to the next minute with a mechanical shudder. Almost two minutes now, and Director-Homicide Neumann complained monthly about their long-distance telephone bills.

The sound of a door slamming, rapid footsteps, and a breathless "This is Lyford!" came through Gleick's earpiece in succession.

"Mr. Lyford, this is Herman Gleick . . . in Kiel." He was naturally shy. "I sincerely hope I haven't interrupted something."

"Just a hell of a good dump is all. Other than that, I've been hoping someone nice would call me today."

Gleick paused. Was this American humor? Or was it sarcasm? He wasn't sure, but it sounded as if maybe he'd interrupted Lyford in the lavatory. It was always so difficult to be sure with these Americans. "If I created a problem, I'm sorry because the lady who answered your telephone never gave me a chance to leave a message for a callback."

"Hey, think nothing of it. I can go back and finish up after we talk. Maybe I'll invite her to join me, and next time she'll learn how to handle the phone properly."

Surely it was American humor and, he noted with amusement, at its crudest. But as far as he was concerned it was preferable to the European habit of not expressing what you were really thinking. "Perhaps it will improve your day if I tell you I may have a fantastic lead to follow."

"I'm all ears."

Gleick enjoyed their slang. If Lyford had made a comment about his wandering eye, it would have been even funnier. "I received a telephone call from Captain Preminger's widow this morning. She found a box of matches in a coffee-table drawer in her living room from a restaurant in Hamburg called As-Sa'iqa. Since she knew nothing about the place, she wondered if it might mean anything to me."

"As-Sa'iqa." Lyford pronounced it a few more times. "Certainly not German, is it?"

"Not at all. As a matter of fact, the only reason she didn't throw them away was that they were in Arabic. I stopped by

Mrs. Preminger's home and picked up the matches right after her call. Then I took them over to one of our Arabic specialists here at the central office. That name, As-Sa'iqa, goes back more than twenty-five years. It was a name Mr. Paddha had mentioned when he was trying to remember various Muslim terrorist groups of the past. It's Syrian and means thunderbolt. As-Sa'iqa was a terrorist group that grew out of the Palestinian branch of the Syrain Ba'ath Party. During the 1970s, they performed a few reasonably successful terrorist operations, but since then they've sort of disappeared."

"Doesn't it seem rather odd to name a place of business after a terrorist organization?"

"There are a number of equally strange situations in Germany these days," Gleick answered. "We've got neo-Nazi organizations thriving again, and we seem to look the other way. Who would ever bother with the name of a tiny foreign restaurant on the Elbe River in Hamburg that no Germans bother with to my knowledge?"

"I take it you've already checked this place out."

"I called a friend who is an investigator in Hamburg. He called me back an hour later to explain that it was a nondescript place on the riverfront, not too far from the airport. No alcohol is consumed there, so he doubts any Germans ever visit. Other than that, he knows nothing."

"And naturally you're curious as to why the commanding officer of a German submarine should have had matches from there." Lyford made a sound somewhere between a snort and a laugh. "Especially since he seems to have been joyfully banging away at this Soraya, who knows something about terrorist groups herself."

"Yes," Gleick answered, once again amused by the American slang. Obviously, Lyford was referring to Preminger's sexual dalliance. "I'm going to drive down to Hamburg this afternoon to see this restaurant for myself, and I would appreciate it if you could see what else you can learn about this As-Sa'iqa group from your sources. I'll call you back this evening and let you know what I've learned. Would that be satisfactory?" Gleick inquired politely.

"No problem. I'll get someone on that name right away,

but how about if you wait a few hours until I can hop a plane and meet you in Hamburg and we can both visit this place?"

Gleick paused. The director had said he wanted Gleick to visit the As-Sa'iqa right away. It seemed that the navy was causing political pressure to be put on the mayor's office, and that, in turn, was coming to the chief investigator's office. "Your offer is very kind. If I wasn't experiencing pressure here, I'd be pleased to have you join me. But I don't have that luxury today."

"Mr. Gleick . . . Herman . . . I hope you don't mind me using your first name . . . the older I get, the more I look over my shoulder. That includes going into strange places alone. I'd sure like to be there to back you up if there's something worthwhile."

"Hamburg is just ninety kilometers south of here. I appreciate your concern. But it's just an hour's drive, and I really haven't been given a choice of when I can go down there. I'm sure you understand office politics."

"A great American tradition," Lyford noted. "Okay, let me wish you luck then. And don't keep me waiting. Call anytime. Maybe I'll have something else for you by then."

"I promise. I'll call no later than my return home this evening."

"No, seriously, how about earlier if you have a chance? Don't wait. I'm going to stay right here all day."

Gleick was warmed by the obvious concern in the American's voice. "All right. Earlier, if there is an opportunity."

The As-Sa'iqa was a kilometer east of the airport and a hundred meters up a side street from the Elbe River, which coursed through the middle of the city. Although Hamburg was about a hundred kilometers inland from the North Sea, it was a port city. Like most port cities, the section near the docks was run-down and unattractive. Bars and small ethnic restaurants were wedged between warehouses and grimy shipping and clearing offices.

The tiny Arabic restaurant had no sign on the street. Passersby would never have noticed the entrance unless they were searching for it. Only As-Sa'iqa, appearing in the same Arabic script as on the match box, was painted on a single dirty window set in the door to identify the place.

If Herman Gleick had been asked beforehand to describe what he thought the interior of the As-Sa'iqa might look like, he would have been quite accurate. It was dark. Foreign fragrances permeated the air. Exotic coffee machines filled the space where a bar would have been in a German *gasthaus.* Light filtered through the thick air from what he assumed was the kitchen in the rear.

There were two dozen customers at the most, all seated around wooden tables in uncomfortable-looking wooden chairs. Gleick was the only European there, and his appearance attracted instant attention.

When no one appeared to assist him, Gleick seated himself at an empty table under the hostile, watchful eyes of each person in the room. Picking up what might have been a menu, he saw that once again he had been correct in his assumptions about As-Sa'iqa. The page was covered with flowing Arabic script. The management did not anticipate that European customers would appear there.

He looked up as a tall, fierce-looking, mustachioed man appeared in front of his table. Without expression, the man said in a thickly accented German, "I have no menu for you. I can say you what to eat if you in right place." His black eyes never wavered from Gleick's as he glared unsmilingly at him. The eyes said what the man could not—Europeans were not welcome.

"As-Sa'iqa?" Gleick asked, pronouncing the name exactly as he had been coached.

The man's head barely moved in a nod of affirmation.

"This is what I would like." Gleick handed the man a sheet of paper with the food he desired written out in Arabic.

Once again, there was a barely visible nod accompanied by a tightening of the lips. The European had no intention of leaving. The man disappeared toward the back with Gleick's request in hand.

The other customers spoke in hushed tones as Gleick waited for his food, their unfriendly eyes never staring directly at him, never quite avoiding his presence. What, he wondered, had it been like for Preminger? Perhaps if he had been here with the woman called Soraya, they'd found him acceptable after a while. But an overt sense of hostility permeated the room. Germany existed only outside the walls of As-Sa'iqa.

After eating what he decided was an overly spiced, vegetarian meal, Gleick asked the man waiting on him for coffee.

"Not like your coffee. Won't like."

"I will like it." Gleick smiled pleasantly. "Please."

A piece of dirty paper was slipped under the tiny cup of thick black coffee. It appeared to be the bill; the only part he could identify was the total at the bottom. "May I smoke in here?" He already had a cigarette in his hand. There were also others smoking.

He was rewarded with a barely distinguishable nod from the man who was apparently waiting for his money.

Gleick took the As-Sa'iqa matches from his pocket and displayed them in the palm of his hand. "I have a friend who liked your food. That's why I came here." He lit the cigarette and inhaled distastefully. It had taken so long to quit tobacco that he hoped this would not be the revival of the habit. "Hans Preminger. Do you remember him?"

There was a negative, but more pronounced, shake of the head. "You pay now."

"Would you remember a lovely lady he was with? Her name was Soraya. Long black hair. Beautiful eyes. *Soraya*"—Gleick pronounced her name slowly—"often mentioned your food."

The man's face reflected nothing, no recognition, no interest in the question. But his eyes mirrored something else, an increasing hostility. "I ask," he said, and was gone without taking Gleick's money.

The coffee was excellent, thick and syrupy. Two swallows and there was only black sediment caked on the bottom of the tiny cup. "May I have some more coffee?" Gleick asked as the man once again approached the table.

"No more coffee. All gone. No one knows names. You pay now."

There was only one other name he could think of and he had no idea why it came to him. Gleick took his wallet from his jacket pocket. "How about a man named Walter Erhardt?" he asked, as he finished counting out his money. "I think Soraya brought him here also."

The man was a consummate actor, but there was no masking his reaction. He said nothing, but he was unable to restrain a slight frown that emphasized the lines around his eyes and caused his forehead to wrinkle ever so slightly. There was no doubt of recognition even as the man replied, "No names I know." He added, "We close now," even though half a dozen people remained inside. He scooped up the money and the box of matches before he turned away.

"May I have a receipt?" Gleick called to his back.

"Close now." The man disappeared into the kitchen in the rear.

As he walked down the street toward the Elbe River, it occurred to Herman Gleick that, unlike Hans Preminger, he had nothing to show that he had ever dined at the As-Sa'iqa. If something happened to him, Roland Lyford would never know whether or not he'd been there, nor would he know that someone in As-Sa'iqa not only was familiar with Preminger and Soraya, but also had reacted strongly to the name of Walter Erhardt. That was something neither he nor Lyford would have anticipated.

Gleick wondered why there were so few people on the streets, until he realized that the few ships alongside the docks were grimy freighters, mostly foreign, and the residents had no reason to visit unless they had business there. That reminded him of Roland Lyford's concern. The CIA agent said that he looked over his shoulder more often as he got older, and Gleick was tempted to do exactly that. He kept his eyes fixed directly in front of him until curiosity got the best of him, and he glanced quickly behind. No one. But he had learned something that was maybe of great value to the case, and Lyford was waiting to hear from him.

Gleick turned right by the river and headed down toward a more modern section of the city where there had to be phones. He crossed the street twice to make sure that he wasn't being followed, and each time he was relieved to see that his imagination was playing tricks on him. As he approached a parking area by an aging shopping mall, he saw a bank of three pay-phone booths. Certainly, it made sense to pass on his information, even if there was no danger.

Since he had no change and the Director-Homicide's office had no telephone cards, Gleick was obliged to make a collect call to Lyford's office.

"I'm very sorry, sir," came a nasal feminine voice, "but we can't accept collect calls . . ."

Gleick recognized a car that had been just down the street from As-Sa'iqa pulling into the parking lot and speeding up as it came toward the bank of phones. "Well then, it's an emergency. Tell Mr. Lyford that Inspector Gleick must speak with him immediately. This is an emergency."

The window on the driver's side of the automobile was rolled down, and the driver waved his hand to someone. Gleick looked to his left and saw two men approaching from the direction he'd just come from. *Yes, indeed, I've struck a nerve.* But why did this remind him of a cheap television movie—approaching him in this manner? He removed his Beretta from the holster set in the small of his back. Would it have made any difference if Lyford had been with him at As-Sa'iqa? Not really. If they'd killed others so easily, two more wouldn't make a difference.

"Sir, if you can hold just a moment, Mr. Lyford will be with you. He's just finishing a conference—"

"Fuck the conference!" he interrupted, screaming into the phone. He was certain that's how an American would attract attention. "I'm going to be a dead man in a moment. I need him now."

The car stopped ten meters away. The reflection on the windshield prevented him from seeing inside the car, and no one stepped out. Once again, the driver waved his hand. The men coming down the street were a block away but had picked up their pace. Gleick held the Beretta just inside his jacket, his finger on the trigger.

"Gleick, what the hell?!" Lyford's voice boomed over the phone. "What's this about being a dead man?"

The operator in the background cut in: "Sir, will you accept the call?"

Gleick closed his eyes. How could this happen? Then he

heard the car doors open. The others were half a block away now and running purposefully in his direction. Two men emerged from either side of the car, both very dark, both with the same hostile expression as the man in the As-Sa'iqa.

"I accept," Lyford bellowed. "Gleick . . ."

"Be quiet!" Gleick shouted into the phone. "I was there . . . As-Sa'iqa. What I didn't expect was that Walter Erhardt's name was recognized. Erhardt!" Each of the men from the car had guns in their hands and were moving cautiously toward his phone booth. The men approaching from the other direction were close and now had guns also. "That means . . ."

One of the men from the car raised his gun. Gleick shoved open the door with his foot and brought the Beretta up, squeezing the trigger as he did so. Their shots seemed to go off together. The man he'd shot at appeared to vault backward.

Gleick felt something slam into his shoulder and knock him back against the telephone. He knew he'd cried out in agony.

"Gleick, what?"

"Erhardt . . ." This was Herman Gleick's last word. It began as a shout and ended in a groan.

Lyford's voice howled out of the earpiece as Herman Gleick whipped his Beretta around in the other man's direction. But he was never able to level it. Something pounded him in the stomach. He cried out in anger. The glass in the phone booth shattered as one of his arms went numb. Something seemed to explode in the back of his neck. As he plunged helplessly through the door of the phone booth, he saw his rimless glasses land on the pavement and shatter. But he never felt himself land on top of them.

One of the men from the car stepped over Herman Gleick's corpse and picked up the receiver dangling by its wire. "Hello, who am I speaking to, please?" he inquired in broken German.

"Who the hell is this?" Lyford asked.

The man let the receiver swing free and fired twice into the heart of the telephone.

Lyford called, "Gleick?" But the phone in Hamburg was dead.

"First, Mr. Schroeder, if you are going to join me in this flight through the Mediterranean alps, you must imagine when there was no Mediterranean." Walter Erhardt spoke expansively, almost hypnotically. "That was long ago, maybe a hundred, maybe even two hundred million years ago." He spread his arms. "Imagine a vast continent tearing itself apart, great plates of land colliding, one sliding under the other, earthquakes, volcanoes—a great cataclysm." He nodded in satisfaction. "That's what it was. That's why this sea-floor map looks like this."

Schroeder studied the relief map of the Mediterranean on the chart table. Erhardt was right. It reminded him of when he was a child in the classroom and of the raised maps of the Alps, the kind you could actually touch.

"If there was no water in the Mediterranean, you would see mountains and valleys, wide plains, streams, deep rivers, and cataracts dropping a thousand feet." Erhardt's index finger tapped the area between Tunisia and Malta. "That is exactly what this area is like, except we are going to cross it in a submarine. You and I, Mr. Schroeder, we have to imagine we are on a cross-country hike. We're going to climb mountains, descend into valleys, and search for passes to make our trip easier. Except . . . except we are never going to touch anything solid. We are going to swim through. And while we are making this dangerous passage, we don't want anyone to notice us. Do you see?"

Hugo Schroeder marveled at why he wasn't already a dead man. Yesterday, when he'd incited Ismael, he was certain his days might be over, but it was a chance he had to take. He was still certain that it was only a matter of time before he'd served his purpose with Erhardt. If only he had one more opportunity—just one—to signal headquarters, to let them know that *Heinz Waller* was alive and dangerous.

"Always it has been down and up," Erhardt continued. "Dive—level off at three hundred meters. Up to the surface. Down two hundred. Always—just like an elevator. Nothing to challenge you. Thin soft air above the surface. Nothing beneath because you were never deep enough. Now you and I are going to change that, Mr. Schroeder. We're going to navigate this submarine through that mountain range before us, and we're going to make sure no one knows we are doing it. This is what you've been trained for and you have the talent to do." Erhardt clapped him on the back. "We'll tell the computer what we want to do, but we will also plan each maneuver ourselves."

What could he say? "Yes, sir." Maybe . . .

When they had finished, Schroeder realized Erhardt had no intention of coming to the surface again. Air-independent propulsion systems would allow them to remain submerged for much longer than the apparent time they had left. Should he attempt to destroy *Waller* now? If they were near test depth, maybe he'd have a chance to get to the fair-water planes . . . jam them down. Whatever he did, it had to be final. It had to be the end of *Waller*. Either way, he'd be dead. He couldn't fail! So he had just one more chance. He had to make the right move at the right moment. Hugo Schroeder understood that he was the last hope in stopping this insane, suicidal mission of Erhardt's.

"So you see," Erhardt noted triumphantly, "we are a true submersible because we can remain beneath the surface for extended periods of time. But we must be constantly aware of water temperature because of the currents through this mountain range. We must always try to have a temperature layer between us and any surface ships, so we will take water-temperature readings every fifteen minutes."

Erhardt took the first two-hour watch, insisting that Schroeder rest. And when Schroeder relieved him, the captain spent the next two hours coaxing and encouraging the younger officer until he was sure he could take the pressure. Although the computer could bring them to their next contact point, Erhardt was going to balance the computer with human input.

Before he finally allowed himself to sleep, Erhardt cautiously brought *Waller* to periscope depth to confirm their exact position through the navigational satellite. Once back at a safe depth, he studied the distance to be covered to reach their position east of Malta.

"Please wake me, Mr. Schroeder," Erhardt said gravely,

"if we appear unable to maintain our speed. We have less than twenty hours to reach our destination." Then he instructed the diving officer, one of Michael's men, to keep a close watch. Schroeder seemed almost too cooperative.

And after Erhardt had left the control room, Michael had appeared. "Don't allow him to touch anything. If he makes one move you don't like, shoot him."

"The captain?" the diving officer began tentatively.

"Fuck him. I'll take care of the captain."

Heinz Waller sped through the inky blackness of the Mediterranean, scaling peaks, dropping into valleys, prowling across open plateaus, always beneath the temperature layers that distorted the sounds that might reveal her presence.

Never once did the diving officer take his eyes off Schroeder during the two hours they were on watch together. When Schroeder decided to test the man and suggested they should lower their speed, the response was the appearance of a pistol in the man's hand.

Roland Lyford slowly placed the telephone back on the receiver. He continued to stare at it as if he might hear what he wanted to hear if he picked it up again. But that was too much to expect. The actual facts of Herman Gleick's death would take another day to sort out. Kiel's Director-Homicide Neumann confided during their conversation that he was the one who insisted that Gleick travel to Hamburg right away. Certain politicians close to the navy had been pressuring him and it had seemed a good idea at the time for Gleick to follow up immediately on the As-Sa'iqa restaurant. Now, Neumann was having a difficult time of it because he knew Gleick should have gone there with Lyford.

There were no clues other than the seven bullets that had penetrated Gleick's body, and the one that had destroyed the phone. It was certain that, while the type of weapons used would be easily identifiable, there would be no way to trace the guns involved.

Members of the Hamburg homicide squad had visited the As-Sa'iqa twice that day, once after Gleick's body had been removed to the coroner's and once that evening when there were customers. They encountered only two people who knew any German, one being the owner, and both spoke the language so poorly that the detectives quickly grew frustrated questioning them.

As far as the director's office could determine, Gleick had never been in the restaurant that day. The names of Preminger and Erhardt meant nothing to him. The owner explained that Europeans did not frequent the As-Sa'iqa. Soraya's name, too, was met with a mystified shrug. There were many women with that name. With an emotional finish to their phone conversation, Neumann had explained to Lyford that he would get back to him the following day.

The CIA agent was unhappy also. He'd become fond of the diminutive investigator the few times they had talked. Gleick was one of the only Germans Lyford had encountered who was genuine with Americans. There'd been no chip on his shoulder, no ax to grind over an American intelligence agent in their midst. Gleick had actually welcomed the assistance that his own people were unable to provide. And the man had died calling an American, rather than first reporting what he'd concluded to his own office!

Lyford had already booked a flight to Naples because Will Riley was going to meet him there that night. Now he knew he had to see Tom Davis first. The only way he might get his point across would be face to face.

His first words when he called Davis from the airport were these: "Herman Gleick was murdered this afternoon. He was shot while he was calling me from Hamburg. It has to have something to do with that peace conference. There's so much pointing toward that German sub."

When they were facing each other, Lyford explained the strange turn that had led to Gleick's murder. "Gleick called me before he called his own office. His last word, after he'd already been hit, was *Erhardt,* the one who replaced Preminger on *Heinz Waller.*"

"That is ominous, I suppose," Davis responded casually.

"Murders almost always make sense," Lyford said. "The murderer usually has what seems like a sound reason to kill at the time. Gleick had obviously learned something the murderers didn't want someone else to know. Logic follows logic—that something was Erhardt."

"Who commanded a submarine that went down five hundred miles from where it was supposed to be," Davis murmured.

"Uh-huh. Have you got anything more on the *Waller?*"

"My people have been working with the search and rescue team in La Rochelle, and I don't think there's anything else they can pick up there. They also offered their assistance to the commanding officer of the German submarine force. The Germans are happy to have our submarine recovery team searching the bottom of the Bay of Biscay for them, but they're not saying a word to anyone about that other signal. Rumor has it that they're convinced it must have been a computer glitch." Davis wrinkled his forehead in disgust. "It's almost like they don't want to consider that they might have a rogue sub on their hands. You know—the old it-can-never-happen-to-us routine. Has Gleick's boss, that director of homicide, contacted their navy?"

"Director Neumann said that he called the admiral shortly after I talked to him the first time. All he got were condolences on Gleick's death and a closed mouth about everything else."

Davis was cautious. "What are you thinking?"

"Has this submarine recovery team found anything that might indicate a submarine was down there?"

"Christ, no. There's twenty seven hundred fathoms of water. We have sonar readings of something down there. But it could be anything. That depth just tears a submarine apart. Could be there's just pieces spread all over the bottom for miles. It may be weeks before we come up with anything for the Germans. Maybe we never will. Who knows?"

"Maybe that signal was real. Someone in the German navy must think so. After all, they've been searching that area off Lisbon, too. Who can say that submarine was ever in the Bay of Biscay?"

"The German navy says, officially. They found a *Heinz Waller* life jacket. Of course, that's the only hard evidence in this whole mess."

"I could go out and buy a life jacket, stencil *Rollie Lyford* on it, and toss it off a boat. Does that mean I'm dead?"

"The odds are pretty good if someone saw you go out in

the boat, and you're not in it when they find the boat and the life jacket. Definitely, if you're still in the life jacket."

"Nobody's found the submarine, or a corpse," Lyford persisted.

"Hell, a human body bursts apart at that depth. There wouldn't be any corpses. They're automatically chopped fish food."

"Can you come up with a better theory than I'm building about where that sub may be?" Lyford asked.

"You've probably already ruined my sleep."

"Are you going to bitch at me because I've ruined your sleep, too?" Roland Lyford had just shaken hands with a puffy-eyed Will Riley.

"No, I'm not going to bitch at you, not yet at least." They were in Lyford's Naples hotel room, which the CIA agent had just scanned electronically. "But I didn't like taking off from the *Wasp* and I'm going to enjoy landing on it even less."

"So this better be good, right?"

Riley took a good look at Lyford and found it hard to believe that the man was with the CIA—rumpled suit, graying hair in need of cutting, a heavy beard definitely in need of a shave, and an eye that seemed to wander on its own accord. "You come very highly recommended. I was told that if you thought you had proof that aliens were landing, that I should take you seriously."

Lyford pointed at a soft chair. "Make yourself at home. Something to drink first?"

"What are you drinking?"

"Soda water these days."

"Make it two."

Will Riley listened and sipped slowly at his soda water as Lyford told him about Herman Gleick's investigation, weaving in his theory about *Heinz Waller*. "My friend, Gleick, was murdered this afternoon while we were on the phone. He was explaining to me that he got a solid reaction from Walter Erhardt's name at the As-Sa'iqa today. Now when I put that together with what Mr. Paddha told him about Erhardt's lost love, I see the man tied right in there with these terrorists."

"That's pretty far-fetched," Riley noted wearily. "Why didn't you just work this out with the guy you mentioned—ah, Davis—with Sixth Fleet intelligence?"

"I did. He's sympathetic to terrorists. However, he deals only in facts. He's already convinced the navy to tighten up its antisubmarine effort, but that's as far as it goes unless I show him hard proof."

"I'm aware of what they've already done. I could look off the bridge of *Calm Seas* this morning and see that for myself."

Lyford stroked his chin thoughtfully. "I know you can't call off this conference right in the middle. But what about the President's visit? Maybe you should persuade him to stay away? I'll bet the Secret Service would be nervous."

"You know . . ." Riley began thoughtfully. "I think you've got something here that's worth chasing down—if there was time," he said, wagging a finger at Lyford. "But not only is there no time, this could just be the centerpiece of the President's re-election effort. President Salkin would walk through fire to be there when they sign that accord. I need something a hell of a lot more solid before I can even start to recommend that he stay away." Riley looked at the CIA agent ruefully. "Get me something else . . . and maybe I . . . shit, I don't know."

They talked for a few more minutes before Lyford finally said, "Why don't you get yourself back and get some sleep. I'll see what I can do on my end."

There are no visible events that take place around the White House that are allowed to go unrecorded by the news media. At about nine fifteen that night, the President's helicopter settled down on the pad near the White House. The stairs were folded out in anticipation of passengers.

Fifteen minutes later, President and Mrs. Salkin stepped through a side door of the White House and strode across the lawn to the helicopter. They were observed in leisure clothes, the President in slacks, an open-necked shirt, and a light gold jacket. His wife was always in a skirt, but her outfit was decidedly sporty. They were accompanied by the ever-present Secret Service, Bill Herbert, Salkin's director of communications and a scratch golfer, and three members of the White House staff. Two other staff members carried golf clubs, which were handed up into the helicopter. As soon as they were airborne, one of Herbert's assistants provided a handout for the duty press corps. It had been prepared in a humorous vein:

> (For immediate release) President and Mrs. Salkin have departed on a surprise four-day golfing vacation in Scotland. During their visit there, they will be residing at a vacation home belonging to the Royal Family that had been offered by the Queen, who enjoyed the President's vacation home in the Caribbean last year. The Secret Service recently reported the fact that the Queen's home in Scotland is accessible to three golf courses. The President has never been known to turn down vacation time near a golf course.
>
> The President's golf partner will be William Herbert, White House director of communications, who regularly gives his boss free golf lessons while winning five dollars a hole. Both the U.S. and British press corps have been asked by Mr. Herbert to cooperate and allow as private a vacation as possible since the President's game has been known to fall apart under close observation. Daily reports of golf scores will be released if the President has a good day on the links.

At Andrews Air Force Base, as soon as the rotors were still, two stretch limos and a pickup truck appeared alongside the helicopter. The baggage and golf clubs were placed in the back of the truck. The Secret Service, along with President and Mrs. Salkin, climbed into the first limo, the vacation party into the second.

Both vehicles drove out to Air Force One's secure parking area. Within minutes, vacation personnel and gear were inside the huge aircraft. Half an hour later, Air Force One was airborne, her flight plan filed for a British military airfield in Scotland.

The limos and pickup truck returned to the hangar where they were normally stored to await the return of the presidential party. But ten minutes after the lights in the hangar had been extinguished, two men were led out to a darkened air force transport jet by the Secret Service. An hour later, when only security forces moved about Andrews Air Force Base, the cockpit lights of that jet came on. Once the engines had been tested, the aircraft taxied out to the runway, received clearance for takeoff, and roared into the night sky. No flight plan had been filed.

Phil Salkin and Bill Herbert were on their way to Naples. From there, they would be transferred under cover to a navy plane that would fly them directly to U.S.S. *Wasp,* steaming east of Malta.

Only the flickering taper of a lantern lighted the single room at the base of the mountains that had become Hussein's new headquarters. The communications equipment had been wired less than an hour before he arrived. Camouflage had been erected, and the scene presented to any aircraft flying overhead was a deserted village. His security force had sanitized the small town so there was no direct threat to his life. It was as comfortable as could be expected, yet Hussein would have preferred the serenity of his beloved mountains. That was where he achieved peace of mind.

But that opportunity had passed as quickly as time. From this moment forward, he was required to be by his source of communications. As simple as it was, this camouflaged mud hut was Hussein's flag plot, and it was from here that he would coordinate his battle.

"We don't know how it was done, but he has left the United States on time," the courier reported.

Hussein looked at the man with a frown. "You weren't told how it was done?"

One of his aides handed him a sheet of paper. "He brought this," he said, indicating the courier.

"This says that the President is taking a golfing vacation in Scotland." Hussein's frown increased. "And does everything point to that?"

The courier nodded. "There's nothing from our people in the United States to indicate otherwise. His wife left with him. Golf clubs were placed in his helicopter. Yet we have been told that there is an aircraft still reserved in Naples to carry someone important to the *Wasp.* Talal is certain it has to be the President, no matter what that press release claims."

Hussein considered this for a moment. If he was about to play such a great big trick on the world, why couldn't the President play a small one on him?

Nothing had changed.

CHAPTER FIFTEEN

DAY SIX

Jake Steele had decided within the first thirty seconds of the intelligence briefing that he should keep his mouth shut. The only people who liked such gatherings were those who produced a short and successful one, and that was not happening now.

"I . . . the situation . . . is confused for the moment," Lieutenant Germond said unhappily. "That's why I thought I ought to be honest."

It was a rare moment when Rear Admiral Turner's young intelligence officer was ill at ease during a briefing. He normally exuded confidence. Peter looked good in a uniform—blond, broad-shouldered, penetrating blue eyes, and he carried himself well—when he was confident. But as he spoke to the half-dozen men in Turner's briefing room, he paused often. His eyes blinked self-consciously. He rocked from left foot to right foot and found it difficult to look the others in the eye.

"Maybe you ought to be talking with Sixth Fleet," the admiral's chief staff officer commented acidly.

"I've talked with Captain Davis at Sixth Fleet intelligence three times today. He says his boss has ordered two of the six hundred eighty-eight submarines in the Med to join us . . . just to be on the safe side."

The young officer's eyes skipped around the briefing room. Rear Admiral Turner, Captain Black, *Wasp*'s commanding officer and executive officer, Jake Steele, the squadron operations officer—each of them watched him intently. "There's not a trawler in this part of the Med right now that Sixth Fleet intelligence figures is the least threat. You remember all the photos I showed you?" And to answer his own question, he said, "Forget them. There is none that appears to be a threat in the least."

Jake Steele spoke for the first time. "So much for training."

Germond smiled weakly. "Captain Davis in Naples said he wouldn't even consider the story he was about to tell me if he didn't have a great deal of respect for the source. There's a CIA officer in Berlin who's come up with this crazy idea about Arab terrorists and submarines . . . and part of it has to do with a German detective who was murdered in Hamburg yesterday investigating the murder of the captain of that submarine." He looked up helplessly at Turner. "It goes back to that German submarine that sank in the Bay of Biscay. This CIA agent said maybe it didn't. The German navy is absolutely bullshit that our CIA is even inquiring about it. They won't even talk to them." Lieutenant Germond, his eyes blinking rapidly, looked to Rear Admiral Turner for help.

"Is Sixth Fleet particularly worried about us?" Turner asked.

"They can't come up with anything absolute to worry about," Germond replied. "We're already in an advanced readiness state. We've got the sky covered, the surface covered, we've tightened up the ASW screen, and now—just in case—we're going to have additional cover underneath."

"Thank you, Peter," Rear Admiral Turner said kindly. "What you've got to learn is that you're never going to know everything. You've done your best. It would appear to me that we're in a pretty good situation. Our op area is sanitized. Our coverage can only get better. We'll take advantage of those nukes if they happen to show and let us know they're around. If Sixth Fleet isn't worried about us, then I'm not going to worry. Any comments?"

No one spoke.

"President Salkin will arrive this evening after it's dark.

He and Mr. Herbert will be dressed like any other naval officers dropping by. They will go immediately to my quarters. With luck, no one will know they're here until tomorrow morning, unless the Secret Service blows their cover by being overzealous with our people. The Secretary of State, Mr. Griffey, estimates that we should be ready to transport them to *Calm Seas* shortly before noon tomorrow for the signing ceremonies. If for some reason everything falls apart, we'll sneak them off tomorrow afternoon."

"Is there any reason to think it will fall apart, Admiral?" Jake asked.

"None at all, according to Mr. Griffey."

The diving officer placed a hand on the planesman's shoulder without taking his eyes from Hugo Schroeder. "Fine job. Fine job. You've worked hard the last hour." The diving officer stood between the planesman and Schroeder. He'd remained there for the last hour, one hand resting on his pistol.

Heinz Waller had just maneuvered from the deep waters of the Malta Trough up through a subsurface mountain range that had released them to the deeper water of the Malta Plateau. It would not have been a complicated process except for the fact that it had been done at full speed.

Moments later, Walter Erhardt, his face and hair shining from the lukewarm water he'd splashed on his face, entered the control room. His eyes were still red from his stolen hour's sleep. He licked dry lips. "Depth?" he asked.

"Ninety meters, sir," the planesman called out promptly.

"Very well. Sonar contacts, Mr. Schroeder?"

"Nothing subsurface, sir. Merchant shipping, no destroyers." Sonar had reported the distinct sound of destroyer propellers a few hours before, but those had disappeared.

"You would take her up then?" Erhardt asked sharply, rubbing his eyes.

"Yes, sir." He felt a surge of excitement. *Maybe . . .*

"I have the conn," Erhardt barked, then gave his orders. "Periscope depth. I want an accurate fix before our final run."

The ESM reading found no errant radar signals from military planes in the area. The periscope revealed nothing more than three freighters at a safe distance and a Maltese dhow fishing well away from the home island. The satellite navigational fix was in agreement with the computer placing them slightly more than a hundred kilometers from their next radio contact point.

Erhardt watched Schroeder fidget, his eyes darting from the depth gauge to the ladder leading up to the bridge. *What would Schroeder do if we . . .* "Do you think we should come to the surface, Mr. Schroeder?" he inquired playfully.

"If you think so, sir." Schroeder bit his lip and stared straight ahead. "I imagine the crew would appreciate some fresh air."

Erhardt smiled wickedly. *So Mr. Schroeder wants to get to the surface.* "Yes, I agree. But . . ." He hesitated. "I think not. Take her back down to ninety meters," he ordered. Erhardt looked at the straight line on the surface display unit from their current position to the one designated by Hussein. "There we are." He gave an order to slow their speed. "We'll arrive shortly after midnight."

An exhausted Schroeder, now certain Erhardt was toying with him, inquired innocently as he studied the plot, "Have you ever been to Malta, Captain?"

But before Erhardt could respond, an obviously contentious Soraya stepped through the hatch into the control room. "Your captain knows Malta well, don't you, Walter?" Soraya remarked sarcastically. She looked tired, too, and there was a distant, faraway cast to her eyes that hadn't been there before.

Erhardt appeared agitated by her comment. He refused to look up from the chart. "What do you want?"

"Malta is a beautiful place," she continued. "I'll bet you knew all the beautiful beaches, didn't you, Walter?"

"Many of the beaches are rocky," he answered calmly, his attention still fixed on the chart.

"Do you have regrets about returning to Malta?" she persisted. Her voice was slightly taunting now.

"We're not returning. We are passing in the night."

"That sounds romantic to me," Soraya murmured in a husky voice, but even that was calculated to be disparaging.

Her facial expression, though, remained passive as she spoke.

Erhardt sensed something was coming. "Tell me what you want," he said reasonably, "and then you can get back to where you're needed." His voice remained controlled, but his face reflected anger.

"I came to find out what other drugs you have on board, Walter. Ismael still doesn't respond properly. Who knows the drugs?"

Erhardt snorted. "When Ismael killed the cook, he also killed the pharmacist. The cook feeds the crew, then he gives them pills to survive his cooking." He chuckled unpleasantly. "Maybe he hurt himself more with his own stupidity."

Soraya stared back at him curiously.

"That's right," Erhardt continued. "On a submarine, everyone has a couple of jobs. Go on. Take a look. The locker for our medicines is in the galley. Look in it for yourself. See if there's anything Ismael might fancy. Maybe something to improve his personality?"

"Without Ismael, you may have to remember Malta for however long you live," she snapped viciously, then stalked out of the control room.

Will Riley stepped into *Calm Seas'* pilot house and squinted in the darkness. "Where are you, Francis?"

"Out here."

Will turned in the direction of the voice.

"Bridge wing," Waters coaxed. He waved his arm. "It's easier to stay awake upright."

Riley recognized Waters's figure in white outlined by the moonlight. He stepped out to the starboard wing. "Where are we tonight?"

"Come on, Will. Same place as last night. Same place as the night before. We steam back and forth in this little box. We get as close as sixteen degrees east of Malta and as far away as seventeen degrees east, give or take a little more each way. That means the box is about sixty miles long and maybe ten or fifteen miles wide."

"Sounds nice and safe."

"It ought to be. We've always got the *Wasp* in sight. And

I've watched destroyers and cruisers charging around every time we change course. The radar tells me there's more ships I usually can't see. So, tell me. What gives?"

"You're letting everything get to you, Francis. I came up here to relax you. You've been getting tight lately. You're not your usual laughable self." Riley held out a silver flask. "Go ahead, have a snort."

"I never drink on watch." But he eyed the flask appreciatively.

"Mr. Griffey said to make you take a couple. He says there's a couple of thousand sailors on watch in the Mediterranean and you need this."

"What is it?"

"Cognac. Five-star. The best. Mr. Griffey only drinks the best."

"Why doesn't Mr. Griffey like Spanish brandy? That's my favorite. A little Carlos Primeros makes the moon a little brighter."

A voice came from the radio speaker inside the pilot house.

"Oops. There we go again. Another complicated naval maneuver." Waters called into the pilot house for the helmsman to reverse his course. "You now have the pleasure of sailing west for about sixty miles or so." He reached for the flask. "If it's Mr. Griffey's orders, then I'll have some."

"It's his flask, too, Francis. Enjoy."

"Hmmm. Doc Jock drinks nothing but the best."

"Doc Jock?" Riley murmured curiously. Then he said, "You're right, Francis. I was already thinking about the closing ceremonies. I guess I'm kind of tired, too."

Waters took another small pull on the flask and handed it back. He wiped his mouth with the back of his hand. "Your boss had a wonderful idea, but keep it away from me till the party's over."

The two men remained silent, studying the moonlight on the water until an inquiring voice came from behind them: "My flask still up here?"

"Yes, sir." Riley turned and extended the flask to Lou Griffey.

"I hope our captain had a couple," Griffey said, lifting it to his lips.

"Just a snad," Waters answered. "But I thank you for the thought. A few more swallows and I'll be sleeping on my feet."

"Why don't you get some rest?" Griffey suggested pleasantly.

"I will. I usually try to grab an hour or so during each leg."

"Try for more," Griffey replied. "Tomorrow's going to be a busy day."

"Does that mean you've accomplished what you hoped for?" Waters asked.

"Maybe more. Our guests are all in the main salon right now. Dinner's over. The drinkers are sipping a little cognac. The rest are comparing coffees. The lady from Lebanon is at the head of the table. They obviously don't need me. I think maybe they're even telling each other jokes."

"About the Jew and the Arab?" Waters asked.

"They've been trading jokes since the second day. What amazes me most is that there's no offense taken when they become the butt of the same joke they used to tell about the other. When they're away from their own turf," Griffey noted, "what was once insulting becomes funny. It doesn't matter how many Poles or Mexicans or Jews or Arabs it takes to screw in a light bulb as long as it's told in the right tone of voice. Right now, the American Secretary of State seems to be a popular target, and, to me, that means they've bonded together."

"Will says tomorrow looks good for a signing," Francis said.

"God willing," Lou Griffey murmured. "God willing." He unscrewed the cap and raised his flask aloft. "Here's to a peace accord tomorrow . . . for if we don't achieve it, I fear for our world in the next century." He took a pull and handed it to Francis. "Thank you for helping us."

Waters stared at Griffey in the darkness. *He really means it!* "God willing," he agreed softly. He took another pull before passing the flask to Riley.

"God willing." Will Riley finished the last of the cognac.

His mind drifted back to Roland Lyford's theory, and he whispered, "God willing," one more time.

"What's the matter, Bill?"

Bill Herbert was peering through the helicopter window. "There's nothing down there. I've never been in one of these before when I couldn't look down at the lights."

"Scared?" Phil Salkin teased.

Herbert glanced over at him with a furrowed brow.

"Just a teeny bit?"

"I like solid ground. And if I can't have that, I like to see some indication that it's beneath me."

"No problem, Bill. Believe me, Mother Earth's right down there below us. It's just that it's the wet part." The President chuckled at his own humor.

After a few moments, Herbert pointed out the window. "What are those lights? Looks like an airport."

At that moment, the pilot's voice came through the overhead speaker. "We're approaching the *Wasp,* gents. It may be a little bumpy as we come down, so grab your asses."

"The man's in for a surprise someday," Bill Herbert commented. Their helicopter crew had no idea of the identity of their passengers. They'd simply been ordered earlier that evening to be ready to fly out to *Wasp* with two officers. When the copilot asked why one of the small transports that made regular flights wasn't used, the response was that it was a security matter. That was as good a reason as any for avoiding further questions.

The helicopter swept around the carrier's stern in a wide circle and floated down to a landing circle near the island. The pilot was told that as soon as his passengers were on deck, he would be towed to another location for refueling. To his surprise, as soon as the rotors stopped, the deck lighting in the area was extinguished.

The helicopter's side door slid open. Salkin and Herbert saw the blond head of a young officer peer inside.

"Gentlemen, I'm Lieutenant Germond, Admiral Turner's intelligence officer." His voice was high-pitched and nervous. "I'll be your escort to the admiral's quarters."

Phil Salkin and Bill Herbert stepped down onto *Wasp's*

deck. To anyone who happened to notice the two new arrivals, it would appear that two navy commanders had just arrived aboard. They followed the young man who warned them about stepping over the high coamings of watertight hatches and to avoid bumping their heads on the top of the hatch when they did so. The corridors were deserted.

"I haven't been aboard this ship before, Lieutenant. Can you tell me where we're going?" Salkin asked.

"Admiral Turner's quarters, sir," Germond answered, but his voice came out in a squeak. He cleared his throat self-consciously. "Second deck below the flight deck."

When they were at the bottom of the ladder on the deck just below the flight deck, Bill Herbert sniffed the air. "Smells like a doctor's office."

"The ship's hospital is on this deck, sir," the blond officer responded.

"This is the admiral they call 'Happy Jack,'" Herbert said. "My people told me he smiles even when he's angry. Isn't that right, young man?"

"I just know him as Admiral Turner, sir."

They descended a second ladder and followed the officer through two hatches with signs that stated NO UNAUTHORIZED ADMITTANCE. Germond stopped at a door at the end of the passageway and knocked before pushing it open. He found enough of his voice to say, "President Salkin, sir," as he held the door open for Salkin and Herbert.

Rear Admiral Turner was standing in front of his desk. He saluted. "Welcome aboard *Wasp,* Mr. President. I'm sorry I wasn't allowed to meet you when you landed, but we didn't want anyone looking more closely at our guests."

"Relax, please. Everyone relax," Phil Salkin said, surveying the other officers in the room. They were all at attention and saluting, their eyes fixed on a point in space before them. "I'm not supposed to be here. Remember? If you make a habit out of this, we may blow it. Now relax," he said assertively. "You're going to make me as nervous as Lieutenant Germond."

The salutes dropped. Eyes turned curiously in the President's direction.

"That's better. I've been looking forward to this visit.

And don't worry about not being on the flight deck, Admiral. The lieutenant was quite charming, except," he said with a grin, "he seems to have lost his voice. This is Bill Herbert, my director of communications. Once we have those signatures tomorrow, he's going to coordinate the media representatives that we allow to come out here." He turned to Peter Germond. "You said you were staff intelligence officer, Lieutenant. Did we get here without the world knowing about it?"

Germond's eyes blinked faster. "You almost got here without us knowing it, Mr. President." His voice was still a level higher than normal. "I had to run to get to your helicopter in time."

Rear Admiral Turner introduced the other officers—*WASP's* captain and executive officer, his own chief staff officer, the staff operations officer, and Jake Steele. "Right now, the only people who know you're here, sir, are in this room."

"He's not in Scotland."

At first, Hussein's response was silence. His eyes bored into Talal's. Then he said, "You're sure of that."

"His wife arrived there. She came down the steps of Air Force One on the arm of someone who was supposed to be the President. But I know it wasn't Salkin."

Hussein remained mute. His eyes never left Talal's, an indication that he wasn't satisfied.

"It was early morning, barely sunrise. The man's collar was up. He wore a hat pulled down. Salkin never does that." Timing was so delicate now that Talal had anticipated Hussein would require proof of some kind. "I have a photograph. It was taken with a telephoto lens. You can see how little light there was at that hour." He passed it to Hussein, then placed another clear photo of the President and his wife alongside it.

Hussein hooked the glasses he rarely wore around his ears and bent forward to study the two photographs under the flickering lantern light.

Talal pointed at the photo that was clearly of President and Mrs. Salkin. "Compare the two. The man getting off the plane is a bit taller, and certainly he isn't so broad in the shoulders. But even in the winter, Salkin doesn't wear one of those hats."

"It's not the same man. I agree. So where is Salkin?"

Talal took a deep breath. "I don't have absolute proof yet," he admitted. "But I am sure he is on the carrier *Wasp* or will be soon."

Once again, Hussein remained mute waiting for his intelligence officer to provide substantiation.

"He hasn't been seen anywhere. I must admit I have absolutely no hard indication where he is." Talal's voice was firm. He possessed an uncanny ability to sort facts from the overwhelming mass of information he received. His reputation had been based on saying nothing if he didn't believe something himself. He'd never lied to Hussein, and Hussein understood that. Talal's importance in the organization was second only to his leader's.

Hussein nodded, but he wanted more. His gaze never wavered from Talal's face.

"The original scenario scheduled Salkin to appear aboard that ship only if an accord appeared certain. I never learned how they would get him there, only that he would appear. The Americans are very good at moving their President around when it's necessary to maintain absolute secrecy."

Hussein removed his glasses and rubbed his eyes. It seemed that those glasses always started a headache over his temples. "I agree, Talal. Salkin has to be aboard *Wasp*. He should transfer to *Calm Seas* sometime tomorrow. They must have reached an accord or he wouldn't be aboard that carrier now." He sighed and massaged his temples. "What time is it?"

"Almost midnight."

No wonder he had a headache. He hadn't slept well the last two nights and he wouldn't sleep this one either. It was more than the glasses. He rose to his feet and stretched. "Michael should be calling soon. Join me . . . please."

The process for establishing contact was the same each time, exacting and precise. Talal had compromised too many security systems over the years to allow the same mistakes. Once the appropriate code words had been authenticated, Michael confirmed his position to Hussein.

Hussein knew exactly what he wanted to corroborate. "What have you been able to pick up on your sonar?" Hussein inquired.

"The normal shipping between us and Malta. It's heavy, but not impossible to track. What we do have," Michael continued enthusiastically, "are military ships to the west." He'd been excited by them. *Will we actually have the privilege of destroying some of them?* "Erhardt's nervous about being at periscope depth with so many of them nearby. Sonar has classified an American amphibious group with at least one cruiser and one frigate, maybe more, and they can hear a much larger ship which they believe to be an aircraft carrier."

"That will be the American carrier *Wasp,*" Hussein responded. "The Spotlight photos show they've remained in the same area." Spotlight was a French photographic satellite whose owners sold high-resolution photos from space at an attractive profit. "Unless something unusual takes place, you can be assured those same ships will remain within that location. They should continue to go back and forth. Talal will relay their positions at the end of this contact. You should use your sonar to confirm these, of course."

Michael's anxiety overwhelmed him. "I assume we are to sink the carrier." That was a target worth dying for.

"No. There's a civilian motor vessel surrounded by all those American ships." Hussein gave a description of *Calm Seas.* "She will be the only white ship seen through the periscope. Sometimes, it's in front of the carrier, sometimes behind. It depends on their direction. Have you loaded the torpedoes you transferred from the trawler into the tubes?"

"Affirmative."

"Ismael was given a program for performing the tests between the submarine's attack console and the weapon. Did they all conform to the test results we provided beforehand?"

"Ismael is ill," Michael replied hesitantly. "*Waller*'s torpedoman is learning how to perform the tests from Ismael."

"What's wrong with Ismael?"

"His eyes," Michael answered. Without hesitation, he added, "We expect him to be ready when he's needed."

Hussein's voice remained even, but his anger was obvious. "The detonators and the propulsion system must be checked one more time. Those mechanisms are delicate and untried. Only Ismael knows what has to be done. A stranger can't . . . no, it has to be Ismael."

"Believe me, everything will be ready." Michael was growing anxious. They had come so far. Why couldn't they complete the mission without Ismael?

"Shortly after noon local time tomorrow, you will sink *Calm Seas* with those torpedoes. When they detonate, the ship will instantaneously be swept by fire. Your mission is a failure if there are any survivors. And you can't run after you shoot, Michael. You must do whatever is necessary to guarantee there are no survivors."

"It would mean even more to my men if they know what they are sinking."

Rather than answering, Hussein asked, "Is Erhardt there?"

"He's listening."

"Captain Erhardt," Hussein said, "my men undertake this mission in the name of Allah. They know they will be rewarded in heaven for eternity. But I want you to know once again in your heart that sinking the *Calm Seas* will bring you the revenge that you deserve, just as I promised. The names of the people aboard would mean little to you, but you will accomplish more in this manner than you could ever have hoped to in your remaining years. The *Calm Seas* is carrying people who were actually involved in shooting down that plane and taking Darra Paddha's life. The loss of her young life will be avenged. My men look forward to their reward. I wanted you to know yours beforehand."

Erhardt had been promised that vengeance for Darra's murder would be overwhelming. He was satisfied.

PART FIVE

APRIL

Calm Seas: The Attack

CHAPTER SIXTEEN

DAY SEVEN

Walter Erhardt's low whistle was totally out of character, especially over the past few days as his temper vaulted from one end of the spectrum to the other. "Come here, Mr. Schroeder." He beckoned without looking away from the periscope's eyepiece.

Schroeder hesitated. Erhardt had taken pleasure in badgering him for the past few hours. That could only mean that his time was very short and he would soon have to make one final, desperate effort to destroy *Waller.*

"Don't be nervous. Come. We're almost where I want us to be. They're still a safe distance from us." Erhardt was pleased with how the American formation actually matched his own assumptions. "Wait. First look at what I've laid out."

Schroeder saw the rough formation diagram the captain had sketched on a separate sheet of paper from Talal's description. *Wasp* had been placed in the middle. There were two ships—marked CG and DDG, a missile cruiser and a missile destroyer—at either end of the formation. There were eight others in various locations.

Erhardt had first matched *Heinz Waller*'s course and speed to *Wasp*'s. Since he essentially became part of the formation from the moment their movement paralleled the carrier's, the angle of bearing of the other ships from *Waller* would remain the same. Then he deployed *Waller*'s passive sonar, a listening device towed well behind them on a cable.

It was the sonarman's job to isolate and identify the bearings of ships' sounds—cruisers, frigates, destroyers, LSDs, LSTs. Erhardt then varied his position enough for the sonarman to obtain two lines of bearing that crossed. This gave them the approximate ranges of these ships from the submarine. With that data, Erhardt was able to confirm the positions on the Spotlight photo that Talal had relayed by radio.

"Do you understand why I've selected this side of the formation—the south side?" Erhardt asked of Schroeder.

"No, sir." There was no reason to massage Erhardt's ego.

"Sonar reported that the active towed array sonar on the frigate on this side has been retrieved. Apparently, they're having a problem. Without that sonar, it makes our job a bit simpler, although nothing will be easy from now on. But, it was the one I was most concerned with." Erhardt stepped back from the periscope. "Go on, Mr. Schroeder, take a look."

Schroeder peered into the eyepiece. *Wasp* was well lighted. The captain had brought the periscope up to full magnification so that the amphibious carrier looked much closer than it really was. Even in the darkness, he could see the carrier's outline, the height of the flight deck above the water's surface, the bow lights on either side of the deck delineating her width, the six levels of the carrier's island, and the truck light at the top of the mast. She was immense.

"I know it's hard to distinguish the other ships, but tomorrow you'll have a final chance to see them all. We are going to make one of the most daring daylight attacks ever undertaken by a submarine. And it most certainly can be done. What do you think of that?"

Schroeder saw a light in Erhardt's eyes that he was certain hadn't been there previously. It was the piercing glint of the hawk, the eye of the hunter . . . the eye of a man who in his own way was just as crazed as Ismael.

"No response, eh? Well, my young-and-inexperienced number two, you are going to become one of the first German submariners to be part of a daylight penetration of such a formation in more than fifty years. And by the time we are finished, you shall be qualified for command. What do you think of that?" he asked, as if that was something that could actually happen.

Schroeder hadn't been able to sleep during this transit, even when Erhardt sent him to his bunk. He'd been sent to sea to look for a killer and instead he'd found himself in the midst of a nightmare. The strangers who now possessed *Waller* were real. Erhardt was once again taking great pleasure in tormenting him. Death was an instant away. He must find an opportunity to . . .

"Come, Mr. Schroeder, aren't you impressed?"

His eyes swept the control room. Except for himself and Erhardt, the others had all come aboard with Michael. And they never stopped watching him, never let their hands stray far from their weapons. When his gaze returned to the captain, he was treated with a triumphant smile. Erhardt understood—he was toying with him.

Erhardt clapped his hands. "Now we're going to allow them to maneuver around us. We don't want to make any noise that might make them think someone else was out here." He clapped his hands again, pleased with the control-room audience hanging with rapt attention on each word. "You are going to be able to tell your children someday about your part in one of the greatest missions ever, Mr. Schroeder." His eyes and his voice radiated a cruelty that had been hidden until now.

Schroeder remained silent.

Erhardt gave orders to slow the submarine until the formation passed. Then he spoke to the control room as a whole. "Every one of you has a vital responsibility now to see us through this operation. No one can relax at his post." He continued to compliment each man as he moved from one to the next, explaining how critical he would be to the success of their mission. "What we do tonight will be exciting. But tomorrow, in the daylight, you will be making history." He then excused himself to speak to the men in the engineering spaces, then went forward to the torpedo room to do the same.

Once astern of the final cruiser, Erhardt dove beneath a sharp temperature gradient, leveling off at a hundred meters. Then he came around in a wide circle away from the formation, increasing his speed until *Waller* once again matched the formation's course and speed at a distance of ten kilometers from the nearest ship. They were listening, but there was nothing to hear, for *Waller* remained quieter than the American submarines the U.S. sailors were accustomed to training with.

Now came the frustrating part—the waiting. Erhardt had prepared a plastic overlay of the box the American formation appeared to remain within. He placed it over the automated surface display and ordered his quartermaster to mark each course change of the formation. Assuming they remained within that box, Erhardt was certain that he would be able to predict with accuracy where his target would be at noon that day.

It was now time to confront the problem of Ismael. Hussein's two torpedoes must function properly.

Lou Griffey followed Captain Black down the ladders and darkened corridors within *Wasp*. It briefly occurred to him that he was descending into the catacombs. He preferred the comfort of *Calm Seas,* the broad windows around the main salon, the carpeting, the colors, the appointments, but especially Francis's bridge. That was like a home at sea, at one with yourself and nature. You could close your eyes and sense the vastness of the ocean. These immense carriers were much too confining. *Wasp* seemed more an extension of his office inside the State Department building.

Griffey had known he wouldn't sleep that night because the hour was at hand when an historic contribution would be made to world peace. And it came as no surprise to him when Phil Salkin had contacted him less than an hour before. As soon as a rough copy of the accord was available, he wanted to review it.

It was close to three in the morning when Lou Griffey was ushered into the President's quarters aboard *Wasp.* Bill Herbert lifted a hand in greeting from an easy chair next to Salkin's, then pointed at a coffee urn.

Griffey shook his head. "A good morning to you, Mr. President," Griffey said. "I expected to see you in pajamas."

Salkin grinned. "Not quite yet. Too anxious."

Griffey handed him the first draft of the peace agreement.

After perusing the highlighted sections of the accord, Salkin looked across to his Secretary of State with a warm smile. "This reads like Rupert's Christmas list." He made an effort to curb the strong emotion evident in his voice. "It's exactly what he would have asked for himself."

"The delegates unanimously agreed to call it the Daniels Accord."

"Unanimous . . ." The President mused. "Even a year ago I wouldn't have dared to anticipate unanimity of any kind from those individuals . . . amazing."

"I wish they'd agreed unanimously to use your name," Herbert said. "You wouldn't have had to campaign next time around."

Salkin smiled wistfully. "One might just get too overconfident if that happened. Campaigning's part of American tradition, Bill. But you've always known how to take advantage of these things. Right?" he concluded on an upbeat note.

Bill Herbert gave Lou Griffey the thumbs-up sign. "Take no prisoners."

Herman Gleick's murder had a profound effect on Roland Lyford. The concepts of death or murder or violence had little to do with this reaction because such things had long been a part of his life. There were many people he'd encountered who deserved to die unpleasantly and it was always pleasing when they did. Rather, it was the fact that the small unassuming detective had been a nonviolent individual who'd succeeded by using his mind rather than a weapon, and he'd garnered the CIA agent's respect as a result.

Lyford therefore immersed himself in a search for a clue to the apparently impenetrable terrorist organization responsible for Gleick's death. He made contact with every source who'd ever known anything about the terrorist underground. None of them, no matter how much he was willing to barter, could tell him anything more about the woman named Soraya. Yet he made it known that he would remain in his office by his secure phone if anyone decided they had information to exchange.

It was during the evening of the second day, after nine o'clock, when Lyford's phone rang. "Mr. Lyford, this is Tyro."

Tyro was the code name of a former agent in the Stasi, the once-dreaded East German secret police. "You're supposed to be dead," Lyford commented. Tyro had been a very deep mole for Lyford many years before.

"I still am." He made a soft noise that might have been a chuckle. "I've come back to haunt you."

"I'm probably a fool to inquire why you're calling me."

"No doubt you already know why I've risen from the grave. You are seeking information about a woman named Soraya and what she had to do with two German submarine captains . . . and where that missing submarine really is right now."

Lyford exhaled slowly. "Ghosts," he whispered. Then, in a normal voice, he continued. "I'm sure you've learned that I'd kill for that information. So, considering your resurrection, that must mean you have a specific deal in mind."

"I can tell you exactly what you want to know—probably more than you bargained for—if you can arrange the release of Heine Witscher."

"Witscher? You only want the impossible?" Heine Witscher was once the head of the Stasi directorate responsible for political assassinations. He'd been sentenced to over three hundred years in prison.

"Nothing's impossible, not when I can assure you that an organization named As-Sa'iqa knows where your President Salkin is at this very moment."

As-Sa'iqa!

"Your President's not in Scotland."

Lyford closed his eyes. If Tyro knew Salkin's whereabouts . . .

Tyro interrupted his thoughts. "I think my information will be a fair exchange for Heine."

How the hell? "I'm not sure how to go about this," Lyford answered quickly. There was no time. Tomorrow . . . "Let me think for a moment." Tyro would never make such a proposition unless he really had the information he was offering. Who could help now? "Let me make some calls. Give me a number and I'll call . . ."

"Come now, you're getting forgetful in your old age. Even though you're my favorite American, I'd never give you a phone number. I'll call you back in exactly sixty minutes. I'm betting you'll have a deal."

The phone went dead.

Who the hell am I to . . . ? Riley! Will Riley! Other than Gleick and Davis, he was the only other who'd really been sympathetic to his ideas. And he was as close to Salkin as . . . it was the only way to get to the German government. They'd have to promise Bonn that Heine Witscher would disappear forever and . . . no, Tyro would make sure of that.

"I should tell you my life story, Will, but you might not buy that either." Lyford's approach on the secure radio net was direct. "So let me just tell you a short story—one line. I had a call a little while ago from an old contact, one of the baddest of all the bad guys in the world, and he told me that a terrorist organization named As-Sa'iqa knows where President Salkin is at this very moment, and it's not in Scotland."

Will Riley stared hard at the smudge on the wall of the tiny compartment that served as *Calm Seas'* secure communications center. "I see. Go on."

"He also mentioned the woman named Soraya and the two German submarine captains, and hinted that the *Waller* is very much alive."

"How nice that you have friends willing to provide us with such information gratis."

"Have you ever heard of Heine Witscher?" Lyford asked.

"I think I remember a trial in Bonn. Am I close?"

"My man wants him freed. Witscher is Bonn's plum. They wanted him locked up as an example more than anyone else in the world. Release him and we get information that will save a peace accord and keep our President out of danger. That's the deal. Is that a reasonable exchange?"

Riley made a clicking sound with his tongue. "I assume that this deal is the last thing in the world that Bonn would consider. Am I safe in thinking they'd even crucify Christ in front of Parliament before they'd release Witscher?"

"Right. And they'd probably still insist on keeping Witscher afterward. The only thing I can suggest, since I think you're as twisted as I am, is to let me set up an arrangement wherein Witscher dies in prison. It'll be splashed all over the papers. Maybe we'll have him commit suicide. Whatever, my man promises the world will never see or hear of Heine Witscher again—and my man has been considered dead for five years."

"Sounds like a bad movie."

"We've done it before."

"How soon do you need an answer?"

"I'm going to be called back in twenty-three minutes."

"Tell your man I'm working on it. Will that get our information?"

"It'll get me another callback, a little more time."

"Tell him Witscher's probably going to die tomorrow, before noon."

Ismael's sleep was troubled. "When did you give him the last shot?" Captain Erhardt asked.

"Maybe ten hours ago," Michael answered.

"You gave it to him?"

"Soraya did."

Erhardt glanced at Soraya. The defiant look that had been a part of her personality since she came aboard had been diminished by lack of sleep. "How long will he be like this?" Ismael's body seemed in motion. Fingers twitched. Muscles jumped. An occasional soft moan escaped his lips.

"I've been cutting back the dosage. It's probably half of what it was when he was in so much pain."

Ismael's breathing became rapid for a second. Then he relaxed, a low moan escaping his lips as his head twisted from side to side.

Erhardt raised his eyebrows questioningly. "Why does he need it at all then?"

Soraya looked at Erhardt with annoyance. "Because before we were able to sedate him, he was going to get even. Kill your man Schroeder. He can't see shit, so he probably would have killed each person he ran into until he was sure he had the right man." She looked at Erhardt as if he'd forgotten something. "Ismael's crazy. He'll do anything.

But you already knew that, Walter. And he's also mostly blind. Michael and I decided you needed Schroeder more for the time being."

Erhardt shrugged. "Schroeder's served his purpose. How much can Ismael see?"

"Light and dark," Michael said. "Forms. Shapes. If we took him completely off the drugs, he'd probably kill the first person he saw, thinking it was Schroeder. It might be you. Perhaps one of us. He wouldn't care. We had to keep him this way."

"Can he run the final checks on the torpedoes?"

"I doubt it, at least not by himself."

"Can Neuner help him?" Erhardt asked.

"I don't know. That's something we'll have to find out," Michael answered. "The detonators in these torpedoes are quite different from the ones you normally carry."

Erhardt was caught by surprise. "They looked exactly like ours when we brought them on board!" he exclaimed.

"Walter, I'm not an expert in torpedoes," Michael said in exasperation. "I know only that they employ the same basic shell. They fit a five hundred thirty-three millimeter tube. I was told the warhead is much bigger. The only one who can tell us more is asleep and will probably awaken just as blind as he was when Soraya gave him the last shot."

CHAPTER SEVENTEEN

There had been no sleep that night for Lyford or Riley. Twice Tyro had to be reassured that everything was being done to arrange Heine Witscher's release. Will Riley had flown over to the *Wasp* to confer with President Salkin and Lou Griffey. The President had been adamant about remaining aboard the *Wasp,* claiming that his absence the following day would be a slap in the face to the peace accord. If he displayed fear, then fear would rule and the accord the delegates were to sign would be nothing more than worthless sheets of paper.

The idea of releasing Witscher had initially been firmly rejected by the German government. Witscher's imprisonment was a symbol of total unification. There was no room for bargaining until Griffey had explained to his counterpart in Bonn in no uncertain terms that proof was forthcoming that not only was *Heinz Waller* still afloat but also that she was now a threat to international peace.

At three in the morning, President Salkin had personally guaranteed the German chancellor that Witscher would never be heard from again, and if ever there was a trace of him the United States would assume full responsibility. Arguments and counterarguments ensued for another hour until Bonn was finally appraised of the conference aboard *Calm Seas.* An hour later, Lyford and Tyro had agreed upon a means of spiriting Heine Witscher out of Germany.

The sun was peeking over the horizon when Lyford,

sitting on a bench in Berlin's Tiergarten, watched as an old man with a cane hobbled down the path and sat down on the opposite end of his bench.

"Been a long time, Mr. Lyford."

"Yes, it has. Death becomes you."

"My passing has been rather a pleasant experience. I've accomplished a great deal since my demise, and made a great deal of money also. I've decided to retire after this."

Lyford smiled. "You wouldn't know what to do with yourself."

"Probably you're right. But I'll give it a shot. Witscher?"

"He'll be committing suicide before breakfast this morning. The evening papers will explain that he hung himself in his cell."

"No need for an autopsy then. Nice and clean."

"That's the idea. Burial will be later today in an unmarked grave at the insistence of the chancellor." He explained the means for transferring Witscher to a secluded place outside of Berlin where Tyro would then assume responsibility. Lyford looked into the sharp eyes that had been studying him. "The President and the Secretary of State have been up all night arranging it. My word's always been good before. It's guaranteed."

"Accepted." For the next fifteen minutes, Tyro explained exactly what he had promised over the phone.

"We haven't found any trace of a submarine yet," Lyford said.

"Believe me, it's somewhere out there." Tyro explained Hussein's mission. "You know my old associates and you know the information they obtain is correct. Once we got wind of this thing, my people went to work. When they told me what they had, I knew it was good enough to spring Heine. It wasn't easy. No one in this As-Sa'iqa knows everything, but we worked over enough of them to get what we needed. That submarine is alive. I honestly don't know where and I can't say they'll succeed, but . . ."

"I understand." A deal was a deal and there was still so much to be done.

Walter Erhardt stood behind his sonar operator. He'd given the exhausted young man a hearty pat on the back. "I know you're tired, my friend. I am also. But our mission is almost at an end." Earlier, he'd been called when the sonarman had picked up traces of an American nuclear submarine. But it had been well away from the formation and Erhardt had to assume it would continue to patrol at a distance from the amphibious group, since that was a standard American tactic. If for some reason one of the nukes came close to him, he would face the problem at that time.

He came around to one side and dropped to one knee so he could look directly into the sonarman's eyes. "Now, listen carefully . . . close your eyes. That's it. You can feel the tension draining away. Your muscles are relaxing. You know the sounds of each of the ships in the formation. Now, have you heard anything else, anything at all?"

"No . . . not from the formation . . . nothing has changed."

"Ahead of the formation?"

The operator shifted his concentration to the forward hydrophones and listened. "Distant . . . merchant . . ."

"Behind them?"

"Ah . . . merchant again . . . not close . . ." The operator raised his head and rotated it like an athlete. "Nothing seems to come close to the formation, Captain. I think maybe they chase everyone away." His accent was Portuguese. When he attended the German submarine school, he was considered to have tremendous potential by his instructors. He'd been serving aboard a Brazilian Type-209 submarine and was overjoyed when he learned that he'd been selected for this mission. There was little he could do for Allah in Brazil.

"You are the finest sonar operator I've encountered," Erhardt said heartily. "Now, once more. On our starboard beam. Do you have anything close, anything that might see our periscope?"

"Closest contact is small, maybe a coastal freighter, maybe a fishing boat . . . weak . . . not close . . . and one other thing, Captain . . ."

"Yes?"

"This frigate, the closest one, it still has trouble with its towed array. They've retrieved it twice more. I'm reading weird sounds again. I think they just slowed to haul it in again."

Erhardt rose to his feet. "That settles it. We definitely penetrate the formation in front of that frigate. That's just like climbing in a window." Erhardt clapped the sonarman gently on the shoulders. "Thank you. Not long now. Not long and you will be able to claim what none of your peers will ever boast. Stand easy, my friend."

Erhardt strode confidently back into the control room. "Periscope depth . . . gently," he ordered the diving officer. "Not like a cork. I don't want to attract any prying eyes."

Waller's deck canted upward slightly. There was a barely recognizable rumble as water was pumped from the ballast tanks. The only sounds in the control room were the voices that issued orders and those that responded. The silence was a combination of hours on watch and the anticipation that Erhardt had been building in his diverse crew. He'd been certain that in just seven days he could mold them into a singular force that would respond efficiently when the time came. And now it was upon them.

Erhardt moved over beside the quartermaster at the chart table. "I'm going to take a final look at the formation while you record your satellite data. We know where we should be in relation to the carrier." He indicated the overlay. "I'll give you a mark, bearing and distance to the carrier, to double-check our accuracy."

The diving officer, a Muslim from Brazil who was half Arab and half Spanish, turned his eyes from Schroeder to the bubble on the control panel to the depth gauge. They seemed to be rising too fast, more like the cork that the captain had warned against. He reached for the valves to decrease the outflow from the ballast tanks and said, "We're rising too fast . . ." He turned back to the planesman to complete his sentence: ". . . your bow angle . . ."

But Hugo Schroeder had reached an inescapable decision. There would be no more opportunities for him. But they were near the American formation and it was daytime. If the submarine could break the surface, this horror would be ended.

Schroeder lunged, reaching over the planesman for the control wheel, clawing the air as the man cried out and struggled to shake him off. Schroeder's elbow slammed into the planesman's neck, and as the man recoiled, he literally leapt over his shoulder, grasping for the controls.

Erhardt whirled just as the crack of the diving officer's pistol shattered the air. His first shot hit Schroeder under the left arm, driving him sideways. Schroeder's right hand was on the control, his fingers desperately clawing for a handhold. He had it . . . almost. The pain was blinding. He could feel his body slipping, floating. The control panel appeared to drift behind a deepening mist. *Which way? Up? Down? Left? Right?*

Two succeeding shots knocked him backward, away from the control panel. He sensed the impact, but there was no longer pain. Nor was there feeling. Did he have the control? He was falling . . .

"Level!" Erhardt shouted.

But the diving officer was already beside the terrified planesman. "Forward!" he bellowed. "Push the controls forward . . . make the planes level!"

The planesman reacted automatically, both hands back on the control wheel, eyes on the bubble, as he eased the planes. The diving officer returned to his valves. Then, while a grateful Walter Erhardt observed, the submarine rose gradually to periscope depth.

"Periscope depth, Captain," the diving officer called out, as if nothing had happened.

"Very well." Erhardt paid no attention to Schroeder's corpse. He pushed the button for the periscope and bent slightly from the waist as the eyepiece rose to him. Yet it was an effort to calm his shaking hands as he began to swing around with the periscope in a complete circle. Nothing of concern. Just as the sonar operator had reported.

"I have the satellite data, sir," the quartermaster reported.

"Very well. Just a . . . there she is . . ." He manipulated the dials on the periscope. "Standby . . . mark."

The quartermaster recorded the bearing and range from the periscope dials. "I have it, sir."

Erhardt pressed the button and the periscope descended. He turned to the diving officer who had just shot Schroeder. His cool reaction under stress had saved the mission. "Dive,

Mr. Esquimal," he said, using the man's name for the first time. "Gently again." He moved back toward the sonar room, careful to step around the body and the spreading pool of blood, and he stuck his head inside. "What depth was the last thermal layer?"

"Eighty-two meters, Captain."

"We'll level at a hundred. Let me know if there's any significant change." Returning to the control room, he said to the diving officer, "One hundred meters."

Each individual in the control room concentrated on their assignment. No one looked at the corpse. No one spoke unless required to do so. How could their captain act as if nothing had happened—like Ismael?

Back at the chart table, the quartermaster had calculated their exact position. "What were the surface conditions, Captain?" he asked Erhardt.

"Slight seas out of the northwest. No whitecaps, very calm, wind probably less than ten knots."

The quartermaster indicated a mark on the surface display. "That's where we should have been. That's where we are. Too little difference to note. We're being set very slightly to the southeast, Captain. But no more than a couple hundred meters. I'd say the surface ships should be experiencing just about the same thing."

Erhardt bent to the display. The quartermaster had written the local time beside their position: *0958*. Two more hours. "What time is their next course change?"

"Approximately an hour and a half. Eleven thirty. Reverse course to two seven zero. They should stay on that course until fourteen thirty."

Erhardt studied his diagram. "I intend to enter the formation here." He indicated a position well ahead of the frigate that was experiencing problems with its towed array. "I expect that they'll use helicopters to cover the frigate if it still has problems. No matter. We'll let them steam over us. I intend to rise slowly. We should be at periscope depth here. . . ."

"Walter!" Michael's voice rang out sharply against the restrained calm of the control room. He'd stopped just inside the hatch, eyes riveted on Schroeder's corpse. Heads snapped involuntarily in his direction.

"Do you wish to speak to the captain?" Erhardt responded with barely controlled anger.

Michael acquiesced. "Yes. I wish to speak to the captain . . ." He eyed Schroeder's corpse. "In the torpedo room, if that would be all right with you."

"Very well." Erhardt indicated Schroeder. "He was dangerous. I'll be forward, Mr. Esquimal. You have the watch." As if it was an afterthought, he added, "Have the body removed and the deck cleaned up. I intend to move slightly ahead of the formation to make my approach, so you should follow the quartermaster's speed recommendations as soon as he has a solution. Please check with Sonar to make sure we remain below the thermal layer." For Erhardt, these final minutes were all that really mattered. There was an attack to be completed, and until that was accomplished, reality had no place in his mind.

"Ismael's awake now," Michael said nervously, as they left the control room, "but there's something wrong with him. I'm not sure how to explain . . ."

Erhardt stopped outside the torpedo room and grasped Michael's arm firmly. "We're not going in there until you explain."

"Perhaps it's the drugs we gave him. Maybe his system has trouble with them. But he's not coming out of it like he should. He's awake, Walter, but the Ismael we know isn't quite there. In a way, he frightens me more."

"Is he threatening?"

"Not really. He's more like . . ." Michael's only fears were with those things he didn't understand. "Like one of those caged animals you see in the zoo. You know what I mean, pacing back and forth, head down, as if you're not really there. But they do know you're there and you have no idea what they're going to do. I don't know what's going on in his mind. Except, Walter . . . except he keeps talking about the torpedoes."

"You didn't mention about Hussein?"

"Nothing. But there's something in his mind, like someone had planted it there, that's reminded him he must do something."

"Tell me, Michael, how much do you know about the

torpedoes?" Erhardt asked. Was it possible that Michael could be hiding something from him?

"Very little, believe me. My job was to get them here, just like yours is to launch them. Ismael was supposed to be a trouble-shooter, the one to make certain they worked." He recognized the uncertainty in Erhardt's eyes. "Believe me. That's the way it is."

"What's so different about them?"

"I'm not really sure . . . other than . . . well, the explosive is special . . . some kind of incendiary reaction that Hussein mentioned last night." Michael was hesitant. Then he shrugged. "That's all I know. That's the way Hussein works with us."

When they entered the torpedo room, Ismael was in a sitting position, his head cradled in his hands. A frightened Neuner, who had been ordered by Erhardt to remain on watch in the torpedo room, had wedged himself into a corner behind a rack of torpedoes. Neuner intended to stay as far away from the Turk as possible. He peered warily at Erhardt from behind his perch. Soraya had a hand on Ismael's arm and was speaking softly to him. Ismael's body swayed from side to side as he moaned rhythmically, but very softly, apparently to himself.

"The captain is with me, Ismael," Michael announced.

Ismael gave no recognition of the fact.

"Is he in pain?" Erhardt inquired cautiously.

"No," came a muffled response from Ismael. "No . . . no . . . no . . ." he repeated until the word deteriorated back into the unintelligible moan.

"His eyes?"

"His sight?" Soraya responded. "I think it may be a little better, but not good enough to accomplish what he wants with his torpedoes."

"What has to be done that Neuner can't do?" Erhardt asked.

Ismael raised his head slowly. Somehow, he sensed that Neuner was in the corner. He pointed in that direction and shook his head menacingly, much like a great caged cat. Then he turned to Erhardt, his acne-pitted face made uglier by a deep red flush. What little could be seen of his eyes through barely open lids appeared as a pink stain. "My torpedoes," Ismael responded in his broken German.

"Yes, Ismael, your torpedoes," Erhardt said. "Do you know who I am?"

"Captain."

"That's correct. I am your captain. I need your help. I want to know if certain tests should be accomplished before firing—"

"My torpedoes are good," Ismael interrupted with a growl.

"Michael says they're very different from what we normally shoot," Erhardt countered.

Ismael rose to his feet with difficulty to face the captain. "Propulsion system same . . . but smaller . . . for shorter range . . . I tested." His body swayed in rhythm to the clipped phrases he spoke. He turned toward Michael. "It is . . . it is . . . it is . . ." His voice increased in intensity as he searched in his cadenced speech for the lost word, his eyes closed, his large head swinging slowly with his eerie rhythm.

"Does he mean *compatible?*" Erhardt asked.

Michael translated the question and Ismael nodded. "Yes . . . yes . . . yes . . ." Ismael's head continued to bob up and down as he repeated the word silently to himself.

"No problem then. Ismael, I plan to shoot the torpedoes from a position slightly ahead of the target at a range of about three thousand meters." Erhardt watched closely for a reaction. "I'll set the depth for three meters, and . . ."

"No . . . no . . . no . . ." Ismael's body swung from side to side in concert with his head. "Detonators set . . . no . . . no . . . no . . ." Suddenly he stopped and his eyes opened, two ugly red holes accenting his broken nose. His hands balled into fists. "Depth one meter. No more. One meter . . . one meter . . . one meter . . ."

And on and on like a dangerous, ugly metronome, Erhardt thought. "All right, one meter," he agreed loudly. He glanced uneasily at Michael. "I don't know why. That close to the surface, we'll lose much of the explosive pressure, but there must be a reason."

"Ffffiiirrreee . . ." Ismael drew the word out until he closed his eyes and returned to his rhythmic swaying. "Fire . . . fire . . . fire . . ." he chanted.

The torpedo room was packed with equipment—mechanical, electrical, and hydraulic—that made the torpedo tubes functional. Torpedoes were stored on racks on either side. The overhead was a mass of piping and cables.

Erhardt untied one of the drop-down bunks. "We should all sit down," he said matter-of-factly, indicating that Michael should assist Ismael. He glanced quickly at his watch. Ten twenty-eight. He wanted *Waller* to be in position in an hour and fifteen minutes. "I'm concerned about Ismael," he said in an exaggerated voice for the Turk's benefit, "but I'm glad that his torpedoes are ready. I'd still like him with me when we're ready to shoot." When his gaze settled on Michael, he made no effort to disguise his concern, but his voice remained even. "I'd also like Ismael to be more comfortable than he is now. Do you understand me, Ismael?" Somehow, Ismael had to be drugged into unconsciousness. He was too threatening in his current condition.

"Can't . . . can't see . . ." the Turk managed.

"I understand that Ismael. That's why I want to help you. If you feel better, you will be able to help me. We both want your torpedoes to work perfectly. I'm going to see if our pharmacy has something that will help you." It was similar to talking to a child. But Ismael had been so ravaged with pain that he still appeared to be in shock. In actuality, he was a child, and an extremely dangerous one. "Will you let me give you something that will make you feel better, so you can help me?"

Ismael turned his head toward Erhardt, as if he could actually see him. He opened his mouth as if to speak, but there were no words. Yet it seemed as if he was nodding his assent.

At that moment, Neuner decided it was now safe to extricate himself from behind the torpedo rack. As he wriggled to free himself, squirming out feet first, a stray tool was dislodged and clattered to the deck. In the time it took Neuner to step from behind the rack and bend over to pick it up, Ismael had leapt to his feet and hurled himself across the space between them. He landed with a savage scream on top of Neuner, driving him to the deck.

"My torpedoes!" Ismael howled. There was no wasted

motion or speech this time as he pummeled the frightened torpedoman.

Neuner uttered a scream of terror and attempted to wriggle out from underneath. But Ismael wrapped a thick arm around his neck and began to force his head back.

"My torpedoes, my torpedoes," Ismael repeated, as he applied pressure.

Neuner's head was twisted in an impossible fashion. He was unable to breathe. His terror-stricken eyes bulged.

Erhardt dove for the wrench that had fallen to the deck. In one motion, he swept it from the deck, raised it above his head, and swung it savagely, hitting Ismael as hard as he could.

The blow struck at the base of Ismael's skull. His stranglehold relaxed, but he still held Neuner, who shrieked horribly as he sucked air back into his lungs. Ismael flailed about with his other arm in a wild attempt to locate Erhardt. The cries that issued from his mouth were no longer intelligible, but they blended with Neuner's screams and filled the torpedo room with a dreadful sound.

Erhardt ducked a wild swing and smashed down again with the wrench, catching Ismael just behind the ear. Blood spouted from a deep gash. Ismael released Neuner and stumbled blindly forward toward Erhardt. But the Turk's head was lowered now by pain and confusion, and the wrench descended yet again, striking Ismael on the temple. He fell forward, crashing to the deck. Erhardt swung once more, hitting him on the skull with the broad side of the wrench.

"That's enough, Walter. You'll kill him." Soraya was on her feet between Erhardt and the Turk, who lay facedown on the deck in a spreading pool of blood.

"I hope I have." The wrench dropped from his hand and landed with a clatter. "That's what I was trying to do."

"But the torpedoes . . ." Michael said. "Hussein insisted . . ."

"There is no more time, Michael. We're beyond Hussein's control now. We have our mission. Don't you understand?" Erhardt said in a low voice. "There is no more time. We are positioning ourselves to penetrate the formation. I'll fire them when we're in position." He bent down and gently touched Neuner's shoulder. "How are you?"

Neuner had raised himself into a sitting position, his back against a torpedo, his arms wrapped around his legs. His entire body shook. He moved his head up slowly until he was looking at Erhardt, but he said nothing. He stroked his throat, and tears ran down his cheeks.

"I need you, Neuner. I saved your life seven days ago because you are the finest torpedoman in the fleet. And now, I've saved your life again. I need you. Will you help me?" And then, to remind the terrified man that there were other lives more important than his own, he added, "I don't want to be forced to radio ashore for someone to visit your family."

Neuner looked slowly toward Ismael, then back to Erhardt. "Is he dead?" he croaked.

"I don't know. But I won't let him bother you. Now will you help me?"

Neuner assented with a nod of his head and a choking sob.

"Soraya, give Ismael a shot of whatever you were giving him before." Then he looked to Michael. "Then get some men to move him out of here. I don't care whether he's dead or alive and we have no time to worry about that. Neuner and I have work to do in here." He had another thought. "Put Ismael in the galley. No one's going to eat anything for the next few hours. Get a good rope and secure him to something in case he's alive."

Michael stared uneasily at Erhardt and was about to speak, but thought better of it. Until that moment, he was sure he was in charge. But now he didn't know. By attacking Ismael, Erhardt had altered the delicate balance between them.

Erhardt reached a hand down to Neuner. "Come, my friend. Let me give you a hand. I think you need a good shot of schnapps before I put you to work. We only have an hour to find out about these torpedoes."

Rear Admiral Turner had issued a top-secret intelligence report to all ships in Amphibious Squadron Four concerning the existence of *Waller* along with the information reported by Lyford that morning. Since there'd been no report of submarine activity from his nuclear submarines well on the outer perimeter, he had no reason to believe there would be. It was simply that Will Riley had said that Roland Lyford's mind worked much like his own, and Lou Griffey was willing to accept Riley's word—there's a maverick German submarine somewhere out there.

Now they were in PHIBRON FOUR's intelligence space for a final briefing. Although the Secret Service had cautioned against it, the President still intended to fly over to the summit at the appropriate time. Phil Salkin had made it clear to everybody that unless they could come up with a submarine before it was time to leave for *Calm Seas,* he would take part in the ceremony. He owed that to the participants—and to Rupert Daniels.

Rear Admiral Turner glanced at his watch then moved his wrist farther away. "My eyes aren't working the way they used to. It's a bitch getting old." He looked over at Jake Steele. "Well, it's eleven fifteen. What do you say, Jake? Do you want to be with your boys over on *Ashland?"*

"No, sir," Jake answered. "I think I'll stick close. If something goes down, it's easier to see the big picture here. There's a helo on deck if I have to make a fast getaway." Steele had changed in his quarters before he came back to the staff area. He was wearing web gear and life jacket, and he carried fins, mask, and a holstered .45-caliber along with personal weapons. His automatic weapons, a SIG-Sauer 9mm and an H&K MP5, had been left in the helicopter. He had six men ready to fast-rope with him from the helo down to *Calm Seas'* deck, along with a sniper to cover them. "You know my platoon leaders, Admiral. Nichols and Harrison. They've done everything they can to prepare their men and it would be wrong to get in their way."

"Fine by me, Jake," Turner agreed. "I guess I'd kind of like having you around anyway if anything happens, so I know what you decide."

The briefing was nearing its end and Lieutenant Germond was concluding: ". . . liftoff at eleven forty-five on the button. The President will put down on *Calm Seas'* flight deck exactly four and a half minutes later. Allow another sixty seconds to secure the engines. The delegates will be assembled in *Calm Seas'* main salon at eleven fifty-five for the signing. Mr. Griffey and Mrs. Mehari will greet President Salkin when he steps out of the helicopter. There'll be some small talk and they'll show him the exterior of *Calm Seas* as they head forward. They should enter the main salon about eleven fifty-six, so the President can witness the signing. Mr. Griffey says there's a pecking order as to who signs the accord first and where their signatures go, but that should be complete almost exactly at noon. Then there will be private pictures. Then"—he spread his arms dramatically—"the world receives the good news."

"Standby," the quartermaster noted calmly. "Mark. Time is eleven thirty. We should reverse course to two seven zero." And as he spoke, the computer concurred with the human—to Erhardt's satisfaction.

Esquimal called into sonar to confirm the depth of the thermal layer. They were still well hidden beneath it. The frigate nearest to them had still not been able to put its towed array sonar back in the water. They could hear the sound of the helicopters' dipping sonars, but Erhardt had little concern about being detected by a sonar beneath the layer. He knew the helicopters would also be dropping passive listening devices, but *Waller* was almost silent under electric power, and the mix of sound from the formation would cover him.

"Recommend we add two knots, sir," the quartermaster said. "That should place us at formation entry point in about ten minutes."

"Do so, Mr. Esquimal."

Waller had reduced speed well before the formation reversed course. Now she was in a waiting position, barely moving, totally silent, with the forward segment of the formation approaching her. There would be no need to race to arrive at her position ahead of the carrier. Below the mask of that thermal layer, she was as invisible as she could ever be.

Walter Erhardt was back in the torpedo room peering over Neuner's shoulder. One of Hussein's torpedoes had been extracted from its tube. It lay just outside like a surgical patient on the hydraulically operated slide used for loading the tubes. Neuner had opened the detonator section and was studying the interior curiously. Soraya and Michael, who had assisted, were behind Erhardt.

"That's the depth setting," Neuner murmured. "He was right. Just below the surface. But I can't understand why."

"It's the enabling run I'm concerned with," Erhardt snapped. He shouldn't have waited. This should have been done earlier. But, then again, he was not aware of it until the last radio contact. "What range can I shoot from? I'm planning on a forward angle shot from three thousand meters. Can I do that?" Why was such vital data hidden within minds like Ismael's?

"I can't tell," Neuner mumbled. "The propulsion system is the same. I . . . I don't know what . . ." He was pointing at various components within the casing with needle nose pliers, as if he might find an answer by counting each unit. "I . . . it's going to take more time to . . ."

Erhardt slapped his hand against the torpedo's metal hide. "We don't have any more time. In five minutes, we have to have this buttoned up and back in the tube. I want to flood the tubes and open the outer doors before we are in position. I don't want some American sonarman to suddenly wake up and say, 'Hey, I hear a submarine flooding its torpedo tubes which must mean that maybe that submarine's going to shoot!' Range, Neuner!" he shouted. "Tell me the range."

"Walter," Michael interjected, "what does it matter? It's going to explode on contact anyway."

Erhardt whirled and faced him. His eyes were narrow slits. "Yes. It will do that, if it's not running around in circles because my attack solution couldn't input the correct range. Do you understand that?!" he shouted. "Do you understand that maybe, because the torpedo can't accept my solution, it might just come back to its source and destroy us and our mission?" He remembered Hussein's last words—people aboard *Calm Seas* had been responsible for Darra's death. *The mission . . . the mission . . . the mission was for Darra.*

Michael had no idea what Erhardt was trying to say. "Does it look similar to your own torpedoes, Neuner?"

Neuner was perspiring freely and his entire body shook. "Yes . . . yes, I think so. I'm trying to do what we were taught in school . . . by the numbers," he answered. "Please, just another minute."

Erhardt leaned farther forward to watch Neuner, who continued to touch one unit after another with his pliers. His lips moved silently.

Finally, Neuner said, "It seems to fit our own model, Captain." He closed his eyes and took a deep breath. "I would need hours to familiarize myself adequately, but I think someone has compressed this design in order to expand the warhead." He brought his hands up and began to stroke his temples as tears of fear and exhaustion rolled down his cheeks. "I think," he concluded.

Erhardt jumped to his feet. "That's it, then. Let's get this back into the tube so Neuner can prepare himself." He bent down and whispered in Neuner's ear. "It's all right, Neuner. You've done a good job. Now get control of yourself. You and I—we're going to show the world what the German navy can do."

The process of slipping a torpedo into its tube was no longer a muscle-and-sweat evolution. It was efficiently controlled by complex instrumentation operating hydraulic equipment. The torpedo was raised to the level of the tube, automatically aligned with the tube opening, then mechanically inserted inside. When they left the torpedo room, Neuner was already going through his check-off list to prepare the weapon for firing.

Chief Bewick shifted position so that the sunlight shone over his left shoulder onto the magazine he was reading. He was sitting on *Ashland*'s deck, his back propped against the reinforced fabric gunwale of one of his RIBs. Other SBU crew relaxed nearby, playing poker with matches. The SEAL platoon members amused themselves with a spirited game of hacky-sac.

"What you reading, Master Chief," Lieutenant Junior Grade Nichols asked. "A skin magazine?" He was outfitted like the other SEAL, his face darkened with camouflage paint.

"Nope. Investment opportunities for the next decade," Bewick responded. "I'm thinking about changing the weight in my portfolio from information services back to defense contractors. And, of course, I think it's wise to always keep a third of your available cash in treasuries." He finally looked up over the top of the magazine. "You and your sidekick," he continued, indicating Lieutenant Junior Grade Harrison, "care to read it after I'm finished?"

"Sorry, Master Chief," Harrison answered. "They don't pay us enough to save anything. It's just older gentlemen, like yourself, who should be worrying about that stuff."

"Yeah, I guess you've got something there," Bewick agreed. "I suppose I ought to put a little paint on this dome so any bad guys don't see the reflection and start shooting at you."

"Hey, I'm just kidding, Master Chief."

"I know that. But you know," Bewick continued philosophically, "us old guys have to set an example. Think I'll check out those engines one more time. Never can tell. You know what I mean?" He rose to his feet and carefully stuffed the girly magazine he'd been reading in a leather briefcase that was always with him.

Master Chief Bewick moved slowly about his RIBs, checking the blocks and lines that would support them if *Ashland*'s cranes lifted them over the side. Then he climbed into his small boats and rechecked gauges, equipment, weapons, mentally reviewing check-off lists that he'd already gone over time and again.

"Think they'll float, Master Chief?" one of *Ashland*'s third-class boatswains called out.

"With luck. A couple of them will . . . with luck," Bewick answered. "Depends on the crews, though." It was the same question and the same answer as the day wore on. The SEALs no longer paid attention to them.

"You're sure of that, Master Chief?" Nichols asked with a grin as Bewick stretched out nearby again.

"You know," Bewick said, exhibiting his lazy smile, "after this is all over, I think I'm going to lay out an investment program for the two of you. I hate to think what would happen to your families if one of my boats sank."

"We're not married, Master Chief."

"Doesn't matter. I'm thinking about your poor gray-haired mothers. They're my generation, you know." He reached back into his briefcase and pulled out the girly magazine, opening to the page he'd turned down. "How about this?" He looked over the top of his magazine at the two officers. "This market specialist recommends a forty-percent balance of chemicals and software companies against pharmaceuticals and automotive. Would you buy that?"

Harrison was about to respond when one of the ship's sailors monitoring the ship-to-ship communications handed him the phone. "Go ahead, Jake," he responded. "Yeah, we're all set here, checked and double-checked and triple-checked, and the master chief's into tits and asses again. Everything's copacetic over here."

Rear Admiral Turner, at the behest of the Secret Service, had made the final effort as respectfully as possible to dissuade the President from transferring to *Calm Seas.*

Salkin had studied the admiral's face calmly as he spoke, knowing it was for his own benefit, then answered quietly, "This is the most critical moment of my administration and certainly the most important one in my life. There's no indication of a submarine anywhere in our vicinity, is there?"

"No, sir." Turner had ordered helicopters and aircraft ranging out to a hundred miles from the formation since before sunrise that morning. He'd followed the book, covered every possibility, and then reviewed everything again in depth after Lyford's report. There had been no indication that one existed.

"Your concern is appreciated, Admiral. I have to go."

Since Phil Salkin was about to leave the ship, there was no longer a need to conceal the fact that the President was aboard *Wasp.* Turner escorted him up to the flight deck. Sailors in the corridors pressed themselves against bulkheads in rigid salutes as the two men passed, unable to believe a moment later that the Commander in Chief had reached out to shake their hand or clap them on the shoulder as he moved on.

There was a light breeze across the flight deck as the two men stepped out into the open. "Mr. President, you haven't seen much since we had to hide you in the closet for the night. Let me show you where you're headed." He escorted Salkin the hundred yards back to the fantail and pointed at the brilliant white vessel six thousand yards astern. "There she is—*Calm Seas*. She really deserves her name on a day like this."

It was a brilliant day. A bright sun warmed *Wasp*'s flight deck. Fair-weather clouds sparkled brightly against a blue sky. The Mediterranean, a darker blue, lay smooth like a spring pond. The ships in the formation rose and fell lightly on an almost imperceptible swell.

Phil Salkin waved to the groups of sailors that formed as word spread that the President was aboard. "This is a nice life out here, Admiral. Wish I had more time to spend with you." *Just a day or two would be nice,* he thought, *enough time to talk to these men, to get a handle on what mattered to them. With no wars, we've been shortchanging them.*

"We'd sure welcome another visit, Mr. President, when you could stay a little longer. I'd like you to meet our men, see how they operate. They have a lot to offer in a crunch."

Salkin looked thoughtful as they meandered back toward the waiting helicopter. "That's a hell of an idea. Maybe I'll just do that when I come back." Perhaps the admiral was a mind reader. He looked questioningly at Turner. "I do have to come back to this ship when I head for home, don't I?"

"That's the plan, sir."

"I'll talk to Bill Herbert." The communications director had flown over to *Calm Seas* an hour before.

Rear Admiral Turner came to attention and saluted as President Salkin climbed inside the helicopter with two Secret Service agents.

Waller maintained a deathlike silence. Sound, being subject to the oddities of nature in saltwater, was highly respected by submarines. The air-circulating equipment had been turned down to minimize noise. Each man aboard remained in his assigned position unless permission was granted to move. No one wore shoes. No one was allowed to handle anything that could send a signal, called a "sound transient," through the water if it was dropped. Proceeding under electric power, S-252 moved silently and invisibly through the water at four knots.

When Erhardt had considered his choices for the approach to *Calm Seas,* he'd determined it was safest to enter the perimeter of the formation from the front, then slide silently toward his target. While he took into consideration the danger of being heard as he passed in front of the frigate and her weaker, keel-mounted sonar, he gambled on water conditions and the fact that her towed array wasn't functioning. As he approached his decision point, he'd brought *Waller* gradually up to sixty meters, then down to one hundred twenty, searching for the optimum depth. They'd confirmed a sharp temperature drop was at seventy-two meters. That would now be his shield.

Go ahead, Walter. Be aggressive. Don't go back on your decision. Yet a prudent voice of caution had said to enter the formation behind the frigate. *It's much safer!* But then he would have to put on a last-minute burst of speed that might be heard over passive sonar. The aggressive self eventually overwhelmed the cautious self and he stuck with his original plan to penetrate ahead. *After all, Walter, isn't every attack both a gamble and a work of art?* And this one was also for Darra.

Erhardt had explained his intentions to the crew before *Waller* entered the screen slightly behind the forward LST and almost seven kilometers ahead of the frigate. Now he allowed their progress to be relayed to each space over sound-powered phones.

Four thousand seven hundred meters from the frigate! That was their closest point of approach to that ship. Each man waited in silence.

Walter Erhardt pursed his lips. "Relative position of the frigate?"

"Her signal is broad on our starboard beam."

"Should be about four seven zero zero meters according to our display," the quartermaster noted, "and opening."

They'd successfully crossed the bow of the frigate!

"The captain is smiling again." That reaction was passed on to each man in each space. "We're opening our range from the frigate."

"Perhaps we are home free," Erhardt commented. "Those sonars on the frigates are just extra baggage."

Captain says we're home free!

"Range to come to our base attack course?" Erhardt asked the quartermaster.

"Three seven zero zero meters, Captain."

Erhardt glanced at the ship's chronometer and did some rapid calculations in his head. He expected to be in position in fifteen minutes. The computer agreed. "Increase your speed two knots." That would make their relative speed to the formation sixteen knots when he turned to their attack course. Perfect.

"Time to come to zero nine zero?" Erhardt questioned.

"Six minutes, twenty-five seconds." There was accord once again by the computer.

Just about noontime!

The overlay of the formation was on top of the display, centered on a dark line showing the formation's course. *Waller*'s path was in red. It followed a neat line that displayed her angular course to a second line that paralleled the formation's course. That was the opposite of their course and would carry them three thousand meters off *Wasp*'s and *Calm Seas'* beam. The line ceased at a large *X*, a point slightly ahead of *Calm Seas*.

There was absolute silence in *Waller*'s control room, broken occasionally by the reports from sonar and the quartermaster, and Erhardt's own conning orders. Each minute seemed to expand to an hour as they approached their target.

"Mark!" said the quartermaster in a hoarse whisper.

Walter Erhardt gave the orders to come to zero nine zero.

Moments later, sonar announced, "Carrier passing to port."

Erhardt took his position at the attack console.

CHAPTER EIGHTEEN

Will Riley's voice resonated with the emotion he was feeling. "Mr. President, it is a distinct honor to introduce you to Mrs. Mehari, the delegate from Lebanon and the elected chairman of this conference." The three individuals stood on *Calm Seas'* flight deck beneath the now still rotors of the navy helicopter. The two Secret Service agents hovered discreetly behind the President.

Isabel Mehari shook hands with Phil Salkin. "Mr. President," she said warmly, "from my heart I would like to thank you on behalf of the peoples of our respective nations for making this historic day possible." She had written a short welcoming speech, then rehearsed it that morning, for she had never dreamed she would ever meet the President of the United States. But when Phil Salkin alighted from the helicopter and smiled at her, the few words she uttered came from deep within her, totally unrehearsed.

Phil Salkin, instinctively aware of the inner strength of this small, neat, attractive lady, replied, "Mrs. Mehari, it is you people to whom I owe a debt of gratitude. We simply provided the means for you to come together. You were the ones to achieve the accord on your own."

Riley shielded his eyes against the bright sun. "The delegates are assembled in the main salon for the signing. Mr. Griffey is reviewing the protocol at this moment. He asked us to briefly show you *Calm Seas* and introduce you to the captain since things should be rather busy afterward with the media." Will would have preferred to say, *Let's get on with it, start the ceremony, do your thing, and get the hell off while we're still in one piece. Your Secret Service staff is beside themselves.* But that was a dream. Phil Salkin was adamant. Will could only pray fervently that if there was indeed a submarine nearby it would remain beyond torpedo range and be detected before it could become a threat.

The party climbed the ladder to the port wing of the bridge. Riley looked into the pilot house. "Francis, come on out here. There's someone I'd like you to meet."

Francis Waters had been shaking hands and smiling pleasantly for a number of people Will Riley had brought to his bridge that week. But now, seeing the President out on the bridge wing, he hesitated for a moment. He'd had no idea he would be introduced to Salkin. Francis stepped out into the sun, blinking against the sudden brightness.

Phil Salkin shook his hand warmly. "I've heard a great deal about you, Captain, from Will. You've done quite a service for your country."

It was more a matter of his past catching up with him. Until that very moment, it had seemed more like being drafted again. "Thank you very much, sir."

Walter Erhardt listened calmly to Neuner's report. It was a repetition of the check-off list, but it was necessary to him. Thank God he'd made a point of keeping the youngster. Erhardt was sure all steps had been followed, but Neuner's report was an integral part of attack procedures.

Tubes flooded.

Pressure equalized.

Muzzle doors open.

Torpedoes warmed.

Neuner, driven by fear and the ever-present guns that had so often been pointed at him, had done everything he'd been trained to do.

"Two thousand meters to firing point, Captain."

"Very well." There'd been a hush in the control room as they drifted down *Wasp*'s beam. *Waller* was seventy-two meters beneath the surface protected by that sharp temperature gradient, and *Wasp* had no sonar.

So close to a carrier—the temptation!

As they'd passed astern of *Wasp,* Erhardt had given the orders to commence a slow ascent. Water was pumped slowly from the ballast tanks. The planes were at an easy up angle. Esquimal was coordinating Schroeder's part of the process with relish.

If they were going to be detected, this would be the time. They were leaving the protection of the thermal gradient, their pumps were operating, water was flowing—if anything, passive sonar would hear sounds that were not supposed to be nearby.

Erhardt stepped over to the attack console to recheck the inputs to the fire-control solution. This was the third time he had done so. The attack was simple, a textbook procedure—a surface target on a steady course of two seven zero, a constant speed of ten knots, and her aspect would be port bow at three thousand meters when he fired his torpedoes. The weapons were preset to detonate at slightly less than a meter beneath the surface.

"Depth, five zero meters," Esquimal reported.

"Range to firing point, fifteen hundred meters."

"Depth, four zero meters." They were naked now, in open water for every American sonarman to hear.

"Very well."

When *Waller* was five hundred meters from the firing point, Walter Erhardt would slow and bring her bow around in the direction of the target. *We're almost there, Darra.*

Lou Griffey met Phil Salkin at the door to *Calm Seas'* main salon. His welcoming grin seemed to double the size of his round face. "It's going to be a great day. Rupert deserved to have been here to witness this."

"Somehow, he knows." President Salkin, with his Secret Service retinue never more than a step away, was led into the room by Isabel Mehari and was greeted by an ovation from the other thirteen delegates, the aides who had been at their right hand during the conference, and their ever-present bodyguards.

One of the dining tables had been prepared for the signing with a large floral display in the shape of a dove with an olive branch in its beak. To the side was the symbol of the conference that had been created by Isabel Mehari—

interlocked hands in the center of a circle with the names of each of the fourteen countries emanating clockwise from the center alphabetically. She'd made up her mind to design it after the close of the second full day in response to the overwhelming enthusiasm of the delegates to reach an understanding among themselves. It had been unanimously accepted by the delegates the following day when they also elected her chairperson. Will Riley had sent her design off to *Wasp,* where the machine shop had cut and welded a replica and returned it the previous evening in time for the farewell dinner.

Before the uncertain delegates could decide whether they should come to him, Phil Salkin waded into their midst. He made a point of shaking hands with each individual before raising his hands for their attention.

"Ladies and gentlemen, this is your day. I'm here merely to witness the signing of this historic document and to congratulate you for your vision. It will mean more to me right now if you will allow me to step aside and watch you affix your signatures to that document. Mrs. Mehari, please continue with your ceremony." With that, Phil Salkin humbly backed away to a position behind the table.

"Depth, thirty meters," Esquimal intoned. "I will hold my depth at twenty-five meters," he said, as he gave orders to the planesman and made valve adjustments to the ballast tanks.

"Range to turning point, five hundred meters," the quartermaster called out.

"Very well," Erhardt responded. "Slow to four knots."

"Ninety seconds, Captain," the quartermaster said.

Heinz Waller slowly maneuvered into position twenty-five meters below the Mediterranean's placid surface.

"I have a new man-made sound bearing . . ." The sonar operator in one of *Wasp's* helicopters gave the bearing from the carrier of the sound he'd picked up.

"Roger that," came the report from another helo. "I have a sound classified as water bubbles . . . sounds like ballast tanks . . ."

The staff antisubmarine coordinator aboard *Wasp* noted the point where the two bearings crossed and checked the radar. "Bearing is clear visually," he reported. "Recommend emergency turn!"

Erhardt depressed the intercom switch that connected all spaces in S-252.

"Stand by tubes one and two," Erhardt ordered.

"Torpedoes are ready," Neuner responded.

"My solution is ready," Erhardt said.

"My rudder is left." Esquimal was as involved in the process as the others—an integral member of the team. "Coming to course zero five zero."

"Tube number one . . . on my command." Erhardt was barely breathing.

"We're at the firing point, Captain."

"Steady on course zero five zero," Esquimal reported. "The ship is ready, Captain."

"Shoot."

A shudder ran through *Waller* as the water slug propelled the first torpedo out of the tube.

"Tube number two . . . shoot."

Another noticeable shudder.

"Slow to two knots."

"Two knots, aye."

"Both units running properly."

"Time to target?"

"One minute, forty seconds."

It was an antisubmarine helicopter from one of the frigates that had just moved into its assigned sector off *Calm Seas'* port quarter that gave the initial warning. The pilot caught sight of an unfamiliar object in the water. The sun's reflection temporarily screened it as he banked slightly to get a better view.

"Emergency!" he shouted into his transmitter. "Torpedoes. Port beam *Calm Seas.* Seven hundred yards. Repeat, torpedoes in the water. Port beam *Calm Seas!*"

The turn signal from *Wasp* had already been issued. But the warning came much too late. There were less than thirty seconds to impact. The helicopter circuit had been patched into the controller's circuit on *Calm Seas'* flight deck. The controller raced into the security shack and fumbled for the correct button on the interior communications system. He was able to shout a warning to the bridge. "Torpedo, port beam."

There were ten seconds to impact when Francis Waters heard the frantic cry. He lunged for the wheel and threw it hard left.

The last of the signatures had been affixed to the document. Isabel Mehari asked President Salkin to say a few words.

"You each represent a momentous shift in world power. In the past, power and leadership have been identified by wealth. That is changing. Today, your countries have forged a union that creates a new era of peace and understanding among more than one-fifth of the world's population. In the simple strokes of your pens, you are accepting that shift in power and taking on the immense burden of showing the rest of the world that peace is indeed possible." He steadied himself as *Calm Seas* began to heel to starboard. "I thank you for naming this agreement the Daniels Accord, for you have named it after a man who died in order that you might come together for this signing today. Maintaining that peace is sometimes a lonely . . ."

A tremendous crash filled the main salon, drowning out his last words.

Phil Salkin was hurled off his feet as *Calm Seas* seemed to leap sideways. His eyes widened in amazement as each of the people he was speaking to appeared to fly toward him as one. He landed hard on the carpeted deck, rolling when he saw the heavy white-clothed table tumble in his direction.

Salkin heard a second deafening noise that coincided with the deck beneath slamming violently upward. There was instant pain in his side as his body was heaved involuntarily into the air. He came down hard on the back of his neck. Light and dark flashed in his head to complement the sharp pain in his side. His first thought was that he was unconscious, until he realized the screams and shouts around him were real. He struggled to rise on one arm. Lou Griffey was crawling toward him, blood dripping from his scalp.

Walter Erhardt flushed a deep red as the report from sonar sunk in—both torpedoes had hit the target. *Neither one had exploded!* Something had been drastically wrong with the detonators.

Michael and Soraya appeared in the control room together. "What the fuck did I hear?!" Michael screamed.

Erhardt's head turned slowly. "Your torpedoes were shit," he said, hissing quietly. His eyes were full of rage. "They are sitting somewhere inside the hull of that white ship . . . absolutely useless. They didn't explode." He saw Soraya for the first time. "And we are sitting out here waiting to be sunk. Are your orders to kill someone now?" he asked bitterly.

Shock reflected momentarily on Michael's face before anger returned. "You fired them incorrectly," he raged. "Ismael said they were ready."

"Ismael was full of shit," Erhardt snapped. "The mission is a failure, and now . . . now we are all dead men," he concluded philosophically. He could see in his mind's eye the frigates and helicopters racing in his direction.

Michael stepped hesitantly toward Erhardt, unsure what he should be doing. His fists were balled. The cords in his neck bulged in rage. "You have your own torpedoes. Load them and fire again."

Erhardt snorted. "Forget it, Michael. There's not enough time. Right now, that frigate that didn't hear us pass knows where we are. He must be bearing down on us. He may already have his weapons prepared to fire. Helicopters with torpedoes are going to be directly over our heads in moments. We had only one chance. By the time we could prepare an attack solution and fire again, we would have been sunk three or four times."

"Come to the surface, Walter." Soraya's expression remained passive. But her words were sharp. "It was always possible this would happen."

"What do you know . . . ?" Erhardt began.

"I know that those warheads weren't tested under actual conditions. And I know that others always worried they might fail." She confronted both men. "What do you think all those extra crates were brought on board for? They're full of explosives that were to be used if the torpedoes malfunctioned."

Erhardt glanced at Michael, recognized hesitation, then turned back to Soraya.

"Walter," Soraya snapped, "bring this submarine to the surface. We are going to ram the white ship. Then we are going to blow it up."

Erhardt's voice rang through the control room. "Emergency surface. Flank speed. Sonar, give me a bearing on the target." Then he glared at Michael. "Have your people break out the weapons and demolition equipment."

A bored Nichols was dozing when Jake Steele's voice boomed into the earpiece of his communicator. "Torpedoes in the water on *Calm Seas'* port side. On the way!"

"Let's go!" Nichols bellowed. Harrison, the other SEAL platoon leader, had heard the same words.

Chief Bewick's crews were into their RIBs and signaling for the crane operators to hustle as each four-SEAL element hefted their remaining equipment into the inflatable boats. As quickly as the cranes on each side of *Ashland* lowered the first RIB into the water, the second was ready to be hoisted over the side.

"Nick, you under way?" Steele asked over his communicator.

"Roger. The second RIB is hooked up to the crane. Steve," he called to Harrison, "status?"

"Same. Second RIB is in sight above *Ashland*'s deck. We'll be ready in about a minute."

"Copy, Jake?" Nichols asked.

"Roger. I copy you both." Steele and his men were in the helicopter. "I'm airborne with six men. Tactical picture is muddy. *Calm Seas* appears to have been hit by two torpedoes. Neither one detonated. Uncertain of status. She's dead in the water. The formation has slowed to five knots and flag is coordinating an emergency plan now. RIBs, rendezvous one thousand yards off *Calm Seas'* starboard beam and wait for orders."

Calm Seas was listing to port.

Francis Waters had been knocked to the open bridge deck by the impact of the first torpedo. Before he could move, he was thrown against the pilot-house door by the second. Even in his first dazed moments, as he struggled to maintain his senses, he realized there'd been no explosions.

Vision began to fade when he struggled to his knees. As he kneeled, waiting, he saw that the helmsman had lurched to his feet and was leaning against the wheel. "Do we have power and steering control?"

The man spun the wheel, then pushed the engine controls forward. "Negative on both."

Don't pamper yourself, Francis. You've got some valuable cargo aboard—get your ass below and assess the damage. Then get your ass to Griffey and Riley, tell them the exact situation, and coordinate a plan for that cargo. He climbed unsteadily to his feet and headed for the rear of the pilot house, where he splashed some water from the urinal on his face. As he scurried down the ladders, he was acutely aware that his right knee ached.

The first torpedo had penetrated the crew berthing area on the deck just beneath the kosher galley. The impact had torn a five-by-three-foot hole in the hull. Two *Wasp* sailors were already attempting to stuff rolled mattresses in the jagged hole where water flowed in around the base. *Thank someone's genius for giving me men from the* Wasp. The torpedo lay in the far corner of the compartment, its badly damaged propeller slowly turning.

"Jam something—anything—under that thing so it doesn't roll!" Waters shouted, as he limped out of the compartment.

The second torpedo had burst into the upper level of the engine room below the main salon, hurled itself across the open space, and smashed through the main electrical board. It had wedged itself beneath one of the huge diesel engines. Water poured into the darkened space through a gaping hole larger than the forward one. The two civilian crewmen who'd been on watch in the engine room had disappeared. On his way to the main deck, Francis grabbed two *Wasp* sailors and sent them after mattresses and damage-control timbers. "Anything that can slow the engine room flooding!" he shouted.

Waters encountered Will Riley on the deck outside the main salon. Will's pale face was highlighted by a stream of blood that ran down his cheek from a gash on his forehead. But there was also an effective-looking weapon, an MP-5, hanging from a sling around his neck and a pistol tucked in his belt.

"Talk to me, Francis, quick. What have we got?"

"Two torpedoes penetrated the hull. Neither one detonated. We're trying to neutralize the flooding."

"How bad is it?"

"No immediate danger unless one of those torpedoes decides to blow. Is the President injured?"

"Shaken, but okay. Mr. Griffey and his Secret Service people are in the salon with him. There's a lot of frightened people in there. Bruises and cuts. No serious injuries that I know of. We've got everyone in life jackets. Once again, Mrs. Mehari has everyone under her wing. First thing's to arrange to get the President off super quick." Riley slipped a miniature headset over his ears. A tiny mike hung to one side of his mouth. "I'll have an explosive-ordnance demolition team sent over, too."

Waters noticed the screen around *Calm Seas* for the first time and saw that they were closing in protectively.

Riley spoke briefly over the radio, then said, "The admiral needs a preliminary damage report."

Waters took the headset and detailed the damage. "We might be able to plug the hole forward," he concluded. "I don't know about the one in the engine compartment."

"We'll send you submersible pumps."

"We can use everything, but flooding's not critical yet. The major concern's the torpedo warheads. We need EOD assistance super quick."

Riley took back the headset and spoke directly again to Rear Admiral Turner. After a short conversation, he turned to Waters. "EOD's airborne shortly. When the rescue helo makes its approach, I'll start the President and Mr. Griffey toward the flight deck. Navy small craft are on their way to help offload delegates. They'll worry about the pumps after we're evacuated. You control your side from the bridge. I'll join you up there shortly. We'll have a tight screen around us during the evacuation."

As Francis climbed the final painful step onto the bridge wing, he came face to face with the helmsman, a look of stark terror on his face. "Captain . . . the submarine," he uttered, pointing off the port bow.

Waters stared in disbelief. No more than seven hundred yards away, the conning tower of a submarine was emerging from the depths. White water gushed back on either side of the sail. It was heading directly toward *Calm Seas.*

There wouldn't be time for the few guns in the screen to isolate the target. Francis reached for the radio transmitter. "This is *Calm Seas . . ."* he began, but stopped in midsentence. *No power!* He grabbed one of the portables that Will Riley had left in strategic parts of the ship. It was preset for the tactical net. "This is *Calm Seas!"* he shouted. "Any helicopters close to me, submarine surfacing my port bow. Do you have any weapons?"

"Roger, this is one four, your problem in sight. Am currently closing target, but all I have is a couple of machine guns. All stations this circuit, emergency . . . emergency . . ."

Waters grimaced as the submarine's menacing black hull broke the surface like an angry whale, foam boiling down either side. He dashed over to the interior communication system and depressed the button for all stations. "This is the captain. All hands move to the starboard side. Repeat, starboard side. Stand by for collision port side."

Then he watched as the lone helicopter approached the submarine. Its 7.62-caliber bullets raised sparks as they danced off the hull and sail, but they had no effect as it plunged on toward *Calm Seas.*

"That noise!" Soraya exclaimed at the incessant clanging that filled the control room.

"Bullets," Erhardt responded calmly, without removing

his eyes from the periscope. "Helicopter's firing at us. There are others approaching, too. But it's like throwing pebbles at a brick wall."

"How much . . ." Michael began.

But Erhardt cut him off. "Less than thirty seconds. The target is still dead in the water. Steer zero six one."

Walter Erhardt watched *Calm Seas* until she seemed to fill his eyepiece. Even when he turned the magnification down to the lowest level, all he could see was her white hull. The helicopters had turned away to avoid hitting *Calm Seas.* There was a man in a white uniform on her bridge wing watching him with binoculars. When he saw that man rear back and heave the binoculars in his direction, Erhardt knew there were just seconds left. "Prepare for collision." He reached upward for a handhold.

There were two distinct sensations as the vessels came together. The first was a jarring impact magnified by an incredible sound, as if two railroad trains had collided. This was followed by a surge forward as *Waller*'s bow ripped through the skin and ribs of *Calm Seas'* hull and rolled the white ship almost onto its beam.

Then came the horrible screech of tearing metal as the weight of *Waller*'s bow inside *Calm Seas* settled and the yacht fought to right itself. The two craft shuddered, struggling against each other's weight.

As *Calm Seas* heeled to starboard from the impact, the submarine had surged upward into the gaping hole it had punctured in the yacht's side. Now S-252 rested with her bow raised about ten degrees while *Calm Seas* leaned about fifteen degrees to starboard. The twisted wreckage remained so tightly interlocked that there was little immediate flooding in the white vessel.

Erhardt scampered up into the sail and opened the hatch. Except for the grating of metal against metal, as the two vessels continued to settle against each other, there was an eerie silence. He stepped up onto the bridge, raising his head tentatively above the railing. A helicopter stood off about a hundred yards, unwilling to fire so close to the yacht.

They'd struck *Calm Seas* just forward of midships. Almost twenty meters of *Waller*'s hull remained embedded inside the white yacht. With most of the submarine's bulk below the surface, much of the damage to the yacht remained unseen. But *Calm Seas'* deck was buckled upward near the point of impact, and there was a jagged tear in the bulkhead visible to the next level above the main deck.

There was a large room amidships on the yacht's main deck that must have been enclosed by glass, for bright shards of it lay everywhere. The room was open but there was no one visible to Erhardt on the inside.

Craning his head, Erhardt saw helicopters in every direction keeping a respectful distance until they received orders. Turning, he saw a frigate, probably the one they had managed to evade as they made their approach, standing half a kilometer off his stern. The neatly positioned screen had fallen in around them. To port, he saw what was likely the cruiser from the front of the formation steaming in their direction. He was sure that ship would also stand off until the Americans determined their next step.

Erhardt looked at his watch. Less than two minutes had passed since the collision. He depressed the intercom button to the control room. "I want four men with automatic weapons on deck. Exit through the forward trunk. Michael, what's the status on the explosives? There's an entire task force around us and they're not going to let us alone for long."

Waller lurched, sliding backward a few meters with an accompanying screech of grinding metal. Bubbles foamed around the jagged hole in *Calm Seas.* Good. They were taking on water. He remembered Hussein's admonition about survivors. Those helicopters would close in at any moment if he didn't give them reason to stay back. People would be able to escape if they didn't blow her up soon.

Will Riley assumed instant command of the rescue operation. They would move the President to the starboard side until the helo touched down, then hustle him up to the flight deck if it was safe.

"Number *one seven* should be closing you now," Lieutenant Germond called. His voice remained unruffled, his words measured. "Pilot asks if President can be lifted by sling in an emergency."

"He's in pain. Secret Service says it may be broken ribs. We can't take the chance of additional internal injury from something like that. We'll have to plan on a landing for now."

"Roger that. Pilot should be on this circuit. Do you copy, *one seven?*"

"I copy. Time to touch down approximately one minute, three zero seconds. I have backup helo, *one eight,* with me. Will remain on this circuit for instructions."

"Will." This time it was Rear Admiral Turner's voice. "Have you seen any sign of crew from that submarine, or any activity?"

The nearest helicopter had reported nothing. But nothing was logical—nothing would be logical. Two torpedoes had been fired to destroy *Calm Seas.* When neither one had detonated, the sub rammed. Whoever was in command would now try somehow to finish the job.

"Negative on that," Riley answered. "Wait one. I'm on the opposite side with the President and Secretary."

Another pilot broke in. "This is *one four.* My copilot has one person in sight in the submarine's sail. Hatches have been opened both fore and aft. My ammunition has been expended. Suggest we coordinate further action with *Calm Seas'* bridge."

"I'll take it here, Will," Lou Griffey said. "Get up to the bridge and coordinate with Waters. I'll get the President to the flight deck."

"Calm Seas, this is SEAL team commander, call sign Sierra Tango One. You have small craft carrying navy SEALs approaching from starboard to assist." It was Jake Steele's voice on the radio net. "I am aboard one of the helos approaching low on your starboard side. All stations—Sierra Tango One will now assume tactical command on this circuit. Switch to circuit bravo for general communications. Out."

At the moment of the collision, Isabel Mehari had been sitting on the deck with her back against the far bulkhead. Beyond the fear that affected everyone as the yacht seemed to heel over at an impossible angle, she'd found herself unscathed. Once the movement of the two vessels had settled, she began to martial the others in her perpetually calm manner. There was no longer anything in life that could intimidate her. When she saw the man in the submarine's sail, she'd moved them forward beyond his view. She radiated confidence as she circulated among the delegates, now gathered on the starboard side of the main salon.

With the Secret Service hovering at his side, Phil Salkin was now standing erect, almost exaggeratedly so. A glimmer of pain clouded his eyes with each breath.

"Mr. President," Lou Griffey suggested quietly, "do you feel capable of moving on your own?"

"Right, Lou." His speech was slower than normal and he was unsteady on his feet. "We got a couple of good jolts there, didn't we." He patted his right side gingerly. "Believe me, I'm better off moving around . . . clear my head a little . . ."

Griffey maneuvered the President far enough away to say, "It will be time to head aft shortly, sir." His voice was low as he added, "We have a helicopter coming in to pick you up. You have to go."

"How many of these people can we get on board?" Salkin inquired softly.

Griffey's expression was firm as he turned to Salkin. "Just you and your bodyguards, Mr. President. I know what you're thinking, but you got a good whack in the head. Your mind's still cloudy. But as the President of the United States, your safety is paramount. You are aboard a U.S. ship under attack and a U.S. helicopter is coming in to remove you." His voice became firmer. "I am remaining aboard to help Mrs. Mehari and coordinate rescue activities for the others." He leaned close to Salkin's ear. "You have no choice."

Erhardt raised the binoculars to his eyes and swept them in an arc from port quarter to starboard quarter. The American warships were of no concern to him. There was nothing they could accomplish as long as he and the white ship were locked together. He noted the small high-speed boats and decided they were secondary for the moment. His major concern was helicopters. They were hovering nearby, lethal. He attempted to keep track of them when he first climbed into the conning tower, but there were too many now. Some were rescue helicopters, harmless. But others were sent out to kill him? Which ones? *It doesn't really matter, does it? You want to die anyway.*

There were three that seemed to be sneaking up beyond the white ship, flying low. They must be trying to rescue the people aboard. Were they armed? They weren't like the ones designed for combat that bristled with guns and missiles. Would they dare to fire when the chances were just as good to hit their own ship? He doubted it, even if they carried laser aiming devices. He and this white ship were a single target and that gave him just a little more time.

Four men had emerged from the forward trunk with AK-47s. "Shoot anyone who moves on that ship," he called down. "There will be no survivors."

Erhardt called below to the control room. "Michael! Time is short. We are surrounded by helicopters. By the time you get yourself ready, they're going to be like vultures." He glanced at the helos approaching astern of the white ship. "Send a man up to me with the Stinger."

"Calm Seas, this is *one seven,"* the copilot of the rescue helicopter called. "I am making my approach for pickup. Now fifteen hundred yards off your starboard quarter. Do you have me visually? Over."

Francis Waters and Will Riley were on the open bridge on the yacht's starboard side away from the submarine. *"One seven,* all I see are helicopters," Riley answered.

"Standby. Will flash a white light from my cockpit."

"There it is!" Waters exclaimed.

"One seven we have you now," Riley answered. "Your pickup is ready."

"Roger. Do I have a clear approach?"

Waters moved cautiously through the pilot house to the other wing. Peering over the edge, he saw there were now four armed men on the submarine's deck.

One of them shouted and pointed toward *Calm Seas'* bridge. Automatic gunfire filled the air.

Bullets ricocheted off the metal around Waters as he

dropped to the deck. The windows in the pilot house shattered, covering him with glass.

Will Riley called, *"One seven,* this is *Calm Seas.* Break off. Automatic weapons fire from the sub."

"One seven, this is Sierra Tango One. Hang back until we give you a clearance. One of my RIBs will provide cover on the landing area for you." Jake called Nichols in the closest RIB. "Nick, clear the deck of that sub so *one seven* can pick up his party. My team will fast-rope aboard as soon as rescue helo is airborne."

"Roger, Sierra Tango One. On the way."

Steele had kept the RIBs idling just beyond small-arms range until the President's rescue was clarified. Now Nichols's inflatable roared off at flank speed, balancing on one gunwale as it swept around *Calm Seas'* bow and turned directly toward the submarine.

Erhardt directed his men's fire the moment the RIB appeared. But it was an impossible target racing in low in the water at thirty knots. Nichols's M-60 machine gun swept back and forth across the submarine's deck. Two of Erhardt's men were blown into the water before they could take cover behind the sail.

The RIB swung out to pass off the sub's stern to the opposite side. *"One seven,* enemy fire has ceased temporarily. You may begin your approach."

Lou Griffey and the Secret Service agents moved toward *Calm Seas'* stern with President Salkin.

As the inflatable boat moved behind *Waller,* Erhardt lifted his head just high enough to peer through his binoculars at the helicopters. He knew there was a specific reason for the RIB's attack. There were two helicopters approaching. His eyes stopped on the helicopter with the flashing white light approaching from *Calm Seas'* starboard quarter. "Where's that Stinger?" he shouted into the intercom. "I have a target."

At that moment, one of Michael's men crawled through the hatch into the conning tower, carrying the shoulder-aimed missile launcher.

Erhardt pointed at the helicopter approaching *Calm Seas'* stern. "Lock on that target. You've got one chance before it merges with the white ship."

A rope dropped from the other helo approaching low on the yacht's opposite side.

One seven was two hundred yards off *Calm Seas'* port quarter when the copilot recognized the telltale puff of smoke as the missile motor ignited. Both men in the cockpit could actually see the missile bearing down on them, but the distance was much too close. There was no opportunity to evade.

Phil Salkin stared in horror as the helicopter blossomed into a brilliant orange fireball that plunged into the ocean less than a hundred yards from where he waited.

Out of the corner of his eye, Erhardt saw the other helo halt briefly over the white ship. As he tried to blink away the dark halo of the missile burst, seven men exited that helicopter in a controlled jump down that rope. He blinked once more and saw that the rope was now swinging freely as the helo banked away. Only seconds had passed, but Erhardt realized seven dangerous men were now aboard *Calm Seas.*

CHAPTER NINETEEN

Like a second sun! Phil Salkin's eyes closed involuntarily when the helicopter's fuel tank exploded in a brilliant yellow-orange burst.

When he opened them, the burgeoning black spot against his eyelids had melted into a flaming mass plunging toward the sea. One moment men were flying in to rescue him, and the next they no longer existed. *Brave . . . daring . . . dead* were the only words that came to mind—and they kept repeating themselves.

"A Stinger! Had to be." Jake Steele's voice boomed over the circuit. "All helicopters—down on the deck. Stay out of the sub's line of sight until . . ."

Another explosion filled the air behind the yacht. The backup rescue helicopter had been well off *Calm Seas'* stern but high enough to be isolated by the Stinger's range finder. The pilot had heard Steele and had been evading at the time, but the Stinger missile was much too fast.

"Nick . . . Steve . . ." Steele called out. "Tell me what you can see on the sub."

"We have the deck clean and covered. It looks like the missiles are coming from the sail," Nichols answered. "Pop up, lock on the target, missile away, duck down. The only way we might get 'em is from on top, or maybe arch a grenade into the sail. That means a close-in run. We can't fool with anything bigger with *Calm Seas* and the sub locked together."

"Wait one," Jake answered. Rear Admiral Turner would be monitoring the circuit. "Admiral, you heard the status from Nick. Our passenger is still aboard *Calm Seas*. Recommendations?"

"Secret Service reports our passenger is still safe for the moment, but we can't mess with explosives as long as he's there," Turner answered. "They'll remain out of sight on the starboard side, main deck. Peter Germond is convinced they have explosives aboard the sub. That goes back to that trawler that loaded out in Benghazi. So why couldn't they have transferred those explosives to this sub? Let's expect that while we expedite the rescue."

"My men will clear a defensive area around the President and provide security to the delegates. The RIBs will keep the sub's deck clear."

"Jake, I'm assuming these are fanatics standing in line to meet Allah. There's only one reason they come on deck if your guys are going to blow them away. They want to keep our birds clear until they blow *Calm Seas* along with themselves."

"Roger that," Steele replied. "I can get bodies on that sub under cover fire."

"Number-one priority is to get our passenger off *Calm Seas* safely. Wait one for instructions. Out."

Erhardt sensed a trembling just before the sub shifted again. For a man used to the sea, it was disconcerting, almost a tickling of the soles of his feet followed by an odd, jerky motion. Esquimal called up to him seconds later, his deeply accented voice calm. "Captain, we have heavy flooding in the voids beneath the torpedo room. The added weight is forcing us down onto wreckage. That's cracking the hull on the starboard side of the torpedo room. It could flood before we're ready."

"Can you man the pumps?" *Just a few more minutes!*

"The pumps are inoperative, Captain."

There was no time, nor was there really a purpose for damage control. He couldn't see the men who'd fast-roped aboard *Calm Seas,* but he had no doubt they'd be coming shortly. "Status of the explosives?"

"Ready, but Michael doesn't want to take the chance of losing them if we bring them on deck under fire."

Erhardt's voice was even. "Send Michael to the bridge."

Erhardt scanned the ocean area beyond the submarine in ninety-degree quadrants, popping his head up, no longer needing binoculars, turning quickly, then dropping down again to avoid automatic weapons fire. No matter where he turned—helicopters, more than he had missiles for. The crewman with the Stinger squatted below the top of the sail waiting for orders. *How much time?*

When Michael heaved himself through the hatch, he saw that Erhardt's lips were a thin gash in his face.

"Take a look for yourself," said Erhardt. "Quickly—don't be a target!"

Michael briefly poked his head above the bridge rail, ducking as he drew fire from the racing small boats.

"What you see out there are frustrated Americans. They're not sure what we are going to do. The helicopters are wary of our Stingers. Those little boats that killed our gunners are keeping our deck clear." His arm swept in a semicircle to indicate the American ships. "But they don't have a plan yet, or we'd already be dead. There's some reason . . . they're scared of something. So maybe we have a couple of extra minutes . . . maybe less. The one thing you can be certain of is that they're going to make a move. If we're still alive when they do, we've failed."

"If only Ismael had been able to . . ." Michael began angrily, but stopped in midsentence. *If only.*

Erhardt's deep-set eyes studied him carefully and he spoke as if he hadn't heard Michael. "I wanted you to see this . . . so many of them. We have no more time. I'm coming below with you now and we're going to do whatever is necessary to set off those explosives from inside," he said decisively. "How it's done doesn't matter. We're not going to be around to see it. Esquimal can come up here and report to us whatever is happening out here."

Steele's voice came over the tactical circuit. "Steve . . . Nick . . . Sierra Tango One . . . swimmer team is ready to splash. They'll come in low on the starboard side of *Calm Seas* to stay out of range of that Stinger. They have snipers aboard the helos who will come down on either side of the sub, but give them cover, too. I want RIBs to sweep in on each side to keep the sub busy. When they're aboard, we'll move on the sub. Commodore, do you copy?"

"It's your call, Jake," Turner responded.

Erhardt came to the conclusion that they had to decoy the Americans to buy time, even a few minutes. "We're going to send a team aboard the white ship. Maybe only a few will make it, but we've got to make them think that's the way we're going to hit our target. They've already put special forces aboard the white ship and they're the ones we have to keep busy. While they're occupied with our people, we buy a little time to set the explosives up forward. Our torpedo tubes are inside that ship."

Michael frowned. "It would still be more certain if we set the explosives aboard that boat. There would be no doubt and Hussein—"

"Walter's correct," Soraya interrupted matter-of-factly. "There's no other way."

Erhardt continued. "Think about it. Half a dozen men aboard *Calm Seas* with AKs. Divert the Americans. That will give us more time here. We have almost no chance if we try to set the explosives there. Here, I think—no, I'm certain—we buy time . . . have a better chance."

"Captain!" Esquimal's voice boomed over the intercom. "I've just seen a helicopter on the other side of the white ship come in close. There were men who jumped into the water."

"You see, Michael. They're not wasting any time," Erhardt said triumphantly. "Those are divers. To join the ones who roped aboard. It won't be long now," he said. "Too many of them."

Michael's eyes swung from the boxed explosives to Erhardt to Soraya.

Esquimal's voice intruded. "I have those small craft approaching again, one on either side."

Erhardt pushed the intercom button for the bridge. "They looked like inflatables on that first pass," he called to Esquimal. "I'm sending up some snipers. I want them to aim for the pontoons on those small boats instead of the men. If that works, they'll be dead in the water, or at least a better target. Hold the automatic fire until they're close." He turned to Michael and Soraya. "That should give our men time to get aboard the white ship."

Michael's dark eyes darted from one to the other. "I don't—"

Soraya interrupted softly. One hand rested on Michael's arm. The other now held her pistol. "No survivors, Hussein said. Walter understands that." Hussein's special orders to her had been clear. *If you have any doubts, make certain no one—no matter who—stands in the way.*

Michael drew a deep breath. Deep in his mind, there had never been any doubt why Soraya had been chosen by Hussein. They would all die anyway. "I'll take the men over to the white ship myself." He glanced down at her pistol. "You're in charge here." Then he shook his head sadly as he looked back into her eyes. "You always have been," he added wistfully. "I'll divert the Americans." He turned toward Erhardt as if to speak, then turned away.

Michael selected five men from the group remaining in the control room and told them which weapons he wanted them to use. Then he disappeared through the hatch without looking back.

The RIBs cut sharp turns, riding up on one pontoon and then the other, as they closed the submarine. Their automatic fire chased spouts of water toward the sub, sparked across the hull, and bounced off the submarine's sail. But there were no easy targets this run.

Master Chief Bewick was the first to notice a form with a rifle lying prone beside the sub's sail. He glanced quickly over to the other RIB as water spouted up just in front of it. Seconds later, it veered as one side deflated.

"Sniper on the sub," Bewick barked into his mike, "going for our pontoons." He saw the man squirming around on his belly, bringing the rifle around in his direction. "Timing our turns. Do your own thing." He yanked the wheel on his RIB wildly from one side to the other as they closed the submarine. "Concentrate on the base of their sail, port side. Worry him a little." But it was impossible to aim as they bounced from side to side.

The voice of the coxswain from the other boat came into his earpiece. "Got a man hit up forward, too. We're out of it."

Michael and his men scampered across the submarine's hull as the withering fire from the boats subsided momentarily. He was the first to reach up to grasp the railing on *Calm Seas'* deck.

Will Riley crawled through a shattered glass door on the starboard side. "Mrs. Mehari," he called, "I have rescue craft on the way. . . ."

But Isabel Mehari waved a hand to quiet him and hissed, "There!" She pointed through the shattered glass doors on the port side.

There was no time to call the SEALs who had surrounded President Salkin. Riley saw a man climb up over the yacht's railing from the submarine. He was leaning back over the side to assist a second when Riley opened fire with his MP5. The second man was knocked back over the railing, but two others provided covering fire with AK-47s as the rest vaulted aboard.

Riley ducked back out of sight.

"Will, you okay?" It was Waters calling over the radio from the bridge.

"Francis, could you see how many came aboard?"

"I saw five, all with backpacks. I saw two go forward through the laundry, probably headed below. And I can hear shooting . . . wait one." Seconds later. "I've lost communications with my damage-control people."

"This is Sierra Tango One. I copy. We are moving the President to a more secure position beneath the flight deck."

Waters peered over the bridge railing to see a man staring back at him from the submarine's sail. He ducked back as automatic weapons fire shattered the quiet. "They've got our port side covered, too, Will."

"Admiral," Will transmitted, "we're under fire again from the sub. We're pinned on the starboard side. They put five men aboard, all with backpacks—maybe explosives."

"Your call again, Jake," the admiral responded.

"Nick . . . Steve . . ." Steele's voice was clear. "I will stay with the President until the swimmers are aboard. Your remaining boats are going to have to close the submarine again and try to keep her deck clear."

"Roger that," Nichols responded. "Commencing another pass now."

"You armed up there, Francis?" Will asked.

"Nine-millimeter automatic—sixty rounds."

"The RIBs are making another pass to try to keep the sub's deck clear, but they can't get the one in the sail. I'm going after the guys who went below through the laundry." The only entrance to the laundry was on the port side. "Give me some cover."

Riley made it up the port side and edged into the laundry room. Empty. He moved cautiously down the passageway toward the forward entrance to the engineering spaces. A sailor lay dead by the hatch. Will dropped to his hands and knees and leaned forward extending the MP5 in front of him until his head was below the hatch opening. Two men with backpacks, their backs to him, were near the evaporators. Riley couldn't back down the ladder. Instead, he eased his rump onto the edge and placed his feet three rungs down the ladder. Then he lowered his body through the hatch with the MP5 in front of him, switching to single shot to limit ricochets.

Both men whirled in unison at the sound of one of Riley's boots scraping the ladder.

Riley jumped from the ladder, squeezing off two quick shots as their weapons turned in his direction. The one to his left fell to the side, his AK-47 tumbling into the bilges. The other was knocked back into the evaporator, yet he held on to his pistol and managed to bring it up toward Riley. Will's next two slugs caught him in the throat.

Riley put two more in the first man before he kneeled down and gingerly went through each backpack. *Nothing! No explosives!* He took the ladder rungs two at a time.

Phil Salkin, the ever-present Secret Service bodyguards, and Lou Griffey were on the starboard side beneath the overhang of the flight deck surrounded by the SEALs who'd fast-roped from the helicopter. Jake Steele was at the President's side speaking over his radio as a form appeared on the surface twenty yards away. Jake pointed. They could see a dive mask, then a black wet suit. Then a second head appeared, then another, until there were eight of them. The leader gave hand signals to the others as they approached *Calm Seas.*

"There's enough explosive here to blow a hole in the Mediterranean!" Erhardt exclaimed, as he watched Soraya and two others prepare the detonator for the plastic. They placed the explosive in the starboard torpedo tube and very gingerly slid it forward until the door could be sealed shut.

"No one's going to get into that," Soraya said proudly. "When it blows, it's going to be absolutely beautiful."

Esquimal's voice came over the intercom. "Those small craft are making another approach, Captain. Heavy fire . . ."

"What else . . . helicopters . . . ships?" Erhardt asked.

The sound of gunfire grew louder over the torpedo room's intercom. "They're closer . . . not turning away this time . . . I . . . our sniper on deck has stopped firing . . . keeping our missile man down now . . . I'm taking fire from a helicopter . . ." His voice ceased.

Erhardt understood. The sniper on deck had been cleared off by the machine guns on those little high-speed boats and the helicopter had silenced Esquimal. That meant the Americans would be boarding them soon. He depressed the intercom button for all spaces. "Secure all access hatches. The only person I want outside is the man with the Stinger."

Riley's jaw muscles relaxed when he came to the starboard side. A SEAL, mask and mouthpiece dangling beneath his chin, hoisted himself onto *Calm Seas'* deck, followed by seven others.

Jake Steele came forward, beckoning the squad leader to his side. "President's back there. I've got five men with him. We've got some bad guys aft on the port side, maybe in the engineering spaces. We know they have AKs." He turned to Riley. "What about the explosives?"

"I nailed two of them up forward that I figured were

setting plastic." Will shook his head. "Nothing. Empty backpacks."

"Decoys!" Jake closed his eyes briefly before nodding to himself, then looked back to Riley. "Wasting our time. They're gonna blow that sub and try to take us with them."

Steele assigned the squad leader and three men to the main salon, then headed aft again with Riley. "Mr. President," he said firmly. "I have the responsibility for getting you off safely. We have another helo on the way."

Salkin nodded.

"I'll make the decision on whether a helo evacuation is safe. If not, then we have to bring a boat in. We now have terrorists aboard this ship. Their positions and ability to resist or hazard your safety are my main concern. Nick," he called into his transmitter, "status on the sub."

"Clear. At least, I don't see anybody. But they've closed the hatches. Sealed up tighter than a drum."

"No Stinger?"

"Can't be sure of that. He could be playing possum."

"You and Steve stand by. I'm calling in another helo extraction for the President. Riley reports explosives that appeared to be brought aboard here were a decoy. If the sub is buttoned up, I'm betting they're turning that into a bomb." Steele switched circuits and instructed the closest helicopter to come in just above the surface off *Calm Seas'* starboard quarter and pop up on the deck on his command. "That Stinger may still be active. We'll do our best to cover your approach, but the President's our number-one priority. I make the decision on whether he boards once you're in position."

"Roger, this is *two zero,"* the pilot answered. "Will close and pop up on your command."

Steele had to gamble. With at least three terrorists still aboard and the sub a probable bomb, he had to get the President off quickly. "Mr. President, Riley will cover you until you're aboard that helicopter with your bodyguards. Mr. Griffey, if that bird can land, I want you both to jump in."

"I understand."

"If you get aboard that bird, I'll make sure there's no hostile fire from that sub." And if he couldn't do that, Steele would either extract the President aboard a RIB or, as a last resort, he'd take the man for a swim!

A *Calm Seas* sailor stepped through a hatch in the after deck house on the port side just as Michael came out on the main deck. He saw Michael, saw the AK-47, and froze for an instant too long. Michael's burst knocked him over the side.

The familiar sound of the AK-47 galvanized a SEAL in the main salon. He vaulted through the opening on the port side, dropped low, and turned with his CAR-15 in Michael's direction. But as his finger tightened on the trigger, half a dozen rounds hurled him backward.

Then Michael signaled his two remaining men to approach the opening to the main salon slowly.

It was eerily quiet in *Heinz Waller*'s sail. No bullets rattled off its thick metal hide. The deep rumble of the RIBs had receded to blend with the rhythmic impulse of helicopter blades. The rattle of automatic weapons aboard the white ship had ceased. The lone man in the sail contemplated his final moments on earth, preparing himself for everlasting peace. He was pleased that he'd been trained to use the missile launcher because that had allowed him to face the enemy on a more personal basis. He closed his eyes and began to pray to Allah, welcoming eternity.

But, as he murmured the ritualistic words, a now familiar sound came to his ears. The distinctive *slap, slap, slap* of approaching helicopter rotors increased at a rapid pace. Would they try again? He'd loaded one of the two remaining missiles in the launcher before the last helicopters had withdrawn. A final opportunity!

He rose cautiously to his feet, the back of his head sliding up the cool metal at the back of the conning tower, eyes searching the sky. He remained out of sight of the men on the white ship, his head below the railing, as he cautiously peered up over the edge. Nothing was visible, but the sound was increasing. It had to be low, very low, and approaching from the other side of the white vessel. There was only one place it could land—the small flight deck on the stern—and he knew it would have to rise above the white ship before it could land.

There was no need to make himself visible just to confirm what he was certain of. The next time he showed himself would be the last time. He ducked back down and prepared himself, summoning his courage. It must be done quickly for he would draw heavy fire from the white ship. And he would never know if his missile was true.

But—paradise would be his.

Walter Erhardt and Soraya had just stepped into the control room when a guttural sound—a low alien growl—came from beyond the forward hatch. They turned in unison as Ismael stumbled into the control room. His face and neck were caked with dark dried blood. Two slits in his dreadfully swollen face marked his eyes. Handcuffs dangled off one bloody wrist where he'd broken free from the galley. He raised that hand, pointing it at Erhardt as he advanced toward them.

Walter Erhardt froze for an instant, fearful of the ghastly figure approaching him. How had he . . . ?

Then, before he could react, the Turk charged, hitting Erhardt in the midsection. He was knocked back into the periscope. Then one of Ismael's huge hands lashed out, smashing the captain's nose, crushing his head against the smooth metal. Erhardt slumped backward, sliding to the deck.

Ismael was reaching for Erhardt's throat when Soraya's first bullet hit him in the side. Ismael turned slowly, a look of wonder on his ugly face, as a second shot rang out. Ismael took a step back, pawing at the blood pumping from his chest.

Soraya held the gun in both hands, firing a third, then a forth, shot into Ismael. The Turk took a couple of hesitant steps in her direction. Then, howling like an animal, he charged. Soraya's final shots were higher. Ismael straightened up, hands clawing at his face, then fell at her feet.

Steele spoke into his transmitter. "All stations, I expect the sub intends to blow up *Calm Seas.* I can't take the time to extract the delegates by helo. I'm sending them into the water starboard side. Request helo and small craft close me now to recover swimmers." Four SEALs went back into the water to shepherd the delegates away from *Calm Seas.*

"This is *two zero* in position to make my landing on your flight deck," the copilot called from the rescue helo. "Awaiting instructions."

"Clear on the sub, Nick?" Jake called.

"All clear now."

"On the bridge. Waters?"

"No movement from their sail since the hatches were closed."

No time left. "Go *two zero,"* Jake ordered. "Nick, put covering fire on the sub's sail until *two zero* has made his pickup and is out of range."

The pilot increased his power and the helicopter popped up from behind *Calm Seas.* Automatic weapons fire rattled off *Waller*'s sail. Steele could see the helo's crew chief waiting by the open door.

"Move the President to the flight deck," Steele ordered.

Nichols saw the form pop up above the sub's bridge railing. Sparks flew with the impact of each bullet against the metal sail. There was a puff of flame and smoke from the rear of the missile launcher that had appeared almost at the same moment as the operator's head seemed to burst. "Negative . . . negative . . . break off . . . break off!" Nichols shouted.

The missile was visible streaking across his line of sight. "Get the President down!" Jake shouted.

The Secret Service agents had reached the flight deck ahead of the President. Riley was still on the ladder, leading Salkin up. He turned and hit Salkin full force with his body, knocking him back into Griffey. The three men landed at the base of the ladder, with Riley tumbling on top of the President as the helicopter exploded overhead. Flaming wreckage showered down as the helicopter plummeted into the flight deck in a flaming mass.

Michael's reaction to the flaming helicopter was instinctive. *Time to die! Take as many as you can with you.*

He plunged through the port-side entrance of *Calm Seas'*

main salon, his AK-47 on automatic. The SEALs' defensive position had been set up quickly to cover the delegates as they left the ship on the starboard side. The nearest SEAL was knocked backward. But a second SEAL caught Michael with a burst of 5.56mm slugs from his CAR-15. Then he worked his way toward the port side, firing short cover bursts through the opening.

One of the two remaining terrorists was reaching for a grenade when Steele opened up from the deck above on full automatic. Both of them were hurled backward over the side.

Steele raced across to the starboard side and jumped down to the main deck. *President Salkin?*

Will Riley bodily dragged the President forward with him as burning fuel cascading down from the flight deck licked at their heels. "There's no way we can get him off by helo!" he shouted to Steele.

Time, Jake thought. *I'm out of time. This thing could blow any . . . the safest place for the President was in the water. But can't wait for a RIB.* "No choice! My rescue craft are inbound. You're going in the water with him." Jake called Nichols. "How close, Nick?"

Nichols's RIB was rounding *Calm Seas'* bow a few hundred yards distant. "Less than a minute."

Steele pointed to starboard. "Go," he told Riley. "I'm taking the rest aboard the sub. Schanley," he called out, "set up to blow the forward hatch. I'm right behind you."

Riley could see the small craft approaching. "Okay, sir," he said to Salkin, "you're looking good. I'm worried about your ribs, so I'm going to bear-hug you. You do the same to me. Then we all jump." He glanced toward Lou Griffey. "When we hit the water, we're going to move away from the ship as fast as possible. Mr. Griffey, I hope you're a good swimmer."

"I am today."

"Good. I'm going to stick with the President because of those ribs. Mr. President, I want you to relax. Once we're in the water, put your hands on my shoulders, and I'll start pulling you. If you want to help, you can kick. Questions?"

Phil Salkin looked at him curiously before a little smile lifted the corners of his mouth. "More fun than a game of golf. Let's go, Will."

"Follow us, Mr. Griffey." Will Riley turned to the President, wrapped him in a bear hug, and together they jumped from the deck of *Calm Seas.*

"Fire in the hole!" Schanley bellowed, as he took cover with the others behind the submarine's sail. *Waller*'s entire hull vibrated with the explosion. The submarine's forward hatch no longer existed.

Schanley was the first one to the opening to remove debris. "All clear."

Jake gave a hand signal to Schanley, who dropped straight down, landing on his feet in a crouch. He rolled to one side as Jake and two other SEALs followed him through the hatch.

Jake made hand signals to one of them to follow him. To Schanley, he said softly, "The torpedo room."

The first thing Jake noticed as he cautiously entered the control room was Erhardt, unconscious, facedown by the periscope. Jake's eyes darted about the space, stopping when they registered movement to his left.

Soraya had risen from behind the chart table, a Beretta in her hand. Her eyes widened as she shouted in Arabic. Jake rolled. He was coming up to firing position as her first shot grazed his flak jacket, knocking him off balance. She whirled toward Jake's partner, but he was a split second ahead of her, squeezing the trigger of his MP5 as the Beretta came around in his direction. Soraya was hurled backward by the impact of the slugs that ripped open her chest.

There was dead silence in the control room. Jake came to his knees as his partner approached Soraya, his gun leveled on her body. But she was dead.

Steele rose shakily to his feet and went cautiously over to Erhardt. He rolled the man over onto his back. The face was covered with blood. The body was limp.

"Up forward" were Jake's only words as he turned and headed for the torpedo room.

Schanley and his partner had attempted to force open the

torpedo-tube door. "They've got it jammed shut," Schanley said. "There's no chance of getting into it."

"Clear the sub!" Jake ordered.

Walter Erhardt opened his eyes. White stabbing pain streaked through his skull. He put a hand to his forehead and stared curiously as it came away covered with blood. Then, rising on one elbow, he saw the bodies—Ismael, Soraya—but he was unable to comprehend what had happened. All he could remember was the white ship . . . and Darra. A vision of Darra swam into his consciousness, her figure gray, shimmering in definition with the flashes of intensive pain. *But it is you, isn't it, Darra?*

He rolled over onto his hands and knees. Agony racked his body. Using the chair at the planesman's station, he pulled himself upright. Through sheer willpower, Erhardt hauled himself shakily to his feet. His legs were weak and he put out a hand for support. Why was he alive when Ismael and Soraya were dead? Then a thought struck him—he must see if the white ship was still afloat.

He stumbled through the hatch from the control room. A ray of sunlight came from above, through a jagged opening where the forward hatch had been. As he stared up at the light, Darra gazed down at him, smiling, beckoning. Very slowly, painfully, he began to climb the ladder. Each rung seemed to double the agonizing pain in his head, yet Darra continued to smile, coaxing him toward the light.

I'm coming to you, Darra.

As Erhardt's head came up through the hatch, his first impression was that there was hardly a cloud in the sky. It was a beautiful day. The sun was warm and comforting, and there was still a light fair-weather breeze out of the west—the kind of day it felt good to be at sea.

Where was Darra? Something big, bright, and ominous loomed in front of him.

He shaded his eyes and once again Darra appeared, beckoning, her body floating before him, now turning slightly to point. The white ship contrasted sharply with the dark hull of the submarine embedded in its side.

Had they failed?

Walter Erhardt was conscious of a flash of light, a blinding, vivid blaze brighter than the sun. He sensed the pressure from the blast rather than heard it.

Heinz Waller and *Calm Seas* erupted in a mass of flame.

Rear Admiral Turner had been watching through binoculars from *Wasp*'s flight deck. He saw the bloodied head appear through *Waller*'s forward hatch just before the flash. The glare from the explosion was so bright that he was forced to look away.

When he turned back, both ships had disappeared.

EPILOGUE

High in the Lebanese mountains, Hussein listened calmly to the newscast originating in Beirut. It spoke of the end of generations of struggle and of a new era of peace and unity.

He acknowledged that he had but one choice left as the leader of brave soldiers who had martyred themselves for their cause. He took his pistol from the desk drawer and slipped it under his robe.

"I'm going for a walk by myself," he told the guard when he stepped outside. "I won't go far." But his journey would be beyond that known to any man on earth.

He was going to join his brave soldiers for eternity.

Ashore, the naval establishment will match any other service branch for the beauty and emotional impact of their ceremonies. It is a different matter at sea, for a ship and its crew become a unique and singular entity bound together by their mission. Ceremonies are few, for there is no audience to impress—they are carried out to honor the traditions of the sea service and the men and women who serve. They are over quickly.

The memorial service aboard *Wasp* took place on the fantail just before sunset on that same day. There were no flag-draped coffins, nor was there a military band. Instead, Rear Admiral Turner spoke briefly about the personal sacrifices that had been made that day and acknowledged that the end of the Cold War had little effect on the duty of military men and women. He asked each individual present never to forget the memory of those who had died that day doing their duty. Then, as he had promised, he turned to President Salkin. "You wanted to say something, sir."

Phil Salkin, his ribs tightly bound, was assisted from a folding chair by Jake Steele. "I asked Admiral Turner to speak first because I have no speeches today," he began softly. "This is your day, not mine. Nothing I could say would be adequate after what Admiral Turner has said. Today duty and sacrifice remained a naval tradition and all I will ask is that you each join me in a silent prayer for those who are no longer with us."

As Phil Salkin lifted his head and turned to Rear Admiral Turner, a deep tenor voice began to sing:

"Eternal Father . . ."

The song was immediately joined by the assemblage:

". . . strong to save.
Whose arm doth bind the restless wave,
Who bidd'st the mighty ocean deep
Its own appointed limits keep,
O, hear us when we cry to Thee
For those in peril on the sea!"

As the voices died, a marine bugler sounded taps. With the short ceremony at an end, the participants slowly went their own way—Isabel Mehari and the Arab and Jewish delegates, Phil Salkin with Lou Griffey and Bill Herbert, Will Riley and Francis Waters and the remaining crew of *Calm Seas,* the surviving men and women of the helicopter squadron, the crew of *Wasp,* and Rear Admiral Turner and Lieutenant Germond and the Amphibious Squadron Four staff. The last to leave were Jake Steele and Chief Bewick, who climbed aboard helos to return to *Ashland* with their surviving SEALs and RIB crews.

Taps echoed across the water after them.

At the same time, a separate service, much smaller, much quieter, was taking place in a small cemetery on the outskirts of Kiel. In addition to the uniformed guard from the police department, the commander of Submarine Squadron Four had arranged for a naval color guard to escort the casket from the church to the burial site. It was so much more than Mrs. Gleick and her children had expected.

As the graveside service came to an end, two men, strangers, who had remained quietly to one side, came over to Mrs. Gleick. Roland Lyford took her hands in his and spoke softly, "I want you to know how fortunate I feel to have known your husband, even if it was for only a short time. He did a service not only to your country but to mankind. He was a giant of a man."

Captain Tom Davis was in full dress uniform. "The President of the United States personally authorized me as his delegate to give you and your children this memento in memory of your husband and the contribution he made to world peace." He placed a folded American flag in her hands.

Then another stranger, a woman, moved to her side. Mrs. Preminger put an arm around the grief-stricken widow's shoulders and held her very tightly as Herman Gleick was quietly lowered into his final resting place.